"Two women live uneasily on separate floors of a decrepit mansion in Paris. The younger can't envision any future for herself. The older woman's wish to live is failing. Mary Fleming weaves their stories together in *Civilisation Française*, a haunting novel about the pull of time past and future, and the courage to live fully one's life and death."
—Laura Furman, author of *Tuxedo Park* and *The Mother Who Stayed*

"Mary Fleming brings a fresh, tragicomic view to the Américaine-in-Paris novel, exploring the intertwined lives of two expatriates: a rich widow haunted by World War II, and a young woman struggling to overcome a traumatic childhood. *Civilisation Française* is eloquent, erudite and entertaining."
—Jake Lamar, author of *Viper's Dream* and *Ghosts of Saint-Michel*

"With her deep knowledge of French manners and mores and mischievous sense of humor, Fleming turns the classic situation on its head. There were so many things I loved about this book: the fresh way Lily moves forward as she observes Paris and its markets and cafés and French men, in contrast to her prickly employer who moves backward with her souvenirs of vanished times, good and bad; the secrets, large and small, that the characters live with and keep from one another; the complexity and the burden of French history that governs all. Plus, delightful surprises such as Madame's totally unexpected reaction and solution to the presence of the squatters who invade the vacant rooms of her building. Skillfully crafted and elegant, *Civilisation Française* is a work of *grande classe*."
—Harriet Welty Rochefort, author of *French Toast* and *Final Transgression*

"In Mary Fleming's absorbing and affecting novel, a young American takes a course in French civilization and learns more than she bargains for—about sex, cooking, and a family's unhappy past—and is the better for it. So is the reader."
—Lily Tuck, author of *The Double Life of Liliane* and
   I Married You for Happiness

Civilisation Française

MARY FLEMING

Heliotrope Books

NEW YORK

Heliotrope Books LLC
heliotropebooks@gmail.com

ISBN 978-1-942762-50-3
ISBN 978-1-942762-51-0 eBook

Cover photograph by Mary Fleming
Cover design by Naomi Rosenblatt
Typeset by Heliotrope Books

To my daughter Georgina

Autumn

Wednesday, 15 September 1982

I have found a young person, *une jeune Américaine*, to take the room. *To take the room.* As if the long search for a tenant had finally been satisfied. Does Octave think that because my eyes are failing I can't see through his verbal antics? That I haven't noticed what he and that wife of his really want, which is for me to die? So they can sell this house and spend, spend, spend the money? What I don't see is why, until that day, I can't be left alone. Why Germaine and I can't continue to lead our quiet life. We don't need some girl, American or otherwise, disturbing our peace just because I set a toaster on fire. Accidents can happen at any age.

Octave had barely hung up the phone before he was over here with two men and a bucket of paint. I'd put my foot down where I still have some stomping power and said this stranger could not live in the room next to mine so what did he do but choose the *chambre de bonne* upstairs, right over my head. Two days ago, they came to paint it. This morning they returned to take the furniture—*his* bed, *his* armoire—a physical disturbance of memories I want left silent and unmoved. The girl, Octave informed me, arrives next Monday.

All I wanted to do was escape, which I would have done when I still had functioning eyes and dependable legs. To an exhibition or coffee with a friend. In younger years, I could have slammed my office door and done some work. I had many outlets through which to steer my mind from aggravation. Today the only available exit is putting words in this notebook that I bought—what—three years ago? Was it so recently that my body could be trusted? It already seems another life.

Other than my anger at Octave, I am not sure what I plan to record in my diary, *mon journal intime*. In the present it's fair to say there isn't much to report beyond the growing explosion of black at the center of my vision. And the past—well, wouldn't I prefer to leave most of that where it is, locked up in my head? I have no one to bequeath it to, no one I feel should—or would even care to—know. Even if my mind has been much occupied by it these last weeks. Strangely the long ago past—my childhood, my mother. As if the closer I get to the end, the more my thoughts circle back to the beginning.

And now I'm to have a babysitter. My very own *fille au pair*.

***

*A*fraid I'd be late, I am early. Just ten minutes but enough time to consider what, really, I am doing on this square in Paris, waiting to be interviewed for a job with an old lady. Other people my age find work in restaurants or shops or at least taking care of children. And if this old lady is anything like the other elderly woman I have known, it would be best for me to turn around right now, to start my search for home and employment all over again.

The old stone and brick buildings that line the four sides of the place des Vosges, are similar but not identical. They are stately but in different states of repair. Some look completely derelict, others recently cleaned. The one I will enter is in the middle—neither fresh nor neglected—and I wonder what that might mean about the people who live inside it. About the old lady who may soon be my employer. Stop it. What can you tell from a building anyway?

The gated garden in the middle of the square is all order and straight lines leading to fountains in each corner and a statue of what the sign says is King Louis XIII. Perched on a horse, he's smiling, barefoot, dressed up like a Greek and not even holding on to the reins, which confuses me, makes me think I'm missing the joke. At one edge is a small playground. I sit down on a bench under a line of trees and watch the children digging in the sand, climbing up the small slide and whooshing down, or rocking back and forth on a horse atop an iron spring. Two of the mothers are in intense conversation, while another, one thin leg crossed over the other, hunches over a magazine and flicks through its pages. Yet another appears to be looking intently at her daughter in the sand, but she's probably just lost in her own thoughts. Unless French mothers are different from my American one.

Two small boys run past me, one chasing the other. The leader is laughing, and the other's face strains desperately as he fails to catch up. There's always a winner, always a loser, that's what Madame Flaviche used to say, looking down at us as if we were clearly in the latter category.

It's time.

Under the arched arcade that runs all around the square, the front door is heavy oak with iron studs and is at first glance imposing, even dissuasive, like the door to an institution that lets you in but not out. The top part is rounded with a half circle of rays shooting upward and outward like a rising sun and surely that's a good omen. I press the bell, straighten the waist of my new skirt. In London its floral pattern looked fresh and stylish but here in Paris, doesn't it make me look naïve, unfit to attend to the needs of an old lady losing her sight?

After quite a wait—I begin to wonder if I've made a mistake—a small door within the big one opens. A serious face peers out, a hand beckons vigorously. "*Entrez*," she says, and I step over the threshold onto large and uneven paving stones and blink, try to adjust my eyes to the sudden lack of light.

"*Venez*," the woman says insistently as she opens a paned door on the right to a black and white tiled foyer, a sweeping staircase.

I put my hand on the finely wrought iron railing. It's cold to the touch. The whole place is chillier than the sunny September air outside. I can feel it on my bare arms like the cool fingers of whatever ghosts must be living in these old walls, and I pick up the pace, stick close behind the greying bun and the round bottom in the close-fitting wool skirt in front of me. You're expected upstairs is all I catch.

We pass paintings that clash in style: old portraits in muted tones, then bold, half-abstract landscapes, then a quiet still-life. The juxtaposition strikes me as a challenge, makes me feel an intruder on some private disagreement, but surely that is my irksome imagination already getting the better of me in this strange house. At the first landing she stops and puts a hand to her bun of hair, offering a better chance to examine the face, to consider its level of kindliness. The features are even and handsome but appear severe, until she tilts her head towards me with a smile that melts all the lines. "*On y va*." She knocks on the white doors and enters without waiting for a reply. Beyond a windowless entry hall is a large room with a very high, painted beamed ceiling. At the other end is a stone fireplace that you could walk into. Sofas and armchairs in faded covers, a worn Persian carpet, make it less imposing. It is airy and orderly, completely unlike what I expected, which was cramped quarters, buried under a lifetime of trinkets and junk, the way I assumed all old ladies live.

The man from the notice board, the one whose business card is now stuck in the 4th arrondissement page of my Plan de Paris, the book of street maps that guided me here, steps forcefully across the room.

"*Mademoiselle Owens*," Octave de Malbert says, taking my elbow and guiding me towards the old lady. "*Ma tante, Madame Quinon*." He gestures formally towards her as if we were in a ballroom at a dance.

Gripping the chair arms, the old lady raises herself. She is thin and rigid, her hair wispy white and her eyes an intimidating blue. They are so intense that I cannot imagine they are failing, that she needs my help in any way. In fact, rather than a potential employee, I feel like an obstacle and must resist the urge to turn around and see what I am obstructing.

"*Enchantée*," she says, looking anything but pleased to be meeting me.

"*Bonjour, Madame*," I reply, bringing out my French manners: always *Bonjour, Madame. Merci, Madame.*

"*Tante*," Monsieur de Malbert says, "Mademoiselle Owens is like you. She is American. She speaks English."

His aunt replies by settling again on the hard-backed chair.

"Please," Monsieur points towards an armchair. Despite the softer seat, I sit as tentatively as Madame. He settles deeply into another, crosses one leg over the other and cocks his elbow on the armrest but he looks too impatient—as if at any minute he might start tapping his fingers on his knee—for his at-home manner to be convincing.

"I've told you," he says. "Mademoiselle Owens speaks English and French." He looks at me with a half-smile. His dark face is boyish but getting heavy around the jowls. "Unlike me. I apologize again. We French are terrible with any language but our own."

"So are Americans," Madame Quinon continues in French. "Germaine?" She turns her head. "Are you sure she speaks French?"

The woman who brought me up here and must be the housekeeper eyes me. I did no more than peep *Oui* on the stairs, but she gives me that same reassuring smile. "Yes, Madame, she does."

"But like the French," the old lady says, looking quite agitated, "Americans never speak other languages. Unless like me they've lived in the country for centuries. And even then—" She shakes her head at the hopelessness of it.

"Mademoiselle Owens grew up in London," Monsieur de Malbert adds quickly.

"And?" The imperious woman straightens.

"I had a French," I pause—how to put it? Why not use the word Madame Flaviche applied to herself? "I had *une gouvernante*. And I went to the *lycée français* for several years. When I was small."

"Ah." The old lady folds her hands on her lap, lets her blue eyes wander towards the window, then quick as a bird back at me. "And what are you doing here in Paris?"

"Taking a course."

"In what subject?"

"*Civilisation française.*"

"*Civilisation française*! Yes. I can imagine."

Imagine what, I wonder, looking around. I can understand the words, but the rest is a mystery. The housekeeper is standing stoically in place. The nephew consults his watch.

"Well, *Tante*, what do you think?"

"You know what I think."

"Yes. But—"

"It's apparently as you wish." She crosses her angular arms and looks down.

"Good." He springs from his seat. "Then we'll proceed. Germaine, you can show Mademoiselle Owens the kitchen and the room we've prepared for her." To me he says: "We're putting you right above *Tante*'s bedroom. In case..." Then to the old lady: "I must get back to the office. I'll phone you in a few days to see how you're getting on." She doesn't budge, seems to be doing everything she can to make the nephew twist while he kisses either cheek good-bye.

As soon as he is gone the particles in the room settle, the air lightens. I can feel it, like when a machine stops moaning and you realize how tense the noise had been making you.

The old lady braces the armrests again, stands, says defiantly to Germaine: "I'm going back to my room."

After she's gone, the housekeeper, looking apologetic for Monsieur or Madame or both, says: "Come with me."

We walk through a dining room, dominated by an oval table that could seat a dozen people. I now notice, walking behind Germaine, that her gait is uneven, that one leg seems shorter than the other. Like a swagger but with her it's more as if she were soldiering on. I follow her down a corridor to the left, where she points out the bathroom, the closed doors of Mme Quinon's bedroom and sitting room, from which classical music emanates. Expressing my approval isn't hard. The place is majestic, there's no other word for it.

"And here's the kitchen."

Compared to the rest of the flat, it is compact and humble, with cabinets on two sides, a window over the sink, a table in the middle, a clock on the wall. Like the rest of the place, it's lost in another era, but it feels snug, inviting.

"I'll show you how to prepare the breakfast later," says Germaine from the sink, where she is cleaning a coffee filter. After turning it upside down in the rack, she dries her broad hands, folds the tea towel and hangs it over the bar on the oven. "The back stairs that lead to the *chambres de bonnes*, or *service* as we're supposed to call them these days are here." She opens a door between cupboards and counters, turns on a light.

The stairs to the service, once maids', quarters are windowless and the steps are wood rather than stone, a material demotion maybe meant as a daily reminder to domestics, like I may soon be, of our station. At the top, where a small window lets in some daylight, we enter a narrow corridor with several doors. Germaine stops in the middle.

"As Monsieur Octave said, you'll be right above Madame."

"She's going blind? Is that right?" It's what the nephew told me but there is something shifty about him, something that makes me question his sincerity, his version of the truth. I did not like his hand on my elbow.

"Yes. A condition. Degeneration. No, macular degeneration, that's it. There was an incident with the toaster. He decided she needed more help. A pair of younger eyes, is the way he put it." She shakes her head, draws in her lips.

So neither of them wants me here, I think, with a sinking heart but—

"I wasn't sure at first, but now I think he's right." The smile again. "Here we are." She opens the unlocked door. The room smells of fresh paint and the early autumn light is streaming through the open window, warming the pale blue walls and the dark wooden frame of the bed, the heavy oak armoire, the small table and chair and cabinet.

"Beautiful," and it is, beautiful as a dream.

"Good." Germaine moves towards the door. "The WC is at the end of the corridor. You can use that spare bathroom downstairs."

"I guess I should fetch my suitcase? I've got the job?"

"Well yes. Of course." She gestures towards a small cabinet in the corner. "We've left you some kitchen things. Now let's get you a key."

We rewind our steps, down the service stairs, through the kitchen, down the corridor, music still emanating from Madame's quarters, through the dining and living rooms and back to the entry hall. Germaine pokes around a blue and white cup with a broken handle on the small round table. "This is the key to the *portail*. That's all you'll need." The key at least looks like it fits a modern lock, one that might keep burglars and the like from penetrating this strangely unprotected house. She walks me back downstairs, stopping halfway at a door tucked in the wall. "This is where I live."

On the ground floor, she points to a staircase in the corner of the large courtyard. "You can use that entrance. So you don't have to walk through the apartment every time you come and go."

She sees me back to the *portail*, the front door, and says "Why don't you join Madame and me for dinner tonight. Around eight-thirty. *A ce soir*." And the door closes behind me.

Outside again in the sunny day, I wonder if I haven't dreamt the last hour. A house—what the nephew called *un hôtel particulier*—in the middle of the city, maybe occupied solely by an old American lady who refuses to speak English and her limping, not so young housekeeper.

No, it does not seem real, but I hope that's wrong because I am very eager to leave the avenue de Breteuil, where I've been staying with Dr Fortin, a work acquaintance of my father's. The flat is both office and home. The family living room doubles as the waiting room during the day. Since they do not have a spare room, I was put on a camp bed in the doctor's consulting room. For the last two weeks, I've gone to sleep with the smell of antiseptic in my nose; every morning I've folded up the bed and rolled it into a closet, packed my bag and stuffed it in a cupboard under the tongue depressors and the syringes, thus removing all trace of myself. Although I've tried hard to stay out of the way, I've felt constantly underfoot. The four boys sidestep me as if I had something contagious, and Madame Fortin treats even my offers to help with meals or shopping as an imposition.

Between patients, I extract my bag from the supply cupboard in Dr Fortin's examining room, and he apologizes for not being able to provide better accommodation. I say good-bye and thank you to my hostess, finally getting a smile out of her. Patients look up unsympathetically from their magazines as I lug my large duffle bag through the living-waiting room. It's really heavy but what a great lightness to be out of there and on my way to a place where space is, to say the least, not a problem. To be starting my Paris adventure for real.

***

Monday, 20 September 1982

The girl has arrived, thrust upon me by Octave who sat in that chair—I could feel it even if I couldn't quite see him—like he already owned the place. She, Lily Owens is her name, appears to be shy and discreet so perhaps won't be pounding around over my head day and night. Her French is hesitant, as if the language has been hiding somewhere and is now struggling its way back to the surface. Her accent is good. She says she had a French *gouvernante*. Did she mean a nanny or the head of a large household staff? Either way, beneath a managed exterior, the girl could be a spoiled brat, used to having her every whim satisfied by a slew of servants. Whatever her background, whatever her character, I have no desire to know more, to encourage familiarity of any kind. I was barely cordial, could not even bring myself to speak to her in English, partly out of pig-headedness, partly because I speak it so rarely these days. Though it remains my language on this private page, French has become more natural to my public persona.

Despite English being my mother tongue, language of my mother. Thoughts about her just won't leave me—or more precisely my conscience—alone. She was so awful about François. But that didn't mean I had to be awful back. It didn't give me license to kiss my embarrassed father and brother good-bye with what I believed to be French flourish and to not even look my mother in the eye. Then to never return, even once the Second War was over and there were airplanes and we had money. My own grief was no excuse. A big trip like that, a complete change of scenery and an easing of my conscience, a chance to apologize for my cold, hard departure twenty-five years earlier, could have provided a good antidote. As it had for François after the First War, when he travelled to the US and met me.

I tell myself it's ridiculous to fret over missteps taken decades ago. But it's not working.

***

It was Maude who had the idea.

"So Sister," she said, hunched on her folding stool. "Now that you've finished university, what are you going to do with your life?"

"Good question," I said, prostrate on the grass, *Sophie's Choice* open and face down on my stomach. Shading my eyes, I watched the rhythmic motions of her brush, water-paint-paper, water-paint-paper. The girl who'd been all sharp points, from nose to chin to elbows had become, since the last crisis two years ago, almost plump. I couldn't get used to it, even though I thought it made her look kinder, better intentioned. "I have absolutely no idea. It's terrifying." I closed the thick best-selling novel that I'd been trying for weeks to get through, turned on my side.

"If I were you," Maude said, tapping the brush against the rim of the plastic cup, "I'd go abroad. Far away from here anyway." The roof of the house, The Vicarage, next to the village church steeple, was just visible beyond Maude's head on the horizon.

"That's what Jane said too. But I haven't got much money saved up.

Just what I earned last summer at the pub." From this angle the grass looked gigantic, an impenetrable jungle. I picked a long blade and split it lengthwise down the middle. "And where would I go, anyway?"

"France, I suppose." She turned and looked at me. "You do remember it, don't you?"

"What? The language? Yes. I think so."

Maude turned back to face the stand of trees she was painting. "There you go."

"France? Really? After, you know…"

"You can't blame the entire French nation for the old hag Flaviche. Paris would be totally different from *her* place. It might even be good for you. Change your perspective on past, present and future. Or something like that."

"But what about money? I don't think I could afford much more than the ticket over there."

"You can get it out of them."

"You know how they are about *spoiling* us. Or how she is."

"It's an act." Maude took the board off her lap, held it at arms' distance from her face, then turned and looked at me with her slightly bulging eyes. "You don't think either one of them wants you hanging around here, do you?"

I sat up and looked at the watercolor too. The dark, twisted mass looked nothing like the trees in front of us.

"No, I don't." I lay down again, plucked and split another blade of grass.

"When I went to Florence after art school, I remember, I could feel their relief as I said good-bye." The old Maude, the one with hooded, feline eyes flashed again. "Too bad for them I had to be brought back in an ambulance."

"Maybe you're right. I'll think about it."

Going to Paris seemed a strange, possibly dangerous course of action. Yes, I'd known the language as a little girl. Madame Flaviche, with help from *le lycée français*, had seen to that. But I had not exactly enjoyed the French period of my life so why would I go to the source, so to speak? Was Maude right it might be a help? I wished Jane, my other sister, the one I had counted on my whole childhood, were there. Earlier in the summer she too had told me to get far away from here but what would she say to Paris? Jane was back in New York—I couldn't ask her opinion—and now Maude, whom Jane and I as children had actively avoided, was all I had. And maybe after what Maude had been through, she had changed or gained wisdom or whatever it was that ordeals and suffering are supposed to generate. In any case, they were both right about one thing: I needed to get away from here so why not Paris. Even Mrs Hooper, our housekeeper and cook, someone generally suspicious of foreign lands, said: "Go, Lily, go."

The next evening, when our father came home from work, I trapped him in the narrow entry hall.

"Hello," he said, then put down his case and unbuttoned his Mac.

"I was wondering," I said. My father paused, looked as if he might re-button his coat and turn right round, out the door and into the rain again. "About my future."

"Ah!" he said, giving his wet hat a shake.

"I was thinking of going to Paris."

"Paris!"

"Yes, Paris. I thought some time abroad might do me good. I do speak the language, remember."

"Yes, of course." He passed a hand over his head to refix the strand of hair that had come unstuck under his hat. Maude had been right: make him feel guilty by bringing up those years. "What would you do there?"

"I thought I might take some courses, get a part-time job." I could see him look beyond me, probably thinking about his evening whisky, but I didn't budge from my strategic position in the middle of the passage. In fact, I widened the planting of my feet. "I thought maybe you could help me. Just to get started. I never took a gap year, remember."

He nodded, smoothed his hair one more time.

"It's an idea," he said.

Despite the tepid reaction, I sensed it was a done deal. As Maude had pointed out, they wanted me gone. I felt it every day when our mother ventured from her bedroom. Or when the four of us—father, mother, Maude and me—sat around Mrs Hooper's evening meal.

So I moved into action and a few weeks later the plan was all in place. I would take the *Civilisation française* course that started end of September at the Sorbonne. I'd go over a couple of weeks earlier, stay with the Fortin family, and get myself sorted.

Now here I am on my way to occupying a room in a large house on the place des Vosges, preparing to help a crotchety old American lady who refuses to speak English. My first lesson in *la civilisation française*, it seems, will include some strange form of expat Americana.

∗∗∗

Tuesday, 21 September 1982

It's been many years since I used my writing table for writing anything more significant than a quick letter and even that, given my
bad eyes and my ancient or dead friends, is becoming a distant
memory. Today, with this notebook, it is—I don't know—comforting.
Almost exciting. It is bringing back the nervy anticipation at the start
of a translation, the challenge of rendering the soul of another's work in
that mother tongue of mine. Once the bubble of concentration formed
around me, hours could pass in what seemed like minutes. Now—even
with nothing much to say—the bubble forms easily, because of how little
I can see beyond what's inside my head. It's an odd sensation to be unable to discern much of what I write—whether or not I am even staying
within the lines—but this is not an exercise in penmanship or a docu-
ment I want anyone else to see. *Tant mieux* if no one can read my scrawl.

At this desk, in this room, I don't need sight. The picture of it is
imprinted in my mind's eye. The window and bookshelves, the two
armchairs in front of the fireplace. I insisted on cushioned furniture,
telling François that I'd had enough of hard French chairs, no matter
how elegant or valuable they were. I know, I know, he said. You Americans always want comfort. To which I replied: We certainly prefer it to
discomfort. That had made him laugh, by then a rare occurrence. The
reason it has stuck in my mind, I guess.

But I don't want it sticking there now. It hurts too much, remembering. The happier memories induce one kind of pain, the unhappy
ones another. Looking back causes an ache *tout court*.

Yesterday, before I could completely discourage hospitality, Germaine launched an invitation to dinner—

—to which she has just called me. More later.

***

By the time I arrive back at the place des Vosges, my shoulder is burning from the straps of the duffle bag that contains almost everything I own. Which admittedly isn't much. Just enough to be carried awkwardly and painfully across town. I pause in front of the *portail*, as Germaine called it. But I also heard her call it the *porte cochère*, the big entrance for vehicles with a little door inside for people, *la porte piétonne*. Do I really speak French? The vocabulary that I do not possess is vast. And even what's there is rusty. It strikes me that my language skills—and my life itself up to this point—resembles the Gruyère cheese in the sandwich I had for lunch, defined as much by its holes as by its solid matter.

I walk as quickly as I can with my heavy bag over the bumpy paving stones in the courtyard. I feel as if someone is watching me—there are windows everywhere—and am relieved to be in the windowless staircase, which I climb like a snail, advancing slowly with my home on my back. At the landing is the door to the kitchen. To the right. But there is also a door to the left, and I wonder what, who is behind it. Not a sound and the light, on a timer, goes out. I grope towards a red glow on the wall and push it back on, walk up one more flight and head down the corridor towards the room the housekeeper had shown me. I pause, listen again. Again nothing, just the silent hall and the line of doors. It's a little spooky. But when I open my room, drop the bag off my shoulder, every muscle of my body relaxes in the fresh paint and Indian summer air. Whatever else eludes me in the house, I am certain of one thing: I love this room.

The oak armoire door creaks open. There are shelves on one side and hanging space on the other. I've never been a good packer or folder and my clothes are a crumpled mess. Since Paris is supposed to be a fresh start and I haven't got anything else to do, I attempt to arrange my things in an orderly fashion on the shelves. I hang up my other skirt, a dress, a coat and a jacket.

The day after I cornered my father, my mother came to my bedroom and, smiling as if the sun never stopped shining on the Owens' household, said:

"I hear you're going to Paris. What a good idea."

"I hope so," I replied, jumping up from the bed. Her very presence in my room caused a nervous reaction, as if I'd been caught smoking or reading a porn magazine.

"You'll need some new clothes," she said, looking me up and down. "Some things to help you get started on the right sort of Parisian foot."

"I guess," I said, resisting an urge to retract into a ball under her inspection.

Even more unusually my mother then proposed a day in London together the following week. The prospect put me in a state of high nervous tension during the intervening days. Would she succumb to one of her bouts and cancel at the last minute? If not, what would it be like? Had we ever even spent a whole day alone together? I couldn't remember such an occasion. Though the prospect scared me on the one hand, on the other, a corner of my heart filled with hope that the day would change everything, make us closer.

Come Monday my mother was up, bright and normal. The two of us boarded the train to Victoria Station, went shopping around Sloane Square and along the King's Road, had a delicious lunch in a little French bistro on Pont Street that she knew. I was reminded that on her good days my mother is very congenial company—chatty, even confidential. "You know," she said, leaning toward me over lunch, "there are times when I'd just love to give it all up and move back to this big, humming city." She swung her fist at the air. I wasn't sure what the *all* was that she wanted to give up, but mixed in with the incomprehension was a twinge of pride at being let in on her secret desires.

She directed the whole expedition, choosing the shops to enter, rifling through the racks and pulling things off for me to try on. Her excitement was contagious; I followed all her advice, sure that everything was just perfect. It was only afterwards, back at the house and pulling the clothes from their bags, that I wondered if I really liked them, if they were really *me*, whatever that might be. When I look at them now, here in Paris, they could well belong to someone else.

Next to the sink there is a little wooden stand with a black and white marble top, on which I firmly plant my toothbrush, toothpaste, deodorant and skin cream. I am chuffed and relieved, knowing that I will not have to put them back in my duffle bag until the day I leave.

In the small cabinet there is, as Germaine said, everything I need to make my own meals. On top is a heating plaque. Inside are two of everything: glasses, plates, knives, forks…thoughtful of them, those pairs, but the idea of bringing someone into this strange arrangement, especially with the old lady, Madame, right underneath me, is unthinkable. Assuming I make some friends.

A soft breeze wafts through the window. Leaning on the ledge, I have a view of the whole courtyard. The rectangle of buildings that wraps around it seems to be apiece. There's the taller, front section that gives onto the square. That's where the *salon* and dining room are. On this side, underneath me, are the rooms off the corridor: Madame's quarters, a couple other closed doors, the bathroom and the kitchen. Across the way, the windows look blank and empty, same as the ones on the ground floor when I walked through the courtyard. Ditto for the back section of the building. As for the courtyard itself, from up here I can fully appreciate how neglected it is. Urns are filled with dry earth, the odd weed. The stone basin is empty, and moss outlines the paving stones.

I pull away from the window, walk to the door and open it slowly, quietly, just in case there are other people living up here, and walk into the corridor holding my breath. Nothing. I put my ear to the next door. Nothing. I slowly turn the handle. The room is like mine but stuffy, dusty, with walls last painted—who knows—centuries ago. There's no way anyone else can be up here, I think on the way to the loo. With all its different staircases and corridors, you could get lost in this place and not be found for years. But back in my freshly painted blue room the house seems full of potential excitement, a hopeful start to the gap year I never took between school and university because I didn't know what to do with it and that I'm taking now because I don't know what to do with the rest of my life.

Just before eight-thirty I head back down the stairs and smell food. Something in wine sauce and my mouth is watering when I knock on the kitchen door. Germaine opens it, an apron over her skirt and shirt.

"Come in, come in," she, waves her hand, as she'd done when I arrived, as if a terrible storm were raging behind me. "No need to knock. Food's just about ready. We eat right here," she points.

"Can I lay the table?" I'm relieved that we won't be sitting in the grand dining room.

"The cutlery's here, the plates up there to the right." Germaine is back at the stove stirring something vigorously.

The silver is heavy but simple. The plates are heavy too, and slightly yellowed, with an old-fashioned floral pattern. They have the weight of a different era; the sound they make when in contact with one another resonates more deeply than the plates I know.

"*Bon*," says Germaine, wiping her hands on her apron, loosening the bow and pulling the strap over her head. "I'll get Madame. Don't forget the glasses. They're in that cupboard."

There are tumblers of different sizes and wine glasses. Which type did Germaine mean? The Fortins always had a symbolic glass of red with dinner, but Madame is American and so severe it is difficult to imagine her drinking anything but water. I look around the counter for a wine bottle and finding none, I opt for tumblers, fill the jug that is sitting near the sink with water.

"Here we are, Madame," says Germaine. "Mademoiselle Owens is already here."

"I can still see that much," says Madame Quinon, holding a glass with the watery remains of what looks to be an *apéritif*. "What's your first name again?"

"Lily."

Germaine moves towards the cupboard and pulls down some wine glasses.

"I'm sorry," I say. "I didn't know."

"Didn't know what?" asks Madame.

"About wine glasses," says Germaine as she puts a platter of meat with a creamy sauce on the table. Some mixed vegetables and a few slices of baguette in a basket.

"Americans never do."

"Please," Germaine smiles at me, points at the meat, passes the vegetables to Madame, who cocks her head and looks sideways, hard as a hawk, at the serving bowl before spooning herself a small portion. Ditto for the meat. As usual I am starving, and Germaine's food looks delicious. Unlike Madame Fortin's, which tasted as if it too had suffered from her short temper.

Germaine opens another cupboard and pulls out a bottle of red wine. Without asking, she pours me a glass too.

"Thank you." At the Fortins', I was considered one of the children and given water.

"Octave seemed in unusually brisk form," Madame Quinon says to Germaine.

"Hmm."

"Such a shame," she answers, takes a bite of food, chews it carefully. I try to slow down, focus on the conversation and resist my habit of eating fast as a dog. This food is really, really good.

"I always told you…" began Germaine.

"Yes. Yes, you did. I didn't listen," Madame cuts in. She turns to me. "Tell me about this *civilisation française*."

"It's a course for foreigners and lasts a year." I can feel my face reddening at the direct questioning. "It starts tomorrow."

"How is it then that you speak passable French and know nothing about the culture? This *civilisation*?"

"I've never lived here." My pores prickle as the conversation heads in a direction I am forever trying to avoid.

"Ah, yes, the *gouvernante*. The *lycée français*." Madame wipes her mouth on the white napkin, thankfully turns again to Germaine. "They were saying on the news that perhaps it wasn't the Irish after all."

"I don't know why it would have been..." Germaine puts down her knife and fork, looks at her oddly splotched hands as she turns a wedding ring round and round on her finger. "What do the Irish have against..."

"Who's to know. There have been eight attacks these last months, lots of them unclaimed. Anarchists, Armenians. Terrorists, they're saying."

"Terrorists," says Germaine, letting her hands drop on her lap. "I don't like that word."

"They are angry men."

"Not all angry men are shooting people right around the corner on the rue des Rosiers."

Germaine's face has turned grave as stone. Her grey eyes have frozen, and she seems to have forgotten the food in front of her. And Madame's bony hand can't stop fiddling with the stem of her wine glass.

"No. No they aren't." Madame's voice has softened.

"It must have been the Arabs," Germaine says, picking up her cutlery again.

"It could have been the Iranians. They're not Arabs."

"Well, they're all from that part of the world." Germaine jabs her knife in the imagined direction of the Middle East. "Oooh. All those police crowding around."

"It was unsettling," says Madame. "And I agree it's hard to believe the Irish, even the IRA separatists, would be interested in a Jewish delicatessen."

"When it comes to this kind of thing, the French..." Germaine seems to be looking for the right words.

"The French have trouble blaming the right people," Madame finishes for her.

"Yes," nods Germaine.

In August I saw footage of the rue des Rosiers attack on television. There was a cluster of policemen in their blue shirts and kepis, looking bewildered on a narrow Paris street. The newscaster had described grenades being thrown and machine guns fired at people eating lunch at Jo Goldenberg's, a Jewish delicatessen. To learn it happened right around the corner from here makes the back of my neck tingle all over again, but I have to say the sensation this time is not unpleasant; the thought of nearby danger now, here in Paris, is quite stirring.

Still, looking from one woman to the other, I wonder what I've missed. I've understood the words. It's what has not been said, the geological substrata to the conversation that I am unable to grasp. The reason why both Madame and Germaine seemed so unsettled. Even after Madame has returned to her room and I'm helping Germaine wash up, silence seems in order. I take the stairs as lightly and quietly as I can, walk quickly down the corridor of empty *chambres de service*. Inside my room I close the door with care, turn on the bedside lamp. The softly lit space feels as safe at night as it does in the day, even with that grumpy old lady and all her mysteries right beneath me. I step over to the sink and the marble-topped washstand, pick up the toothbrush and toothpaste Mrs Hooper gave me before I left ("In case they don't clean their teeth over there"). While brushing, I open the window. It's dead quiet outside and hard to believe I'm in the middle of a major city. The dark windows all around are eerie. I turn back to the sink, spit out the toothpaste and rinse out my mouth, undress quickly and climb into the plump bed, which is bigger than a single, if not quite a double. The sheets smell fresh, feel crisp on my legs; the mattress is forgiving where the bolster pillow is not. I pull the duvet around me and tuck the pillow under my neck and stare at the pale blue wall.

Though I stopped by the notice board at the American Church regularly, it always seemed that other people had been there first, had already found the rooms or the babysitting jobs. That I was too late. It made me feel hopelessly lacking in some key survival skill. That, and knowing I'd have to answer Madame Fortin's daily questions about my house-hunting progress, really got me down. To stay out of the way, I walked the streets.

First, because there was never enough to eat at the Fortins', I'd dish out some precious francs for a croissant, take tiny bites, make it last as long as possible while I sat on a bench and consulted the Plan de Paris that I'd bought at the newsagents next to the Duroc métro station. My itineraries were often based on streets with evocative names: the rue de Sèvres, for example, to the rue du Cherche-Midi to the rue Saint Placide to the rue Notre-Dame-des-Champs to the avenue de l'Observatoire. In the Luxembourg Gardens I'd watch children on the caged green swings or atop the mean-eyed ponies. Following my itineraries did help pass the time and I was lucky it didn't rain much, but I felt lonely. I worried as I walked that I'd made a big mistake. The city—even its smell—felt foreign, except when I'd occasionally catch a passing whiff that reminded me of the *lycée français*, in which case my gut would seize up, the association was so powerfully toxic. I'd ask myself how I could have come to a place that had anything to do with those miserable years. You're a glutton for punishment, Mrs Hooper would say to Maude, when she'd stay out beyond curfew or skip school. What had I been thinking, how could I have believed that "getting away," especially to France, would actually get me anywhere?

Until that day, when the man in the coat and tie, the soft cotton shirt and the grey wool trousers, all the way down to his polished black-tasselled loafers—unmistakably French—faced the board next to me. I could see him looking at me out of the corner of his eye, sizing me up, until finally:

"Are you a student?" I nodded. "American?"

"Yes."

The man held up the chit he was about to post. "You wouldn't by any chance be looking for work?"

"A room and work in fact."

"Ah!" The man raised his head, directed his dark eyes towards the heavens, as if God had answered his prayer without his even having to enter the church itself. "We are perhaps solving one another's problems." He thrust out his hand. "Octave de Malbert."

He explained that his aunt had a degenerative condition whereby she was losing her sight. Recently she had set a toaster on fire. "The housekeeper saved the day. But it's too much for one person. She needs help. Just with breakfast. Really nothing at all."

I wondered then and still do about that "nothing at all." It was too breezy. I turn off the light, snuggle more tightly into the duvet. How many people looking for rooms or jobs on that notice board have ended up in a situation as strange and intriguing as this one, in a bed this plump and comfortable. Maybe it's been worth the wait.

***

Wednesday, 22 September 1982

So much for "later." Though at this point now or later, yesterday, today, tomorrow, what matter. Time has become almost as blurry as my vision. Dinner with the girl. It is strange that she speaks the language so well, even attended the lycée in London, yet feels the need for a course in *la civilisation française*. A course she apparently knows little about. A subject she claims to know little about. What is her real purpose in being here? The facts add up to something fishy. Odd at least, even if she does not appear to be the spoiled nanny's girl I feared. But it's hard to judge someone whose face I cannot quite see and of which I have no memory.

I have to agree with Germaine on the rue des Rosiers. Why would the Irish attack a Jewish delicatessen? It does seem more likely that a Muslim group of some kind was behind it. I can't help but worry about a new surge of Jew-hating. Whenever anti-Semitism raises its ugly head, bad times are around the corner, or at least within walking distance. It's practically scientific.

Of course, I couldn't quite see Germaine at supper, but I sensed her anguish. It's not the same thing at all, I tried to tell her, but how can I expect her to believe me. How could she not feel terrified by an attack on Jews, especially so close to home?

Meanwhile, when I'm alone with my thoughts, my mother keeps intruding—barging—right into my head, just the way she would rush into the kitchen and yank open the oven door to make sure the roast wasn't overcooking. At first, she practically flirted with François, a Frenchman sent out by one of Father's fancy cousins from the east to work on the ranch for the summer. She was full of questions about his life, about France. Always an extra helping for François. But once she understood what was happening between us, she became all bitter lips and narrow eyes, full of dire warnings about the slippery ways of Frenchmen, their rampant desires and liquid morality. No more solid than the wine they drink with every, single, meal, she'd say. As François behaved exquisitely and appeared to be surviving just fine on the ranch without a drop of wine, I laughed away her scaremongering.

And what had happened to her? She'd been the one who encouraged me to want more than ranch life. To read the good books in my grandparents' library, to appreciate fine things. It was she who argued with Father for me to attend university, she who proudly told everyone her daughter was studying literature. But I guess marrying a Frenchman and moving to another continent was taking her hopes too far. Maybe it was jealousy. Certainly she'd never got over her parents' move to Wyoming. They had to pry my fingers one by one from the front door jamb, was how she melodramatically described the departure from New York State. I guess seeing me escape the life she so disliked was more than she could bear.

That's how I see things now. Unfortunately, at the time, the only effect her Cassandra doom and gloom had was to throw me with greater ardor into the solid French arms of François Quinon, who would indeed take me away from her and the ranch, forever.

***

When the alarm goes off, I have no idea where I am. I haven't slept this soundly in weeks. After the initial disorientation comes relief. I am here in a room of my own. At the Fortins', it not only smelled of antiseptic, there were no windows. When I turned over on the narrow camp bed, I felt like a pig on a spit. This morning I spread my legs in the almost double bed, throw an arm out, just because I can. The air coming in the open window has a thin edge of autumn. Birds chirp in the distance. I swing out of bed, go to the window and peer again into the courtyard. Abandon has different aspects, according to the time of day. On a sunny morning it radiates a certain charm.

In the kitchen, the breakfast tray is laid out.

"She gets very worked up if she can't find something," Germaine said. Since I would like to avoid seeing the woman get any more worked up than she already is, I carefully take note of the items and their position: the plate in the middle, knife and spoon at its side; yogurt top middle; the honey pot and fig jam jar in the left corner, next to the butter; the coffee cup and saucer to the right.

I boil the water, slice a piece of yesterday's baguette down the middle and put it in the toaster, the way Germaine showed me. I make the drip coffee directly into the thermos, then take it all down the corridor to Madame's study. With my hands holding the tray, how to knock? My voice gets stuck in my throat, but I can't stand here forever so I put the tray on the floor, rap lightly.

"*Entrez*," comes irascibly through the door, beyond radio voices. I turn the squeaky brass handle, open the door a crack, pick up the tray, look furtively at Madame, but of course Madame can't see that I've picked up the tray from the floor. I must remember her blindness gives me certain advantages.

"I've brought your breakfast." The room is vertical, like its resident, with bookshelves to the ceiling, one long window, a door into what must be her bedroom. There is a fireplace with two armchairs in front of it, a television to the side. It's surprisingly comfortable, given how severe she seems. Near the window Madame Quinon is seated at a writing desk, listening to a news show on the radio.

"Put the tray here. Thank you."

When no further instructions come, I ask: "Can I get you anything else?"

"Just come back in a half hour to collect the tray. Then you can get on with your *civilisation française.*"

The carpet in the corridor looks more worn this morning than yesterday. Everything in the place looks well past its prime. But because it's kempt, it takes time to notice the fraying edges. I make myself some coffee, open the old fridge. Germaine has told me to help myself, but there's not much to choose from here or in the cupboards, except an extra jar of honey.

A substantial piece of the baguette remains, and I toast it, as I did with Madame's, and butter every millimeter. I used to watch Jane slap butter willy-nilly on the middle of her toast and could never understand how she could leave the four corners high and dry. I asked her once and she looked at me with no idea what I was talking about. I spread honey over the surface with equal care, then tug off a bite with my teeth, and as I chew, my taste buds jolt into life. The salty butter, the slightly bitter honey, with the spongy-crispy baguette. Alchemy.

Bread and butter doesn't taste like this in Britain, even with Mrs Hooper's homemade jam. At the Fortins', the baguette tasted like cardboard, the butter was not salted and the jam bland. Here I savor every bite, lick my fingers, then the knife, and wash it all down with the strong coffee, softened with milk and sugar, so much tastier than the Nescafé from home or the Fortins' weak tea. When I finish, I feel perfect. Or balanced. Or something I'm not used to feeling after a meal of toast and coffee.

Everything feels different today because today I have purpose. Breakfast for Madame and *civilisation française.* Registration is this morning. After picking up the tray, tidying up and getting myself ready, I walk out onto the place des Vosges. It seems much longer ago than yesterday that I was sitting under the trees, waiting for a job interview, if that's what you would call the scene in the living room. Though I know the way to the métro, I pull out my Plan de Paris anyway—like a shield against the unknown day ahead of me—and flip to the 4th arrondissement, the *quartier* that I guess I will be calling home for the year ahead. Yes, it's still there, the place des Vosges in green, the arrondissement in pink. It feels good to situate myself, to validate my new living quarters, on a map.

At the Saint Paul station I stick the orange ticket of my *carte orange* pass into the turnstile and get on the train, direction Charles de Gaulle Etoile. From Châtelet I walk across the Seine and the Ile de la Cité to the boulevard Saint Michel and the Sorbonne. Yesterday I'd spent half an hour planning the route with the help of the Plan, which includes maps of the métro and bus routes, plus lists of post offices, churches, administrations. It's like carrying the whole city in the palm of my hand.

There are a lot of people already milling around the registration office in the daunting, domed building that is the Sorbonne. My stomach is in knots when I take my place in the line amidst my fellow students who appear already to have made friends, formed little groups. In front of me is a mass of long blond hair, like a mockery of my own thin, light brown straggle.

When it's the blond hair's turn, there appears to be a problem. The mane is now being flicked irritably over her shoulder, wound into a loose knot, then abandoned.

"My father pay." Not only is the conjugation incorrect. There isn't even a hint of a French accent.

"So you say," the woman behind the desk replies. "But we have no record of any payments made."

The blond hair's husky voice says in English: "What are you saying? I don't understand." She turns. The face too is gorgeous.

"Can I help?"

"Is this lady saying I'm not paid up?"

"Tell Mademoiselle 'anson," the woman says, "that there's no sign of a transfer. These payments must be made by bank transfer."

The woman shoves the papers into my hands and explains that Mademoiselle must contact her parents or someone in the United States and resolve this problem quickly or she won't be able to stay on the course. As I translate, the beautifully blond Meredith Hanson eyes me with interest.

"How come you speak French so well?"

"I had a French…" I can't say *gouvernante* with this cool person. "I had a French babysitter."

"So why are you doing this course?"

"I've never lived here. I thought it would be nice." Squirm. Nice is an idiotic word, said Miss Bonner, my favorite English teacher. She forbade us from using it in our essays. "I've just finished university and don't know what I want to do. You know, with life."

"I'm just a junior, but I can definitely relate," Meredith nods. "I have *no* idea what to do once I graduate." She looks around and wriggles her torso. "I need to get out of here. When you're finished, let's go to a café."

"Sure," I say, handing my own papers to the woman behind the desk.

Meredith waits for me to finish, tells me again how much she envies my French. On the way out we run into her college friend and flatmate, overweight and heavy-faced Carol. It occurs to me that Meredith may be the type to surround herself with the ugly and the un-cool, to highlight her own superior looks and manner. But this is just a fleeting notion. I'm happy as a puppy to be tagging along with others. To be charming them over *cafés-crème* with the broad strokes of my story. My American parents who came to study in England on Fulbright grants and never went back, my hybrid sort of childhood.

Meredith is from California. Santa Barbara. And Carol is from Chicago.

"I've been there," I say.

"Really?" says Meredith. "To Chicago?"

"That's where my mother grew up."

"So we could have run into each other on the street once upon a time," says Carol.

"I doubt it. We only went once."

"What did you think?" asks Carol.

"It was cool," I say, nodding vaguely.

"We both go to Northwestern," says Carol. "You know, in Evanston." No, I don't know, but I keep nodding like those fake dogs with the articulated necks that bob along in the back of cars.

"Yeah, Dad wanted me to go east," says Meredith.

"You can hardly call Illinois east," says Carol.

"It seemed east to me. And it was the best place I got into."

"Not only did I grow up right next door, my parents also both went to Northwestern. So how pathetic am I?" Carol opens her fleshy arms, looks around the café. "This is my rebellion, I guess."

"Is that why you came?" I ask. "To rebel?"

"I just needed a change," Carol shrugs.

"For me," says Meredith with a little smile, "it's ever since I had this suave French teacher in high school. I got a thing in my head about learning this language."

"We're about to get some more practice," says Carol looking at her watch. "The landlord's coming over to see about that dripping faucet, remember?"

"Let's hope I deal with him better than I did with that asshole lady behind the desk." Meredith stands up and stretches, exposing a swathe of midriff. She is almost plump, but the extra flesh just adds to her overall appeal, seems part of a zest for living, rather than a lack of self-control. "Where are you staying?"

"I have a room at an old lady's place. In exchange for making her breakfast."

"Sounds like a pretty good deal," says Carol.

"As long as she leaves you alone," says Meredith. "Old ladies have nothing better to do than get overly interested in other people's lives."

"She's going blind."

"Still," Meredith persists. "I hope she's not knocking on your door every five minutes, crowding your space."

"No. I can't imagine her doing that."

"Well, let's go." Meredith throws a bill on the table and turns to the door. "What do I owe you?"

"Forget it. In exchange for your help. Really nice to meet you, Lily."

"Yeah," says Carol. "We'll see you around."

Why didn't I tell them more about the place des Vosges? Was I afraid they wouldn't believe me? Or that they'd insist on seeing it and I would have to deny their request? When I told them about Chicago, why didn't I mention that I never met my grandparents, that the trip was made after they'd died? I said it was cool, a word that besides sounding completely uncool coming out of my mouth, was untrue. It was steaming hot and it was there, in Chicago, that I began to lose Jane.

My mother is always saying: "*The less said the better.*" In fact, if we had a family motto that would be it. Don't discuss anything that clouds the blue skies of normality. Ignore the past, no matter how troubling it might have been. For the first time I wonder if my mother isn't right. Forget the bad stuff; let this year be a fresh start on a clean slate. I've already made two friends. Or two people who seem well-disposed to me anyway. Meredith even called me exotic, is envious of my French. Both allowed that this was their first time outside the United States.

"Hawaii," said Meredith. "Dad loves Hawaii and that's where my family goes on vacation every year."

"Beats Michigan," said Carol. "Every summer two weeks in Michigan. On the lake. How dull is that?"

Here in Paris, I am clearly walking under a different sun, so why not follow its lead?

*＊＊

Tuesday, 28 September 1982

Maybe this journal is not a good idea. Instead of being a repository that frees my head, it's more like a cauldron where memories heat up and bubble to the surface, then crowd my nights and play havoc with my sleep. Writing makes me think and remember more. Now not just my mother but the whole damn family, my life on the ranch. It comes back in snatches. Like photographs or film clips. Helping my mother cook for the men. Helping my father with the horses. Winter air smacking me in the face, making my cheeks sting and my nostrils tingle, then summer air that felt like it had come straight through the gates of hell. Our stone house, built by the grandparents I never met, was a cool refuge in summer and a warm one in winter until day after day of snow and forced internment made it feel more like a prison. The little schoolhouse, one class for everyone, and poor Miss Elver trying to overcome all that ignorance and indifference. As I got older, I would watch her stiff movements at the blackboard and imagine my bookish self ending up just like her. Or there I am riding behind Ted, his body fused with the horse, as if he'd been born on its back. Or there we are the two of us, escaping when we had a free hour in summer, running on the red soil next to the mountain creek; there he is, jumping straight as a pencil from the boulder into the icy pool. Or there I am, alone on the rock outcrop next to the pond letting my horse graze, while I stare across miles and miles of rolling plains at those mesas until I wonder if they are real or merely a mirage expressly designed to torture me, to feed my frustrated wanderlust.

When I emerge from these reveries, it's as if the last sixty-five years never happened. As if I have been taken out of my body, and I find myself wondering who is the real Me? The perky farm girl or the bag of bones in this Paris chair?

*＊＊

My shiny new electric kettle begins to whoosh as it heats up its first cup of tea.

Following Germaine's advice, I went to the BHV department store, not far from here, to buy it. The place has everything, including entertainment. Under a wide overhang are all kinds of merchants, selling their wares. One woman turned large, silken scarves from neckwear into shirts and skirts and belts with smooth, unbroken movements, like a dancer. Next to her a man already surrounded by mounds of chopped, diced or sliced cucumbers and carrots delivered his sales pitch at the same break-neck speed as the blades of his device kept chopping, dicing and slicing.

Everything is more dramatic here, from this strange living situation to my newly active social life. Last night for example, after the BHV, I went to Meredith and Carol's three-room apartment near Saint Michel for dinner. The flat is more expensive than its run down condition and five flights of narrow, uneven stairs deserve, but as Carol said, you pay for dilapidation in the heart of the Latin Quarter. "What else are Americans good for in Europe," she shrugged. "We're here to be ripped off."

Meredith said: "I bought this chicken fresh off the spit. You can't do that in the US. Just taste it."

The chicken was good. But the salad. The dressing was sweet and the ingredients, which included large chunks of raw red peppers, were indigestible. Though that is only occurring to me now. During the dinner I was too busy drinking red wine and talking to mind about a silly salad. Here in Paris, it's good-bye to thy shy self.

I didn't roll in until after two. This morning, when the alarm went off, I had a reeling head. After giving Madame her breakfast, I crawled right back into my cottony, feathery heaven, and when I woke up again it was mid-day and time for a picnic in the Tuileries that Meredith had organized.

There were eight of us. An English guy called Ronnie, a Canadian girl called Una, another Californian called Lara who's nothing like Meredith—dark-haired, delicate and good at French—and the very wealthy Luisa from Trinidad. Then there was the New Yorker Gary, who spewed information like the fountain spouted water. We learned that the gardens had been designed by Louis XIV's gardener, Le Nôtre; that the obelisk at the Concorde was the oldest monument in Paris, having been brought back by Napoleon from his Egyptian campaign; that Napoleon had planned to put a statue of a giant elephant instead of the Arc de Triomphe at the top of the Champs-Elysées. The extent of his knowledge was impressive, I guess, but it was his overbearing delivery that fascinated me. Watching Gary was like observing a different species. My father is American but very subdued, by nature and maybe too from so many years abroad. And the Englishmen I am used to, even if just as pompous underneath, cloak their self-importance with a silvery tongue. Gary's is all brass.

While he talked and talked, I also observed Meredith. At first, she looked on with a wry smile. Then she closed her eyes and tilted her face to the soft autumn sun and appeared to stop listening altogether. Until she suddenly opened her eyes, leaned forward and said in her husky voice:

"It's Sunday, Gary. The day of rest. Here—have a swig of wine." She nodded at Carol to pass him the bottle. Leaning back again and looking around with a smile, she added: "And what better way to spend it than sitting in this green chair, sipping wine and watching Paris go by."

I have never met anyone as naturally cool and uninhibited as Meredith Hanson. Thoughts seem to travel from her brain to her lips without stumbling over worries about what is right or wrong, good or bad, to say. I set down my mug of tea, pick a piece of lint from my cardigan that, following Meredith's lead, I've started wearing shirtless. It feels deliciously soft against my skin. This city is old, but life here feels as fresh and novel as my shiny new kettle.

***

Sunday, 3 October 1982

Why Octave had to choose the room right above mine. She may be quiet as a mouse, but even mice can be heard when they scratch around a place. When I am in my bedroom, I can hear her walk, stop, walk again on the old floorboards. The armoire creaks open, moans shut. I can even hear the water running and splashing in the sink. The sink that is there because when we began renovating this building, François had them installed—along with a raised toilet rather than the squat-down Turkish kind that used to be at the end of the corridor—in the shamefully rudimentary service quarters. He had the idea of renting the rooms out to students like her. His prescience can be eerie, even now.

Her door has just closed. Silence. Blessed silence. She must have gone out, presumably on her way to learning something first-hand about *la civilisation française.*

I too was lapping it up at her age. The good years of Paris, the good years with François. Even by Quinon standards, it was a prosperous time. The family soap business was booming, had started exporting to New York, after François had noticed how clean Americans were and how much they liked things French. We spent a week there, before the ship sailed for Le Havre. It was more of a cultural shock to American, farm-girl me than to Parisian François. All those people and buildings crammed so close together. The noise. The smells. The city assaulted my every sense, and the first two days I felt numb from the shock. But by the third day the buzz began to hum through me, wake me up. We had dinner with Father's cousins, the ones who had sent us François. He was a lawyer and his wife just the kind of woman my mother wanted to be. Elegant and cared for. I could feel their surprised approval of me, and it seemed to bode well for the future. The day before we sailed, François bought me a fur-lined coat at Saks Fifth Avenue, and I felt the luckiest woman on the planet.

That week was good preparation for Paris, another dense city. It was odd. I immediately preferred it, even if I couldn't understand what was being said around me. Or maybe that made it easier. There was no pressure to fit in; as a foreigner I could feel comfortable as an observer. And Paris in the twenties felt like the center of the universe. Every artist who was anyone was here. There was room, and it was affordable, for the old guard and the avant-garde. Past, present and future felt reconciled. Civilization felt perfectly balanced.

The Quinon apartment on the rue de Tournon was in the thick of it, not far from Le Dôme and La Coupole at Montparnasse and a ten-minute walk from the Deux Magots and the Café de Flore at Saint Germain des Près. It was just a fact of life in those days, passing well-known artists and writers in the street, sitting next to them at cafés or dancing side by side at the clubs. They'd be at the same parties, or we'd get invited to theirs. Gertrude Stein and Alice Toklas threw huge soirées, though François didn't like those. Too many people on the make, he said.

Shakespeare and Company was right around the corner on the rue de l'Odéon. Sylvia Beach, with her bird-like, distracted manner, was nice to everyone, regardless of their standing in the world. It was she who encouraged me to study at the Sorbonne, as she had in her early days of Paris. Ernest Hemingway, who arrived not long after I did, often stopped by for a chat. He wasn't yet famous, but his self-confidence travelled across the room and penetrated your skin. His eyes undressed you. The flirtations were titillating, but I was too in love with François, whose forearms were just as strong and hairy, to be drawn in. James Joyce stopped by the bookshop often too. If you saw him on the street, with his hat and cane and scruffy tennis shoes, you could almost think he was down and out. But not once he was sitting and talking to Sylvia with that lyrical Irish voice. His face breathed intelligence even through his thick glasses or the patch he sometimes wore over his eye.

Of course, for me Paris glowed. François and I were in love. Sometimes a smile would melt his face, and he'd grab me, twirl me around and say how lucky he was to have found me. There were always parties with lots of dancing, and he was a very good dancer. Sometimes, after his mother and sister went to bed, we put records on the Victrola and twirled around the living room. We went to the clubs too—the fancier ones on the Champs-Elysées or the seedier bohemian ones at Montparnasse—and everyone would watch. Everyone would clap. I felt like a princess, and it was something of a fairy tale, to have been swept away from that hardscrabble ranch to the careless luxury of Paris. My hands became as soft as chamois, my nails clean and unbroken. All I had to do was give orders to the servants employed by any house with means in those days. In a way that was the hardest part, getting used to telling other people what to do and watching while they did the work. Sometimes out of habit at the end of a meal I'd stand up to help clear, only to be stared back into my seat by my mother-in-law. François would laugh. You're witnessing the future, Maman. Be happy someone in the household is prepared for it.

Oh, how good those years were. I didn't see any reason it couldn't last forever.

***

Every morning I give Madame her breakfast, eat my own baguette-butter-honey magic and, weekdays, head off to classes at the Sorbonne. There are lectures on grammar, on phonetics and on *civilisation*—history, literature, philosophy, art. There is a writing class called *expression écrite sur textes littéraires*. We have smaller classes as well, TD, *travaux dirigés*, tutorials to back up the lectures or clear up what we haven't understood, though even these are pretty *dirigistes*. It's assumed we understand everything already. Same as at the *lycée français*, my first experience of school. Apparently there's no room for the slow or the slothful in the French education system at any level. My reports always read: *pourrait mieux faire*. But then Jane, a very serious student, also got the could-do-better comment. Now, whether I get a nine or an eighteen out of twenty, it doesn't matter. There's no one to be disappointed in me.

We've been studying Romanesque architecture, reading *Tristan et Iseut*—so tragically romantic in their ill-fated devotion it made my heart ache—and learning about the ideas of Descartes. *I think therefore I am.* I like that philosophy, his generally positive attitude.

Then there's Paris herself. The light shining down a narrow street, the harmony of the façades, behind which hum thousands of stories that I can still feel reverberating. Like the one Gary told us on the way back from the Sunday picnic about Marie-Antoinette in what is now the palais de Justice, a building I walk by once or twice a day on my way to and from the Sorbonne. The deposed queen, stripped of her finery and her hair, was imprisoned in one of its towers. The days must have been interminable, but finally the guards come to get her—she hears their boots tromping up the stairs to her cell. She is thrown into an open cart that rumbles towards the place de la Concorde, then named place de la Révolution, and the guillotine. An angry crowd hurls insults at her bonneted head; she apologizes to the executioner for stepping on his foot…sometimes when I snap out of it, I am surprised to see cars rolling by me in the streets.

After class I often help Meredith and Carol, especially Meredith, with the homework. Or a group of us sit at Chez les Gaulois, drinking coffee or wine. Maybe not people who would naturally be friends, but we are all in the same small boat, strangers in a strange land.

On my way back to the place des Vosges, I pick up a baguette at the bakery, buy some cheese, tomato and saucisson at the Félix Potin around the corner. Evenings I eat in my room, do whatever homework there is.

Nothing wildly exciting—the way I guess a year in Paris is supposed to be—but exciting enough for me. Especially after that amorphous post-graduate summer, when I slept as long as I could just to pass the time and was forever trying to finish *Sophie's Choice*. My room here feels like the first home of my own. No family, no other students. Just me, on my own. Madame's gruffness puts a bit of a damper on things—I like to be liked—but she's a small part of my day, my Paris life. And I have to keep in mind that there's plenty of time for bigger things to happen. My year has just begun.

***

Thursday, 14 October 1982

Germaine took me to the hairdresser yesterday. It was a soggy, mournful morning but the outside air, the sound of spoons clinking against cups and the voice of an impatient waiter as we walked by the corner café were a welcome distraction from my now largely indoor life.

My old hairdresser retired recently, and her replacement is a young man whom I imagine from his high voice is a homosexual. Octave has told me in plangent tones that the Marais "is filling up with them." Another sign, I guess, of how the world I knew has changed.

He told me that his name is Marcel. Then he said proudly Proust. Really, I said. It's a *un nom de ciseaux*, he said, snacking his scissors—at least he could make a joke of sorts—but I wondered if such a personage really knew how to cut hair. Especially when he began gingerly touching what's left of mine.

It's not contagious, I said.

He removed his hand.

Old age, I mean.

I'm just trying to imagine what we might do.

We might cut it, I said. A little shorter than it is now. The scissors began to snip. After a moment, I asked him if he lived in the neighborhood.

I wish, he said. It's way too expensive.

I almost laughed out loud. Until not so long ago, no one wanted to live in the Marais, except my husband François. It was falling to pieces and poor, still known as the Jewish ghetto.

One day, though, he said, I hope to have a salon of my own and move here. It's the best *quartier* of Paris. By far.

From his voice I thought he was very young. His wishful optimism confirmed it.

I'm sure you will, I said.

When Germaine got me back, through the *portail* and up the stairs to my sitting room, I sat in an armchair and closed my eyes and I was right back there in the taxi with François on the way home from the theater in the late nineteen-fifties. Our talkative driver told us that he lived on the place des Vosges, that his father had bought the place right after the war for a song. That property was still a steal.

I guess that must be right, François said, leaning forward in the seat.

I could see him thinking. His eyes darted busily, his jaw muscles got to work. A month or so later, he came home all excited—in itself remarkable then—and told me over supper that he had a plan. He was going to sell Pallet et Fils, the family soap business, and purchase a house on the place des Vosges. Magnificent, he'd said breathlessly. I want to do it up and turn the building into apartments. It wasn't until sometime later that he mentioned selling our current home too and moving to one of the new apartments ourselves. Not only is it an excellent business opportunity, he said. It's also a way to put all this, and his hands waved like a man surrounded by wasps, behind us.

By then the rue de Tournon was indeed crammed full of stinging memories, and he convinced me that this was just the new start we needed.

But when he brought me over here, my heart sank, down and out through my shoes. Yes, under the grime the buildings had a certain inherent elegance, traces of their noble origins. But the place des Vosges then was sad as a beaten dog. Every façade was decrepit, and the middle of the square was bare earth with only four lampposts. We walked under the arcades while the rain came down. He stopped in front of the arched *porte cochère*, the heavy rectangles and the fanning sun—surely it is setting, I remember thinking—and pulled out a heavy key. When he opened *la porte piétonne*, it stuck, and he had to ram the door open with his shoulder.

Inside was no better than out. Paint peeling, plaster falling, window-panes broken. The apartments at the back still had tenants, people so poor I felt ashamed in my silk shirt and cashmere cardigan. Don't worry, said François, I'm going to help them find better accommodations. No matter how hard I tried to ride the wave of his enthusiastic imaginings, I felt bleak to the point of despair that day he led me through the dusty, dilapidated rooms and outlined his vision for restored grandeur.

Afterwards, we argued.

You can't do this, I said. The place is a nightmare. There is talk of tearing down the whole *quartier*.

I know there is, he said, that's why people like us need to move in.

You can't fight the French state, I said, the whole Modernist movement.

You'll see, he said. The *quartier* will survive and re-discover its former glory. One day people will be longing to live in the Marais.
As usual he was right, and now it's beyond the means of hairdressers who rename themselves Marcel Proust.

***

Meredith and Carol are giving a party tonight to lift their spirits. It's been raining a lot and "It's *sooo* depressing," says Californian Meredith. I have spent the day inside my room doing some homework and sleeping, writing a short letter to my parents, an answer to the vapid biweekly missive I receive from my mother. That shopping day in London, I have concluded, meant nothing.

Early evening, when I catch sight of myself in the spotted mirror over the sink, I do not like what I see. My face looks like the man in the moon gone pink. How can I possibly go to a party with a face like that? Who would want to look at it much less converse with it? The groaning armoire clearly agrees, and I would like to crawl into a ball inside it, instead of choosing clothes to wear from within it. But how can I not go? What would I say to Meredith? I just didn't feel up to it? No. Meredith would never accept that excuse.

I put on the black jeans bought with my mother and a black pullover Jane left behind. I drape a blue cotton scarf, also a mother's-day purchase, around my neck but take it off again. I can't decide if the splash of color is an improvement or a hopelessly failed attempt at panache.

I should have known better than to spend the whole day inside and alone. It leaves too much space and time for The Mood, the thing that bubbles up like crude oil, smothering me in a dark, slippery coat of gloom. With The Mood comes self-doubt, self-loathing. The certainty that I will never amount to anything, that I am a Loser with a capital L, who will bumble through life, miserable and alone. Just like Madame Flaviche predicted. There's fear too. Fear that I will end up like Maude. Like our mother.

Once I asked Jane if she ever felt anything like The Mood and she looked back at me as if I were indeed batty.

"These things can be genetic, you know," I said.

"Yes. They *can* be. They don't *have* to be."

"You never feel low?"

"Not like *that*. Not like *them*." She sat down next to me on my bed, put a hand on my knee and looked at me with those hazel eyes that had been protecting me my whole life. "You're just a sensitive soul, Lily. A sensitive soul and a dreamer. And not all dreamers are nutters."

"Maybe," I answered, only mildly reassured.

This evening I will defy The Mood and carry on as planned. I rewind the blue scarf around my neck, put on my jacket and leave, before another wave of doubt can send me into the armoire. On the way over there I push myself out of myself, force my mind to think of nothing but the stone streets that have been standing here for centuries and the light from the streetlamps twinkling on the Seine. It does lift my spirits an inch or two. Until I'm outside Meredith and Carol's apartment. Party voices sound menacing, mocking. Surely their laughter is directed at me—or it will be—and I cannot bring myself to ring the bell. Heart pounding, I turn away, take two steps down the stairs and hear other partygoers coming up. It's Ronnie, Lara and Luisa. I'm trapped.

No sooner am I inside than Meredith's hand is on my shoulder.

"Hey!"

Carol is there too with a young man. "Hi, Lily," she says. "Glad you're here."

"Oh, Carol, Carol," says Meredith. "Come with me. The teaching assistant I invited has no one to talk to."

"Meet Thibaud," she says as Meredith pulls her away by the arm.

There we are, thrown together, and I am terrified, thanks to no brothers and an all-girls school. At university I made not a single male friend. If I am shy in the best of circumstances, with members of the opposite sex I become paralytic.

"A glass of wine?" he asks, in heavily accented English.

"Sure."

We snake our way to the table with the wine and the peanuts and the raw vegetables with dip.

"White or red?" he asks, taking two plastic cups from the stack.

"Red, please," I say, eying him while he pours. His brown hair is almost chaotic, just a little too short to allow the curls full flourish and a little too long to tame them completely. His delicate face, with a high, broad forehead and triangular nose, tapers towards the chin. "What brings you here?" I ask.

"Sorry?"

"Why are you at this party?" I enunciate slowly, loudly.

"I meet Carol before the university."

"Are you a student?" I soldier on. He leans his ear towards me; I try French. "I suppose you have no need for a course in *la civilisation française*."

He laughs, replies in English: "No one ever really understand *that*. I study the law."

I nod, take a sip of my wine. "I studied law too." I do not add that it had been the wrong choice. As Jane said once the decision had already been made, my mind is too fanciful, overly prone to flights of imagination. "Though you have every right to be a stickler for justice," she added with the reproachful look she always got when referring, however obliquely, to family matters.

"You did? Where?"

"In England. Undergraduate."

"You are not American?"

"Technically, yes, I am."

"Technically," he repeats.

"My parents are American. But I grew up in England."

"And you speak French?"

The pink face deepens to pulsing red. I say very fast, hoping he won't understand: "We had a French nanny when we were young," then change the subject and speed. "Are you from Paris?"

Now it's Thibaud who looks uncomfortable. He shifts and looks down, crosses his arms over his chest and hoods his brown eyes slightly. "No."

I sip my wine, waiting for further information. "Then where?"

"Well. My father is a diplomat. I—"

"Okay everyone!" Meredith shouts above the crowd. "Time to dance!" The music on the cassette tape deck Meredith bought last week is turned up. A deep and sexy American voice sings: "Everybody's got a hungry heart, everybody's got a hungry heart, uh-uh." I do not recognize the song, but its energy is irresistible. Some people, singing along, start dancing immediately. Others step back to leave space and watch. I assume this is Thibaud's cue to ditch me but instead he leans towards my ear and says with an avid but childish smile:

"I love to dance. Let's go."

As is quickly apparent, Thibaud is indeed a very enthusiastic dancer though not a good one. Flailing might be a better word to describe his interaction with the music. We hop around for quite a few songs, never touching. At one point I wonder if he has forgotten my presence altogether. When a slow song comes on, we and others ebb away from the dance area. Now, I think, it's now he's going to excuse himself and start chatting up someone else. But—

"From where is your family in the USA?" he asks as we retrieve our plastic cups.

"My mother's family is from Chicago. My father's from Oklahoma."

He appears to be concentrating very hard. I doubt he's ever heard of Oklahoma.

"One day I will go there, to the USA," he says.

"Why? Don't you like France?"

He shrugs like the country makes his skin itch. "It is too old. There is no future here."

"That's what I like about it. The old, I mean, not the no future."

He laughs, leans towards me again. "Do you like parties?"

Since I don't know whether or not I like parties, I look to see what answer he might like to hear. It is not apparent, so I say: "Sometimes. It depends. What about you?"

"Same. Depends."

The music's gone upbeat again. "*Allez*," he nods towards the dance floor and we're back to hopping around.

There is a loud knock on the door. Someone turns down the music. "Please," says an agitated middle-aged man. "It's midnight. We can't sleep."

"I apologize," Meredith says in English, which throws him off his irritation. She puts her hand to her heart. "I am so sorry. We'll turn it down right now." He smiles at her big blue eyes as she closes the door. "Okay, guys, music off."

Thibaud says: "I must go now. The last métro depart soon."

"I should get the last train too," I say, though other late nights I've walked back to the place des Vosges.

"I go here," he says on the street, at the Saint Michel station. I could join him and change after one stop at Châtelet. But the connection is labyrinthine, including a moving walkway in a mile-long corridor that I always avoid. Plus—new self—I want to resist my tendency to be overly eager:

"I'll catch the train on the other side of the river."

There is an awkward moment. Finally, he leans forward stiffly and kisses me on both cheeks, causing a tingle that stays with me well beyond my trip back to the place des Vosges.

***

Sunday, 17 October 1982

When I arrived in Paris late 1920, Proust was still (barely) alive, and *la Recherche* was being published volume by volume. He'd won the prix Goncourt the year before for *A l'ombre des jeunes filles en fleurs,* and he was the talk of the town, though at that point I couldn't understand any of it, either the books or the chatter. François, who thought the writing brilliant and the person a fop, would say to me: The conversations that people are having and their opinions about the book provide living proof of the perfect tableau Proust paints of Paris society. He'd shake his head, adding: It's all there, right down to the half-turn of a heel.

My early efforts to read the books, once my French got good enough, were abandoned because I found the sickly narrator overly precious. Maybe also because I was too busy discovering first-hand the world he so microscopically depicted. François' family was *de la haute bourgeoise,* not aristocratic—the Verdurins rather than the Guèrmantes—but the circles overlapped in real life too. Having grown up in a place where the nearest neighbor was uncouth and miles away, where friendships were recent and expedient, where the land had only been settled by us white people for a generation, I was mesmerized by the sophistication, the friendships that went back generations, the intimacy, the proximity of people and their coded interaction. For me, Paris was the New World and I wanted to live it, not read about it.

Maybe too my own sense of time and memory and loss was not yet well enough developed to connect with Proust. If that was the case, the Second War took ample care of those deficiencies.

In the early years, I was embarrassed by the remembrance of my own past. What other writers—Henry James and Edith Wharton, for example—described as the Franco-American dynamic of the wealthy American woman recruited to *redorer le blason,* as they say, put the gold back on the family crest of a spendthrift French aristocrat, did not apply to me. I was poor as a church mouse, and it was François' family that was prosperous. Though the soap company was founded by his Catholic grandfather from the south, François was the one to make a success of it. He put this down to the Protestant, Alsatian blood on his mother's side. Our money goes into the bank, he said, where it accumulates and comes back out in calibrated drips. We do not waste hard-earned cash on mistresses and card games.

Now, as more of a spectator than a participant in my own life, I wonder why I didn't put my origins to good use. The wild west, guns and cowboys and Indians—all that rubbish. The chronically ironic French love a dash of exoticism in their generally spice-free diet, and I could have fashioned my story into a zesty dish. Instead, I allowed myself to feel cowed by that more potent ingredient in Parisian nourishment: snobbism.

Fortunately, my social life was not limited to those incurables. During the twenties there were throngs of other nationalities, and many of them by no means rich. Walking in our *quartier* I was just as likely to hear English or Russian as French. I made friends in the expat world too, which delighted François, who found too many of his compatriots closed, arrogant and spoiled. We should have stayed in Wyoming, he sometimes said after a dinner party. Bought a ranch. You wouldn't say that if you'd spent a winter there, I'd reply. If you'd met more of our neighbors. As for me, I felt happy with a foot in each world, the French and the expat. The city was so vibrant and open, anyone could find a place. No project, artistic or otherwise, seemed too wild. It was Sylvia, after all, who brought Joyce's *Ulysses* to the larger world when no publishing house would have him. François and I contributed money to the project.

It was no wonder black Americans like Josephine Baker felt at home here, along with homosexuals like Proust or lesbians like Sylvia and Adrienne, Gertrude and Alice. It was a time of Tolerance with a capital T. Of course there were plenty of Octaves then too—there's never any shortage of them—and after a certain time, with the help of the Nazis, their Intolerance took hold again. The aesthetes were run out of town, all the way to New York, and Paris' moment, like mine, was over.

***

I t's a lovely early autumn day. The air pricked my nose when I walked out this morning, but a soft sun has taken the edge off and put the Paris stone in a honey yellow light that warms my soul while I wait for Meredith and Carol on this bench outside the Sorbonne.

If only I could stop thinking about Saturday and that man, that Thibaud, and what our dancing all evening meant, if anything. Dancing, even when you're not touching, is an intimate, fusional experience, but once it's over, I guess, so is the we-are-one feeling. At least in this case, apparently. I have not heard from him since—though how and why would I have? We did not exchange *coordonnées*, addresses and telephone numbers.

Something interferes with my musings. I look up and it's him, Thibaud, standing stock still and staring at me. From this distance his oval face looks flawless. When he sees me seeing him, he walks towards me. I stand up, hike my bag onto my shoulder, squint into the sun.

"You looked lost in thought," he says.

"I was thinking about the lovely day and how good it is to be in Paris."

"It is a lovely day."

"But Paris is terrible, right?"

He smiles. "No, I was not thinking that right this minute." When speaking French, he sounds more—I don't know—manly, more grown up.

"I think it's the most beautiful place I've ever been."

"Hey, anybody up for some lunch?" It's Meredith, with Carol in tow, saving me from my own idiotic comments. "Let's grab a table at Chez les Gaulois."

With Meredith there, all awkwardness vanishes. Shyness is as foreign to her as the French she's so keen to master. "What did you think of our party, Thibaud? You sure looked like you were enjoying yourself."

"It was re-all-y fun," he says.

"Jean-Paul, our teaching assistant, said he had a good time too," Meredith says, leaning back, making a knot of her hair.

"He's cute," says Carol.

"I think he's gay," says Meredith.

"That's what you say about any guy who's not fawning all over you," says Carol.

The waiter appears. Like me, Thibaud orders a *Paris beurre*, a ham and butter sandwich, cheapest item on the menu. Meredith and Carol order *salades niçoises*. "*Sans anchois*," says Carol to the waiter and to us: "Those are two words in French I'll never forget—no anchovies. Yuck. With those bristles it's like having someone's eyebrows lie on your salad."

"That's so gross, Carol. Stop it," says Meredith.

"What was Jean-Paul saying this morning, Lily, about Notre Dame?" asks Carol. We are now on to Gothic architecture. "I didn't get all the details."

"He said that the cathedral was built on the ruins of a Gallo-Roman temple. He talked about how much it's changed over the centuries. There were times when it was neglected and damaged. During the Revolution, for example, it was pillaged, then later renovated by some guy called Violet-le-Duc. He added the spire." I shrug. "Stuff like that." I had been riveted by the story of the cathedral and now feel slightly embarrassed—I don't know why—maybe for Jean-Paul and the super personal way he was talking about it. He could have been describing the ups and downs in the life of a human friend. "He finished by saying: 'She is the pulsing heart of our city.'"

"Wow. We'll have to go again and have a closer look," Carol says.

"I told you he was gay," says Meredith.

Our food comes. Carol pokes her salad with the fork to make sure no anchovy is lurking under a lettuce leaf, like it was last time. Meredith digs in, says to Thibaud before she shoves salad in her mouth: "You said you knew some Americans from last year. How do we compare?"

"Good," Thibaud says.

"How did they meet you?" Carol asks. "It seems like here we are in Paris and besides you and Jean-Paul, we never meet any French people."

"I walk out of my lecture to the place du Panthéon and they ask me if *le Panthéon* is a church. The girl, Cathy, had very white teeth. How do you Americans find such white teeth?"

"The dentist does it. With a machine." Thibaud gives a blank nod, almost as if not quite sure about the practice of dentistry in general.

"My English become much better with them. I hope further better with you."

So that's why he is spending time with us, to improve his English, undoubtedly in the context of his grand plan to go to the US. My heart, I admit, sinks a notch. Though his little story sounded charming, with the accent and the mistakes, I do not like speaking in English to Thibaud. Trying to slow down, speak clearly and use easy words makes me feel even more awkward and boring and exposed than when I speak normally.

But this thought doesn't stay long in my head. Meredith and Carol are recounting their trip to the post office. The long wait, the lack of a queue.

"Do people in this country even know what a line is?" asks Carol.

"Of course we *know*," says Thibaud. "But we do not like to obey the rules. We like to make a big circle around them," he stretches his long arm around. "It is, how you would say, *une spécialité parisienne*."

"Well, you certainly have to have sharp elbows," says Meredith.

"Yes, that is better," says Thibaud. "At the post office maybe you learn a more important lesson in *la civilisation française* than a careful study of Notre Dame." We laugh. His eyes light up. "You know, *sans anchois* is maybe a more useful phrase than the name of Violet-le-Duc."

This moment, sitting at a sunny café in front of the Sorbonne with—okay, let's call them friends—feels like paradise. Like I couldn't ever want anything else in the world. For a few seconds I can even forget my constant worry about money and dose out the francs for my sandwich without regret. Before Thibaud heads back up the hill to the Panthéon and the law faculty, the four of us agree to meet again on Saturday evening, a plan for the future that makes a prefect ending to the present.

As we settle into our seats for the afternoon lecture on the Age of Enlightenment, Meredith says: "You make a very cute couple."

"We're not a couple."

"He's obviously not interested in me," says Carol. "Even though I'm the one who met him first."

"He told us. He just likes hanging around Americans," I say.

"But you're not," says Carol, "a real American."

"Who is a real American," says Meredith. "We're all mutts."

"Speak for yourself," says Carol.

I don't know how mutt and Meredith can even be uttered in the same sentence. But I keep quiet, know that I have to be careful not be seen as interfering in their friendship. I feel a little sorry for Carol. She is picking up the language. Even her accent isn't bad. And if she weren't so heavy, I think she could be pretty. As it is, her face crowds her nice hazel eyes with extra flesh; her body is bulky and her step lumbering. Her hair needs a good cut.

The professor enters, puts his papers on the lectern and begins explaining to a hall scattered with Americans the Enlightenment ideals on which their country of mutts is founded. Meredith called us a couple, which of course we're not. But he was staring at me. I keep seeing his gaze locked on me as I sat on the bench and what a start it gave me. His dark eyes are intense and beautiful—the perfect distance apart. During lunch they lingered in my direction. Maybe he was astounded at how unattractive I am, really not much better than Carol. That's obviously not what Meredith thought, and I have got to start thinking more like her if I am going to get on in life.

"*Ecoutez-vous vous-même*," the professor is saying. Listen to yourself. "It is one of the founding principles of *Les Lumières*." So far that policy hasn't got me very far, but maybe your thoughts need to be headed in the right direction already before you can believe what they're trying to tell you.

Meredith and Carol's pens are poised above their blank notebooks. I'm not surprised they haven't understood much. The professor is not taking into account his audience's shaky grasp of the language. I shift in my seat and start taking notes so that I can share them later. French tutor is an important function of mine in our relationship.

He is now quoting Montesquieu. I write: "Today we receive three different, conflicting educations: that of our parents, that of our teachers and that of the world. What we learn from the last overthrows all that we've learned from the first two."

Thibaud could be right. Maybe we are learning more at the café or the post office than in these chairs. And if I could overcome some of my parents' instruction, that might constitute real progress.

**

Friday, 22 October 1982

T he girl—in a hurry now to get on with her day—has just come and gone with the debris of my breakfast. She is dependable. Every morning, lying in my own bed, I hear her getting up at seven-ten (my new clock with the extra big numbers tells me), moving around, back and forth like a dormouse in the eaves. At seven-twenty-five I hear her in the kitchen, putting away what was left to dry in the rack the night before. Soon I can smell coffee and toast and at seven-forty-five there's a polite knock-knock, then a pause as she waits for my irascible *Entrez*. She puts the tray down on my writing table, says *à-tout-à-l'heure* and does indeed return a while later, eight-fifteen, to collect the remains. Dishes clatter in the sink. More noise upstairs, then silence for the rest of the day.

Today I asked her about the weather outside, though I could tell it was cloudy even through my shrouded eyes, could feel an autumnal dampness in my bones. But what else does one talk about to a stranger, which I make sure she firmly remains? I think she avoids invitations from Germaine to dine with us and why wouldn't she? I asked Germaine, who said: I hardly ever hear or see her. She's so discreet, so shy, Lily. But yes, she'd probably just as soon not eat with us old ladies.

I bustled once too in the morning, also on my way to the Sorbonne, though it wasn't a course for foreigners. I had to learn French. It was my only means of communication at home with my mother-in-law, the servants Anna and Sabine, François' younger sister Agnès and soon even with François himself. It became so natural that eventually English felt strange coming out of my mouth. But that was much later.

What a time. Both busy and careless. I had few daily tasks—Anna the cook and Sabine the housekeeper took care of all the details—and could focus on my course, on wandering the streets and sitting in cafés—often in disbelief at my luck in having landed here. At night we'd go out or have friends over ourselves. Staying up late and drinking too much wine never seemed to slow us down. Did the sun really shine every day?

***

I've eaten my salad supper and done my grammar exercise on prepositions. I've brushed my teeth and got undressed and into bed. But I can't get Him out of my mind. How he was staring at me in front of the Sorbonne with his handsome, almost beautiful face. The eyes but also his large, rounded forehead, his triangular nose and sensitive mouth. Meredith, the voice of experience in the matter, called us a couple. Maybe, just maybe, there's hope.

A bang downstairs. I listen—nothing else. Has Madame fallen? My heart is pounding in my ears. Nothing. I should ignore it. I turn off the light, hug the bolster pillow. What if she's had a heart attack? A stroke? I get up, slip on my shoes and go downstairs. The kitchen is dead quiet, its edges outlined by the glow of distant city lights. The narrow corridor is windowless and dark. I feel my way along the wall, see a light under the door—not the sitting room, where I deliver her breakfast, but the bedroom. I knock softly. If it isn't a heart attack, I don't want to give her one. Nothing. A little harder. Nothing. I pause, hand on the handle. Holding my breath, I ease the door open a crack but can only see the wall. I push the door a little farther. There is a notebook on the floor and a fountain pen not far from it, as if a crime has been committed. Peeking my head around even farther, I see Madame propped up in bed, head to the side, mouth slightly open. I am sure she has indeed had a heart attack or a stroke, until finally she starts slightly and shifts position. She must have fallen asleep. Relief. But should I pick up the pen and notebook, turn off the light? No. She might wake up. She'll at least know I've been here, witnessed this scene. Very quietly, I pull the door closed again and creep back down the dark corridor, through the eerie light of the kitchen and up the stairs. My heart has stopped pounding, but I feel off-kilter. It was unsettling, walking through the night-time world of Madame Quinon's flat, witnessing her slack-mouthed in bed. She looked haggard and vulnerable. It was an intimate moment, but all the intimacy was on my side, almost as if I had seen her naked. Though I'd like not to feel sorry for the grumpy old woman, I do. It's not something I think much about, being old, but seeing her in that bed, notebook on the floor, it seemed even lonelier than being young. At least at my age, there's still time for improvement.

I climb back in that safe bed, get myself all tucked up. How did Madame end up here in this house, in this city? With her delicate nose and high cheek bones and confident air she looks like one of those New York heiresses, sent to Europe for polishing. Undoubtedly her handsome husband—I know there was one because of the rings that roll around her bony finger and the photos I saw when I looked in the spare room on my way to the bathroom one day—was well-born but short on funds. Maybe his family already owned this flat, but it was her money that allowed them to restore and maintain it. This flat or this building. It's still a mystery. On the ground floor, there are some tall windows. I've peered in while walking through the courtyard. Just empty space. Then there are the stairs that continue upstairs, past Madame's quarters. Could people be living up there and I just haven't seen them? What about the two other sides of the rectangle that wraps around the courtyard, which must be empty too. I've seen no sign of life, day or night. Are they owned by other people or does it all belong to Madame? Once upon a time this place must have been very grand indeed. I can picture the balls and the long, sleek gowns and glittering jewels. Liveried servants with white gloves and magnums of champagne. Maybe Thibaud's grandparents, also diplomats, were among the revellers. Now here Madame is, all alone, looking dead in her bed.

***

Monday, 1st November 1982

When Louise D. telephoned yesterday and said Amenia? my reply got stuck in my throat. It's been a long time since I've heard my name—so many friends and acquaintances are gone or too old to communicate—that I found myself asking: is that really it? Is that really who I am? Funny to keep asking that adolescent question at my age, but now that I think about it, one's never too old to doubt. And the mind lags way behind the body.

At school, amongst the Marys and Janes and Wendys, I was mercilessly teased, especially once it came out that the name derived from a town in the east. My classmates would take on what they assumed to be English accents and pretend to be sipping tea with their little fingers in the air. Ame-e-enia.

My mother named me after the place her family had forced her to leave, Amenia, New York. By clinging to that east coast past, she was being, according to the neighbors and their children, a snoot. When I looked it up on the map, I couldn't figure out what she was so proud of. Amenia is hardly a suburb of New York City. It's way up the Hudson, and from the spaces between the towns, obviously not a densely populated center of culture and refinement. She always tended to hyperbole and melodrama, to an exaggerated self-importance.

It was evident everywhere. The furniture in our house had to be a little more comfortable, a little more elegantly upholstered. Mother would order material all the way from Chicago, then sew it herself. She made the curtains and my dresses. It was the same with food. One wouldn't go so far as to say she approached any kind of European cuisine, but her cooking, with whatever herbs or sauces she added, was a cut above ranch fare.

Anyway, it was only when I brought my odd name over here that I became proud of it. By then everyone was following the flights of Amelia Earhart and my name, close to but distinct from the most famous American woman, was admired in that ironic French way. Now it's back to sounding oddly silly in my ears; embarrassment flushes up my neck and cheeks as if I were once again being taunted in that one-room schoolhouse.

***

It's finally Saturday evening and time to meet Meredith and Carol and Thibaud at the Saint Michel flat. The rain has been falling gently all day, but I was determined to keep The Mood at bay so consulted my Plan de Paris and walked to the place de la Bastille, which is practically right next door. I was hoping to find some traces of the ignominious old prison that I read about in *A Tale of Two Cities* with Miss Bonner, but it's just a big, ugly roundabout with a towering column in the middle of it. The gold angel on top looks silly, hovering above all those hooting cars. But the excursion did pass the time, keep The Mood away and even got my mind off men, or I should say a man, for more than an hour.

On my way down the back stairs, I smell something oniony and delicious coming from the kitchen. There often is at this time of evening. The aromas are an almost irresistible temptation to accept Germaine's invitations to dinner. She's really kind, always has a smile for me, a piece of advice, when I run into her. Madame appears resigned to my presence now. Her thank-yous when I deliver and remove her tray no longer seem to stick in her throat. Once or twice, she has made an effort and mentioned the weather. Still, it's not exactly encouragement to share the evening meal.

In the courtyard a fine, cold drizzle wets my face. I wrap my blue scarf around my head and look up at the yellow light emanating from the kitchen window. It's somewhere between sad and comforting, the image of two women sitting alone but eating yummy food and drinking good red wine.

I must hurry now. After all that waiting, I'm now running late and walk briskly to the Saint Paul métro. I hope at least that we can just sit around their place. It's hard keeping up with Meredith and Carol financially. They have parental money, plus what they've earned from summer jobs. I keep telling myself that I need to find more part-time work but so far haven't been able to force myself back to the notice board at the American Church.

About to push open the door, I hear:

"*Salut.*"

"Hey, Thibaud!" I say but regret immediately trying to imitate Meredith. I sound ridiculous. To shelter himself from the rain, Thibaud stands very close to me. I can smell his wet jacket. It's an old, settled smell, not clean and fresh, like the shampoo smell that constantly hovers around Meredith and Carol.

As we climb the stairs, Thibaud asks me if I know what the plan is.

"Either sit around or go to a café, I guess."

"I'm happy to stay here," he says.

"Me too."

"Let's go," Meredith says, turning off the music, the second we're inside the door. "I'm going stir crazy."

"We haven't been out all day," says Carol. "I noticed a jazz bar around the corner that looks nice. I don't think there's an entry fee."

We hip-hop around puddles on the narrow streets. Men outside the Greek restaurants urge us in broken English to come in, come in, eat here. We—or at least Meredith and Carol, with their compressible umbrellas and Nike trainers—are unmistakably American. Water has seeped through my shoes and my socks. I squelch with each step and wish we could have stayed at the flat. These streets are tawdry in good weather, lurid in the rain, and entry fee or not, I'll have to pay for my measly glass of wine.

And here it is wedged in between a tourist shop and a kebab joint, the basement jazz club Carol was talking about. Inside it is thick with cigarette smoke and crammed with as many tables and chairs as the space can hold. Most are already full but over near the wall, under a photo of a perspiring trumpet player is an empty spot. Once we finally manage to squeeze and excuse our way over to it, I feel better. It's dry. This is a genuine Paris experience. Stuff the cost of the wine.

"The waitress said the musicians return in a minute," says Thibaud. "They take a pause."

"At this point I don't much care about the music. I'm soaked," says Meredith. "I need something to drink."

"God it's crowded in here," says Carol.

"It is not like this in America?" asks Thibaud.

"No way. Personal space is very important to us."

Meredith pours red wine from the liter carafe and has us clinking glasses convivially. To view the band Carol and I must turn our backs to the table, while Meredith and Thibaud are lined up against the wall. The quartet sounds lyrical enough, but I know even less about jazz than pop music. In any case right now I'm having trouble concentrating on it because behind me Meredith and Thibaud are whispering and giggling. Meredith, like a bored cat, has instigated the flirtation. There's no way she is really interested in Thibaud. Nice-looking he may be, but cool he definitely is not. Even I can see that. How could he be so easily drawn in? It's exasperating and how I could have wasted so much time thinking about this mouse. I steal a look at Carol to see if she finds the scene behind us irritating. But she is listening intently to the music, appears not even to notice. She must be used to it.

When the jazz band takes its second break, I am tired. Of the smoke. Of the flirting that is still going on behind me. Of my wet feet. It's nearing midnight.

I stand up abruptly. "I'm going."

"Ah, come on," says Meredith.

"I must go too," I hear Thibaud, at whom I am absolutely not looking, say. "To make the connection. On the train."

"Let's all go," says Carol.

"Yeah," says Meredith. "I guess it's time."

"God, I hate this rain," says Carol, snapping open her umbrella. "Good night!"

Thibaud looks at me for the first time all evening.

"Do you go to Châtelet?"

"Yes, that's where I'm headed," I say in French. I'm in no mood to play his language lab right now.

"How do you pass your weekends?" he persists in English as we walk.

"I walk around a lot," I answer in French. "Catch up on my course work."

"And the old woman?"

"Just breakfast. That's all I have to do."

"Not so bad, I guess."

We have arrived at the station and will go our different ways.

"Tomorrow I go to the cinema. There is a five-franc cheap ticket this weekend for old films. You want to come?"

"Oh," I answer. "Why not."

"Good. See you at four o'clock at the Champollion, rue des Ecoles."

Champollion, Champollion, rue des Ecoles, I repeat over and over in my head. Drizzle is still falling, and Thibaud does not kiss me good-night but that's okay. We're going to the movies. All is forgiven.

***

Monday, 8 November 1982

Octave and company came to tea yesterday. To think I used to be fond of him. I like to blame that horse-faced wife for his ruin-ation but then I remember his mother, poisonous Agnès, and his dreary *petit marquis de Bordeaux* father Georges, and I realize the odds were stacked against him before the poor man was even conceived. Germaine always warned me that I had a blind spot about him. I guess it wouldn't take Sigmund Freud to figure out why.

They were late and from Octave's flustered manner I gathered that the Horse had intentionally delayed them. Tante! he said. So happy to see you! Anyone inflecting two exclamation marks in a row like that must be disingenuous. The Horse's Tante was curt and cold and followed by kisses to my cheeks that felt more like cool stones approaching my skin. They came with their two little girls, Violette and Chloé, who are better behaved and more cordial than their mother. Germaine had pre-pared everything, to protect me from possible embarrassment, such as pouring hot tea on the Horse's lap. Octave waits like a vulture for a jus-tification to put me away. The toaster incident almost did it. It was most un-strategic of me to tell him, and I have to remember that the girl living over my head is infinitely preferable to being forced into some home for the old. Germaine had the kettle ready to boil, the pot with tea in it. A jug of juice for the girls and a plate of little pastries from the bakery. She even offered to stay and serve but I couldn't deprive her of Sunday with Flora and the grandchildren.

I asked how things were going at Pallet et Fils. I've never quite known what to think of Octave's working at the old family soap business. Whether it's laudable or warped. He currently has an upper middling position, but I know he has designs to one day direct the company.

Quite well, he said. The old guard is resistant to change. But I'm hopeful. Tell me, Tante, he cleared his throat. How is the girl getting on?

Fine, I said. She's very discreet.

Yes, that's why I thought you'd like her.

I didn't say I like her.

If you don't like her, we should think…

She does a fine job.

Stupid me, almost falling into another trap already. He'll try anything to get me into an old people's home. To think that this house will go to him—to him and the Horse. They'll probably sell it before they can even toss me in a grave. The Horse would not find the Marais palatable, despite its rising chic. Like so many of her ilk, she'd hate the Jews who still live here and is undoubtedly even less charitable about homosexuals than her husband.

He *was* a more tolerant, thoughtful person when I first met him at François' funeral, or I would never have told him to look me up when he came to study in Paris the following year. When he did knock on my door, after a couple of months in a mice-infested student hotel, I liked him enough to let him move in, which I otherwise wouldn't have done, rodents or not. I even let him stay in the room next to mine, use the furniture that was *his*. We often had dinner together. He talked and talked, as if no one had ever listened to him before. Everybody at Sciences Po, he said, has known each other since before they were born. They don't need any new friends. Certainly not a bumpkin from Bordeaux.

I'd hardly call you a bumpkin, I said, but I knew the type of Parisian he was talking about. They were the children of the ones who'd turned up their Gallic noses at me.

When he was still lonely and untarnished, he would say: My parents were on the wrong side of the war.

Things weren't so obvious then, I'd reply.

But Pétain, he practically spit out the word.

You mustn't forget. He had been a hero during the First War. Some people stay loyal to their heroes.

Not when they're selling the country's soul. Uncle François saw that.

In those days Octave was the religious face of the rebellious sixties. Particularly in the provinces there were plenty of them who believed the world had become too materialistic and needed a radical change of course in the direction of a humbler version of Christianity.

That was the young Octave. Underneath his tidy clothes—always a jacket and an ironed shirt—he was all passion and conscience. Until he did make some friends. Until the horse-faced Marie-France Coursault entered his life and all the humanity in his conservatism got hollowed out. After Sciences Po, he attended business school.

Thankfully, they didn't stay long—hardly long enough for the tea to cool and for them to ask if *l'Américaine* could do some babysitting. We must go, said The Horse. The girls have homework.

And you have designs on all that I have left.

***

I wish I hadn't arrived first. Being first makes me feel too eager. Conspiring too. For once the sun is shining, but the air has a discouraging cold edge that might make Meredith and Carol decide to eat at Chez les Gaulois, rather than come here to the Vert Galant, as Thibaud suggested. I keep hoping that if he and I are alone together something will happen. Hope based on nothing because if sitting in a dark cinema together and watching *To Have and Have Not*, with Humphrey Bogart and Lauren Bacall falling in love on the screen as well as in real life didn't inspire him to take my hand, what possibly could?

The real question that plagues me is: Will anyone, ever, fall in love with me? Or phrased another way: Will anyone ever be moved to put an end to my mortifying condition?

By mortifying condition I mean that in this year of nineteen hundred and eighty-two, I am probably the only person in the western hemisphere if not the entire world who, at the advanced age of twenty-one, is still a virgin. Needless to say, I haven't even done much kissing. There was Tom Willoughby at the school dance when I was sixteen, but I never heard from him again after that evening. It caused weeks of pining and misery. At university there was some half-hearted groping with Alan Stirling, but he had bad breath. It was disgusting. For at least a month I actively avoided him and his rank smell.

What's wrong with me, I wonder for the umpteenth time, my egg salad baguette sandwich right under my hungry nose. What puts men off? My looks? My awkward manner? Some animal signal I give off? I mean, why can't I be more like flouncy Meredith? She hugs and kisses people with abandon, exudes a carnal warmth. Maude says cats that have no contact with people in the first three months of their lives will never accept human caresses. Is that my problem? Early physical deprivation?

Here comes Thibaud ambling along the bridge, with his slight body and beautiful forehead. I'm always surprised how tall he is.

"Hi," he says, squinting into the sun, shattering the geometry of his face. "The other girls do not accompany you?"

"No." One sentence in and his clumsy English is already grating, making me wonder why I would want him to get anywhere near me anyway. And it's not just that the awkwardness and mistakes are jarring. I like his personality better when he speaks in French.

We walk in front of the huge statue of Henri IV on his steed that lords over the Seine. Unlike Louis XIII on the place des Vosges, this king is dressed in armor and has normal hair and a serious face. He is holding onto the reins, not looking goofy like Louis. Does this mean something historically, or is it just artistic interpretation? We haven't yet studied either of these kings.

Down the steps of the Vert Galant, the bushy triangle under the Pont Neuf, we sit on the stone edge, legs dangling over the edge. We eat our sandwiches in silence.

"Doesn't this stuff bore you?" Thibaud finally asks, thankfully in French. Pointing across to the Left Bank. "I mean, look at that old pirate ship parked there. It's stupid."

"No it's not." I had just been admiring the dark wood and intricate crafting of the vintage Dutch sailboat.

"It is. Look at it. Out of a film, not real life."

"There's nothing wrong with old things," I say. "And it *is* real life. Someone lives on it. I just saw a man go inside."

He frowns over his sandwich, pulls off a bite with his teeth, then, with his mouth full: "Why didn't you go to America, instead of coming here? You're so lucky you've got a passport. You could have taken care of an old lady in New York."

"My sister went to New York," I say. "But I'm not interested in going there."

"Why not?"

"I told you. When I went to the US with my family, it was weird."

"And Paris isn't?"

I guess this should be the case. But it's not. "Sort of. Not really."

"What does that mean?"

"When I was in Chicago—I don't know—everyone's been telling me my whole life that I'm American and once I finally got there, it seemed completely foreign. I felt almost guilty about not loving it, not feeling like I'd come home, like my sister Jane did. Here in Paris there's no pressure to feel at home, to fit in. Here I feel like I connect, even if I don't fit, and that seems okay." I pause, wondering if I am making any sense. "Anyway, how do you know you're going to be so happy over there? Since you've never been."

"I just know," he says quietly, eyes half closed. "You see, here I don't connect. And in the United States of America, I think anyone has the chance to fit. I just need to find a way to get there." He kicks the heels of his scruffy shoes against the stone bank. "I want to go there because the US is a country that can still be talked about in the future tense. Whereas this place," he tosses his head towards the old boat, "is all past tense. The imperfect."

He seems deeply unhappy, which makes me uneasy. I search my brain for something to lift the mood. "Why don't you apply for a Fulbright?"

"What's that?"

"They're…" I don't know the word for grant. "They're things you get to pay for your studies abroad. It's how my parents came to England."

"Really—*une bourse*? Do you think I could?"

"Why not. You're a good student, aren't you?" His doubt really surprises me. "There must be an office in Paris."

He nods, smiles for the first time. "That's a good idea. Shall we go? It's freezing down here."

As we turn away, Thibaud throws his sandwich wrapper in the water.

"You're throwing your wrapper in the Seine?"

He shrugs. "The river's filthy already."

We walk up the stairs to the bridge in silence. Thibaud says he has an afternoon lecture and is heading back to the Panthéon. I say I'm done for the day and am returning to the place des Vosges. He heads south; I head north. Maybe I can connect with a place, but people seem beyond my grasp.

***

Wednesday, 10 November 1982

Since Louise lives alone and is almost as infirm as I am, I went *chez elle* yesterday, accompanied by Germaine. She is English, my first friend in Paris, met at the Sorbonne. Later she married Robert, and they had an art gallery on the rue Guénégaud. The four of us spent many an evening and weekend together. During the war we lost touch. The friendship was rekindled when François and I were buying art for the place des Vosges.

After François had his accident, Louise was very kind, phoning me regularly, inviting me to dinner, when so many others avoided or conveniently forgot the as-good-as-widow.

She still lives in the little house on the rue Vaneau. It is off the street, behind another building that until recently was a derelict block of flats—more what you would expect to see here in the old Marais than in the patrician *7ème*. Developers gutted the insides, leaving only the outer walls, and rebuilt luxury apartments, a modern foyer. Very deluxe, all this polished marble, if you like that kind of thing, said Germaine as we walked through and into the garden beyond. Louise and Robert designed it *à l'anglaise*, a controlled lushness. When I could still see, I would marvel at its volumes and nuances. Yesterday I could just feel the presence of plant-life around me, make out blobs of verdure.

Louise now lives on the ground floor of the house and rents out the upstairs to a family. It's of course what I should have been doing on a larger scale at the place des Vosges for the last fifteen years, but no use, at this point, adding that to a list of things I should have done. The foyer had the musky smell of the scented candles she used to burn before the War. It gave me a Proustian jolt, as if it were François at my side and we were coming over to eat one of Louise's good dinners.

Germaine left for the Bon Marché department store to buy some clothes for her grandchildren, and we two old ladies were left to our shrunken world. As she hung up my coat, I suddenly felt deflated, wondered why I was here. What's the point of rehashing stale reminiscences of better times?

What's new, I asked rather wearily as she poured me a cup of coffee.

I wish I could say nothing, but there's a group of smug, young *7ème* people in that soulless new building pressuring me to chop down the hawthorn tree in the garden. It was the first thing Robert and I planted. They say it blocks their light.

But it was there when they bought their flats.

They say it was winter when they visited. I've offered to trim it. I'm not cutting it down.

Good for you.

Please let's change the subject, give me something else to think about. How are you?

I told her about the toaster and Octave wanting to put me in a home, about his and the Horse's designs. About the girl and what it's like having a young person living over my head. As I spoke, I felt lighter and lighter. As if I were taking each event, stone by stone, physically out of my head. I'd forgotten that other people, friends, can do that, unburden you from yourself. Clearly I'd done the same for Louise, listening to her garden woes. Maybe that's what friendship provides, a mutual unburdening.

And I was reminded that there's always a present, even at our age.

When we did reminisce, about our time at the Sorbonne, about some of the weekends the four of us spent at Robert's family house near Milly-la-Forêt, it felt comforting rather than stifling. What a shame so few of my friends are left.

***

A few days ago, as I gave Madame her breakfast, she said: "Would you be interested in some babysitting? My nephew Octave mentioned it at tea the other day. I thought it might give you some extra pocket money. The girls," she emphasized, "are very sweet."

Both Meredith and Carol talk all the time about babysitting. They speak competitively about their brattiest charges. But I have never taken care of children, not even for an hour. In general, they make me almost as nervous as men do, and two little *Parisiennes*? But I could use the money.

Armed with my Plan de Paris, I am on my way this Wednesday evening to the Malberts' flat in the 16th arrondissement. The train ride, after a change at Franklin Roosevelt, lasts forever, like I'm going to a different city, which is what it feels like when I finally emerge from the métro. The buildings are very tidy and turn of the century, which I know because many of them have date of construction and the architect's name chiselled into their clean façades.

After turning my Plan de Paris this way and that, I locate and make my way to the rue George Sand. I punch in the code that Madame gave me and the door clicks open. At a second door, I press a second code.

There is a lot more security here than at the place des Vosges.

A carpeted staircase wraps around the elevator shaft. I push the button and the lift descends noiselessly. Inner accordion panels sigh open automatically; I pull open the metal cage door, step inside. The car holds no more than three, a sign informs me. Three French people, it should read, maximum two Anglo-Saxons. The machine glides upward, lands gently. The panels sigh open again. When Monsieur answers my ring, opens the door, a golden dog lunges at me.

"Calm down, *Achille*," he says. "You'll have plenty of time to get acquainted in the course of the evening."

"*Bonsoir Monsieur*," I say.

"*Bonsoir*," he thrusts out his hand. "Come in. Let us be rid of these horrid French formalities. Octave, please."

The apartment is very orderly with a massive red velvet sofa dominating the living room. Monsieur—Octave—points to it: "Please, sit down. I'll get the girls." And he disappears down a corridor, calling "*Chloé ! Violette !*" The dog rests its golden head on my knee. Its eyes are irresistible, as is its furry head, soft as chick fluff. We never had pets, and they are another category of life form with which I have uncertain relations. I stroke its head gingerly, take in the room. There is a glass coffee table with sharp aluminium edges, not a smudge in sight. A large chrome light reaches over the middle of the sitting area. An off-white carpet covers much of the parquet.

Little feet patter down the corridor, young voices giggle. "Don't run," I hear Octave warning. The girls, ten and eight, Germaine told me, enter the living room. They both have ash blonde hair and big eyes, the elder blue, the younger brown, and they are already dressed in matching nightdresses, cut from the same soft cloth as their father's shirts. The dog switches loyalties and bounces towards them. Octave introduces blue-eyed Violette and brown-eyed Chloé. Each girl points her face up for a kiss. It comes back to me from the *lycée*, how all French children are kissed hello, even by strangers.

"Do you want to play a game with us?" asks Violette.

"Good idea," I say. Trying to sound chirpy, I come off as insincere, I can hear it.

"Chloé, go get a game from the cupboard." The younger sister hops up from her crouch next to the dog. "No, not that one," when Chloé returns with *Jeu de l'Oie*. Madame Flaviche had one of those, but the board was so ancient it was taped together in the middle and had to be handled with extreme care. "That's for babies. Get Ludo."

As Violette sets up the board on the coffee table and I am wondering how this self-possessed child could possibly need a babysitter, Chloé asks me: "Are you American?"

"Yes, I am."

"We have an American in our class, but she doesn't speak French very well."

"She'll learn, I'm sure."

"No one likes her."

"You can roll first," says Violette, just as Octave returns.

"The girls must be in bed by nine, teeth cleaned, hair brushed. Their homework is done." He looks at his watch with a barely audible sigh. "We need to go."

Out saunters a tall blonde woman, just on the right side of feline so as not to look gangly. "Ah," says Octave. "Marie-France, this is Lily Owens, the young American who is helping with Tante."

"*Bonsoir*," she says putting forward a limp-wristed hand, while looking at the girls. "Good night, my angels." She bends her long, beautiful legs, made longer by super high heels. With clenched knees—necessary because of the short, close-fitting dress she is wearing—she kisses each of them. "Be good for the babysitter."

"*Bonne nuit, Maman*," they chirp in unison.

Octave already has his coat on, is holding hers open and ready. She is taller than he, especially in those heels, and must again bend to get each slender arm into the coat sleeves.

"We won't be too late," Octave says, also kissing the girls goodnight. "School night."

Once they are out the door the air settles, just as it did when Octave left the *salon* at the place des Vosges the day of my interview.

"Let's go play with our horses," says Violette, who had a bad first roll of the dice in Ludo.

An hour later the girls have gone to bed, and I have learned quite a bit about the Malbert household. The girls unsurprisingly go to a private Catholic school. "Sister Odile is a witch," says Violette with dismissive certainty. The dog Achille, French version of the Greek hero pronounced A-sheell, is a cocker spaniel. They have a Filipina maid, thus explaining the spotlessly clean flat. "She babysits sometimes," said Violette. "But Papa doesn't like it. He says she can't speak French," said Chloé. "Maman says it's okay," said Violette defensively. Almost every weekend they go to Normandy, where their maternal grandparents have a horse farm. "But we don't ride those horses," said Violette, making her purple plastic stallion with the flowing white mane jump over an imaginary fence. "We go to the pony club."

Chloé looked up at me, tears welling in her brown eyes. "I hate the pony club."

"Stop being a baby," Violette said. "You know if you want to be in our family you have to like riding. Do you know how to ride?"

"Yes," I answered. Our parents sent us to the local pony club. Maude, already sixteen, loved it. She seemed to connect better with her horse than with humans. Jane and I, thirteen and twelve, weren't bad, though as usual we felt out of place because our parents weren't horsey like everyone else's. Our father would drop us off and flee, rather than stick around for a chat with the other parents, who used the occasion for their own socializing. "But I wasn't very good," I added to make Chloé feel better.

They went to bed with only the mildest opposition, and I have spent the rest of the evening wandering the flat, followed by the dog. On a table in the living room, there are many family photos in silver frames—most of them appear to be of her side, in Normandy. A couple of horses merit their own portraits. I poke around the kitchen, which is situated at the end of the long corridor. It too is impeccable, except for the heap of washing up in the sink, which I suppose has been left for me to do. After I've dried everything in the rack, left it stacked on the counter, I help myself to a couple of Petit Prince biscuits from the cupboard, being careful, now that the dog has got tired of following me, not to let any crumbs fall on the spotless floor as I make my way back along the corridor, stopping at Octave and Marie-France's bedroom, even their bathroom, which is the exact same blue as my room. They must have used the leftover paint. The furnishings everywhere are very modern, the opposite of the place des Vosges. Back in the living room I turn on the large television and keep the volume way down, since no one told me I could watch, but there's nothing of interest and I turn it off.

My mind returns to Thibaud. It can never stay away for long. I run through the times we have spent together, think about ways I might engineer an encounter. One tactic has been sitting in the Sainte Geneviève Library, where I know he studies between lectures. I do my own homework. Or try to. I can't keep the corner of my eye under control and every time someone walks in, I look up to see if it's him. For all the effort, I've only ever crossed his path once. It reminds me of when I was in school and had a crush on Miss Bonner. I was always trying to meet her in the corridor, to strike up a chat. It rarely worked either.

It's after midnight when the door opens.

"Everything all right?" asks Octave.

"The girls were very good," I say, standing up.

"Let's sit down for a minute," he says, settling into an armchair on the other side of the glass coffee table with the sharp aluminium edges. Marie-France kicks off her high heels and sits in another armchair, drawing her legs underneath her so she forms a Z.

I am worried about catching the last métro from this outpost and sit lightly on the very edge of the red sofa.

"Just quickly," he says, leaning forward, elbows on knees, tie dangling between his legs. "You know we hired you because my aunt set a toaster on fire. So tell us," he looks at me intently, as if not wanting to miss the slightest nuance in my countenance. "How is she getting on?"

Suddenly I feel not just delayed but trapped. "Fine," I say.

"No more incidents?" asks Marie-France as if she were referring to a crime. I shake my head. "Because we honestly feel," she continues, looking at me for the first time, "that she should be living under professional supervision in an accommodation suited to her age, instead of rattling around in that lugubrious old *hôtel* with the housekeeper."

The strangest thing happens. No matter how grumpy she is with me, no matter how perfect the Malbert life around me appears, I take Madame's defense, feel quite offended by their insinuations. "I assure you. She's just fine. In fact, given her bad vision and age and all, I'm amazed at how well she manages."

"Well, good," says Octave but I can feel the disappointment, from both of them.

"I really have to catch the last métro," I say.

"Right." Octave slaps his knees, rises. He looks at his watch with a worn leather strap, pulls out some bills, puts them in my hand. Marie-France is examining her fingernails, seems to have forgotten that I'm there. "Here you go and thank you," says Octave.

I run to the métro, as much to put quick distance between myself and this inquisition as to catch the last train.

***

Thursday, 18 November 1982

I didn't need the doctor to tell me that my eyes are getting worse. I can see that for myself, so to speak. He said the treatment did all it could, whatever that means. Germaine was more distressed than I at this news. Or than I appeared to be. In the privacy of these pages, I can admit that his words came down on me like a hammer. Thump. Truth from someone else's lips can finally stamp out the hope that otherwise springs eternal in one's head.

When I came back to this room lined with books, I wanted to sweep them from the shelves, forget I ever had anything to do with the words that I can no longer read on the page.

It started when Pallet et Fils began exporting to the US. I'd help François with letters or information about the soap. That led to similar work for other companies. One day Sylvia asked if I could translate a short story for a writer that her friend Adrienne Monnier was trying to promote.

Fortunately, it was a short short story because it was immediately obvious to me that translating a work of fiction was practically a different *métier* than what I'd been doing. In fiction the words have hidden or multi-layered meaning, the sentences a cadence. The ensemble must be interpreted harmonically into another language. I spent a very long time on *Le Coing*, the story of a woman making quince jelly as her marriage was faltering. I got François' advice. He may have been a businessman on the outside, but like any good Frenchman he was *un littéraire* at heart, a voracious reader of all genres. I've even wondered if he was good at predicting the future because he had read so much about the past. When he said You're good at this, I handed *Quince* to Adrienne with confidence, even pride.

She started giving me more and though I never broke into the really big league, the Prousts and the André Gides, or later, the Sartres and the Camus, the writers who have lasted, I translated many who were popular at the time. Valéry Larbaud, René Crevel (translating his surrealist prose was like guesswork), Irène Nemerovski, a wonderfully lyrical writer, banned from publication in the thirties because Jewish. She was deported during the War and never returned. There were a couple of Colette's lesser-known works. What a rich vocabulary that woman had. I needed a dictionary on every page of her slim books. After the war there was Michel Butor, Hervé Bazin and Robert Pinget. Le nouveau roman almost killed me.

Quite quickly I developed a system. I'd read the book once, marking words I didn't know or writing snippets that seemed to translate themselves, right in my head. So much of it was finding that inner rhythm in the text and giving it the right beat in English. I'd note paragraphs where I could practically tap my foot to the words, work on those first. I'd read passages aloud, translate them, then read them aloud in English to see if the harmonics rang right. So much of it was hearing the music.

Before the War, François read everything I translated. And after, not a word.

***

On my way up the main staircase with the salted butter Germaine asked me to buy, I pause on the landing to the apartment, look at the steps that continue upward.

Curiosity has led me to spend a fair amount of time exploring the other *chambres de service* along the corridor, running my hand along the old wallpaper in one or testing the springs of the small bed in another. Or, on my way to or from the bathroom, to examine the spare room in Madame's flat, whence my furniture appears to have come. It's the only place in the house with photos. Of Monsieur Quinon, I suppose, and of an unidentifiable boy whom I don't think could be Octave because the photos look too old and the child is too fair. Even more oddly, it holds a large collection of old records. The room, without furniture, feels more like a mausoleum.

Today Germaine has taken Madame to an eye doctor's appointment. No one is home. I walk up the stairs to the next floor. The door here looks the same as downstairs, but the brass handle is not polished. From the street, I have noticed that the wooden interior shutters are closed, meaning, I suppose, that if this flat is owned by someone other than Madame, its residents are not at home. When I turn the handle, the door gives way to a dark entry, like downstairs, then a living room, which is illuminated by the late autumn sun filtering through the spaces and cracks in the shutters. White sheets drape the furniture. The ceiling is lower than downstairs, the beams not painted. A chandelier hangs in the middle like a big spider. There is a fireplace here too, also smaller. I lift the edge of a sheet. The furniture appears more formal, more Louis-something French, than downstairs. Through a set of double doors is what looks like an office, with a large writing table in the middle. On another fireplace, this one mottled marble, an ornate clock is stopped at eight-forty. I imagine its ticks getting weaker and weaker, like the heart of a dying person. Was it morning or night when the clock stopped? How many years ago?

Through another door is an antechamber set up as a bedroom. Who lived or lives here? There is no sense of human presence; it smells musty and hollow and sad.

Unhappiness is a feeling I recognize all too well, and there is layer upon layer of it in this place.

***

"Germaine," I say a few days later. I have noticed that people are generally more receptive when addressed by name. "Does anyone live upstairs?"

We are sitting at the kitchen table on Saturday morning, and I'm in no hurry to finish my breakfast. Germaine has come upstairs with the post, is sorting it into bills and junk, reading glasses perched on her nose.

"Oh, no. It was Monsieur's quarters."

"Madame Quinon's husband?"

Germaine nods.

I sip my coffee. "Has Monsieur Quinon been dead for a long time?"

"Since 1967." Germaine slices into another envelope with the silver opener. "And for several years before that—well, he was as good as." She pauses, gathering the mass of paper in her hands with the funny spots, like scars, on them. "Tragic. He was such a vital man. A war hero. And that's how he ended his days."

I can hear the tremor in Germaine's voice. After a respectful moment of silence: "What happened?"

"An accident."

"An accident?"

"Mmm." She tosses the crumpled the envelopes in the basket at her feet. "He was hit by a truck while crossing the street." She takes off her glasses. "Then he lingered, in a wheelchair, for four years. Madame never wanted to finish doing this place up." Her eyes draw a large circle. "Or move. I suggested it more than once, but she wouldn't hear of it. I'm too old to change, she'd say, even when she wasn't. At this point she's probably right."

"She owns this whole building?"

"Yes. Monsieur wanted to renovate it, rent or sell the apartments.

They hired my husband to manage the construction and me to run the household. Only this place and the one upstairs were finished. The others still had tenants, several families. It took a while for them to move, and Monsieur didn't rush them. In fact, he helped them find better accommodation. It's hard to imagine now, how poor and run down this *quartier* was. This building," she grimaces, "was in such a state. Michel my husband was about to start on the other side when Monsieur had his accident." She shakes her head, looks quite lost. "Now, talking about all that empty space, it sounds strange. Unnatural even. Most of the time I don't think about it." She pauses, fiddles with the stems of her reading glasses. "I guess you get used to things as they are, and they don't seem odd anymore."

Up in my room, the dead Monsieur Quinon is still lingering in my mind. From the photos I know he was very handsome. Now a handsome war hero. Married to a beautiful American. The images that begin to form in my mind make Humphrey Bogart and Lauren Bacall's story, on the screen or in real life, pale in comparison. But then there was a terrible accident. That makes the back of my neck tingle. Madame has suffered. Maybe that's what's made her such a grouch.

My eyes land on *The Adventures of Huckleberry Finn* next to the bed. Thibaud told me about it, told me it was his favorite book, though he's only read it in French. I used some of my babysitting money to buy a copy at Shakespeare & Co, across from Notre Dame, on my way back from the Sorbonne the other day. A great American novel that never made it to the syllabus of my English school. I think Jane read it. She's always reading. It's a good story with, *justement*, lots of adventure for a literary novel, but I cannot understand why the son of a French diplomat would relate to it with such intensity. Romantic attraction for the fantastically foreign, maybe. Nor can I understand why his father can't introduce him to someone who will help him conquer America. I mean, why should Thibaud need a Fulbright? Furthermore, how could the son of a diplomat throw his rubbish in the Seine? He is another mystery.

Fortunately, I must hurry to meet Meredith, Carol and Thibaud near Odéon, at the *papeterie* Duriez. Meredith and Carol, whose American notebooks have filled up, want to buy *cahiers Clairefontaine* with help from the Frenchman and the French speaker.

As I arrive, I see Thibaud coming down the boulevard Saint Germain. He's just a dark form, his willowy body outlined by an oblique ray of sunlight, but I recognize his walk from quite a distance. Our cheeks touch hello.

"*C'est con, cette histoire de cahiers*," he says frowning.

"It's not stupid for them," I answer. "Buying French notebooks is a French experience. Remember? More important than Notre Dame?"

Meredith and Carol arrive. More cheeks touch and in we go.

"They're so many kinds," Meredith says in front of the long row of notebooks. "I mean, do I want spiral or bound? Big or small? Little or large squares? I'm used to simple lines. French paper is as confusing as the language."

I wait for Thibaud to offer advice, but he has his hands in his pockets. I say: "Go for the big squares."

"Yes, that is better," Thibaud adds.

"And spiral," I say. "So you can tear out pages if you want."

"What do you think, Thibaud?"

He shrugs Gallicly. "Paper is paper."

Thibaud is here to '*ang owt* with Americans, but I guess he'd rather be doing something more exciting than buying supplies. Still, I'd have thought he had a stronger opinion on notebook paper, after twelve years in a French school. I remember getting the right supplies being a big deal, my years at the lycée.

Meredith looks a bit put out by his apathy. "Well, come over here and help me choose an agenda for 1983. Ronnie showed me the one he'd bought the other day, and I was jealous."

"Okay," he says, finally with some enthusiasm. He is caught in Meredith's paw again, and I turn away, hopelessness and jealousy fighting for top spot.

Carol has taken her own counsel on the notebook front, preferring bound and small squares, but she would like advice on another purchase and beckons me. "I've noticed a lot of people over here—you, for example—use fountain pens," she says to me. I have seen Carol eying mine during lectures. "We don't use those in the States," she adds with a tone that could be interpreted as defensive or apologetic. "But they look kinda cool."

"How much do you want to spend?" I ask. "Prices can vary a lot." Madame's fountain pen, for example, looks very expensive. I have seen it lying obediently on the writing table and awry on the floor next to the fallen notebook, that night I thought she'd died.

"Not too much. But I want something nice. Not too cheap either. What kind's yours?"

"A Parker."

"Let's ask to see some of these," Carol peers at the glass case.

I ask the saleswoman, who is acting as if our very presence is a great inconvenience to her, to open the case. Carol fingers pen after pen like chocolates.

My father gave me the black Parker with the gold trim for my sixteenth birthday. He doesn't usually give presents, and he looked so pleased when I opened it that I felt all warm inside. But also uncomfortable, embarrassed even—there go the cheeks right now—by this rare show of emotion. Nothing with him or my mother is ever straightforward and simple. But I do cherish that pen.

"What about this one?" asks Carol. The saleswoman is returning the Parkers with demonstrative irritation. I look over at the agenda rack. Thibaud is leaning over Meredith's shoulder as she flips through the pages of a diary. She turns and laughs at something he has said, a sentence that is no doubt riddled with mistakes and badly pronounced. I turn back to Carol.

"That's a Waterman. They're French," I say. "Maybe you should buy one of those. Since you're here in France."

"Good idea," Carol says. She goes the whole way, opting for a pump and a pot of ink instead of cartridges. She's really pleased—in fact, I'm not sure I've ever seen Carol look so chuffed. It can be such a little thing that makes you feel good. Or not. An equally small matter—flirting between Meredith and Thibaud, for example—can make you miserable.

The purchase itself is quite a production. The sour sales lady fills out a chit of paper that we must take to the cashier, where we meet Meredith, who is carrying her own chit. Thibaud has remained with the agendas, like looking ahead at the next year is the only thing that could possibly interest him here. There's a queue of four people holding their chits in front of us. The person directly ahead, when asked how she will pay, says *par chèque*. Laboriously she fills it out, tears it carefully out of her *chéquier*, hands it over and rifles in her bag for her *pièce d'identité*. The woman behind the counter then copies the long number of her identity card onto the back of the *chèque*. In the middle of this Meredith says rather loudly: "Do you think my nineteen-eight-three agenda will be of any use by the time we've finally paid?"

Once they have, each returns to their respective sour sales lady with a stamped receipt, which gets stamped again, and their purchases are at long last handed over.

"That was quite an experience," says Carol. "Just for school supplies."

"Maybe worse than *la Poste*," says Thibaud.

"Kind of a toss up," Carol laughs. Thibaud gives a confused smile. He will not have understood "toss up" and I am not going to help him.

Back at the flat, Meredith immediately puts on some music. It's always the first thing she does on arrival; turning it off is the last thing she does before going out again, as if she can't stand silence. Sometimes Carol is bothered.

"Can you turn it down? I can't hear," she'll say extra loudly, even though we can hear just fine.

But today she's too happy with her fountain pen, in which she immediately puts ink. "Hello, new pen, how are you?" she writes in her very sloppy script in the new notebook.

Meanwhile Meredith—head tilted up, eyes closed—is singing along to the Beach Boys, "I wish they all could be California Girls," as if they'd written the song for her. I look at Thibaud, who is enthralled by Meredith's self-absorbed moment. I wish I had left, gone back to the place des Vosges, home of Madame and her now dead vegetable husband. Anything would be better than sitting here.

"Okay," announces Meredith at the end of the song. "Wine time. Are you coming with us to Luisa's party this evening?"

Thibaud says: "I don't know. Are you going?" He looks at me.

I'd forgotten about the party. "Not sure."

"Come on, Lily and Thibaud," says Carol, coming out of the kitchen with a bowl of crackers and a bottle of wine. "It'll be more fun if we all go."

"Okay," we say at the same time.

Luisa lives with her older sister Clara, who is working at an art gallery. It's on the Right Bank, in the 8th arrondissement, the rue de Surène. Clara has been living there for three years and it's a very grown-up place. As if she were already forty and married. The strangely formal setting affects the guests. We're all on good comportment. Despite the ultra-bourgeois setting and the stiff atmosphere, seeing the sisters together makes me miss Jane, causes an actual physical hurt. It can grab me from seemingly nowhere, the heartache of our having drifted apart.

But I have an okay time at the party. Meredith is swept up by the owner of the gallery—this time definitely gay and very suave—and Thibaud sticks with me and some of the others. Carol tells us about her and Meredith's neurotic third roommate first year of college. Una comes over to talk to us, tells us a story about her grandfather being seasick on the boat from Ireland to Canada and losing his set of false teeth overboard. That prods Ronnie to tell us how his grandparents escaped from

Nazi Germany just in time and changed their names to Deal because that was the name of the coastal Kentish town where they spent their first night after crossing the English Channel. Then Ronnie and I talk about England for a while. Parties are so easy when you feel part of the group.

Thoughts of Madame and her vegetable husband only crop up again when I bring her breakfast the next morning. After what Germaine told me, it's as if one of those shutters upstairs had half-opened. I can view her in a different light. Even if I still can't imagine her young, I can now detect sorrow—some of the unhappiness that hovers around here—where before I could only see ill-humor.

***

Monday, 22 November 1982

It had been a while since Flora and family came to lunch—not since early September. Being close on the heels of Octave et Compagnie I couldn't help but compare, wonder how two families could be so different.

Tanta, Flora said, pushing her warm cheeks hard on mine. I'm so sorry. It's been way too long.

Hello, Tanta, Roger said, bending down to greet me. He is very tall and Flora very short. They seem very happy.

Tanta. It warmed me up, hearing that name again. When Flora was a child and Tante Amenia was an impossible mouthful, Tante A became Tanta.

Germaine got the four of them helping with this and that. The two children are still small enough for us to squeeze around the kitchen table. The proximity felt unifying, not claustrophobic. The chatter, not very consequential, never faltered and caused frequent bouts of laughter. We talked about the haughty headmistress at Rachel's school, Roger's trip to Amsterdam for an economics conference, Flora's going back to work next year—Michel will go to the *maternelle*, she says, Maman can help on Wednesdays, maybe sometimes after school—of course she can, I said—I could feel Germaine beaming. The only time, I think, that she is truly happy, is when she is with her daughter and family. And I must say, the same could be said for me these days.

Flora has always been such a bundle of energy, a positive force. I don't know how, given the clouds surrounding the lives of the elder generation in this house. Maybe it was a reaction. As a child she wouldn't sit still—always dancing, dancing. She was accepted at the *conservatoire* and would have become a professional if she hadn't also been a strong student and dissuaded by her mother. Germaine, monstrously deprived by history of so much, including her education, was determined things would be different for her only child.

At university Flora met Roger, a young lecturer. They married after she finished a double degree in economics and psychology. She worked in the human resources of a big company—an only child seeking out people, perhaps—until their second child Michel was born two years ago.

What if I asked Lily about some babysitting in the evenings, Germaine offered as she sliced the chocolate cake. Poor thing. All she's seen is Octave's version of family life.

Uh-oh, said Roger.

He's okay, underneath it all, said Flora, who'd been quite taken by Octave the student, six years her elder, when he lived here.

You have to dig deeper and deeper to find the okay, said Germaine.

Maybe she can teach them some English, said Roger. You really need it these days in the world beyond our Hexagon.

The schools certainly don't see it that way, said Flora. They treat English like an existential threat. Very good idea, Maman.

You can forget what it's like, to feel in synch with a group of people, to enjoy their company unconditionally. How sad the opposite is the case with my nephew.

***

W hen I put down Madame's tray on her table, she says:

"I forgot to ask you. How was the babysitting?"

I hesitate, unsure whether to provide an honest or a polite answer.

"I know," she interprets my delay. "The girls are sweet and the parents less so, *n'est-ce pas?*"

On several occasions since that evening, I have envied Marie-France's slim arms and leggy legs, but he hadn't paid me as much as Germaine said they should. "They were okay."

"Did they mention me?"

"They asked how you were doing."

"Hmph."

"They said they were worried about you."

"They will inherit this house when I am dead, you know." I start slightly at this raw declaration. "I don't mean to be crude." Maybe because she can't see she has an uncanny way of feeling what is going on in a room. "It's just that their interest is not disinterested, shall we say."

"Their questions did seem quite keen," I say.

She sighs, shakes her head. "They think I should be living in some kind of home."

"I said you were doing very well, that you didn't need much help at all."

"Thank you." For once she looks sincerely grateful, even pleased. "Thank you very much."

Inheritance, what happens after you die—I did not consider that part of the equation when Octave and Marie-France were questioning me, but I can see now how Madame would have it on her mind. In fact, I can imagine thinking about it quite a lot at her stage in life.

Since my first lecture isn't until late morning, I go back to my room after breakfast with a cup of coffee. It's chilly—the heat that gets pumped out of the radiators in this house feels as old and frail as Madame—and I hold the warm cup between my hands, under my face, and look out at the abandoned courtyard. Germaine is taking Madame to another appointment. It occurs to me that I'm all alone in this massive space, including the other wing, destined for the nephew but currently, I now know for certain, completely unoccupied.

Once on my way up the back stairs, I jiggled the handle on the other side of the landing, and it was locked. But there's the Delft blue teacup with a broken handle on that little table next to the front door of Madame's quarters, whence came my key. Coffee finished, I make my way down the stairs, through the kitchen and the empty flat and fetch the cup. Back at the service stairs, I try the keys one by one in the lock across the landing and on the fifth try, the key turns smoothly. I do pause, say to myself: I should put the blue cup and these keys right back on the table where they belong and hurry to the Sorbonne for my class, which I will now be missing. But what might be beyond the door is immeasurably more beguiling than *le passé simple*.

Inside is an old room with wallpaper half ripped from the wall and a broken chair sitting forlornly in the middle. The thick herringbone planks on the floor are dusty and lackluster. I move through the enfilade of similarly forsaken rooms until coming to a combination kitchen-bathroom. Next to a small counter and a large enamel sink is a bathtub. The wall to the right is stained in streaks of brown where a cooker must have been. Through another door, unlocked, is a landing with an open door, apparently to another flat, and a staircase. But I must go—what if they come back—this wandering has made me lose all sense of time—all sense—and when I've returned the key, am running down the stairs, I already wonder if I'm not just imagining this huge, empty wing of the house. I mean, is it possible to have so much unoccupied space in the middle of a major city? Is it even legal?

If I hurry, I can meet Meredith and Carol as they come out of the lecture. The street bustle is a comfort; so is air that has not been bottled up for decades.

Where am I living?

***

Sunday, 21 November 1982

A lonely Sunday. Germaine's off with her family. The girl has been out most of the last several days and when she is here, I've noticed from her movements upstairs and when she delivers my breakfast that something has changed. Her step is more impatient.

Today it's one of those northern European autumn-winter days with a heavy lead sky and clammy air that penetrates any and all attempts at warmth and these days makes achy joints achier. I nevertheless left the window open, sat down in my armchair with a shawl wrapped around my shoulders and disappeared into the darkening space before my eyes, breathed in that day, the 21st of November 1920 when I walked off the boat in Le Havre. I make my way down the gangplank. I pull the collar of my new Saks Fifth Avenue coat around my neck against the fine rain. My ears tickle from the fur and my nose from the raw air, but I'm not sure I've ever been happier, perched on the edge of my new continent, my new life. Even my new nationality—in those days it was the law, if you married a Frenchman you had to become French.

Or was the crossing itself, the short time between one set of complications and another, the high point? Life on a ship is *sans patrie*, almost *sans histoire*. One is, both literally and metaphorically, floating. Outside the grand dinners and the dancing, François and I spent hours in bed. He would give me little French lessons. Lessons in etiquette: always say *Bonjour, Madame. Bonjour, Monsieur. Merci, Madame. Merci, Monsieur.* He worked on my pronunciation.

What would my mother and father say. Drinking Sham-pain in

bed on an ocean liner with a Frenchman.

Cham-pa-gn-e, he said, the *p* popping like a cork.

How do you say bubbles?

Bulles.

Boule.

No, no. Put your lips together as if you were kissing me, U.

Walking down that gangplank, I had no idea that those memories would become tender to the touch and require handling with care. No idea that youth and hope would be chewed to pieces by history, by what was still awaiting us in this murderous century.

***

Yesterday, at the end of brunch, Gary said: "Let's go to the Marais. I was reading about it yesterday, and it sounds worth visiting."

"That's where you live, Lily," said Una.

I nodded; words had abandoned me at the suggestion of an excursion so close to *chez moi*. I couldn't think of an excuse to bail out, so half an hour later, there we were, standing on the place des Vosges. I'd pulled my scarf up around my ears and chin. I made sure to stand in the middle of the group, terrified that Germaine would return from lunch with her daughter, see me, wave, maybe even walk over to meet my friends.

As usual, Gary was full of information. *Le Marais*, thus named because it was originally a swamp, is one of the oldest *quartiers* of Paris. First religious orders built their monasteries and convents here, then in the seventeenth century, the nobility bought them out to build *hôtels particuliers*, urban mansions such as the ones we've been seeing along the way today. People moved here, Gary said, to be close to the king, Henry IV, who was constructing more *hôtels* to create this square, originally called the place Royale. But he got assassinated, so it was finished under his son, Louis XIII.

"Isn't that Louis?" Luisa pointed to the large statue of the smiling man on a horse, the guy with the flowing hair dressed like a Greek who had perplexed me the day of my job interview. I didn't even know he was the son of Henri, the mounted king on the pont Neuf that I saw with Thibaud a couple of weeks ago.

"Yes, that's him," said Gary. "The name of the *place* changed from Royale to Vosges after the Revolution because the Vosges was the first French department to pay their tax bill under the new regime. But this *square*, the garden part within the gates," Gary swung his arm around, "is still called the square Louis XIII."

"*Place, square,* words that sound like English words but have slightly different meanings in French," said Carol, shaking her head. "How will I ever learn this language."

"They are called *faux amis,* false friends," Lara said. "Words in the other language that you think you know but don't."

"How do all of you know all this stuff? How do you remember it?" asked Meredith, beginning to look bored. "Where do you live, Lily?"

"Over that way." I extended my arm vaguely in the wrong direction.

Gary, who really can't shut up once he gets started, saved me from further questioning. "The writer Victor Hugo," he pointed to a corner of the *place,* "lived over there in the nineteenth century, and the apartment is now a museum. But in the twentieth century, all the nobles and intellectuals were gone, and, the *quartier* became the Jewish ghetto. A lot of people from the Marais were rounded up and sent to concentration camps," he said.

"Yep," said Ronnie, who must have been thinking about his grandparents' narrow escape from Germany. "I've read about that."

"After the War, the architect Le Corbusier wanted to raze the whole dilapidated area and build superhighways."

"Maybe we should visit the Victor Hugo Museum right now," says Carol. "Before some other crazy guy gets his way and tears it down. Do Europeans realize how lucky they are?"

"I'm done with this tourism thing for the day," said Meredith.

"Oh, come on," said Lara. "I'd love to get a peek at what it's like behind these old walls."

Meredith was persuaded to make a lightning tour of the museum. The apartment was on one floor, around two sides of the building, not unlike where Madame lives. Except less grand. And the rooms along the side were all connected, in enfilade, so maybe the corridor in her place was part of the renovation. When we parted ways afterwards, I walked in the wrong direction to throw them off the scent.

Isn't it beyond weird, I wonder on the way to the métro this morning, to have done that? To have two such separate lives, the one with Madame and Germaine and the other with my fellow students, that like a *un faux ami,* I point and walk in the wrong direction? That I am not who my *friends* think I am?

At the beginning of term, once I'd told my fellow students that I lived with an old woman, they thankfully lost interest immediately so did not ask yesterday to see my room. But if I had provided a more complete picture, i.e., that I'm living in a mansion, empty except for myself, an old lady and a housekeeper, either they wouldn't have believed me or they'd have demanded proof. They'd want to verify that I wasn't re-inventing Dickens or writing my own Gothic novel. But I can't imagine bringing anyone there. It's too strange.

On the other hand, Madame and Germaine know almost nothing about what I do all day—the courses I'm taking, the people I see. They don't ask and I don't offer. I wonder, feeding my *carte orange* ticket into the turnstile, if compartmentalized, Cartesian living isn't my norm. I never give anyone the full version of our family story either. Just the broad-brush picture: my Fulbright scholar parents who fell in love on the ship coming over to their year in England during the fifties. How they stayed on because my neurologist father was offered a position at a British hospital. How my mother, an art historian, worked at the Royal Academy until the children were born. Later we moved to a small village in Kent, not far from Tunbridge Wells. Our father commuted to London, where he had a private practice. If asked about my French, I'd say: Madame Flaviche, our *gouvernante*/nanny/babysitter taught it to us, and we went to the *lycée francais* for five years.

Standing in the crowded métro, hand gripping the central pole, I consider Meredith and Carol. They're always talking about their parents. Or Carol is. With Meredith it's always Dad, Dad, Dad. I listen with attentive envy, as if maybe I can learn—like a subject at school—how it should be.

The train lands with a jerk and a screech at the Châtelet station and I barely avoid toppling over. I'm not sure that, like Montesquieu said, you can learn from other people. Or that you can move forward, really. Won't my family stick with me forever? Even if I never tell another living soul the full story, won't it linger as the backdrop to everything I do?

I climb the station stairs, emerge at the place du Châtelet, cross the Seine, the Ile-de-la-Cité, and notice nothing, have no flights of fancy about the fate of Marie-Antoinette. Life is bleak and pointless. No matter where I go, what I do, I will always be Lily Owens, product of John and Sylvia Owens, member of their poor excuse for a family. Waiting at the traffic light to cross the place Saint Michel, I wonder what it would be like to jump in front of a car, if it might not be my best option.

And there is Thibaud at my side. After all my contrived efforts to run into him, here he is, when I'm not even trying.

"*Salut.*"

"*Salut.*"

We walk together up the hill in silence. I am thinking: here's another example of my failure as a human being. I cannot even get myself a boyfriend, will be forced to live like a nun for the rest of my sad life. Then I notice how unhappy *he* seems. The dark eyebrows in fact look dangerously close to atomic fusion. I don't dare ask why, but at the ruins of the Roman thermal baths, where feral cats are curled up here and there, Thibaud stops and looks through the bars. "I'm losing my room. I have to be out by January First."

"What will you do?" A cat unfurls and jumps down to a bowl of food someone has put there.

"I don't know. Rooms are incredibly expensive."

"Can't your parents help you?"

Thibaud starts walking again. "They've decided I need to learn a lesson. Funds are minimal."

He's always saying these cryptic things when I ask about his family. "Maybe you should try the American Church. That's how I got my room."

Even the mention of an American institution doesn't cheer him up today. "Maybe," he says with no conviction as we part ways at the place de la Sorbonne. It's well into the TD seminar on the French heroine Joan of Arc that all the unoccupied space at the place des Vosges rises like a sunny morning in my mind. During another absence of Madame and Germaine, I went over there again, this time downstairs, and I found an entrance on the side street. It's right across from the Félix Potin where I do my food shopping. The key was on a hook in the room that must once have been the concierge's *loge*. If he were quiet, who would find out? There's so much space. In any case, it would only be for a short time, a stopgap until he could find something else. Then again, I hardly know him. Proposing such an arrangement would be brazen, something I am not. But *Jeanne d'Arc* was and maybe I should take a leaf out of her book. Still, if Madame or Germaine found out, I might not be burned at the stake, but I'd undoubtedly lose my job.

These considerations toss and turn in my head, disrupting all effort at concentration, until Thursday, when I will see Thibaud again at Meredith and Carol's Thanksgiving dinner. They've been talking about little else for days. How much it makes them miss home, how everyone will be gathering without them. It's a holiday that we celebrated once, the first year our parents finally moved back to England. Mrs Hooper made the meal according to my mother's instructions, but the food tasted off-kilter. Our parents made a good go at being festive, but it fell flat. Afterwards, when we were getting in bed, Jane said we might as well have been trying to celebrate the Chinese New Year.

Meredith and Carol have planned the meal meticulously. Two pre-roasted chickens to stand in for the turkey they could not find. Pre-packaged stuffing and pumpkin pie mix, bought at the American store on the rue de Grenelle. I went with them to the rue de Buci market this afternoon and we also picked up sweet potatoes and beans—"We have to have some green," Meredith said. Once we get it all back to the flat Carol says: "Now what?" and—it's really weird—I take over. Maybe it was all the hours spent watching Mrs Hooper in the kitchen. I peel and chop the sweet potatoes for boiling, then mashing with butter. I dice the onion that might improve the packaged stuffing mix.

Meredith puts on Bruce Springsteen. She's a big fan and plays him so often, I now know lots of his sexy music. While I top and tail the beans, "Everybody Has a Hungry Heart," the same song I danced to with Thibaud the night of the housewarming party, comes on. The chords rise up in me, inhabit me as if it were once again that first fun evening in Paris, except it's better this time because I know the words, can sing along with the others.

Carol pours us some wine; I breathe in the smell of the cooked food, and it does feel festive. The others—Ronnie, Una, Lara, Luisa and Gary—arrive. Thibaud is the last and I can feel my cheeks turning pink at the sight of him. He is quickly taken over by Carol, who asks him about the right way to cut the cheese that they are serving before the meal, with drinks.

"Our teaching assistant told me there are things you do and don't do. But like what?" Carol wants to know about everything. I practically expect her to take out her notebook and fountain pen and write down the answer.

Thibaud explains that it's important not to cut off the nose, he calls it. Cheese must always be sliced at an angle so that no one gets stuck with the rind. My attention—more focused on Thibaud's dramatic demonstration, cheese knife waving around like a baton, than on the information being provided—is interrupted by Meredith wailing, "We don't have any gravy!" and I return to the kitchen. Mrs Hooper used to take some meat juice, add some water and flour. "I think a previous tenant left some of that," says Meredith, rifling through the back of the cupboard. For good measure, I pour in a splash of red wine too. "Wow," says Meredith, leaning over the pan, pulling the spoon from her mouth, "that's delicious."

The meal is finally ready. People sit around the small living room, some on the floor, some on chairs. It will be impossible, I realize, scooping food onto my plate, to bring up my plan to Thibaud here. So I throw myself into having a good time, into being talkative and fun and mostly ignoring him—all quite easy, given the amount of wine I've already drunk. In a way, since I directed the cooking that everyone compliments, it feels like my evening.

When Thibaud announces he has to catch the last métro, I follow him to the door.

"Hey," I say to the back of his head. When he turns, my heart skips—I'm really very poor at indifference. "There's something I wanted to talk to you about. Could we meet this weekend?"

He looks at me with his sharp brown eyes, a smile hovering between irony and interest. "Of course."

"How about Saturday afternoon, Chez les Gaulois. About four?"

"Sure." He leans forward and kisses my fuelled cheeks.

"See you then." I turn back to the party. I'll not worry about the last métro. Tonight I could walk back on the waters of the Seine.

***

Thursday, 2 December 1982

I am more and more dependent. Germaine had to take me to the toy store for little Rachel's birthday present. She had to escort me in a taxi to Louise D's. So yesterday, when she had gone to look after her grandchildren and the girl was at class, I decided enough was enough. I'm not completely blind; I should at least be able to go for a stroll on the square unaccompanied.

I was careful with the stairs, held the banister tightly and walked slowly over the cobblestones that felt uneven as a mountain path under my unsupported body. I grabbed the handle of the *portail* with relief, until I tried to pull it open, something I have not done for myself for some time. It seemed to have doubled in heft. Although I finally managed, I almost toppled over in the process and my heart was pounding when I stepped over the threshold. Once outside, under the arcade, I froze. I could hear but not see the traffic. The leaf-less trees on the square loomed in gauzy blobs. I certainly couldn't locate the entry gate to the park, though I've been through it thousands of times.

Worse than that, however, was the continued feeling that I might keel over. Terrified, I turned back. As I fumbled at the keyhole I couldn't see, there was a voice, Let me help you. It was her, the girl, back earlier than I'd expected. I felt like a child, hand stuck right there in the cookie jar.

Once we'd got inside and she'd helped me back up the stairs, I swore her to silence. The girl said Of course I won't say anything. Can I trust her? Just because she seems sweet and malleable. You can't spend as many years on this earth as I have without knowing that anything's possible when it comes to a human being. That appearances can be completely misleading.

Here in my *journal intime* I will admit that until yesterday I'd told myself I could, if I wanted, go out on my own. Now I know I can't. I know that I really am as helpless as a small child and it's devastating.

***

I'm still thinking about how to execute my plan for Thibaud, when I turn under the arcade at the place des Vosges and am shaken from my plotting by the sight of Madame standing in front of the *portail*. What kind of emergency could have brought her outside alone? Another fire? Part of me wants to turn around and run away, but I stay put until she turns back to the door and appears unable to open it.

"Are you all right?" I ask softly, not wanting to frighten her.

"I can't get the door open."

I put in my own key, hold the door open. There's no smell of fire, no sign of anything wrong at all. We walk slowly up the stairs.

"Can I help?" I ask.

"No. I can manage." She continues to pull her bird-light body up with the help of the railing.

"Here we are," I say when we reach the landing. "Shall I come in with you?"

"I'm fine. Thank you. But I would ask you not to mention this to Germaine," she says in a confidential tone, while looking both defiant and spooked. "Please."

"All right. I won't say anything."

Madame closes the door behind me, and I am left perplexed and irked. I go back down the main stairs, through the courtyard and *la porte de service*, the servants' door, and up the wooden steps. Okay, I've accepted this business of speaking French—it's even come to seem normal. I understand the woman is ancient and blind and widowed under tragic circumstances, that life must not be much fun anymore. But couldn't the hag have been if not grateful at least gracious, just this once? Mightn't she have suggested, for example, that I walk through the flat to get to my room?

If that's the way I'm going to be treated, I think, stomping around my floor, loudly as I can, I will feel no guilt or remorse for letting Thibaud stay in this obscenely huge house. I am so angry that I am tempted to go back on my word and tell Germaine—but this thought freezes my agitated feet. Telling Germaine, or even making Madame unhappy, might jeopardize my job and if I lose my job, I cannot let Thibaud in next door.

Quietly, I put on the kettle, perch on the edge of the bed and tell myself to get my priorities straight. That's what Jane used to say to me: line them up, Lily. Like ducks, one-two-three. I would listen but still find it hard, harder than it was for Jane, who always had her ducks queued up like soldiers. The kettle rushes and burbles; I pour myself a cup of tea and settle softly back on the bed, wondering what it will be like to have Thibaud just across the courtyard.

***

Tuesday, 7 December 1982

Pearl Harbor Day. I always remember the date because it was also my first boyfriend's birthday. Of course, the boyfriend was before the event, but the date has stuck in my mind more because of Bob than the attack that nudged the Americans into the war. By then the Germans had been holding us prisoner for a year and a half. Everything beyond our urban jail seemed far, far away. Inaccessible and unimportant. To me, at least. Not to François. Thank God, he said. We're saved. For a while it lifted his spirits. But by February we were too cold to feel joy of any kind. By then it was also obvious that our salvation was far from imminent.

Not for the first time on this day, the 7th of December, I wonder what my life would have been like if I'd stuck with Bob, if a Frenchman had never come to work on the ranch and my life had followed the more probable fate of marrying, like my brother, what I would have called my college sweetheart. He was studying history. He aspired to—and achieved, according to my mother's letters—a political career. What if

I'd ended up living in Cheyenne, Wyoming? Or who knows—if Bob had married me, maybe we would have gone all the way to Washington, DC. He was a solid person, and the first man I'd met with a real sparkle in his eye. He too grew up on a ranch—it would have been hard to make a political career in Wyoming otherwise. He had enough natural sophistication and charm to survive in a city like Washington. Not that I've ever been there, but surely I could have been happy in a different center of power, and one from which I'd have watched the horror in Europe at a comfortable distance, instead of being caught in its midst. I could have suffered other tragedies—one is potentially waiting around every corner—but then again maybe not. There is no logical progression to a life. Circumstance, history—events completely beyond one's control—can cause a sharp turn at any point.

I've always believed my mother would have been a happier individual if she hadn't married my father. Because she wasn't in love with him but with his parents, or at least what his parents appeared to be: genteel people who had moved from the east with enough money to build a stone house and enough education to line its walls with books. The trouble was those books held no interest for their son, my father. How could my mother have overlooked that vital point? Their lack of common interest was a recipe for dissatisfaction, unhappiness. It meant that when I was growing up, my mother's life seemed to be defined by negatives: she didn't like the West, didn't much like her husband and frankly, it sometimes wasn't clear what she really thought of Ted and me. So maybe she would have been unhappy anywhere, with anyone.

It's only recently crossed my mind, with this mental assault of my past, that I shouldn't be casting judgment on my parents. After I was gone, they lived for more than thirty years. Maybe in that later phase of life they found balance, common ground, comradeship. Perhaps their life together formed the opposite arc to mine, which started out full of promise and ended—well—will end—in steep decline.

***

"Sorry if I've kept you waiting." For once I'm not over-eager first. Thibaud is already sitting at Chez les Gaulois with an empty espresso cup and a newspaper.

"No problem." He puts *Libération* down on the next table. "Just order something quickly. The waiter thinks I've been here long enough."

"The place isn't exactly full." Only two other tables are occupied, but the hovering waiter homes in, asks gruffly what I want.

"That's the way Parisian waiters are. Unpleasant and impatient." An ironic smile forms. "It's funny how all you Anglo-Saxons order *cafés-crème*."

"It doesn't seem funny to me."

"Did you enjoy the other night? Is Thanksgiving always like that?" He pronounces it Tonks-geeveeng but at least within a French sentence.

I shrug. "I don't know much about it." I shift in my seat. "We didn't much celebrate it."

"But you keep telling me you're American."

"I don't keep telling you anything. I'm neither. Or nothing." This was supposed to be an encounter that would draw us closer together, and instead it's verging on hostile.

"You can't say you're nothing."

"Yes, I can. I just did." I look down. What does he know? "I mean, it's not written anywhere that you have to feel allegiance to one nation or another. Your parents are diplomats. I would have thought you'd understand that."

He shrugs petulantly, says, in a combative tone: "But your parents are American. You have a passport."

"I have dual nationality. That leaves me somewhere midway across the Atlantic, which, since I can't walk on water, is the equivalent of nowhere."

"Okay, okay," he laughs. "But don't your parents celebrate their national holiday?"

"Sometimes. It loses its meaning when displaced. The other night was an imitation too."

"Most of the food was pretty good. But that pumpkin pie." He screws up his face, and now I laugh.

"I couldn't eat it either. Maybe it's one of those things you need to eat as a child to appreciate."

"You mean like Nutella?"

"Who can dislike chocolate and nut spread?" On his suggestion I'd bought a small jar and found it a bit sticky on the palate, nowhere near as good as Madame's honey. "Tell me, exactly, what's happening with your room?"

"My landlords, Monsieur and Madame Yassine, are moving to Belgium, where they have cousins."

"Belgium?"

"They're just tenants, and their lease isn't being renewed. It's not easy for Moroccan people here in this country. For anyone from North Africa. For anyone outside Paris, for that matter." There go the eyebrows again, as if this were all very personal.

"I've been thinking about your housing problem." I stir my Anglo-Saxon coffee. "I assume you're still looking for another place?" He nods. "Well, I might have a solution for you."

"Moving in with some Americans?"

"No," I pause, ignore his disappointment. "I haven't told you much about where I live." I put down the spoon, look straight at him. "Madame Quinon owns a *hôtel particulier* on the place des Vosges. And there are just three of us. Madame, the housekeeper and me. A whole half of the house, closed off from where we live, is completely empty."

"Empty?" His eyes widen. "Half of a whole building?"

I nod. "There's a separate entrance on the side street. But you'd have to be really quiet. If they ever found out…"

"That sounds crazy."

"It is. And you couldn't stay there forever. Just until you find a new place."

"That's—incredible." A smile spreads like butter across his face. "You've saved me."

"It seems like an obvious temporary solution to your problem," I shrug.

We agree that he will come a week from tomorrow, Sunday night at eleven, after most people have gone to bed. When we part ways at the bottom of Saint Michel, he says: "Thank you. Really."

Now we share a plan, a secret.

***

Thursday, 9 December 1982

Between Pearl Harbor Day and something in the air yesterday that whiffed of the War, the floodgates opened. Memories of cold and fear and hunger came rushing in and filled up my being with such force I had to take a deep breath and remind myself that it was all over years ago. Winter was the worst because there was no getting warm, no way to forget a constant pinch of hunger. At the beginning, though, what I remember most is the fear. Fear of the soldiers and their guns, their boots pounding in unison on the paving stones or their vehicles thundering by. Their flags and the spiky Gothic letters of their signs going up all around the city and turning the place into a living horror film. Later—and the War seemed to go on for decades—it was fear that François would get caught.

Though I did not side with Pétain—I thought him a ridiculous old man with a high voice—I also did not subscribe to outright civil disobedience. Seeing the Germans take over the city filled me with anger too, but I wanted us to keep our heads down, just get through the occupation, and even more so when the Americans entered the War. I was French on paper, but persecution was a Nazi sport. Many Americans were arrested. I was frightened every time I walked out the door. François, on the other hand, even before we knew exactly how bad the Germans were, wanted to resist, to do everything in his power to obstruct them. I would say: They'll kill you. They'll kill us. We should just stay out of their way. He would reply: They're criminals, a band of thugs. I cannot sit and watch them marching around our city as if they owned it.

Right now they do own it, I would answer.

François would fly into a rage. Not for long, if I have anything to say about it.

You have your family to think about, I would say.

I can't ignore my conscience.

I'm not asking you to ignore it. Just contain it. Because your conscience won't be worth much if we're all dead.

On and on it would go. We had something of a competitive relationship and were unable to stop ourselves from trying to get the last word. To temper my anger, I reminded myself that François' maternal family was from Alsace. The region had been batted back and forth like a tennis ball between the French and the Germans throughout history. In 1940, the French still hadn't forgiven the Germans for the land they had annexed after their 1871 victory in the Franco-Prussian War. The

Germans hadn't forgiven the French for taking it back after the First World War. Even though Hitler did not reclaim Alsace-Lorraine officially after the French capitulated in 1940, François said: Look at how he's land grabbing. He doesn't need a certified stamp. Alsace is his, de facto. He threw his arm up in the air, paced the room.

I suppose it meant his Résistance activities were a foregone conclusion, especially once Pallet et Fils was requisitioned. François continued to produce the soap that would make the Germans clean of body if not of soul. He used it as a front to do everything he could to defy them. In a secret chamber of the cellar, he hid RAF pilots and others on the run. He had a printing machine on which the Résistance could publish its communiqués.

At first François shared some of his activities with me. But he knew I was nervous, that I didn't like him taking such risks. He became furtive, viewed my hesitation as a low-grade case of collaboration. Which to this day I believe wasn't fair. Things weren't as clear then, in medias res, as they seemed after the fact. In the here and now of the War, the world was not cleanly divided between heroes and cowards, *Résistants et Collaborateurs*. And I did not collaborate, ever in any way. I went out of my way not to speak to Germans. Nor did I encourage François to use his position—and he certainly could have—to get extra eggs or coal from the Occupiers. I stood in line for hours with our ration cards like everyone else. My stomach rumbled from hunger too.

A lot has been written about how the Germans held countries captive. How they murdered millions of people. But in quieter, more private ways, they ruined many other lives too. Countless families were shattered. When his sister Agnès and her husband sided with Pétain, François never spoke to them again. Given my feelings about her, that would have been cause for celebration, if it had stopped there. But a wall went up between François and me as the War went on.

We did talk about it, sometimes, how we were chafing at one another, how conversations too often turned around an accusatory *You*. There would be an effort made on both sides—beyond François' quick temper was a thoughtful, reasonable man. But it never lasted. Resentment built up, brick upon brick, and neither of us seemed capable of stopping the construction. Anger and ill will have a life of their own. No matter how much you tell your head: this is silly, stop it, move on; your lower organs keep right on stoking grievance, fighting the fight.

Between the hardship and the mutual resentment, we simply stopped talking. Or talking about anything of importance. At breakfast he was polite. Yes, please, no thank you, when I passed him a crust of that bland bread, poured him reheated chicory coffee. I hated his good manners then, the mask they provided. Yes, we still sat at the dinner table with the family and had superficial conversations about the day's events. When his mother was dying in late 1943, we both sat by her side.

But it was all a show. A hollow show, right until the end, and then, at least in terms of our personal history, wasn't I proven right?

I cannot think of it without tears of pain and anger pricking my blind old eyes and I don't want to write another word. It was not over years ago. The War is still right here, in the core of my brain, at the heart of my heart.

***

Friday, 10 December 1982

That wasn't much of a resolution. Sometimes I can go for days, weeks without writing, while other times the urge is constant. The girl has just taken my breakfast away. Strange young person. I wish I could see her better. I asked Germaine the other day what she looks like beyond the light brown hair I can make out around her face. Innocent blue eyes, she said. She's very pretty, though at moments she can look quite plain. Or the pretty side seems to take a back seat. I don't know. She's hard to explain. There is something unfinished about her, said Germaine.

Of course, I could communicate with the girl herself, ask her questions about something less trite than the weather. I could encourage real discussion. But something holds me back. Having been let down by Octave?

He came around yesterday. I had a meeting not far from here, he lied. Just thought I'd see how things were going.

Fine, as you can see.

Marie-France and I, he said, sounding as pompous as a prince, were wondering about your plans for Christmas.

(Did he think I'd planned a ski vacation?)

Marie-France has her heart set on spending Christmas in Normandy, with her family. (She has a heart, has she?) Since we stayed in Paris last year, I feel obliged to comply.

All right. (Obliged to comply—really.)

I don't like to leave you alone. You could come with us.

(Help!) That really won't be necessary, Octave. Germaine and I will manage just fine.

The girl? What about *la jeune Américaine* Lily?

She's going home for Christmas. But please, stop treating me like a complete invalid. Tell me about the children. And how things are going at Pallet et Fils.

We then had a reasonable conversation. His voice became eager, lost its arrogance. It's very important to me, Tante, he said, to get the firm back in family hands. Not ownership, of course, but management, I think it's possible. Things are going well.

And at home, I asked again.

Okay, he said unconvincingly.

The girls, I asked. Tell me about Violette and Chloé.

His voice went soft and thick. Violette is fine, he said. She sails through life. I worry about Chloé, sometimes. She cries easily and hates riding and you can imagine how well that goes down in the Coursault family.

I was reminded that Octave is not all bad. He loves his daughters dearly and the fact that he wants to get Pallet et Fils back in the hands of the family is hardly venal. It's a shame he didn't marry someone else; he could have turned out quite differently, I'm sure of it.

After Octave left, I was back to wondering why I wasn't out there defying the Nazis, risking my life, during the War. Because generally I might be described as a plucky person. So why I was passive, not active, I don't know. Except that I felt afraid. Afraid of where bravery would lead. As it turned out, I was afraid with reason, but courage is not about logic. And my inertia might not have averted tragedy anyway, though it certainly doomed François and me.

I wonder if I'd said to him: let me in, let me help, let me do something dangerous. Would that have turned things around, brought us back to our earlier complicity? I'm not sure. There's something about being under siege that deadens feeling. I hardly noticed the people around me who continued to have parties, to sustain a forced or maybe a rebellious gaiety, like they didn't want to admit that the roaring twenties were long gone. And with François, it was as if he were living on a tightrope and I was watching helplessly from the ground. My emotional self had closed up.

Afterwards it was humiliating to learn from newspaper articles about the copy machine and the RAF pilots. His staff—people who didn't lose their jobs, thanks to him—were so loyal, the articles would say. He was never denounced.

What about me, I wanted to scream. He trusted his employees and not me, his wife?

His heroism wasn't enough to satisfy his own conscience. Because he'd never helped any Jews and that, especially when the survivors began to straggle back, was unbearable to him. It was unbearable to all of us—why did he think he was special? And how could he reconcile saving the world while allowing his marriage to shrivel up and die before his eyes?

When my thoughts turn to that time, it's hard to imagine that we ever had fun. That those years when we danced and laughed, when he whirled me around and said how lucky he was, were part of the same life. The same marriage anyway. Joy and laughter abandoned us, migrated to some region beyond our reach. And they never made the return trip.

***

This is the longest weekend of my life. Saturday, I go with Meredith and Carol on an express trip of the Passages of Paris, the nineteenth century pre-shopping mall galleries. The idea came, Carol's guidebook told us, from the place des Vosges arcades. ("Oh," I said. "How interesting"). The most fun was eating charcuterie and cheese at a wine bar and getting a bit tipsy afterwards.

With my own breakfast now finished, the tray fetched and cleaned up, Sunday lies before me like the Steppes of Siberia.

I wander to my window and stare at the space that tonight Thibaud will be occupying. The sky is dull grey, the air is cold and damp. In her latest letter my mother asked if I had visited the Louvre yet. She had pressed money in my hand before I left. If you do nothing else in Paris, she said, you must visit this palace of art. And think of me. I could enter those halls and never come out.

Despite the weather I'll walk over there. It will take up more time. I consult my Plan de Paris and devise a zigzaggy route, *le chemin des écoliers*, the delaying-tactic path taken by the child on the way to school. It includes the rue des Rosiers, which for some reason—maybe because it's not directly on the way to anywhere I've been going—I have not yet been.

On the street of the terrorist attack that Madame and Germaine were talking about my first night at the place des Vosges, I walk practically on tiptoe. I don't know why. It's not like the killers are still lurking. A small group is clustered at the closed Jo Goldenberg's restaurant, reading the messages that accompany the flowers that are piled next to the door. There is bullet-splayed glass on one window. It's as if I'm looking at history and the present at the same time, imagining this violent event, its evidence still on display, in the former Ghetto where Jews were rounded up and deported during the War. I often see Hasidic and ultra-Orthodox Jews in black hats and curls or with yarmulke walking down the street. There are several kosher butchers. How do they feel after such a brutal attack? Scared to death, I'd think.

My walk starts to feel like a scary dream as I follow my schoolgirl itinerary through short, narrow streets, with ancient buildings crowding over my head—left on the rue des Ecouffes, right onto the rue du Roi de Sicile—on this uniformly grey day. I feel like a lab mouse in a maze, and I must find my way out. A young man scurries by me in a hurry, and I think of Jews navigating this labyrinth, on the run from Nazi soldiers. I pick up the pace myself and only relax when the wider, less ancient rue de Rivoli opens up elegantly in my path. Sometimes the history of this old city seems to seep right out of the stone, and what oozes out can smell more like overripe cheese than a freshly baked croissant.

I arrive at the Louvre just in time because Thibaud is starting to intrude into my thoughts again. The thrill and fear behind my plan to house him, of having him so close. I walk across the parking lot, past a few bare trees, to the entrance. This sad Sunday morning there aren't many visitors. It occurs to me buying my cheap ticket with my student card that I have never been to a museum alone before. My mother took us as teenagers once a year up to London, and I visited the Jeu de Paume and the Musée Victor Hugo with our group, but this is my first solo voyage.

The Louvre used to be the royal palace, until Louis XIV built Versailles, Gary told us. It is now a museum. Even with one wing occupied by the Ministry of Finance, it's humongous and houses old art of every kind, but I opt for the European painting section upstairs. In these vast, vaulted halls it is easy to imagine kings and queens and their retinues proceeding ceremoniously in big skirts and powdered wigs. There are immediately signs with arrows for *La Joconde* (Mona Lisa is written in small letters underneath), so I let her, the most famous painted lady in the world, guide me. In the Flemish art section are lots of thin, stiff religious figures with high foreheads and robes. Near the end of the period, Reubens gets a little too flouncy and fleshy for my taste. But suddenly the visual theatrics go quiet. I am in a room of Rembrandts. Portrait after portrait—many of himself—line the walls.

There are lots of art books at our house and I've also seen Rembrandts at The National Gallery, but there's something about this room at this moment that feels completely different—more intimate, more meaningful. The illuminated faces, particularly the eyes, emerging from a dark background exude a warm, glowing light that goes straight to my heart. They are as human and expressive as the real thing, and I am moved to the point of tears.

By the time I have gone round and round several times and am again following the signs for *La Joconde*, I'm in a bit of a trance. Which is maybe why, when I get to the room, I don't even see her at first. But maybe I wouldn't have anyway. I was expecting Mona to leap out at me like a film star, but there she is, unassumingly framed amidst other Italian Renaissance works. I move closer, try to see what is so exceptional. Her eyes are a bit squished together, her nose a bit long. The hint of a smile is nothing to get excited about. I do the thing of going to different points in the room and yes, the eyes follow me, but it doesn't make her seem any more special. After ten minutes of staring, I just don't get it. Unlike the Rembrandts, she leaves me cold.

Back in the cavernous hall, there is Neo-classical David's coronation of Napoleon with the crowd standing straight as pegs, versus Romantic Gerricault's The Raft of the Medusa, with all those bodies falling willy-nilly off the boat and practically spilling out of the painting onto the floor in front of me.

On my way back to the place des Vosges, I am a jumble of emotion. The day has taken me through highs and lows of European *civilisation*. On the lofty side, I have walked through a magnificent palace now filled with art that even when it doesn't move me to tears makes me think. In the nether regions, I have visited the scene of multiple crimes against innocent human beings during times of war and peace. And it was lucky that I was alone. Much of the meaning and intensity would have been lost had I been with other people.

It also strikes me that I am not, after all, disappointed by Mona Lisa. That such a plain-Jane can attain great fame seems a sign of hope. And I'm thankful to this city for filling up my day and my head, taking my mind away from a man and my imminent act of stealth.

***

Sunday, 12 December 1982

Germaine came to see me this afternoon. I could sense her disarray even before she sat down. It's Flora, she said. They've found a lump. They want to, you know, take a piece, to see if it's, you know...

They want to do a biopsy, I said. Lots of people have lumps that are perfectly harmless.

Silence.

It doesn't have to be malignant, I said.

I heard the most terrible sob rise up. From so deep, it sounded like a death rattle, and what could I say? What do you say to a person who knows there's no bottom?

What anyone would say: Don't worry. I'm sure it will be fine.

The only comfort I could give her was an embrace, a creaky old body against which she could lean while she sobbed her heart out. I wouldn't say she felt better when she left. But calmer. She was calmer.

I wasn't. I was furious. Of course in real life Justice is a joke. But my blood boils that that woman should be subjected to more suffering, to this particular Injustice. Germaine, by any measure, has already suffered too much.

***

The shutter to the barred window on the side street is open a crack. On the lookout for Thibaud, I feel like a spy, waiting for the messenger. My eye scans the buildings across the street. Only a few lights. Windows are closed; it's a cold night. I did feel a hint of heat when I put my hand on the cast iron radiator here in the *la loge de la gardienne*, the concierge's residence. Just enough to stop the pipes from freezing. And there's running water. I hope Thibaud won't use enough to make a noticeable difference to the bill.

I keep wondering how long he might stay. A while, I told him. But a while could mean anything. Months, even years.

Where is he? My watch face in the streetlight says it's a quarter past eleven already. I'm freezing. And tired. And beginning to be creeped out by this big empty house. By my duplicity too. Suddenly none of it seems real. That I couldn't possibly have been so bold as to invite a near stranger to trespass on somebody else's property for an open-ended duration. Lily Owens is not that kind of person. Or is she, under that dutiful veneer? She's the type to have taken the key and entered this locked part of the house in the first place. To have entered the closed spare room in Madame's flat and examined its contents with care. Is this unreal house leading her to act out of character? Or is it Paris, city of temptation, that's teasing previously concealed sneakiness from the depths of her inner being?

Heavy wheels are coming down the street and there, finally, is a large old van. It rolls to a halt, brakes whining, in front of the building. After checking the windows one more time—no eyes peering out—I leave my post, open the door within the door of the *portail* and there is Thibaud, rucksack and sleeping bag, like any student traveller.

"I just have one more bag and the mattress," he says, lifting the rucksack off his shoulder.

"Can I help?"

"Not for the moment. Monsieur Yassine and I can get it."

The man who is opening the back of the van has a very worried face—though why wouldn't he—he's aiding and abetting this act of unlawful entry—but he gives me a smile.

The mattress is inside in a matter of seconds. Thibaud says thank you to the man; they shake hands. It is an awkward moment, since it is obvious even to me that this is a final good-bye, that there is absolutely no reason their paths will ever cross again. But it doesn't last long. A car pulls up behind the van and Monsieur Yassine rushes back before the person hoots. My heart is pounding. What if it's someone who knows this street and this empty house?

"If you can just help me with the mattress," he whispers, "I can manage the rest."

It sounds like he can't wait to be rid of me. I already feel disappointed, hurt.

"You take the front," he says. We stagger up the stairs. Mattresses are heavy, awkward, floppy things and I am trying to remember if being on the front end is supposed to be easier or harder, if Thibaud has done the gentlemanly thing, having me go first. If he's behaving like the son of a diplomat. Do diplomats' sons even lug mattresses illegally up stairs in the middle of the night? Maybe the ones who toss sandwich wrappers in the Seine do.

At the top of the steps, I point to the corner room, facing the street. "I thought this place was best. It's about as far away from Madame and the housekeeper as you can get."

"Fantastic," he says, eyes wandering the room.

"Madame's husband had planned to make apartments here. But then he had an accident and died."

"Lucky for me, I guess," he says. "Bigger and better than the one I was paying money to rent."

"Probably colder though." I rub my shoulders.

Silence. Unendurable silence.

"Well," I finally say.

"I really appreciate this."

"It seemed such an obvious solution," I shrug. "Until you can find something else."

His face looks very pale in the streetlight, like one of the marble statues I saw at the Louvre earlier today. "Thanks for helping me with the mattress." He pauses. "Could you give me the key?"

"Oh. Of course." I hand him the big iron key from my pocket. "Good night then."

"Good night," he says. "And thanks so much."

My extremities may be numb with cold, but my face is burning hot as I walk back to my room. What had I expected would happen? That he'd grab me in a passionate embrace, throw me down on the mattress we'd just lugged up the stairs and in swift order finally release me from my virginal prison?

Yes, on several occasions, I'd imagined just that. What a fool. What a hopeless fool. I click my door shut and collapse on the bed.

***

Thursday, 16 December 1982

The biopsy is scheduled for next Monday. They won't know for sure until the new year and an operation would be mid-January at the earliest, but it doesn't bode well that they are acting so quickly. Germaine has pulled herself together at least outwardly. Almost as if she were now clanking around in a suit of armor.

And the girl is in a sulk. She shuffles above my head and brings a whiff of misery in with my breakfast every morning. It must be love. At her age it always is. I hope she gets over it because come January Germaine will obviously want to assist with the children and Roger. I'll insist upon it anyway.

Which means—I can admit it after that foray onto the street—I'll need another pair of hands, of eyes. But not ones belonging to some moping, love-struck child. These days adolescence seems to last forever. Or however long one fancies it should continue. At her age I was running a household, had no time for self-indulgent brooding.

Before I get too high on that "good old days" horse, let's remember that those years were sandwiched between two world wars. Superior they were not.

***

In the lecture hall, Meredith is on one side of me, Carol on the other. I am not listening to this discourse on modifiers, but sitting here is better than brooding in my room. Or being in that house at all, because when I am there, all I can think about is him. It's been five days and we have not met, by chance or otherwise. I wish I'd never had the idea of letting him in. That I'd never hoped. Hope is stupid. Nothing ever comes of it.

"Lily," Meredith taps lightly on my arm. "What in God's name is a COI?"

"*Complément d'objet indirect.* An indirect object."

Meredith notes. "I'll say indirect. Jesus, this is complicated."

Of course it's complicated. Everything is. Complicated and detestable, living is. Why bother to pick apart sentences, to learn about art or literature or philosophy, when just getting through the day is such hard, useless work.

Carol is looking at me. Without realizing it, I have been drawing concentric circles in my notebook, pressing down harder and harder, almost breaking the nib of my fountain pen. I stop, cover the tortured paper with my hand, and lean forward as if paying extra hard attention to the professor, whose voice continues to drone like a swarm of mosquitos for what seems forever. Finally he closes his notes and leaves the lectern.

"He should win a prize," Meredith says, standing up. "Deadest man walking."

"Is that what you'd call his shuffle?" Carol asks. "Walking?"

Meredith laughs and stretches, arms above her head, back arched, still-tanned stomach exposed. "It's Friday," she says. "Let's buy a bottle of wine."

"Good idea," says Carol. "Will you join us?" I interpret her tone and sidelong look as polite but unwilling.

"I should probably go back to my place."

"It would actually be helpful if you came with us," she says. "We got some administrative letter that I'm not sure I understand."

"Okay. I'll stop by for a few minutes."

"Great," says Carol with a big smile.

"We're outta here," says Meredith.

It's almost eight by the time I'm walking under the arcade at the place des Vosges, and only now it occurs to me that no administrative letter was ever produced. After a glass of wine, Carol asked me what was wrong. I said Oh, nothing, but their interest made me feel a lot better. So did talking about other things and getting that stupid man out of my head. The wine helped too, though it's left me a bit light-headed on an empty stomach. Just as I am hoping there's enough cheese and tomato left, who should appear from behind a pillar but Thibaud.

"Oh, it's you," I say, with as much disdainful indifference as I can muster after five days of pining.

"*Salut*," he smiles, says in English: "Sorry I have been quiet."

"Well, I'm glad you've been that," I answer in French.

"I've been setting up."

I am just about to ask: "How long, exactly, do you plan on trespassing?" when Thibaud holds up a plastic bag from the Félix Potin. "I bought a *pique-nique*."

A glint of joy elbows its way into my anger—I can't help it—but I stop in front of the *portail*, determined to resist. "Come on," he says and already I can't muster a bigger protest than:

"I'm tired."

"Aren't you hungry?" he asks, leaning into my arm, pulling me along and before I know it, I've followed him around the corner, through the door. Inside Thibaud lights a torch and we head up the stairs.

"No one's seen you, I hope."

"No one's taken notice, if that's what you mean." He's thankfully slipped into French, and I already feel better disposed towards him.

I stop, but Thibaud keeps going. "Wait. Isn't your room here?"

He shakes his head and up we go to an attic room. He turns on a small light on the floor.

"How did that happen?"

"I hooked up to the Ville de Paris electricity. It's easy to do." He points to a wire running along the stairs.

"But—" The place is all set up—mattress, crates for tables.

"Sit down," he says, pointing to one of two large cushions. "Found them on the street."

"And the heater?" he's just turned on.

"At a flea market. Going for nothing—only needed a new plug. Sit, please," he repeats. Cheese and ham and pâté, a bottle of Vieux Pape, come out of the bag. He lays the spread on the crate between us, opens the wine. "Here," he hands it to me.

I take a sip, hand it back.

"Look," he says and points at the skylight window facing the court-yard and it has black cloth blocking it. "A war-time idea," he smiles.

No wonder he hasn't sought me out until today. He's been too busy setting up for good, by the looks of it.

"So let's eat," he nods, handing me some bread with pâté spread on it.

Thibaud is very chatty—tells me how he talked down the price for the heater at the market, how easy it is to find perfectly good stuff on the street. "I could have furnished an entire apartment." His arm swings out in a wide circle. "This whole house." And I can't help it. My anger evaporates. Food and wine have never tasted so delicious. He asks me about Meredith and Carol. We talk about where they come from, what they are like, as if we are on one side and they on another and it feels good to be on common ground with him.

With this invisible barrier broken, it isn't awkward when our hands touch as we pass the bottle back and forth. "Tell me about the family you were living with," I say. The man's lined face has stayed in my mind.

"The Yassines," he says, still chewing his bread. "Madame cleaned houses and took care of children, even though they have three of their own. Monsieur, who ran a garage attached to the house, wants his two sons to succeed at school, but they're more interested in the Paris Saint Germain football team than their studies. It's the daughter who is mo-tivated." He shakes his head, smiles. "I helped Ahmed and Joucef with their homework, but they were not attentive. Karima, homework done, would come talk to me, tell me her plans for the future. She'd go far if this country weren't so racist. Their lease wasn't renewed, so they decid-ed to move to Belgium, near their cousins."

"Is Belgium better? I mean, not so racist?"

"I have no idea. I just hope they make out okay. They were really kind to me."

The crate has been pushed away and the two of us are looking at our outstretched feet that converged in the middle of this explanation.

"We'd be more comfortable, I think," Thibaud says, "if we sat on the mattress."

Without another word, we change positions, the length of our bod-ies now touching as we lean against the wall. Thibaud puts his hand on my thigh, and I am surprised I don't ignite, right here and now, through internal combustion. Then he kisses me, his tongue probing my mouth, running along my teeth. His hand goes up my shirt, and my skin turns on like a light, though he's somehow managed to switch the real one off. Once our clothes are more or less off, I peep:

"I should tell you. I, I…I…"

"Don't worry," he whispers, taking my nipple in his mouth, which makes me whimper like a hungry puppy. It doesn't take long for my mortifying purity to become history.

Thibaud falls asleep immediately, but I cannot even close my eyes. It hurt a little bit—not as much as I'd feared—and it was worth every affronted nerve. Finally.

He smells of shampoo. The sheets have a rumpled, less fresh odor. Not bad. Comforting, really. Or maybe it's just sharing a bed.

It occurs to me that I must think about getting back to my room across the courtyard. If I wait until morning, Germaine will surely hear or possibly see me. If I get up now, isn't it rude? Wouldn't it be sending the wrong message?

After another half hour or so, I cannot stay still any longer and extricate myself slowly, gently. Thibaud does not wake up, even when my key drops out of my pocket onto the floor while I'm groping around for my clothes. I look down at his sleeping body. His face is turned away and all I can see is the curly dark brown head, the slim form under the duvet, a body I know quite well now.

I walk out onto the street with confidence, as if of course I belong here, make my way around the corner, through the courtyard and up the back stairs. Crawling into the cool, smooth sheets of my bed is delicious. I am at peace, a different person now.

***

Saturday, 18 December

Remembering that Second War, I've started wondering about the pretty picture I've drawn of all the dancing and glitter in the twenties, into the thirties. This morning it is hard to believe, even for me, who lived it. It sounds like romantic exaggeration, if not pure invention. At least a trick of the memory, as if I've sifted the gold to one side of the pan and discarded the dross. But that's what memory is, isn't it? A mental sifting of the past. Conscious or unconscious. In the end, I suppose, what difference. They're my memories and mine alone. They only exist in my head, and now on this page, which is for my eyes (sic!) only. Who's to know or care about their veracity, if there really is such a thing, when it comes to resurrecting the past.

Still, the thinking and writing makes me mine deeper. The glitter of the first years gets stripped away, forces a rawness to the surface. I may have been a good student, but learning French was hard. There were whole dinners where I understood nothing. Even once I could follow the flow, transforming thoughts into my own sentences was like scaling a mountain. Usually by the time I'd clambered to the top, the forever witty conversation had flitted on to something else. I sounded dull, and to the French of that ilk, there is no greater flaw than a slow, clumsy tongue. Their disdain was aroused in part, too, because I was American. Or not French. Or, even more precisely, not *Parisienne*. No, even that's too generous: not from the faubourg Saint Germain, issued from a family that had been living there for the two hundred fifty years, at least.

And all that dancing during *les Années Folles* was as much giddy displacement as genuine joy. Underneath the merrymaking the country was still reeling from the Great War and the influenza epidemic that came right on its heels. No household was untouched. Certainly not the Quinons. François' older brother was killed in the hecatomb of the Somme and his father by the flu two years later. That's why he'd come to the United States, to flee all that death and his sense of guilt for having survived it.

What a thankless task running the household was, even with all the help Anna and Solange provided. My mother-in-law, after losing husband and son, had descended into a mute stupor from which she never emerged, except to criticize me. She couldn't even take care of herself, much less a family, which meant that I, having never laid eyes on a servant, was in charge. How I mustered any credible semblance of authority, I don't know. Though that was easy, compared to caring for the poisonous little sister Agnès. She was thirteen when I arrived and I have never known, before or since, such a proud and self-centered creature. She resented every inch of me and never missed an occasion to demonstrate her animosity. A broken bowl here, a barbed comment there. She stole not just money but my class notes. It was a daily hell.

Still, even after I've dredged up the dross, those years glow because there was an underpinning of happiness. François and I were in love. My life was fuller and busier than I could ever have dreamt it on those long, boring afternoons at the ranch. And I did learn French, and somehow managed to manage the household.

We believed that the worst was over and we had reason to rejoice, to dance. After all the suffering of one war, surely there couldn't be another one right around the corner.

How short-sighted, even with the 20-20 vision I then possessed.

***

These days I cannot even feel the ground under my feet. I float up all five flights to Meredith and Carol's, no shortness of breath. Like a queen being carried on an invisible livery. Nothing and no one can penetrate my aura. Magnanimous, that's how I feel towards the entire human race. At once loving and compassionate and tolerant. Poor, blind Madame, I say to myself when delivering her breakfast. I pity my mother who cannot get a grip. When I look in the mirror, I can see it in my face, the glow that sex has graced upon me. One night followed by another and another and now I'm an old pro, can stand tall next to the likes of Meredith.

I copied the key to the door across the kitchen and every night, once all's quiet, I creep out of bed and downstairs, into the wing. I hurry through the enfilade of rooms, take the stairs at the end up to Thibaud's encampment, which each day becomes more furnished: more crates for his books, a radio, a little stand for his lamp. And one night he takes me down to the kitchen with the bathtub, shows me his *plaques* for heating food and water. Now none of this distresses or irritates me. I'd like Thibaud to stay forever.

With no alarm, I wake and wake during the night, each time consulting anxiously the illuminated hands on my watch. By all logic, I should be exhausted, but fatigue is a condition that does not exist in heaven. In the morning, I'm up and bustling and rushing out to meet the day. The old stone and the moody skies over the Seine touch me physically, like a hand on my skin. It's as if the whole city—and all my experiences within it—are nudging me awake, prodding dormant corners of my being to life. Yes, that's what Paris has been for me these last three months: an alarm clock.

****

Winter

Friday, 24 December 1982

It's nearing midnight and I turn to the page for company. Germaine made me a fire, cooked lamb with rosemary for supper, then left to be with Flora who celebrates Christmas with her Christian husband. She asked me to join them, as I have many times in the past, but this year it didn't seem right. The biopsy was on Monday. The doctors could tell from what they extracted that the tumor may be small but most likely cancerous. Germaine slapped on another layer of armor.

Tuesday was the winter solstice, a day that should provide a note of hope. From now on daylight is gaining ground. Except for me. It's dark all the time. There will never be brighter, longer days and I wonder why the rest of my body won't catch up with my eyes and put out the light.

The girl has gone back to her family for the holidays. I hadn't realized how much life a young mouse could breathe into a place.

***

Saturday, 25 December 1982

I heard Germaine's uneven step in the corridor last night. When she stopped at my door to check on me, I almost called out, but it was late, past time for voices in the dark. She was back this morning, breakfast tray in hand. When she returned to pick it up, I made her sit down, talk to me.

Tell me about Flora. About the family and how they are doing.

She sighed, with a catch in her throat. After a minute: They are brave, for the children's sake, I guess. I try to be brave too, but one can get tired of that. You know.

Not everyone dies from cancer, I said. In fact, these days, I think there's every chance she will survive.

That's what the doctors tell her.

Exactly.

I do not know why I live when everyone I love dies.

Flora is not dead. And the doctors are hopeful. You must be too.

When she left, I felt desperate. Desperate at my inability to help. To compensate for, even in the smallest way, what she's already suffered. We've never talked about it. The story ricocheted from Germaine to Michel to François to me. Fourth hand or not, the bare facts, that Germaine was the only survivor in her family, are incontestably correct. And it's hard to imagine the rest isn't accurate as well—there are so many stories just like it. Germaine was born right around the corner from here, on the rue des Ecouffes. Her father and maternal grandparents were Jewish immigrants from Poland, meaning the family was targeted in the '42 *Rafle*. The parents were arrested and deported. They never returned. Germaine and her sister were concealed in a back room by the father's employer, an antique dealer and a Christian whose atelier was in the Marais, on the rue des Francs-Bourgeois. There they lived, Germaine and her sister, until July of '44—achingly close to the Liberation—when they were denounced and sent to Drancy, then Auschwitz, on the last convoy. Her younger sister, along with the elderly antique dealer, were sent straight to the gas chambers.

Germaine barely survived the pointless long march the Germans undertook near the end of the war when all was clearly lost. Her leg was badly injured, and she has had a limp ever since. Her skin, full of sores, is still scarred. Like the other survivors—as perverse as it may sound—she was taken to the Lutétia, a luxury hotel that just months before had been occupied by their persecutors. Empty eyes to empty eyes, right out of Dante they were, every last one who came back. At least she met Michel there.

Afterwards it was said that we knew. Yes, stories circulated but there were so many stories, and as most of them proved false, one stopped believing anything. I just closed my ears, along with my other senses. And who could have imagined horror to that degree until witnessing it with your own eyes? Then what had been willfully unclear for five years came into morbidly sharp focus. Even for those of us who had suffered our own losses, it caused inexcusable shame. The gavel of history slammed down on us. Boom.

***

Rain punishes the window of the coach; the landscape is an angry grey but that's okay. I am angry. Life without the Hoopers, who retired and moved north at the end of September, just after I came here, was unbearable. Though the new Australian housekeeper has lived in Britain for years, she did not stop harking back to the superior life Down Under. Her cooking could not even be called competent, and it gave the house a smell I found close to repulsive. I couldn't stand it another minute. I changed my ticket—stuff the cost—and am returning five days earlier than planned.

On quite a few occasions, I went out back just to escape the smell and the complaints. With Mr Hooper gone, they've put the garden in the hands of a landscaping company. The vegetable patch had been completely cleared and seeded with grass. The roses, trimmed by unloving hands, were forlorn stubs. I ended up spending a lot of time in the cemetery, where Jane and I used to wander for hours amidst the old stone graves. Though it might sound depressing, I always find it comforting, the quiet and all those people laid to rest.

But this time there was no Jane, and I keep wondering if she'll ever come back. She has loved everything about America from the second her feet hit the tarmac on that trip to Chicago. As if whatever our parents had deprived us of, she found there. I can't explain it, she said to me. For the first time ever, I feel at home. From then on, she had *une idée fixe*, starting with university. She got into Barnard in New York. The parents were proud of her, but they always are. Jane, sensible and clever, is their favorite. Admittedly, Maude was cantankerous and stroppy, but aren't parents supposed to love their children regardless of their less attractive qualities? As for myself, I've always felt a non-entity or, in lower moments, *l'enfant de trop*, the one-child-too-many, the tipping point for our mother.

After Jane left for Barnard, she came back less and less frequently. A couple weeks in August between her summer job and the autumn term, ten days at Christmas. Then just five days at Christmas. To see me, she always said, but we drifted further apart between each visit. Our lives had no common ground anymore except the parents and sister she saw with greater and greater infrequency. After college she got hired into a training program at the Chase Manhattan bank. Last summer they sent her to their London office for a month.

The first evening of Jane's visit was as joyous as it ever gets in the Owens' household. Mrs Hooper—excited as a schoolgirl to have her Janey back—put the steaming food on the table, and our mother was charm itself. She laughed. She addressed each of us, making little personal jokes, but Jane obviously got most of the attention. Our father, forever hopeful when his wife is up, smiled radiantly and paternally at his daughter who shares his clear, practical mind. Even Maude was swept up in the shimmering patina of happiness.

The next day I came down early to have breakfast with Jane before she took the train to London with our father. It was a real shock—I stopped dead in my tracks at the kitchen door. My sister was dressed in a skirt-suit and a stiff white shirt, ugly skin-toned tights and sensible shoes. True, Jane had never cared much for fashion, but this get-up was aggressively unflattering. It sent a deep foreboding to my gut. By the third day, our mother had plummeted into silence. Our father looked down at his plate all the time, fretted with the table mat and fiddled with the cutlery. The second week Jane said the commute was too much and she was going to stay with a friend in London. I went in one day and we had lunch. Jane, severely dressed and career bound on one side of the table; me, recently graduated and seriously floundering on the other.

"Do you have a lot of friends? In New York?" I asked loudly. We were at a pub near her office. It was full of rowdy office men drinking pints.

"A lot of Barnard people stayed in New York," she said, pushing a prawn onto her fork with her knife. "But, you know, I've never had a busload of friends." I nodded. "The bank people aren't really my type. They've known each other since boarding school, if not before, and all they talk about is one another and sports. I haven't got much to add on either front." Jane studied literature. We are not a sporty family. "What about you? What's the plan now that you've graduated?"

I shrugged—no, squirmed. For the first time in my life, I was embarrassed in front of my sister, felt I needed to keep up appearances of control and self-confidence. "I'm giving myself a break for the summer. In September I'll probably come up here and see what I can find." This was a total fudge. Every time I considered looking for a job in London, I changed the subject in my head.

"What if you gave the US a try? If you came to New York, you could stay with me while you got yourself sorted." She really meant it. I could see how much it would please her if I came to New York. I must remember that if I miss her, she probably misses me.

"Maybe." Unfortunately, the idea of New York frightened me even more than London.

"Whatever you do, Lily," she said, pushing her plate aside and crossing her arms on the table, looking at me as if nothing and no one else existed in the world, a look that always made me feel safe. "You've got to get away from *there*. From *them*." She shook her head. "I'm not at all sure London is far enough." She paused, as if calculating the actual number of miles necessary between our parents and me for my well-being. "Just remember. There is life after childhood, no matter how it seems now. I promise. And geographical distance can really make a difference."

So Maude's suggestion of Paris a few weeks later had fallen on primed ears.

We spent a lot of time together these last days, Maude and I. Since

I left in September, she has discovered yoga and meditation. She tried to teach me some moves, but I couldn't stretch that far or keep my balance or my concentration. It made us both laugh and that opened the way to more intimate communication than we've ever had. One evening we were sitting on the floor in front of the fire, and she told me the whole story about her year in Florence, about the international gang of young painters who had gathered there. About the one she had fallen in love with, the American who then started sleeping with her Italian friend. "That was it," Maude said as she poked the dying fire, "I was shrapnel."

And I told Maude about Meredith and Carol, who had swooped through London on an itinerary that also included Amsterdam, Munich, Vienna, Venice and Rome. I told my sister about Madame and Germaine and the huge house the three of us rattle around in.

"Gothic," Maude said.

"I guess it's pretty weird. But it already seems quite normal."

"After this place," she rolled her eyes. "What wouldn't?"

I even told her about Thibaud, including the new living arrangements.

"You have to be careful with these diplomat's sons," Maude said. "Before you know it, they think they're back at the embassy and start throwing big parties."

"Funnily enough," I said, "he doesn't seem to have many friends. He's attached himself to Americans, this year and last. He's obsessed by the US. Even more than Jane."

"Hmm," Maude said. "Sounds like a bit of an odd fish."

That makes me blush even now, remembering Maude's reaction. Though I protested, perhaps too vehemently, that he is really great, I have to admit that there is something most odd-fish-ish about Thibaud. In fact, he doesn't appear to have *any* friends. I have also wondered since being away from him and Paris what attracts me to this strange person. For sure his looks—the sensitive, almost beautiful face—are appealing. I admire his determination to learn English and to do something with his life. Thibaud knows what he wants—or thinks he does—and since I still have no idea, that firmness of purpose is alluring. On the other hand, his insistence on speaking English and his infatuation with the United States can irritate me excessively. As does his way of flailing his arms around when telling a story or dancing. Hard as it is to admit, I sometimes wonder if what really captivates me is finally having a boyfriend, though even there I have to say a boyfriend of sorts. Our relationship remains undeclared, is known only to the two of us, which can make me wonder if it counts.

The rain is pelting the bus window. I hunker down in the seat and rest my head on my balled-up scarf, tell myself to stop it, stop it right now. Such thoughts lead to angst, which inevitably brings on The Mood. I must focus on the good, not the disturbing. I cross my arms over my chest and, with interrupted success, sleep.

After getting off the bus during the ferry ride and back on after The Channel was crossed, after several more hours of road across northern France and snarled traffic as we approach Paris, we pull in to the Gare du Nord at almost nine. It's a raw morning and everything is grey—sky, stone, air. But it feels bracing, energizing. The city has its own thrum, its own long and complicated history that has nothing to do with my pathetic life. While I look out the window of the 65 bus rolling down the boulevard Magenta and the boulevard Beaumarchais, towards the Bastille, it occurs to me that the grey all around—the pavement, the rooftops, the sky—is not uniform, as it had originally seemed. It is as finely nuanced as the paint samples my parents are considering for the living room. As I walk from the stop Chemin Vert towards the place des Vosges, I can sense that I am changing *quartier*, that the Bastille area has a completely different feel from the Marais, something I had only unconsciously perceived that Saturday I walked in search of the prison. This discovery makes me feel that I have begun to know the city at a different, deeper level, and it increases my contentment at being back.

It's only when I'm under the arcade, with my key in the lock of the heavy oak door, that my spirits get a jolt. I didn't phone to warn of my early arrival. How could I have ignored that basic courtesy? Was I that desperate to get away? In any case here I am. On the way up the front stairs, I tap lightly at Germaine's door, but there's no answer.

Being on these stairs reminds me of my first day here. I really do feel different now. Not just more attuned to the shades of Paris grey and her varying *ambiances* but less callow. Stronger too. I packed up and left my parents' house five days earlier than planned. Despite the oddities of this living arrangement and my unclassifiable relationship with not just Thibaud but Madame herself, I am finally beginning to understand Jane's instinctive sense of belonging somewhere else. The *Bonjour* I pronounce to whomever is in the lit kitchen at the end of the corridor has a certain authority.

"*Tiens*," says Germaine. "Aren't you early?"

"I'm sorry I didn't warn you. There was a problem with my ticket, and it seemed easier to return now."

"It's nice to have you back," Germaine says. "Some breakfast?"

"If there's enough, yes, please." An almost full baguette lies on the table, and I can already taste the butter and honey.

I stick my duffle bag in the corner, take off my coat, hang it on the back of the chair. It's very quiet, except for the kitchen clock, whose second hand, when it's silent, you can hear juddering forward.

"*Ca va?*" I ask.

"Well…" she rises, turns to the sink and the breakfast dishes. My *tartine* is halfway to my mouth. "Flora needs an operation."

"Oh." I put the bread back down on the plate. When I last saw Flora, she did not seem at all ill—quite the contrary—she was infectiously full of life. I wait for an explanation, but Germaine keeps washing and rinsing. Finally:

"Madame will need more help." She turns from the sink, dries her hands. Her face is grave and grey. "You can make some more time?"

"Yes, of course."

"You'll be paid, naturally. You'll need some cooking lessons."

"Okay…and Flora?"

Germaine sighs, begins to talk hesitantly, like the words are clogged up in a pipe. A lump. In the breast. They think it's, you know. *Can-cer*. Then she is silent and looks down at her splotchy hands, starts turning her wedding ring.

Somewhere I read so I say: "A lot of women survive breast cancer, especially these days."

"That's what Madame says. That's what the doctors say. But what people say sometimes means nothing."

"Flora seems like a very strong person," I say. "She's got you and Roger, Rachel and Michel."

"I know." She takes a deep breath. "I don't want to burden you with these troubles. But it would be a big relief if you could help."

I assure her that I will do everything I can to lighten her load, a load that somehow seems considerable even without her daughter's illness.

This information accompanies me into a long, hot bath. I first met Germaine's family on the main staircase one Sunday afternoon. I was dropping something off when the door opened. Burst open, actually, with chatter and laughter. Germaine was beaming. Madame was there too. It was a shock to see her smiling. I was introduced to Flora and Roger—never any question of Monsieur, Madame with them—and the children Rachel and Michel. Flora said, Oh perfect timing, we were talking at lunch about how you might like to babysit for us some time. There was such a jolly bustle the whole house felt lifted, like it had received an injection of life-giving serum.

My second experience babysitting was quite different from the first, even the setting. Flora and Roger live near a canal in the 10th arrondissement. The *quartier* is run down, the population too. Roger even insisted on accompanying me to the métro afterwards. They live in a modern block and the flat, a duplex, decorated simply, was untidy, with children's toys on the floor, magazines and books lying on every surface. The same energy I felt on the stairs filled the place. The children were not badly behaved but seemed less like little adults than Violette and Chloé; their pyjamas didn't match. We haven't got a TV but help yourself to something to eat, said Flora. It felt good to be part of their scene.

And now, after this very bad piece of news? Germaine could barely keep her desperation under wraps. I try to bat a selfish question out of my head, but it won't stop flying back in: Would our mother fret with such feeling if one of us had cancer?

After the bath, I get in bed, scissor my legs. It feels so good to be clean and prone, after a night of cramped discomfort on the seat of a bus. I'm back here in Paris. That's what matters. And helping Germaine. I pull the duvet around my shoulders, the bolster pillow into the crook of my neck. She's going to teach me how to cook.

***

Tuesday, 28 December 1982

Last night I dreamt I was back in the apartment, rue de Tournon, hiding in the broom closet, while François screamed at the German soldiers who had broken down the door. Suddenly I felt a gun at the back of my head, and I woke up just as the trigger was being pulled.

If that didn't give me a heart attack, I guess there's no hope anything ever will.

Such a slippery thing, guilt. I can say—have said in these pages— that my behavior during the war was understandable, even defensible, at the time. But was it? Not having done anything for the Germaines in our midst still weighs on me, no matter what we did or didn't suspect then. It's what weighed so heavily on François afterwards. Because we did know enough to do something. We knew that the Jews were forced to suffer countless injustices, from the yellow stars, to moving off the sidewalk when crossing paths with a German. From being forced to close their shops to being banned from much of everyday life. We knew that they were hauled off for no reason and not brought back. Isn't that complete absence of justice, visible to one and all, enough to prompt protest, action?

I cannot get comfortable in my chair with these thoughts in my head. Nor should I.

The girl is back, five days early.

Everything all right, I asked, when she knocked on my door in that tentative way she has and announced her return.

Oh, yes, fine, she said.

That Oh, yes, fine didn't sound convincing—but maybe I'm wrong. There are times when the sound of a voice and a feeling in the air are not enough. One needs confirmation from the eyes, from the body language. But I will admit that I'm glad she's here. It's more a comfort than a nuisance, hearing her footsteps over my head.

Time for my *apéritif* and the evening news. What a relief to have another day almost over.

***

Later, still feeling groggy from overnight travel, I go around the corner to the Felix Potin to buy some food. Fat, smelly Madame Dodé with a bucked front tooth poking through fleshy lips is propped like a sack of flour against a stool next to the cash register, like always. Like always, her husband, cap on his small head, stands attentively at her side.

"You're back!" says Mme Dodé. "And England? How is it over there?"

"Okay. And how was your Christmas?"

"Same as always. We ate too much," she says with a loud, whinnying laugh.

Monsieur lays my gruyère and tomatoes on the counter. I pay, put my change away, grasp the handles of the plastic shopping bag, turn to the door and walk right into Thibaud. We both recoil.

"What are you doing here?" he asks.

"Buying my supper."

"I thought you weren't coming back until next week."

"There was a problem with my ticket."

"I see." He looks down at the tip of his scuffed shoes. "Well, let's get together."

I walk back to the square, stricken. Of course the main reason I came back early was to see him. He's in and out of my thoughts all the time. Then he acts like he hardly knows me. Let's get together—that really, really stings.

I try to focus on my own somewhat mixed feelings and motives. But right now that does not help at all. His chilly courtesy made me feel rejected and abandoned all over again, as if he'd picked me up and hurled me back fourteen years and there I was, watching from the window as my father gets in a taxi. Madame Flaviche calls me. *Lee-lee*, with a warning, scolding voice and I withdraw from the window, feeling empty and terrified and homesick, even though at age seven I didn't yet know the word for it.

As I'm walking across the courtyard, Germaine pokes her head out the window. "You all right for supper?"

"Yes." I hold up the bag. "Thank you."

"Maybe next week we can start the cooking lessons?"

"Great," I say, while wondering why the hell should I learn to cook. Life is sad, lonely, hopeless.

***

Saturday, 1st January 1983

Here we go. Yet another one.

***

After giving Madame her breakfast, I crawl right back into bed with The Mood. How could he have been so cold? After all the things he told me before Christmas. How beautiful he thought I was, ever since that day he saw me sitting on the bench outside the Sorbonne. I realized at that moment, he said, you are stunning. Stunning. No one has ever used that word about me, but I could tell he meant it. I asked Then why didn't you *do* something about it sooner? He shrugged in that embarrassed way he has. I don't know. I haven't got much more experience than you. It wasn't Meredith, I asked. He laughed. Are you crazy? But she's so beautiful and sexy, I said. And you two were flirting all the time. That was just stupid stuff. She's not my type. Really. And he looked surprised, truly surprised, that I would have trouble believing him.

After all that, how could it now be let's-get-together, the thing you say when you want to put off getting together for as long as possible. I will never understand other human beings, I am thinking on my way to the boulangerie for a baguette, when who should pop out from behind a pillar but Thibaud.

"I'm sorry for yesterday," he says. "I hate surprises."

"How long have you been waiting here?"

"Not so long. I thought you might come out around lunch time. Anyway. I am sorry." He closes *Les Aventures de Huckleberry Finn*, stuffs it in his pocket. "Would you like to *'ang owt?*" He smiles at his imitation of Meredith.

I look at the ground. My wounds feel too fresh. He steps towards me, leans into me. The contact, even through two winter coats, feels too good. I let him lead me away.

***

From the long library table, I look at Thibaud through the thick glass of the language lab at the Beaubourg. Headphones on, head down over the text that accompanies the tapes. I have just finished Voltaire's *Candide*. We were assigned extracts while studying *Les Lumières*, the Enlightenment. When I found a copy on Jane's bookshelf, I started reading the whole thing. Candide is a young man, a naïve bastard who is forced out into the world where he discovers its horrors, while learning that he, or man in general, is capable of improving his own fate. He ends up going home and realizing that satisfaction is to be found in your own garden. *Il faut cultiver notre jardin*, he says. It's almost exactly the same story as Samuel Johnson's Rasselas that I read in school with Miss Bonner. Except that Rasselas was a prince who travels voluntarily rather than a bastard who's forced into exile, but both are looking for meaning and happiness in the larger world. Rasselas, a very melancholy guy, doesn't find it. Miss Bonner had us write an essay on the quote: "Human life everywhere is much to be endured and little to be enjoyed."

Like him and Candide, I have come to Paris in search of happiness, or something more than endurance anyway. Though things are off to a good start, I don't know if I'll find it. But I am certain about one thing: it's not to be found cultivating the garden my parents just handed over to the landscaping company.

After Thibaud sought me out, we went back to his room, straight to the mattress. It felt good to be touched all over, to take off my clothes and his and to have sex. It was like all my nerve ends, after being dulled by the Australian's tough turkey and stodgy Christmas pudding, came to life again.

Thibaud is removing the headphones, returning the cassettes. Satchel in hand, he walks towards me and smiles. We have spent a good part of the last few days in the warm spaces of the bright blue tubular Centre Pompidou. Yesterday he took me up the escalator, a clear cylinder that runs along the side of the building, to the top floor.

"This must be the best view of Paris," I said. "Just above roof level. The right height. The right distance. It's magic. Like those planes that fly in between mountains. Or maybe it's more like looking into a giant doll's house."

"I would rather look at your hands," he stroked mine on the railing. "Or your neck. Your long, lovely neck. I like it when you wear your hair up." I get a little thrill now, just remembering his touch.

"Enough English for one day?" I whisper.

"Come with me," he whispers back. He takes my hand, leads me into the stacks. It's still the Christmas holiday, and the place is practically empty. When we get to a corner, not a soul in sight, Thibaud lays down his coat on the floor. "What are you doing?" He points gallantly to the coat. "We can't do this."

He says nothing but pulls me down with him. His hand burrows like a mole under my shirt, making tracks to my breasts, and I put my hand up his shirt and caress his chest, run my hand over the hair. We unzip jeans, wriggle them down to our knees. The act is accomplished quickly, roughly. Within minutes, we are walking out of the library like any two students who have spent the afternoon with their heads buried in the books.

We hold hands through the icy air on the way back to the place des Vosges.

"Let's buy some Poulain chocolate powder and milk at the Félix Potin," Thibaud says. "That's what I used to have for breakfast."

"God, she stinks," I say as we leave the store. Thibaud gives me a quick look, then says: "Yeah."

He puts the key in the front door and shoves it open.

"Are you sure we shouldn't be more careful? More discreet?" I ask.

"No use looking guilty."

Upstairs he turns on the light bulb in the kitchen-bathroom. I put the bag down next to the sink, pull my arms to my chest. "It's freezing in here."

"Let's have a bath then."

"How?"

He points to the water heater, turns it on; I shake my head. "You're crazy."

"Come on. It'll feel good." He turns on the cooking ring. "After our hot chocolate."

We giggle like school children, while I scrub his dented aluminium saucepan and he opens the milk, breaks the seal on the Poulain. "I've only got one bowl, but we can share—and sit there." He points to the shuttered room across the corridor, the room I had designated for him.

We sit side by side on the parquet, against the wall. I blow on the milky mixture, take a sip, pass it to him.

"When I was really small my mother used to give me a bowl of hot chocolate on dark mornings before school," he said. "It was so quiet in the globe of light, the kitchen still edged with cold."

"She did? Where was that? I mean, where were you living then?"

He doesn't answer for so long I wonder if he's angry or even gone to sleep—his chin is resting on his chest.

"Well," he finally says so softly I can barely hear him. "I..." He shifts positions, pulls his knees up. "You know there, in the Félix Potin. I couldn't smell the lady."

"What do you mean?"

"I was drinking my hot chocolate at a kitchen table in the Auvergne where my parents make cheese."

"What?"

"My father is no diplomat. He's a peasant farmer. He has hands like pumice and manners to match. Same for my two brothers. Even my mother."

It's funny how shocking news strikes you. On one level it is like a physical blow. On another—when you've spent time with the person— it's not a surprise at all. There have been hints scattered along the way, incongruities that seem unimportant at the time, but it turns out they have been clues to the truth. There were so many things that didn't fit the only child, diplomatic story, from the rubbish in the Seine to the missing manners to his solitary existence.

"I'm really, really sorry. The words just came out of my mouth. Then I didn't know how to take them back."

"Is that what you tell all young Americans?"

"No. Not at all. Never before." He gives his shrug. "I thought you were pretty, and I wanted to impress you."

While I am trying to fight the temptation to give in to flattery, to adjust to this new picture and decide whether I should be furious or understanding, he looks at me, mouth pulled in, and says: "It's very hard in this city *not* being the son of a diplomat."

"But I don't care where you come from."

"I know. But I do. It's like walking around with a big wart on the end of my nose. The real Parisians know immediately where I come from and avoid me." He pauses. "It's not for nothing that I want to get out of here, go to the US." He wraps his arms around his knees. "But I am sorry. Really sorry."

"It's okay," I shrug.

"Thanks," he says, handing the bowl back to me. "I'm going to start the tub, go get my towel."

The hot chocolate has grown a cold skin on top. I say it's okay, but I do feel hurt, disappointed and betrayed by his confession. Not to mention stupid, embarrassed, really, for having believed the story in the first place. Then again, with his long, fine hands and delicate face, maybe it's not surprising I was thrown off track, that I didn't try harder to make sense of the way he acts and eats, the obsession with the US.

Back in the kitchen-bathroom, I put the bowl down next to the sink and lean against the window frame, peek around the blackout cloth Thibaud has hung here too. I can see my dark window, Madame's and Germaine's illuminated rooms. Thibaud is suddenly behind me, his head peering over mine.

"Things look different from this angle," I say, turning.

"Is that the old lady's room?"

"The higher light, yes. That's her sitting room. If you look one room to the right, that's her bedroom, and mine's above that."

"All that space and you're stacked right on top of her?"

"In case something happens."

"Hope not," he says, moving away from the window. "Thank you for not being angry."

"It's easy to want to be someone else."

"I guess. Let's get in the bath." And he begins to undress.

We have never undressed in the light, and I feel self-conscious, strip off as quickly as possible and climb into the water.

"It's hot," I say, sinking up to my neck, eying his long, slight body. No question he looks more like a diplomat's than a farmer's son.

Finding room for our four legs creates some confusion. "Not exactly the California cool I saw in a sixties film once," he says.

I laugh. "Not if I'm in the picture."

I close my eyes. "You are very beautiful." He leans over, kisses me. I keep my eyes closed. He begins slithering soap all over me underwater and I think: it couldn't get any more sensuous than this, even in California. I'm not quite sure how we manage it in the oval tub, but we have sex again.

By the time we are upstairs in Thibaud's bed, interlocked like two connected cogs of machinery, I'm not sure I've ever felt so close to anyone, even Jane.

He whispers over my shoulder: "*Ca va?*"

"It's nice to be back here."

"In this bed or in Paris?"

"Both."

"You didn't enjoy seeing your family?"

"Not especially."

"Were your sisters there?"

"Maude was. Jane stayed in New York."

"Lucky Jane," mumbles a sleepy Thibaud.

"Yes." After a minute I say: "I hate that place."

The sharp statement stirs Thibaud from half sleep. He raises his head. "What do you mean?"

"I mean my mother is crazy."

"All mothers are a little crazy."

"Not like mine." I pause. "Mine was in a Swiss hospital for five years."

"Before you were born?"

"No. After. They left us with the French woman."

"You mean your *gouvernante*?"

I nod. "It was only supposed to be for one year. But it stretched to five. Them in Switzerland, us in England."

"And what? You never saw them?"

"They visited sometimes. But it was worse, in a way, when they came and took us for a week. It felt unnatural."

"Were they allowed to leave you like that?"

"It was a nice house. We were sent to the French lycée. It looked very respectable. Other kids came and went—I can hardly remember a single one—they were all French, a lot of them children of diplomats, by the way. They went to the lycée too, but their parents picked them up again after weeks, months at most. Not five years."

Thibaud tightens his arms around me, kisses my ear.

"The place was gloomy. There were little trinkets everywhere that she was always telling us not to touch. It was like she'd put them there just to tempt us into breaking one so she could scold us. She made it clear that in taking care of us she was just doing a job she found rather unpleasant. We weren't allowed to speak English. So that we'd learn the language for Switzerland. Where in the end we never went."

"But why did they leave you behind?" Thibaud asks. "I don't get it."

For quite a while I don't say anything—this is too close to the bone of my shame. He readjusts his grip on me, snuggles closer. "She, my mother," I finally say, "tried to…you know…" He kisses my ear. After a pause that is so long Thibaud says: "And?"

"One night when I was seven and Jane was eight and Maude was ten, we were woken up in the night by the sound of a siren, red lights flashing on the wall. We ran downstairs and men were taking our mother out on a white stretcher. Our father's face was the same color. The lights in the kitchen looked bright and white too. When our mother didn't come back, our father said she was ill and that we would live with Madame Flaviche until she got better. The old witch really hated Maude and told her what had happened as a form of torture. Our mother had put a towel under the kitchen door and turned on the gas oven. Our father woke up and noticed her missing just in time."

For a moment Thibaud says nothing, appears frozen or asleep. "That's horrible," he whispers.

A tear drops from my eye onto his wrist under my head. "Yes. Yes, it was."

***

Friday, 7 January 1983

The results came in Tuesday, and I haven't had the heart or the stomach to write a word. Germaine, of course, soldiers on with her duties. She had one more cry, when she told me the news, but other than that she's stoic as steel. The operation is Wednesday week after next. This afternoon I spoke to the girl.

Though the words stuck in my throat, I told her I need more help. I told her Germaine is suffering as much as her daughter. Oh, she said, and it was funny, I could feel her empathy, her genuine compassion for poor Germaine. Up until now, I have felt her reserve, her shy compliance, mixed with mild dislike for me, but nothing else.

Anyway, the concrete outcome of our exchange was her agreement to work two to three more hours a day, doing the shopping and cooking the evening meal. Germaine did indeed seem relieved by the new arrangement, and I could hear her almost forgetting her own troubles as she instructed the girl on how to cut and cook leeks yesterday evening.

I think about the end. Soon. At least relatively soon. Science requires it.

***

"Your first lesson is that good produce is the key to good cooking," says Germaine, picking up an apple at a stall in Les Enfants Rouges market. "And this stall has the best fruit, though this time of the year there isn't much to choose from. *Un kilo*," she says to the merchant, a round man with dark hair and very red cheeks and neck. "Madame likes *compôte*. Do you know how to make that?"

I shake my head. I would sometimes help Mrs Hooper peel the potatoes, chop the carrots or slice the tomatoes. I was always happy helping out in the kitchen, but it was nothing like seeing the process through from start to finish as I did last night, when Germaine gave me my first lesson. How to cut and sauté leeks, quickly fry the veal and whip up a cream and mustard sauce. I didn't see the time go by.

After buying apples and what she calls *clémentines* and what I call tangerines, we stop at the butcher. He and Germaine exchange a few words about the winter weather. All the merchants know her. She says to me: "How about some lamb tonight and a chicken for tomorrow?"

"Sure." My eyes do not leave the butcher's stout hands as he takes a rack of lamb and hacks it into chops, then with a fine knife slices the fat from the arced, pencil-thin ribs. He moves nimbly, despite his sausage fingers. After he's wrapped them in paper, he holds up a chicken for Germaine's approval. He whacks off the head, folds the lolling neck into its body, chops off the claws, before tearing open the torso and ripping out the various organs, which he then returns to the chicken's now empty cavity. With a small gas torch, he singes the legs, and I can smell burning skin and feather stubs. Finally, the butcher makes the bird into a compact hump on the counter and reaches for a suspended ball of string. Tugging the end, he unravels a length and trusses up the chicken with the speed and deftness of a magician.

"I know you've got to get going," says Germaine. "But I wanted you to get a feel of the market."

"I'll help you back with the shopping. I have time."

Classes started again yesterday, but the thought of sitting in a stuffy lecture hall after this live show is not appealing. We walk back, single file on the narrow pavement, with Germaine limping in front and me pulling the caddy. I consider skipping the lecture on Chateaubriand's *Mémoires d'outre-tombe, Memories from Beyond the Grave*, and staying at the house to help Germaine—to cultivate my new garden, in a way— but as soon as the shopping is put away, Germaine rushes off to her daughter's. Radio music emanates from Madame's quarters and I leave too, slipping into a seat near the lecture hall door, just as the professor is opening his notes on the lectern. I wave at Meredith and Carol, higher up the sloping gallery.

Attendance is one thing, concentration another. I can't stop replaying last Thursday evening, starting at the Beaubourg, when Thibaud lay out his coat with mock chivalry on the floor of the library. It arouses me all over again, our groping and humping, and I shift in my lecture seat. It was too fast for me—Thibaud didn't seem to notice—but he made up for it in the bath, where I'd felt like a princess.

Though I now know Thibaud is no prince. He's not even an only child. I'm still not sure how angry to be, at him and at myself for missing the undiplomatic signs that were everywhere. He never opens the door for me—in fact he always barges in ahead. And if we shop for food, I inevitably end up carrying the bag. Even the way he eats. He chews loudly and with his mouth open, downs the food in no time flat, often using the knife as a fork and tosses his sandwich paper in the Seine. Our parents may have been negligent on many fronts, but they did teach us manners and civility. Our father may not make great shows of affection, but he is very courteous. We were instructed not to litter.

But then Thibaud had shown such care and gentleness in the bathtub, prompting my own confession. Here come the tears again, right here in the lecture hall—I fight them down, hide my face with my hand. It takes nothing to trigger the flow when visions of childhood dance through my head. When I am transported back in time, to the terror and emptiness at having our mother gone, of Madame Flaviche's heartless execution of duty towards the children in her care.

That flashing red ambulance light is my first memory. Nothing precedes it, or maybe I should say whatever preceded it was wiped clean by the trauma of our mother's disappearance. Jane's theory, proven, she said, by the white stretcher, was that our mother had been temporarily transformed into an angel and we just had to wait for her to return to earth. Maude would say that's stupid. She's ill. Then why can't we visit her, Jane would say, like we did when you had your appendix out?

Maude would huff away, since she had no answer to that question. Is she dead? I'd ask, voice trembling. No, Jane would say firmly, no, she's not. I'm quite sure of that. But that's the way it felt, like our mother was dead and buried.

In some ways, she was. Jane always thought, and I have to agree, that our mother was given a lobotomy in Switzerland. It was the nineteen-sixties, after all, and she can still go completely blank. Though it's never been said, I've always thought Mrs Hooper was hired to ensure that our mother never set foot near the oven again.

Once we learned our mother was not dead, just "getting better" in Switzerland—and before Madame Flaviche told Maude the full, true story—I would long for our parents to come and sweep us away, but when they did finally appear for one of our hotel holidays, I'd be ready for it to be over within thirty-six hours, to watch our parents from the window as they left, our father opening the door of the taxi for our mother, then walking around and slipping in himself. In later years I would run upstairs the second they left, get as far away from the clunk of the taxi doors as I could.

When I think "family holiday" it's always the trip to Brighton that comes to mind. It rained. The wind blew. The hotel where we were staying was modern and soulless. The arcade, bombarding us with fun, felt sinister. I watched Jane try to ignore Maude, the way she did at Madame Flaviche's, where it was easier to pretend we weren't sisters. I was still a child, but I remember feeling my heart might break, the whole scene was so sad, the situation so irredeemable.

People are slapping notebooks shut and standing up. The open page of mine is blank.

"Hey." Meredith grins at me, puts a hand on my shoulder.

"Hey," I echo, my mind still in the rain at Brighton Pier.

"Do you want to grab a coffee or something at les Gaulois?" asked Carol.

"I have to get back."

"Ah—too bad. But you're coming to our New Year's party this Friday night, right?"

"Sure, yes."

"Great," says Carol. "Oh, and if you see Thibaud invite him too."

If I see Thibaud. Here is my chance to say: Actually, I see Thibaud every night, in his bed. But I do not seize the moment. Why? Partly because his bed lies in illegally occupied territory, and I am not about to tell anyone other than my sister Maude about that. But partly too because of my compartmentalized existence.

"Will do," I say.

This fudge makes me wonder again on the way to the métro what moved me to tell Thibaud my family history. His confession wasn't a quid pro quo. Perhaps the opening of my body has loosened my tongue. Is that good, bad or neutral? Afterwards he fell asleep. I, on the other hand, felt so agitated that I'd got up and gone back to my room. Even my safe haven couldn't calm me. I cried and cried.

In the métro, the turnstile spits back my *carte orange* ticket. It probably wasn't wise, my confession. Sad stories carry the whiff of illness. They can make people bolt. *The less said the better*, like our mother says. She may be crazy, but she's not dumb.

***

Monday, 10 January 1983

Twenty years ago today. Witnesses said that he stepped off the sidewalk just as the delivery truck trundled by. The driver said: He walked right in front of me. It looked as if he were stepping off a precipice, into the void.

Surely that constitutes a voluntary action, though as others pointed out, it was not in the driver's interest to interpret the incident otherwise. Afterwards I would look at him and wonder. Look at him slumped in the wheelchair, arms limply draped over the armrests, hands—once so strong—lifeless on his lap. Look at the drooping head and those dark brown eyes, all the fire and spark extinguished. His breathing was difficult. One lung had collapsed from the accident, the other had already been weakened from exposure to gas during the First World War. Even knowing it was a futile exercise, I couldn't stop myself from hoping he would tell me. Sometimes I even pleaded out loud: Tell me, tell me why you did it.

Why I was so desperate for a response, I'm not sure. Hoping to assuage my guilt, I guess. Because if it wasn't an accident, wasn't I partly responsible? I let him down during the War. Or we let each other down and couldn't bring ourselves back up afterward. Besides a glint of hope when we started doing up this place, we stayed stuck in our ruts, that wall between us. When I think—no, I don't want to think or write about that.

I'm ready to go the way of François. Trucks are no longer an option for me, but yesterday I did come up with a plan, a New Year's resolution. French doctors provide palliatives for everything, so I'll tell Dr Lévy about my sleeping troubles, ask him to prescribe something quite strong. I will then stockpile the pills and when I have enough, that will be that. If it worked for Adrienne Monnier, why not for me.

Octave and the Horse came for tea again yesterday, but no point wasting ink on that visit: it was exactly the same as the last, right up to the girls' homework as the excuse for its brevity.

***

"I would like to see the doctor." She is sitting straight as a metal pole with a look of haughty defiance. "I'm not sleeping at all well."

"I'll tell Germaine."

"No, no," she says quickly. "Germaine has more than enough to worry about. I'd like you to call the doctor. The number's in here," and she slides a worn red leather book towards me. "His name is Dr Lévy. He's known me for years. He'll make a house call. See if he can come this afternoon. Any time."

I wonder, eating my own breakfast, what this is all about. Her manner was very defensive, as if she'd been accused of something, and all she's asking is to see the doctor because she can't sleep. I hope she's not sick. I don't want to sound callous, but that could ruin everything, which at the moment and for the first time in my life, is going very well. I'd even say close to perfect. My days are spent with people I like and who seem to like me. We sing and dance at parties, like last Saturday at Meredith and Carol's. Thibaud and I arrived and left together, but strangely no one seemed to suspect we were a couple.

Even the course work can absorb me. Not long after the close-call visit to the place des Vosges with my friends, we studied King Henri IV, who switched from Catholic to Protestant and back again so many times I lost track. He generally seemed a conscientious, tolerant king. When he wasn't fighting wars and insurrectionists, he promoted the arts and sent people to America. Then we studied his son Louis XIII, learned that he was known as the first absolute monarch, which makes the place des Vosges statue of the smiling guy on the horse who's not even holding on to the reins an even greater enigma. Right before Christmas, we moved on to the long and lavish rule of Louis XIV. Given his spending habits, continued by his descendants Louis XV and Louis XVI, I can't say the Revolution that we've just covered should have come as a surprise to anyone. Poor old Marie-Antoinette got a rough ride from both the professor and Jean-Paul. Remembering Gary's story about the tower and the bonneted head and the executioner's foot, where she seemed so pathetic, I felt a bit sorry for her.

We've also been reading Chateaubriand. I regret having been pre-occupied during the lecture, because I'm enjoying it, have even kept reading after the assigned passages. Like Rasselas, he clearly knows a thing or two about The Mood, had his own problems in childhood. The self-examination, the melancholy voice and the vivid descriptions sound practically modern.

Nights, except when I need a good sleep, start off with Thibaud. Yesterday I went over earlier than usual and helped him with his Ful-bright application. His essay was most instructive. "I decided to be hon-est," he said. "To play the humble origins card. In this kind of situation, it can be beneficial because the French are very proud of what they be-lieve to be an exemplary meritocratic education system. They're wrong of course—really you have to get lucky—but if you do, then the story of your struggle can appeal to their sense of *liberté, égalité, fraternité*, if not to their heart. Should they have one."

In his essay he described life on his parents' cheese farm in the Auvergne. His two older brothers who had become farmers like their father, the generally low level of education and expectations. No one in his family, he said, had even got as far as the Baccalaureate, much less university. If it hadn't been for his mother who understood that books were all he was good at and a teacher at his boarding school, where he was sent during the week for *collège-lycée* because there was no lo-cal alternative, he might be pulling milk from cows' teats himself right now, instead of writing this application. It was Monsieur Morin who introduced him to American literature, nourished a genuine intellectual curiosity and used his knowledge of the system to get Thibaud straight to Paris for university, instead of passing by Clermont-Ferrand.

"It reads like a novel," I said.

"Exactly. A nineteenth century French novel. And you know what happens to all the protagonists who end up in Paris?"

I shake my head.

"They're ruined."

"So that's why you want to go to the US? To escape ruin?"

"I want to be judged for who I am, not where I come from, who my parents and grandparents and great-grand-parents are," he said, looking down at his clean, rounded fingernails. "It's funny, though, how being here makes me think more about our farmhouse. The two buildings were probably built about the same time, and I slept under the eaves there too, except then I had to share with Philippe and Jean-Marie. Until I was twelve there was no WC, just a smelly latrine in the garden. We bathed in the kitchen there too but standing up in a small tub of water that my mother also used for washing clothes. My brothers and father thought I was useless, unable to execute my chores properly. My mother at least," and he looks at me with very serious eyes, "always believed in me, knew my calling was elsewhere."

I felt a pinch of jealousy at his mother's love, but otherwise his childhood sounds unhappy and ill-fitting, several sizes too small.

Now that he's not dodging my questions about his family life, the story burbles out like a mountain spring. "In some ways it was television that saved me. We got one the year after the bathroom, improvements all due to the European subsidies my father had figured out how to obtain. Suddenly, after all those meals where we sat around the table and chewed in silence, just like the cows outside, there was the chatter of the TV in the background. It was a lifeline to something beyond the farm and even the boarding school." His mind seemed to wander. He smiled. "I was so excited when Monsieur Morin helped me get into the Panthéon law faculty on a full scholarship. Riding up on the train," he says, "with a ham and cheese sandwich, our cheese and our ham, and my cardboard suitcase that looked straight out of a Jean Gabin war film." He turned his head to me. "I hid it from you, in the shadows, when Monsieur Yassine dropped me off that night—it was a dead giveaway about who I really am. Stupid. Anyway, on the train I looked out the window and as the rocky terrain smoothed out to the flatter fields of the *Centre*, I felt like all the wrinkles were being ironed out of my soul. I really thought: this is it. I'm launched."

"Until I got here. You cannot imagine," he said, "what a shock it was. Being from a poor family in the Auvergne may have got me a scholarship, but it didn't win me social acceptance. The first thing I learned was not *le droit civique*, but that Parisians want nothing to do with people who were born beyond the *Périphérique*," he said. "And I was very obviously a *péquenaud, un plouc,* a hopelessly uncultivated, unsophisticated barely human creature to be scrupulously ignored. Even once I'd discovered deodorant, I seemed to emanate something that transmitted my origins." He was quiet for a moment, as if his mind were running through every humiliation he'd ever suffered. His eyes got very eager, almost crazed. "I want to get out of this country of backward peasants and incurable snobs so badly. Life has got to be better on the other side of the Atlantic."

"If you want it that badly, you'll get there," I said.

What a different picture I now have. It makes him less daunting in a way. But also more foreign. I grew up in a nice house—no, two nice houses—Madame Flaviche's, even with her trinkety junk all over the place, was physically very presentable—and it is hard for me to imagine standing in a tub in the kitchen to bathe until I was twelve, when my parents finally had enough money to turn a potato shed into a bathroom.

I pop the last bite of baguette into my mouth—always with regret—I could eat all day—and wipe my hands on some kitchen towel, carefully open the address book. The paper is thick and of good quality but yellowed with age. Madame's writing is slanted, as lean and angular as she is. Many of the pencilled entries have faded or smudged almost to the point of illegibility. Dead people, I imagine, with a slight shudder as I sip my coffee. Under the letter T there are several names and US addresses with abbreviations CO and WY near the end. Not the NY that I expected. It makes me wonder again about Madame's family, about the boy in the photo in the spare room. It just can't be Octave. Even if I'm wrong about the date and the fairer hair, neither Madame nor Germaine seems to like him, so why put up his photo to remember his childhood?

We never knew our US family. Our father's parents died before we were born. Cousins were sprinkled around the Midwest. Some still sent Christmas cards. Our mother was an only child and had no interest in her second cousins or first ones once removed. Her parents never visited. A few times a year there would be a phone call. Jane and I could feel our mother's nerves getting fluttery beforehand, which led us to eavesdrop on the actual conversation. She would whine like a child, "But Mummy, I'm doing the best I can. Yes. Yes. We have help." Jane and I would skulk away, mortified by our mother in this pathetic state. After the calls, our parents would hole themselves up in the bedroom. We could hear her crying. Jane's face would squeeze up, as if she were trying to work out an intractable geometry problem. Finally she would say, Come on, let's go, and we'd head out of the house to the cemetery, but neither of us could clear our minds of our mother's tears. We were relieved when our grandparents died within months of one another. Those phone calls were finally over.

At the K-L page, there is Dr Patrick Lévy. The wall clock says it's just past nine and time to call.

***

Thursday, 13 January 1983

It snowed yesterday, leaving the square in cottony silence. The white-
ness filled the edges of my eyes, a light aureole around a murky hole.
On the ranch it would snow and snow until we were confined to the
house and the track we kept shovelled so we could feed the horses in
the barn and bring hay to the cattle in the paddock. In the house, there
was a big wood stove and a fireplace to keep us warm, but after a couple
of snug days, cabin fever set in. I remember thinking I would lose my
mind. Just to get out of the house, I'd huddle in the barn with the horses
and their steamy breath for as long as I could stand it.

Technically it was not as cold in Paris during the War. But it felt
colder because it was impossible to get warm, even hunched in front of a
coal heater, wrapped in shawls, telling myself how lucky we were to have
coal at all. As long as I stayed put right there, my hands and feet did not
go numb, but I was never really warm; I still got chilblains, like everyone
else. It almost seems that I spent the entire war just like that, frozen with
a rounded back in front of a weak heater, while François ran hither and
thither protecting people and becoming a hero.

Dr Lévy came by in the afternoon while, as I'd planned, Germaine
was with her grandchildren. After he listened to my heart (pumping
like a sixty-year old's) and took my blood pressure (steady as a river). Is
there a problem, he asked.

Insomnia, I said.

Hmm, he said.

If you could give me something.

He was silent for a moment, and I worried he might be suspicious.
No amount of straining could give me a good read of his face, so I tried
diversion tactics. Have you uncovered any good books recently? He is
an avid reader, and we always discussed literature.

Ten minutes later I had a prescription. Seresta, the ticket to my
desired destination.

***

On my way to the pharmacy, walking like a stork to spare my shoes in the slushy snow, I wonder why Madame is being nice. Well, maybe nice is too strong a word. Not hostile. When she handed me the prescription, she repeated that it was better not to tell Germaine. "She can be a little funny," she said in a confidential tone. It felt both flattering and uncomfortable, being let in on this quirk in Germaine's personality.

Madame at that moment reminded me of my mother, when she would choose one of us—even Maude—to envelop in warmth and attention. She would make us feel special and loved. "Come and look at this," she patted the sofa one afternoon, wrapped an arm around me, pulled me in close while she turned the pages of a book of John Singer Sargent's watercolors. Sargent had been the subject of the Fulbright project that brought her to Britain. "Look at that luminosity," she half whispered to me, caressing the page. I felt then too as if I were being let in on a great secret. "Let's get a cup of tea." My mother popped up, grabbed me by the hand. At the kitchen table, we sipped sweet milky tea together, shared a piece of Mrs Hooper's plum cake, our two forks pulling off bites. I would hope so hard that it would last, that this intimate encounter meant something. But as always, she withdrew, became as distant as the moon again. The pain her retreat caused never lessened or dulled.

"Is Madame Quinon having trouble sleeping?" asks the pharmacist as she pulls out long drawers.

"A bit."

"She should be careful with Seresta. It's a strong medication."

"I'll tell her."

Everyone in the *quartier* knows Madame, from the Dodés at the Félix Potin to the hardware man to the newspaper seller. That flash of civility with me made it obvious why they all like her. When she turns on even a trickle of charm, one wants to be within her sphere, wants to please and be helpful. Just like my mother, who, by the way, is also very popular with the local merchants.

If Madame were nicer on a regular basis, I think again while dodging slushy puddles on the way back, life really would be perfect because there's also now this cooking thing. I have learned to chop onions finely, to make a béchamel sauce and fruit compotes. I have learned shortcuts and pointers, such as don't make your own single-layer *pâte brisée* quiche pastry when you can order the more delicate *pâte feuilletée* from Germaine's friend *la boulangère*. When I'm in the kitchen with her, the rest of the world falls away. I don't see the time pass. The lessons seem to help Germaine too. The heavy curtain of worry lifts from her face a bit, for a while.

These days I often end up eating with Madame and Germaine so that I can taste the results of our work. In this way I've learned the details of Flora's breast cancer, about the operation next Wednesday and the ensuing radiation and chemotherapy. Because Flora will be feeling weak and sick, Germaine will stay and prepare supper for her family. At this point I will be expected to shop and cook for Madame Quinon on my own. There will be a little purse from which I will pay for supplies, and at the end of every week I'll hand over the receipts. At the end of each month, I will receive the heady sum of one thousand five hundred francs, enough to improve my living standard considerably.

Madame is sitting at her writing table, a shawl over her bony shoulders. A notebook, the same one I saw on the floor that night I came downstairs after the thud, is in front of her, closed. The fountain pen, mottled blue and black, sits next to it.

"Here are your pills."

"Thank you." She pulls the bag towards her, takes out the renewable prescription and slips it into the desk drawer.

"The pharmacist said to warn you that they are strong, and you should be careful."

"Oh, I will be. Would you mind adding a log to the fire? It must be time."

I put on a log, poke the dying embers.

"It's still very cold out," says Madame.

"Yes." I put on a second log, blast the fire with the bellows until it is crackling and soothingly warm on my face. Last week when I came back from class the *portail* was wide open and Germaine was directing a man in a large van full of firewood into the courtyard. He unloaded it into a storage room. It made this place feel both more lost in time—who gets firewood delivered in the middle of a city—and more part of the living, real world where delivery men come and go. "The fire should be fine for a while now. Can I get you anything else?"

"No," she answers softly. "I've got everything I need now. Thank you."

On my way down the dark corridor, I feel almost spooked by her gentle tone. In a way I prefer her being crotchety. It makes me feel less guilty about Thibaud living next door.

***

Tuesday, 18 January 1983

Flora's operation is tomorrow. Germaine can barely contain her anguish and I wish beyond hope that I could do something to soothe her. If there's one thing this long life has taught me, it is how little control we have over anything.

Last week the girl delivered the first Seresta for my stockpile. I felt like a teenager, concealing a cigarette from my mother, except in this case the authority is hardly more than an adolescent herself, warning me to be careful. Oh, I will be.

***

It snowed again today, after last week's had melted. It's beautiful but has again turned the city into a chaotic mess. The kitchen, when I arrive to make dinner, feels warm and snug. I have come to love this room, the space locked in by counters and cupboards, the table in the middle, the old clock on the wall, the window over the sink. Which is strange, given that in the first years at The Vicarage it was a room that terrified me. Especially if my mother got anywhere near it. I was sure she'd return to the scene of the crime, so to speak, to succeed where she had previously failed. Eventually, as Mrs Hooper's domain, it took on similar welcoming associations to here, but that took quite a while.

Tonight we are having roast beef, Brussels sprouts and mashed potatoes. An English meal that Germaine and I will raise to another level. I take the sprouts from the fridge and a small knife from the drawer, a sieve and a board. Following Germaine's instructions, I slice off the bottoms, pluck off the outer leaves, then cut a cross to ensure even cooking. By the time I finish, Madame has been in for her Noilly Prat-cassis aperitif, but Germaine is still not back. So I start peeling the potatoes. It's not until they are boiled—with a clove of garlic thrown in to see if it doesn't enhance their taste—and drained that Germaine finally rushes into the kitchen. Flora's operation is tomorrow, and she looks so distressed that I say:

"I can probably manage. If you'd rather…"

"No. I'm sorry I'm late." She scans the kitchen, looks up at the kitchen clock. "The snow held me up."

"I'll put the water on for the vegetables."

"I'll mash the potatoes."

We are a team, a good team, I am thinking when I tip the sprouts into the boiling water and I see it. I gasp, I can't help it. Germaine, in her anguish over Flora has rolled up her sleeve so it will not interfere with her mashing, and there it is, a number tattooed on her forearm.

"What's wrong?" asks Germaine.

"Nothing. Some of the boiling water spattered. I'm fine."

Germaine returns to mashing the potatoes; her sleeve slips back down her arm. I did not know Germaine was Jewish, much less have I wondered how she got through the War. Does she hide it on purpose or has the occasion for a rolled-up sleeve simply not arisen until now? I think of what Gary told us about the Marais and many people going to concentration camps. I think about my eerie Marais walk via the rue des Rosiers, on my way to the Louvre. But Germaine was never part of the picture. Now she's front and center.

"Don't leave the Brussels sprouts on too long," says Germaine. "There's nothing worse than overcooked sprouts."

I dutifully drain the sprouts and wonder how Germaine, with that blue number on her arm, can say *nothing worse* in regard to an over-cooked sprout.

"How's Flora?" Madame asks as she enters with her empty glass. She is always gentle with Germaine, and I now see that benevolence in a different light.

Germaine sighs, her breath catching as if it were passing over gravel. "Roger took her to the hospital late afternoon. I made the children supper. The doctors say it'll be nothing." Panicked suspicion grips her face.

"And we should believe them. We should have faith in modern medicine." So Madame says, but the wrinkles around her mouth are drawn tight as a balloon knot.

"The food is getting cold," says Germaine, turning to the cooker.

"How is it, out there in the second snow of the winter?" asks Madame once we're seated and served.

"The city is paralysed," says Germaine, her eyes fixed and unblinking. "It took Roger forever to get home from the hospital and for me to get back here."

"Paris can handle many shocks," says Madame. "But a few centimeters of snow is not one of them."

While they discuss how long the snow will last this time and Madame re-assures Germaine that it will not interfere with the operation tomorrow, my imagination does its thing. It only needs a nudge to spin out of control and there I am, thinking how it must have been. Maybe she was running down the streets I walked. Or sitting at home, listening to the soldiers' boots, before the rap-rap-rapping at the door. The family cowered, then snatched a few belongings before being led out the door, most of them never to return. That book, that *Sophie's Choice*, where the mother had to choose which of her two children would go to the gas chambers when the Nazis had arrested her, makes Germaine's story all too plausible, the fear and desperation all too palpable.

"Lily?" Germaine is looking at me with surprise and I can feel my cheeks go pink. "Aren't you hungry? You haven't finished your food."

"Are you ill?" asks Madame.

"I'm fine." And I quickly scrape food onto my fork, into my mouth. "Let me wash up. You've had a long day, Germaine."

"It's so much faster *à deux*," she says, pushing her chair back and tossing her napkin on the table.

While we are collecting plates and piling them in the sink, I eye Germaine. With her head of greying hair pulled back in a bun and her serious, regular face, she is a handsome woman. She is a kind woman, too, though she does not express much emotion, either on her face—except when she smiles—or in her speech. She is an intensely private person, does not like to linger out loud on distressing subjects like her daughter's health, and perhaps that is how she masks the suffering I had not previously detected. Now I would like to ask her but know it's impossible. Being quite familiar with silence, I can sense Germaine never talks about this nightmare to anyone, and certainly not to a stranger like me, one who is practically still a child.

At school we were shown film clips that terrified me, gave me nightmares. All kinds of images run through my mind as I scrape what's left of the Brussels sprouts and the mashed potatoes into bowls for the fridge, as I dry plates and wine glasses and return them to the cupboard. I see the girl Germaine, her eyes grey holes in a shaved skull, arms and legs like kindling, sharing a wooden bunk bed with five others. Ooh—

"Well," says Germaine, giving me a sad little smile. "That's done."

***

Thursday, 20 January 1983

Though I'd been waiting for the knock, it was so faint when it came, I hardly heard it. Germaine entered my sitting room as quietly as a ghost.

Germaine, I said. Is that you?

Yes.

How did it go?

They say they hope they got most of it. It was small.

Well then, we must believe them.

They say they hope, she repeats. Every conversation we have about Flora and the medical establishment is the same. I preach the merits of science and Germaine cannot summon faith. Which is understandable. Who could believe in anything when you've lived through what she has?

She should be home tomorrow.

There you go, that's a good sign. That they're not keeping her longer.

The treatment starts in February.

***

Flora's operation was today and dinner with Madame this evening was a somber affair. The second hand on the clock juddered away while we ate half-heartedly in silence. At the end Madame even apologized, said how worried she was not just about Flora, who is like a daughter to her, but also about Germaine. After seeing that number yesterday, I can see why.

I told Thibaud that I wouldn't come tonight, but once I'm in bed, I don't want to be alone. I take my key, go down the stairs and unlock the door to the wing. Tonight I wish I had worn a coat or at least clothes—it's freezing in the white nightdress I bought the other day at a second-hand shop—but I don't want to go back so move briskly through the dusty, abandoned rooms to the staircase.

Foot on the first step leading to the attic, hand on the banister, I hear voices. Thibaud often listens to the radio. But more softly than this. And these do not sound like radio talk show hosts. I sniff. It smells of tobacco and cannabis. Since when does Thibaud smoke—

By the time these thoughts have worked their way through my head, I have emerged at the top of the stairs and there he is, with two others. The woman has long, straight brown hair and a round, flat face, an imperturbable smile. The man's got that hair, those dreadlocks I associate with black Jamaican musicians, not white French boys. I do not like his smile; it makes me want to hide my head, especially when out of those broad, red lips I hear:

"Angel or ghost?" sparking an explosion of laughter by the other two. Thibaud's face is crinkled-up like I'm the funniest thing he's ever seen. Without another word, I run down the stairs, fly through the enfilade of rooms, back upstairs and into bed. I have never felt so mortified.

I bring my knees up to my chest, pull the duvet around my neck. A nightshirt! I was standing in front of those hippie people in bed-clothes. I might as well have been stark naked. And Thibaud. I do not consider his altered state an excuse for mirth at my expense. It was cruel, cruel, cruel.

In my shock and shame, it takes me a few minutes to grasp the worst implications of the encounter. What were those people doing there? No one is supposed to know about our arrangement, much less be welcomed in to experience it. What are the circumstances and conditions of Thibaud's invitation? Have these friends just stopped by for the evening or are they spending the night? How could Thibaud have let others into our secret? I shift in the bed, look towards the window. What kind of person is he, really? Tonight, he seemed a complete stranger.

***

Friday, 28 January 1983

When we first came to this house the voluminous space, the grand fireplaces, still breathed the aristocratic grandeur of its origins, but everything else had been buried in dirt, dust, cobwebs and the detritus of the less fortunate, more recent occupants. Reminders were everywhere: a bit of torn wallpaper here, an old coat hook there. In the kitchen, there were still pieces of coal in a scuttle, streaks of grease on the wall. These middens spooked rather than reassured me, as did the tattered families still living in the two wings. The whole *quartier* was so poor and neglected. And on top of the grime and dereliction was a film of guilt for what had happened in this neighborhood not twenty years earlier. I wanted to run away.

Cleaning the façade and renovating the apartments where we were to reside pumped new life into the place. Renewal chased away most of the ghosts and restored some of the original glory. François was excited, working hard and using his many contacts to ensure that the Loi

Malraux, protecting historical places like the Marais from the Modernist wrecking ball, would be passed by the National Assembly. With the help of Robert and Louise, we began buying art to cover the walls of the staircase. We had fun for the first time in years, juxtaposing his contemporary tastes next to my more conventional ones. It seemed a sign that our complicity was returning, that there was hope for our future, like there was for the Marais.

But once the law passed and the novelty subsided, François and I sunk back into co-existence. He no longer had a cause to fight for; our differing tastes in art seemed not complementary but symptomatic of an unbridgeable gap. The two floors proved convenient; he often slept upstairs in the antechamber to his office. Between the lingering bad taste of our different wars and the gaping hole left by *him* we just couldn't sustain enthusiasm or joy. Though we carried on as before—went to concerts, the opera, the theater, had dinner parties in the grand *salon-salle à manger*, smiled at our friends who said how brave, how original we were moving here—underneath there seemed to be nothing left. That life only lasted a couple of years. Then the accident. Then another few years, and he was dead. Then Octave for a couple of years. Flora moved out. Shortly after that Michel had his heart attack and died. Then just Germaine and me.

That's it in a nutshell, my life, the life of this building, for the last thirty years.

But each configuration of tenants gives the house a slightly different feeling. Now the presence of the girl has altered the *ambiance* once again. Despite her almost phobic discretion she has generally perked things up. I say generally because there are days when she seems mopey, moody, but most others, I sense that *la civilisation française* is being good to her. Her quick step down the hall, the happy hurry when she takes away my breakfast tray. And lately it's the cooking. When she and Germaine are preparing a meal, their enjoyment radiates from the kitchen.

It cheers me up but only a little. A voice in the background is screaming: Too late for you, Amenia Tucker Quinon.

***

When I knock on Germaine's door, Flora answers.

"I'm sorry," I say, trying to hide my shock. The operation was only a couple of weeks ago, and I'd imagined her still too weak to leave the house. "Your mother asked me to buy her some apples. I just wanted to drop them off."

"You're not intruding. Maman and I have switched places for the morning. Come in."

It's the first time I've stepped over the threshold of Germaine's quarters. As if she protects her rooms as closely as she does that number on her arm. I rummage for the fruit. I don't know what to say to someone who has cancer. It seems those apples will never be found. "They must be in here somewhere," I mumble.

"I came over here this morning because when Maman and I are in the flat together we're falling all over each other," Flora says.

Finally, the bag emerges from the shopping caddy. I put it on the table, look at Flora. She is very short and fine. Even now, with this illness, she beams an energy that fills the space around her. It's hard to imagine there's any room in her for a malignant growth. "I'm sorry about your illness. Your mother told me."

"The operation wasn't too bad. The tumor was quite small. But I start the chemo and radiation soon. I'm really dreading that." She pulls her shoulders up and in. "Would you like a cup of coffee? I was just about to make myself one."

I'd like to flee but say: "Sure."

"Please," Flora says, pointing to the round table, then pouring boiling water over a filter, into a coffeepot. From my seat, I see that beyond the kitchen and dining area, there is a living area with two old-fashioned armchairs and a television, a heavy cupboard.

"You grew up here, right?" I ask.

"Yes." She hands me a cup of coffee, some milk and a sugar bowl. "For almost as long as I can remember anyway. My parents moved when I was seven." The same age I was when our mother disappeared and we were left with Madame Flaviche. "But tell me a bit about you, Lily. Distract me from myself, please." She crosses skinny arms across a flat chest that protrudes like a bird's.

This is usually the question that makes me squirm, provokes a strong urge to crawl out of my skin and leave it in a crumpled heap on the floor while my spirit makes a getaway. But Flora needs help. She is ill and about to undergo a very unpleasant treatment. I must view my response as a rescue operation rather than an escape act.

"I'm doing the course in *civilisation française* at the Sorbonne and trying to sort myself. Figure out what I should be doing with my life."

"And? Is it helping?" she smiles. The kind eyes come from Germaine, but the rest must be her father. The smaller nose and the finer jaw. The curly hair she keeps under wraps by pulling back.

I shrug. "Yes and no. It's hard to say. I still don't really have any career ideas."

"What did you study?"

"Law." Even the word sounds hollow in my mouth. "But that's not an option. For my future."

"Roger was telling me that the Anglo-Saxon system is like that. You can study one subject and do something completely different with the rest of your life." One thin arm flies upward. "Here it's all so rigid. Even if you are a good student in high school and want to be, say, a literary editor, you still need the Bac S, the maths and science degree, or you're judged to be of inferior intelligence. What direction you take at eighteen can decide the rest of your life. Unless the system has already pegged you for a loser." She shakes her head. "So…" she looks for the word…"French."

"What did you study?"

"Economics and psychology. I worked in human resources until Michel was born. Before this," she points to her chest, "I was planning to go back to work."

I nod, hope my smile is sympathetic, not inane.

"But with luck I'll be back on the job market next school year." She drains her coffee cup. "You could do something with your French. It's so good, you could be a translator, like Tanta."

"She was a translator?"

"Yes. For years."

"She doesn't talk much about herself." To say the least.

"Maman told me. You shouldn't take it personally. It's the situation she doesn't like."

"I try to stay out of the way."

"She's angry that Octave imposed help on her. Hard as it may be to imagine now, Tanta used to be fond of him. And he was different, when he lived here as a student. I had quite a crush on him. Also hard to imagine now," her eyes go up to the ceiling. "Sometimes I try to defend him, but he really did turn into a boorish *bourgeois* after he met Marie-France."

"I met her once. When I babysat for the girls."

"Maman says the children are okay though it's hard to imagine how. Anyway, give Tanta a chance." Flora's face goes all soft and lovey. "You know I think the real reason I came over here today is because I feel safe in these rooms, in this house. Like I'm a little girl again, protected by grown-ups, four of them."

I try to picture myself an only child with my parents, times two. A chilly shudder runs through my core. Having sisters saved me, being three against two. Then again, in the company of different adults, the configuration could, I suppose, be enviable, though I'm not sure about getting misty over Madame.

"You grew up in England, right? But you're American."

"Yes, but that's made me feel nothing." This sounded okay when I said it to Thibaud on the banks of the Seine, but right now it resonates as too existentially desperate. "Or let's say I don't really feel either."

"And the French? How does that fit into the picture?"

"A French lady took care of me and my sisters for a while. We went to the lycée in London."

Flora eyes me. "What do you mean, took care of you?"

My face is pulsing with embarrassment. "Our mother wasn't well. This *gouvernante* was put in charge of us." In an attempt to nudge the conversation in a different direction: "I guess learning a language at a young age is like riding a bicycle. It never leaves you."

"I wouldn't know. The French education system is as hopeless with foreign language teaching as it is inflexible. Because what other tongue matters?" She shakes her head, pushes a curl back in place. "Since the *soi-disant* egalitarian system doesn't allow streaming, they put the better students into German classes. Under the theory that it's a difficult language and therefore beyond the grasp of the less mentally gifted. They tried to push me into it, but there was no way I was going to learn German." Her voice lowers, her features narrow.

"The US is bad with language teaching too. Some of the Americans on my course are having a tough time."

"It must be easy for you," she says. "But I hope this year helps you figure things out. I think it's quite brave of you to come over here all alone."

"I didn't know what else to do," I shrug. "It was my sister's idea."

"How many sisters do you have?"

"Two. One in England, one in New York."

"And where do you fit in?"

"Youngest."

"What do they do? Sorry for the interrogation. I'm always overly interested in family configurations. Either the psychology studies or the fact I'm an only child."

"That's okay." I actually don't mind Flora asking. "Maude's an artist. She's living with my parents. For the moment. And Jane is in New York, working for a bank."

"Are you close, the three of you?"

"Jane and I were very close, growing up. Maude was on the outside, but since last summer I've got to know her better."

"And what about Jane?" she asks when I don't continue.

"We've grown apart," I practically whisper. "Since she left for university in the US."

"I can imagine that would be hard," she says. "But life is long. Relationships change." Her voice has quickened, risen—I'm afraid it shows that I'm about to cry. "I had this friend when I was in primary school. Denise. We were inseparable. Then her family moved to the 5th arrondissement, and she changed schools. We tried to keep up—saw each other sometimes on Saturday afternoons. But it fizzled. Then my second year at the Sorbonne, I ran into her. She was studying literature. We became—still are—great friends again. That past counted for a lot. So wait and see. You and your sister Jane might be closer than ever in five years." She looks at her watch, pops up. "Oh, past time for me to head back and relieve Maman."

"I hope the treatment isn't too hard," I say on the way out the door. "Let me know if I can help in any way."

"You're already helping a lot. From what I hear, you've got a knack in the kitchen." She lifts up on her toes and kisses each of my cheeks. "Thanks for the chat. Once this treatment is over and normal life resumes, I hope you'll babysit for us again. The kids thought you were great."

Back in my room, to avoid thinking about Thibaud and whether or not my mockers are still there, I prepare for a TD on the 19th century French novel. We've been reading *Le Colonel Chabert*, part of Balzac's *La Comédie humaine*. This man who had started life as an orphan—like Tristan of *Tristan et Iseut* and Candide—there seem to be a lot of them in French literature—rose to be a rich and prestigious colonel in Napoleon's army. During the Battle of Elyau, he's taken for dead, thrown in with a pile of corpses. He climbs out from under the dead bodies and makes his way back to Paris where his wife, a former prostitute, has remarried and refuses to recognize him. He ends up dying as he was born, poor and in rags. Really depressing, just like Thibaud said most French novels are.

I liked talking to Flora. She is straightforward and sympathetic. Her compliment about my cooking and her children's opinion of me gave a pleasant nudge to my ego. She said I was brave. She held out hope for Jane and me. But she has cancer. Her mother is a Holocaust survivor and Madame a bundle of infirmity and resentment. Thibaud, it appears, has forsaken me, and I am too big a coward to confront him. Who needs fiction, when real life can depress you so effortlessly, all on its own?

***

Thursday, 10 February 1983

The winter is long and dark and reminding me of times I want to forget. Why this year particularly? Because being unable to see, I have more time to think? Because putting words on paper crystallizes thoughts, turns memories into hard, unavoidable objects? Or maybe it's just age, nearing the end.

The house feels unsteady. Germaine is gone much of the time and when she is here—well, I can't say she's a bundle of joy. And the girl. Something's wrong with the girl. Her movements seem nervous when she brings my breakfast. Her mood sits right there on the tray, next to the fig jam. But she's coming along as a cook. I'd say she's even got something of a gift. Nothing overcooked, just the right herb added to elevate the taste.

Sometimes she stays to eat—because she likes food, wants to taste her creation—certainly not for my company. Though I suppose she could feel sorry for me. I doubt it; I'm not nice enough to her, even if à deux, we have begun to communicate in a limited fashion. She tells me her American parents both had Fulbright scholarships in England and afterwards they stayed on. Her father's a doctor, a neurologist who practices in London, though they live in the country. The mother seems a bit slippery. Not quite sure what she has been doing since a stint at the Royal Academy.

The facts of her life sound charming, charmed: expats, private schools for her and her two sisters. But she doesn't sound charmed when relating the information. It sounds as though she'd rather change the subject as quickly as possible. Especially the subject of the French nanny or gouvernante, as she calls her. I can't quite figure out how or why this woman was in the picture. All I know is that when the girl was twelve, the woman was gone. Lack of money? Change of heart? Mission accomplished?

Strange.

I've asked about her course too. Why she wanted to do it (to retrieve and perfect her French) and what it's like (good, she says gamely). She does liven up when describing her Paris friends, two American girls, who sound…well, who sound very American. She described how they tear around on tourist missions. It made me laugh.

***

It's been several days now, and The Mood is pulling me down into its swampy nether-ness. I still haven't seen Thibaud and hope that doesn't mean his friends are still there (though deep down, I fear it does). I am hurt that he hasn't sought me out. But I am also very angry, feel at moments that I could choke. Or choke him, if he weren't avoiding me. I told him things that only Jane and Maude knew. It was the equivalent of ripping open my chest and handing him my heart on a platter. Then what did he do? Without telling or consulting me, he invited other people into our secret. He laughed at me. Our relationship, though undeclared to the larger world, implies a certain loyalty, doesn't it?

How can life seem so miraculous and marvellous one minute and so irretrievably miserable the next?

Thank God for this cooking business. In the kitchen all else is forgotten. In fact, it seems I shouldn't get paid to do something I like so much, but I have to say that part too is a blessing. At Christmas my father topped me up again, and it was awkward. Though he re-funded me without complaint, I hated having to ask. As long as I rely on them financially, I am still beholden. I haven't really grown up. And, I have discovered, a subsidised *salade niçoise* and a glass of wine do not taste as good as an *omelette au fromage* and a glass of wine paid for with money I have earned.

Adult responsibility, i.e., a job, can also be psychologically beneficial. The morning after my humiliation, I had considered staying in bed forever. But Madame needed her breakfast. I had to get up, could not stay reclined and brooding.

I dragged myself to my lectures, mostly because I couldn't bear to stay in the house with my mockers possibly still across the courtyard. And I was grateful on yet another front: Meredith and Carol may have cultural carapaces, but they have sensitive emotional antennae.

"You okay?" Meredith said when I sat down.

I couldn't produce more than a nod. I didn't listen to a word the professor said, just kept seeing the crinkles around Thibaud's eyes.

When the professor left the lectern, Meredith put an arm around my shoulder. "Let's go have some French onion soup for lunch. My treat."

Though the soup burned my tongue, and I was belching onions for hours afterwards, while my stomach tried to break down that rubbery cheese, at least I felt someone cared.

Afterwards they dragged me along shopping. "They say it might snow again and I left my boots in Chicago," said Meredith. "I had no idea the weather could be so awful in gay Paree."

"No place is worse than Chicago," says Carol. "Hot and humid in the summer, bitter cold in the winter."

During our August visit, just after our grandparents died, it was cloying, suffocating. Outside anyway. Inside everything was air-conditioned and I froze. Physically I was constantly uncomfortable, and it was all the more intolerable because Jane seemed oblivious. From the minute we stepped off the plane, she was smiling like some nun on a trip to the Holy Land. Our parents, having just received, Jane believed, a comfortable inheritance, splurged and we stayed at The Drake Hotel, right on the lake. The room and bathroom were grander than anything we'd experienced in England when the parents visited during the Swiss years. Jane marvelled at how big everything was, from the cars to the shops to Lake Michigan. It looks like the sea, she said, shading her eyes as we walked along the beach. We visited my grandparents' apartment on Cedar Street. It had black shiny floors, and my mother got all nervous. Take your shoes off, children. Our father said, Sylvia, your parents are gone. We don't need to worry about scuffing the floor. The living room had a white fluffy carpet, another pitfall for dirty feet, and stiff furniture. Down the corridor, there was his bedroom on the right, hers on the left. Where did you sleep, asked Maude. Down at the end. They turned it into a den the minute I went to boarding school. Though here there was no air conditioning, I found it the coldest place I'd ever set foot in. Jane, however, walked around in fascination, picking up an object here, admiring the view of the lake there.

People and chatter may have elbowed out The Mood earlier today, but as I walk through the *porte cochère*, up the main stairs, past the jarring artwork that still strikes me as a competition, I am again ruminating over that trip to Chicago. I am thinking about Thibaud and possibly his friends across the courtyard. The Mood is trundling right behind me, through the *salon* and the dining room, down the unlit corridor, trapping me on the way to the kitchen. All the tell-tale signs are there: the pressure around my head, the acid rising in my stomach. A slit of light frames Madame's sitting room door. The radio is on. Why bother when in the end it comes to this?

But once I've unpacked the shopping, my mind shifts to the meal ahead, which elbows aside distress. Germaine told me yesterday to buy some scallops. "It's the season," she said. "And if I weren't so distracted, we'd have had them ten times by now. Get some wild mushrooms as well."

When I bought the scallops, they were still in large shells that would have been collectable, if I'd found them on a beach. I watched the fishmonger pry them open with one swift swish of the knife. In another slice, he'd detached the flesh. The scallop and its *corail*, the bright orange phallic tail, went onto the pile, the shell was tossed into a bin where it made a hollow clack against the other tossed shells. It was as mesmerizing as the butcher with his chicken. Since Germaine is still not here, I'll wash them and take out the little digestive tract full of scallop poo that runs along the side of each one.

I am patting them dry on a paper towel when Germaine arrives, all a-scatter.

"Sorry I'm late," she mumbles.

"It's no problem. I got things started." I stop patting the scallops. In my self-absorption I'd forgotten: "How's Flora?" Madame told me yesterday that the treatments started today.

"Okay. So far. It's just the first day," she sighs. "I wish there were more I could do."

"You're taking care of them. That's already a lot."

"I don't know." Germaine's eyes dart around. "Anyway." She lifts her apron from the hook on the door, pulls it over her head and ties the string behind her back. "While I check on Madame you put some flour, salt and pepper in this." She hands me one of the fruit and vegetable paper bags from a folded stack. "Then shake the scallops in the mixture."

I do as I'm told, and out they come, perfectly dusted.

"You can chop up a couple garlic cloves," Germaine says, again in control, as she walks briskly back through the door. "I'll brush the mushrooms."

Within half an hour, the scallops have been seared in a mixture of butter and olive oil with a sprig of rosemary and the *girolle* mushrooms sautéed with garlic and sprinkled with flat-leafed parsley, so much tastier than the frizzy kind of my pre-Paris life. Germaine has cooked some rice. "There we have it," she says, wiping her hands with a tea towel.

"Smells good," says Madame.

The three of us sit down. I look at the white and orange scallops, the tawny mushrooms and the white rice, the green parsley. The visual pleasure raises the whole experience high above the physical need to fuel the body.

As usual, Madame serves herself minute portions. Tonight Germaine does too, and I feel I should follow suit, out of respect for Germaine's suffering, but the food looks too good. Madame also asks about Flora and gets a similarly muted response. She then coaxes Germaine into talking about her grandchildren, but I tune out, am too busy relishing the tastes and textures on my plate to be interested in a six-year-old's judo lessons. I push a bit of each ingredient onto my fork with my knife and am careful to finish it all at the same time, to wash it down with a sip of wine. What a mixture of satisfaction and regret, I am thinking when I scoop the last bite into my mouth. Germaine's voice penetrates:

"Have some more, Lily. There's lots left."

"Thank you, I think I will," I say, remembering that The Mood is waiting for me right outside the kitchen door.

***

Monday, 21 February 1983

Flora's treatment has started, and Germaine says she cannot bear it. They say she'll probably lose her hair, she told me in a wavering voice.

Imagining her daughter pale, thin and balding surely brings back her own pale, thin and hairless days. Those memories she has so effectively stuffed into the deepest corners of her being. Of course I cannot bring it up—that would be cruel—but I am worried. Worried she might finally crack. It's never too late. François showed me that.

So worried I talked to the girl last night.

How do you find Germaine these days?

Unhappy. Very unhappy.

I have never seen her this distraught, I said. Not even after her husband died suddenly from a heart attack.

But this is her daughter, said the girl, quite defensively I thought.

As if I were being insensitive—somehow missing the point.

Yes, but Flora is still alive. Many women survive breast cancer. I think it's something else. Germaine has a difficult past.

I know, she said.

You do?

One day I saw the number.

She hides it normally.

Her sleeve slipped up her arm.

Did you say anything?

Oh, no.

I told her about the *Rafle*, the antique dealer who hid her and her sister, the denunciation so close to the end of the war.

She lost all her family? It sounded as though the girl might cry. I told her about Germaine meeting Michel at the Hôtel Lutétia. It was a happy marriage.

So I said, so I think. But how does one know?

Everyone thought François and I were happy. And we were. Until we weren't. Until it was the *You* and the accusing finger in every exchange when we were alone, the sleeping not just in separate rooms but on different floors. People think you get over the past, move on. But that's not right. The past sticks to your ribs like a heavy meal.

I try and repaint the picture sometimes, imagine the what-if of our still being a family at the end of the War. The War itself might have been forgiven, if not forgotten. But it was one layer of adversity slapped pell-mell on another—we couldn't do it, couldn't get over it. What's the point of imagining a rosier outcome?

***

I dry the last plate, my head still full of Germaine's story. It's unimaginable that she could have survived such—such what? What's the word for savagery to that degree? Horror doesn't even get close. Tragedy, atrocity both come up short, as does every other descriptive word that runs through my mind. I wipe the cloth in circles on the table, collect the crumbs in my hand and let them flutter into the sink. But as soon as I turn on the water to wash them away, I shut the tap. I imagine every crumb a human being, a life thoughtlessly swept away.

It's been three weeks, and I still have not seen Thibaud. I have looked at the windows across the way, listened carefully and heard nothing and have allowed myself to believe that his friends are gone.

But I can't avoid the potential problem forever, so tonight, not wanting to spend the evening in the company of my own head and Germaine's story, I will go over there. Just to be safe, in case the friends are still there, I dress in my coolest, black-on-black, clothes. My shoes slap softly as I make my way down the wooden stairs in the dark. It seems months rather than weeks since I last slipped the key into the door leading to the wing.

Once again, I pass through the dilapidated rooms. At the kitchen-bathroom, I pause. No sound. I walk up the staircase and Thibaud is sitting on the floor with the sleeping bag around his shoulders, book and notebook on a crate in front of him.

"Hey," he looks up surprised but smiling. "Where have you been?"

"I might ask you the same question."

There is a noise on the stairs.

"Must be Jean-Marc and Cécile," Thibaud says standing, shedding his sleeping bag.

"They're still here?" So much for hope.

He looks down, then back up at me. "Just staying until they find something else."

"Like you?" My voice raises, then lowers, comes out in a whine. "That could mean forever."

More noise downstairs. My senses feel muddled from panic.

"Nothing's forever, especially where Jean-Marc is concerned. Come on. Let's go down."

In the kitchen-bathroom, his two friends are standing under the bleak lightbulb in their hippie clothes, dread locks and attitudes, hovering around the cabinet over the heating elements where some packaged food now lives. At least the black cloth is still firmly blocking the window.

"*Salut*," says Jean-Marc, eying me with an amused smile. He plucks a bag of crisps from the shelf. He has a strong jaw and a cleft chin and instinctively I do not like this man. The young woman, Cécile, has almost the same smile but without the mocking backdrop.

"This is Lily, remember?" says Thibaud.

Stop it. Of course they remember—how could they forget? I surprise myself by saying: "I'm really sorry, but you can't stay here."

Jean-Marc, crossing muscular arms across his chest, steals a look at Thibaud. "I understand you're worried," he says in a tone that implies the problem belongs to all of us and we have a long history of collectively sorting out just such predicaments. "We are used to being very discreet."

"I know, but—"

"You haven't heard us, have you?"

"No, but—"

"It's great you're here," he interrupts again. "Thibaud has talked a lot about you. Come and see how we've set up the room." The four of us cross the corridor into the room originally destined for Thibaud, where he and I sat on the floor against the wall drinking hot chocolate and giggling, while we waited for the bath water to heat. A wavelet of nostalgia laps around my heart.

"You see," Jean-Marc says, pointing to the windows, "this room faces the street, and we keep the shutters closed all the time." He turns on a standing halogen light, lowering the dimmer.

Like Thibaud, they have crates for tables, except theirs have candles and ashtrays on them. An old, folded-up quilt serves as a sofa. Cécile's hairbrush, hand mirror and other accessories are lined up along the stone mantelpiece. A photo that appears to be of the two of them is tacked above. My eyes move down to the double mattress.

These people are never leaving.

"Sit down, please," says Cécile, putting a hand on my shoulder. Thibaud has been so quiet, I've almost forgotten he's here, but he sits next to me, puts a hand on my thigh. Cécile takes a pillow from the bed and sits yoga-style, looks across at me with a complicity I resent. Jean-Marc perches on a chair. His left knee is pointing right in my face. It's a big knee on strong, solid legs.

"Do you smoke at all?" he asks politely, like he's the host.

"Not much."

"Well," he pulls a large joint from his Andean jacket and displays it vertically before running the whole thing through his mouth, then holding it up again and making sure the paper is sticking.

I know that I should get up, storm out—do something to object— but I hate scenes, feel too shy. Instead, for the third time in my life, I am smoking cannabis. As it's laced with tobacco, of which I also have little experience, my head feels doubly light.

Thibaud looks different, either to my altered vision or because the drug has changed his demeanor. He shakes his head slightly, coming out of a stupor, and smiles at me.

"See?" he says. "What the old lady doesn't know won't hurt her."

My tongue remembers his mouth when we kiss. Or is it kissed? And would that be in the *passé composé* or *l'imparfait*? I wonder if to kiss, as far as Thibaud and I are concerned, will ever again be conjugated in the present tense. He seems like someone I've never met. I am overcome by doubt. But only for a minute. Now everything seems extremely funny. We're all laughing as Jean-Marc opens the bag of crisps (such a loud noise!) and passes it around. Crisps have never tasted quite this good. What was I worried about? I smoke a bit more, trying to imitate Cécile, the way she holds in the smoke and taps her fingers on her knee as if counting the seconds.

Suddenly there are waterfalls in my ears. Although I would like to stand up and walk out or—better yet—be zapped back to my bed, I can no longer even sit up. The others are still talking; I do not dare open my mouth. Fear rises at the back of my throat. Behind the waterfall, don't I hear someone coming? Aren't we about to be arrested by the police and doubly charged for trespassing and possession of drugs, then handcuffed and thrown in the police van, the *saladier*, before being tossed into cells, kept *en garde à vue*? I look again at the others, feeling weak and queasy. They are having an intense discussion about something I can't quite grasp. I close my eyes for fear I might throw up, an act that would upstage my nightshirt performance by a long shot.

***

Wednesday, 23 February 1983

The girl is still nervous. The other day I almost asked her what's wrong, but the words got stuck, wouldn't come out. I was nice to Octave, but when he met the Horse I was tossed aside like an old sock, as the French say. That doesn't mean it would happen again—she is nothing like Octave—but still I hold back.

Then this morning I wondered if she hadn't been crying. There was a congested cloud that gave a certain timbre to her speech. A cold, perhaps, but I didn't think so. It sounded like loneliness. Like the loneliness I often felt in my early Paris days—it came back to me, whoosh. Between my imperfect French and poisonous Agnès and my mother-in-law's crazed sorrow and François' obsessive work habits, I often felt quite low. At times even homesick for that ranch I'd been so happy to leave.

Until *he* was born. *He*—

I have been sitting here for ten minutes, pen suspended, *allez*, write it:

Henri.

Later: I had to stop. No matter how many years ago it was—no matter how hard the case around my heart has grown—thinking of him blasts me wide open every time.

***

Several days have passed since my second humiliation with those residue hippie scroungers. Between the course work and the shopping and cooking, I am thankfully very busy, and it has helped to keep them, even Thibaud, from my mind.

After a TD backing up a lecture on Napoleon seizing power, I am walking out of the Sorbonne with a small cluster of classmates, thinking about poor Colonel Chabert, rather than the real historical facts, and there is Thibaud.

"Hey," says Meredith, "we haven't seen you in a while. How's your English going to get better if you don't spend time with us?"

"I 'ave been veree busy." I'd forgotten how irritating he sounds in English.

We walk down the boulevard Saint Michel together. I make a point of latching on to Gary, whose brassiness has dulled with the passing months. Maybe *la civilisation française* has rubbed off on him. Maybe being brash is how he deals with insecurity, with new people in a foreign land, and now he's feeling more comfortable, *mieux dans sa peau*, better in his skin. He's telling me how odd it is that Napoleon is so underappreciated in Paris geography. "There's the obelisk on the place Vendôme with him dressed as Caesar on top, but he built that to his own glory. His military campaigns are credited everywhere—avenue and place d'Iéna, rue de Solférino, rue d'Elyau, the gare d'Austerlitz. But he himself gets nothing, as far as I can tell from my Plan de Paris," he pats his bulging coat pocket, "except the narrow, one-way rue Bonaparte, over there, in the 6th arrondissement."

"That's interesting," I say vaguely. Gary is obsessed with Napoleon. Meredith has pointed out that he too is short and perhaps therein lies the attraction. But I am more interested in watching Thibaud whose arms are swinging around his head like streamers as he answers some question of Carol's on correct French practice. He told me one night after his confession that he learned about the polite way to cut cheese not at home on the cheese farm, but at a party in Paris. "That bourgeois *merde* was as foreign to my childhood as the Yassine's couscous."

We all pause at the corner of the boulevard Saint Germain. Meredith and Carol are going to Duriez to buy more notebooks. Luisa is meeting her sister at Odéon. Gary says he's already walked too far—he wants to look for a book at Gibert Jeune.

"Are you returning to the Marais?" Thibaud asks me. Everyone's listening. I nod in a slight vertical way and hope it will be misinterpreted as a horizontal shake. "Good," he says. "I will also cross *la Seine*."

For several minutes we trudge along in silence. I have my hands shoved into my coat pockets, my head sunk into my scarf.

"I am sorry," he finally says.

I stop dead in my tracks. "You know what, Thibaud? If you want to talk to me, please do so in French. I'm not your English teacher. If that's what you are looking for, go spend time with them." I toss my head back, continue walking.

"Jean-Marc and Cécile are old friends. They were really kind to me when I was homeless and living under a bridge one summer."

I don't answer but my curiosity is piqued, which he senses:

"After my first year no landlord would rent to a poor scholarship student and I ended up camping under the Alexandre III bridge, while I worked at a nearby café. Jean-Marc and Cécile were living in a little room in the quayside. They asked me to move in. They put a roof over my head. When I ran into them at the Beaubourg, it was a cold and miserable day. I couldn't very well turn them away."

"Do I have to remind you that you are living in that house illegally and are therefore not in a position to be handing out invitations? That I'm the one ultimately responsible?" Underneath the anger is an open pit of fear.

"Look, they don't want to get found out any more than I do. They're quiet. And I told you, I doubt they'll stay very long. They never do."

We walk by Notre Dame, and for once she leaves me cold. Ditto on the rue Saint-Louis-en-Ile with its ancient, slanting buildings.

"I'm sorry about the other night," says Thibaud. "You didn't react well to that weed."

"No, I did not. And when I woke up you were gone and those people," I say with as much scorn as I can breathe into the word, "were having sex. Loud sex. I'm surprised the whole 4th arrondissement didn't hear them. I had to lie there in their hippie pot smell until he was snoring. Also loudly. Why did you leave me lying there?"

"You were out cold. What was I supposed to do?" He shakes his head. "They weren't always hippie types, you know. Jean-Marc was a star gymnast. Cécile was going to be a teacher."

"So? What does that have to do with their freeloading now?"

He lifts his shoulders. "Nothing, I guess. It's just that they weren't always pothead dropouts. He had a bad accident and they both gave up their career plans, grew their hair and went alternative."

"I don't care, not one bit, that they used to be upright citizens. Right now what they're doing—what you're doing—is illegal and could get me in a lot of trouble."

"I actually wanted to share some good news with you this afternoon," he says, smiling like a child, as we approach the place des Vosges. "I have an interview for the Fulbright."

"Oh. Congratulations." At least that maybe means he won't be trespassing for the rest of his life.

"I can't tell you how grateful I am." He pauses. "Will you come up for just a minute? There's a form to fill out and I don't want to make any mistakes."

I sigh. "I have to make supper." In fact, we're eating leftovers. Cold salmon with dill sauce, a green bean salad and potatoes.

"Please. Just for a minute. I promise."

"All right. But a minute. No more."

"Thank you."

"And I don't want to see your friends."

"Sure. No problem."

Except when we reach the landing there is a new voice coming from the room. My eyes pop at Thibaud; he shrugs ignorance.

"Hey," says Jean-Marc. "Meet my cousin. Laurent, this is our old friend Thibaud and his friend Lily, the person we have to thank for these generous accommodations." His arm sweeps around. "Laurent is a law student too."

"Are you?" says Thibaud.

"Second year. Assas."

"I'm third year. Panthéon."

There is *un air de famille* between Jean-Marc and Laurent, in the broad nose and mouth, the irritatingly ironic eyes. It's only in the bottom of the face, at the chin, which does not jut and cleft like Jean-Marc's, that the resemblance diverges. In other ways Laurent is the diametric opposite of Jean-Marc. He has short hair, classic clothes. Seeing clean-cut Laurent makes it a lot easier to imagine Jean-Marc the gymnast, someone who could perform a handspring without his dreadlocks getting in the way.

"What a spot," he says, looking at me, passing a joint to Thibaud. "I was telling Jean-Marc and Cécile that a friend of mine did a study on property rights recently and got very interested in squatting." At this word my heart jumps into my mouth. "Or putting unoccupied space to good use, as he prefers to say. Apparently, there are many thousands of empty square meters in Paris."

"A scandal, right?" says Jean-Marc, straightening his back and jamming his fists to his sides in mock indignation.

"Well, yes," answers Laurent. "As a student in Paris, it's more and more difficult to find affordable housing. Meanwhile, rich property owners sit on massive empty nests."

"Yeah," nods Cécile with blank eyes.

"Maybe I wouldn't care," Laurent smiles, "if my parents hadn't picked up and moved to Nice. I'd still be living in my old bedroom on the rue du Théâtre." He looks at Jean-Marc, passes me the joint, which I pass directly on to Cécile. "Been back to Dijon recently?"

"A few months ago. I left after one night. Went to stay with Caroline."

"Caroline!" Laurent says. "It was raining the other day and I was bored and I thought of our Monopoly games."

Laurent, an only child, I learn, used to spend every school holiday with his cousins Jean-Marc, Caroline and François in Dijon. They take a long trip down memory lane while the joint that I continue to refuse goes around. I would like to get up and go but can't break the spell. I look at Thibaud, who is glued to Laurent and Jean-Marc's story. He looks both jealous and enchanted at their fraternal ease and maybe at Laurent's self-possession too. Cécile has picked up a book. I wonder if she can really concentrate amidst the reminiscing or if she's just trying to make a statement. These people always seem to be making statements.

Jean-Marc says to Laurent: "Why don't you stay here tonight? You can use our sleeping pads and that quilt Cécile is stretched out on."

"That would be amazing. I've outstayed my welcome on the floors of too many *chambres de bonne* recently."

I want to object, but the but gets stuck behind my lips. It's already gone beyond my control.

Finally, up in Thibaud's room I let loose: "You heard him. He said squat, and I'm going to lose my job. Maybe even get arrested."

"Stop it. You heard how low and measured Laurent le Parisian's voice is. Of course he's at Assas. That's where the chic people go." He shakes his head, envy and admiration crowding his brow and brightening his eyes. "Did you see his slim-line brown shoes? With those crepe soles he'll be quiet as a cat."

***

Monday, 28 February 1983

Everyone loved him; he was one of those children that you couldn't hold close enough in your arms. For me everything changed the day he was born, despite the long labor and the Caesarean and the doctor's pronouncement that there would be no more. With his birth Paris became home, and I became more at home with myself.

They were the best years of my life, his childhood. Mornings with François, sipping coffee and spooning the last bites of breakfast into Henri's mouth, before handing him over to the nanny so I could bike to the Sorbonne. I loved my course. I loved the city. I loved my child. I loved my husband. Everything seemed possible.

There were times when I'd fear something would happen to Henri or François. Premonitions? I don't think so. It just didn't seem possible that such happiness could continue. And of course it didn't.

No sooner had Henri heard General de Gaulle's *appel du 18 juin* after the Germans invaded France than he was ready to make his way to London. François said he was too young—and he was—only fifteen. But the arguments at dinner. First Henri's resentful silence would pervade the room like smoke, choking all efforts at communication. François could not contain his anger beyond the soup—what a hot head he had behind the calm control on display to the rest of the world—and by mid-main course, the words were flying across the table like knives.

A great relief that François prevailed? Not really. Because the resolution of that problem just made way for another. Henri got involved with the Résistance right here, a different branch, but just like his father. The three of us began revolving in our own private worlds, one never really intersecting the other. Afterwards I often wondered if going to London wouldn't have been better. A different path taken, even an apparently more dangerous one, could have changed the course of his fate. Maybe. But maybe not. And why dangle happier scenarios in front of my blind eyes? He was taken from us, and neither François nor I ever recovered.

***

T he next day I am waiting for the lecture to begin, in a nervous fret about the growing problem next door. It's all I can think about. Those people must go, but I feel powerless to make them. Thibaud keeps telling me it's okay, they're quiet, but that doesn't reassure me one bit.

Meredith arrives; Carol has a cold and has stayed in bed for the last two days.

"Guess what?" she whispers, waits, as if I might actually guess.

"I don't know," I finally say.

"It's happened. At last," hands and eyes in the air. "I've met a Frenchman. At a bar, last night." The professor enters the hall. Meredith opens her new notebook, bends the paper around the spiral. "He's married. But that's okay." She shrugs and readies her pen over the paper.

"How old is he?" I whisper.

"Forty-two," she answers nonchalantly.

This seems very old. I'm not sure if it's cool or creepy.

"He works in PR," Meredith adds. "But the main point is now I'll learn French."

The lecture is on grammar. The subtleties of *l'imparfait*, the imperfect, the verb tense employed for the once-upon-a-time and the continual past. The past not linked to a particular moment in time. As opposed to the *passé composé* and the *passé simple*, which are. *L'imparfait* can be a difficult tense for foreigners, as it does not exist in some languages…

Usually, it is entertaining to listen to this professor take verb conjugation to metaphysical heights, but today my mind is quickly distracted by Meredith's declaration. For months she has been talking about her longing for just such an encounter. In the last few weeks, there's been desperation in her cries of I've never gone this long without a man—and I'm in Paris, the city of love! I have heard about the senior who was head of the debating club when she was just a freshman, about the political science professor (once the debater had graduated), who must also have been close to forty-two, though not married. Here in Paris, I have observed her on multiple occasions, flirting with the TD professor Jean-Pierre, with a waiter at a wine bar, with Thibaud. As for the males on our course, none appears to be up to Meredith's standards, and in any case, she's been clear from the start that she wants a native.

I try to imagine what a fortyish PR Frenchman would be like. Sleek suits and low-slung fast cars come to mind. A full head of carefully coiffed straight hair, brushed to the side, a smile of questionable sincerity.

The professor is speaking to us about complex sentences. When the imperfect is in the subordinate clause, in the sphere of the unreal, the main clause requires the conditional, the hypothetical. The professor cites an example: *Si j'étais riche, je t'acheterais un cadeau*…then launches into a word by word analysis.

What about the PR man's wife? I dip into the shallow well of my experience: Octave's wife Marie-France, the French mothers in the playground of the place des Vosges. But not Flora. Flora is too normal, not typically anything. And I certainly can't imagine Roger picking up a young American at a bar. I see a Marie-France type flicking the pages of *Marie-Claire* or *Paris Match*, puffing vigorously at a cigarette, while *petits Pierre et Sophie* play in the sand or teeter and totter on the see-saw.

The mathematics suddenly occur to me. If Monsieur PR is forty-two, the children are not necessarily as young as those in my picture. They might be medium-sized children who come and go from school unaccompanied by their mother. In which case does Madame PR flick her magazine pages and cigarette ashes at home, at the kitchen table? What a depressing image. I switch story lines: Madame PR is an artist in her studio, arm over her palette, head cocked and fully concentrated on mixing a perfect shade of Paris grey. She is above terrestrial concerns, such as her husband's libido.

After the lecture, I go with Meredith back to their flat, where Carol is lying on the sofa with a red nose and a book.

"Since I slept through it," she says with a croaky, congested voice, "let's hear about it. About him."

Meredith smiles, coils her thick blond hair and lets it drop on her back. "I was at the jazz bar with some of the others. Of course, the tables were packed in the way they always are in this country, and our chairs were back to back. He apologized for bumping mine, then asked me what I thought of the music. And that was that."

"What do you mean that was that?"

"You know how these things happen."

"Not really," says Carol glumly.

"One question leads to another. It's hard to hear so your shoulders touch. Then it's the legs. That kind of thing." She throws her hands in the air. "And before you know it, you're leaving together."

"Unbelievable." Carol blows her nose. "I have to say, though, he's kinda old."

"Better than the babies in our class. And he's still very sexy." A mischievous smile spreads across Meredith's face. "He knows what he's doing."

"What do you mean?" asks Carol. What a question, I think, though I am hanging on every word.

"Let's just say," says Meredith, her blue eyes hooding slightly, "he knows where to put his hands." She breaks into a lusty laugh. "And other parts of his body."

"Wow," moans Carol. "You get all the luck." Her heavy jaw sinks and her messy hair falls over face. The cold has not improved her appearance. "But what about his wife? You said he's married."

"She works for a cosmetics company."

My vision cracks and shatters, re-forms: a thin physique dressed in a suit. But not a dowdy one like Jane's. No, Madame PR is French. She'll swish down the corporate corridors in stiletto heels and something sexy, something that highlights her slimness and her femininity, exposes her bony knees. Instead of brooding about her husband's infidelities over the pages of a glossy magazine, she may be designing a business plan to kill him.

"They have some kids—I can't remember how many," Meredith continues. "But as a couple, they've been growing apart for some time."

"That's what they all say," Carol blows her nose. "But how do you do it?"

"You just have to be in the right place at the right time." Meredith gives her shapely shoulders another shrug. "I'm exhausted. I need a nap."

On my way back to the place des Vosges, I wonder about Meredith's conquest. My irksome imagination must have painted an incorrect picture of Monsieur PR and his wife. Although I cannot draw a new one, how could Meredith Hanson's lover not be handsome and cool?

When I walk into the kitchen, Germaine is sitting at the table, reading glasses on her nose, letter opener in her hand. Administrative duties for Madame, I have learned, are always carried out at the kitchen table, often in the afternoon, after the second delivery of the post. At first, I found this odd—why wouldn't she do it downstairs—until I realized the public display has something to do with trust. Or Germaine's perception of it. It's her way of showing that all is above board, even though no one is questioning her integrity.

"Madame used to handle the post herself, and I preferred it that way, I really did," she said to me once. "Opening other people's letters will never sit well with me."

While she sorts, she talks to herself: this we can throw away, that we need to pay, this I'll handle next week. Occasionally I get the odd letter—the bi-weekly missive from my mother or something relating to my course—and they go in another pile.

"*Ça va* ?" I ask, putting the bags on the counter.

"*Oui, oui*," she says. "But look at this *aérogramme* from the United States." The writing on the blue paper is almost child-like in its carefully formed, even loops. The return address, noted diligently in the top left-hand corner, informs me that it is from Richard Tucker in Loveland, CO. I remember seeing that Loveland, CO in the address book, when I phoned the doctor. Germaine has slit it open. "It's in English. You'll have to read it to her."

An uncomfortable tingle rises up my back. I'm pretty sure it doesn't contain good news. "Now?"

"Well, yes. I'll put the shopping away."

I trudge down the corridor. I have no desire to be privy to Madame Quinon's correspondence.

"You have a letter from the United States," I say.

Madame is sitting at her writing table with the new notebook she asked me to buy and her fountain pen. "Come in." She stands up. "Who is it from?"

"Richard Tucker."

"Ah, my nephew in Colorado." She settles in one of the chairs in front of the fireplace, points to the other. "Please." I perch. "Go ahead and read it to me."

"'Dear Aunt Amenia,'" I've always hated the sound of my own voice, especially when reading aloud. And it sounds even worse, reading aloud in English to Madame, using her strange first name. But on I go: "'I regret to inform you that my father, your brother, passed away last week.'" I stop, look up. Madame's face is frozen. "I'm sorry."

"It was to be expected," Madame answers in French, with an uneasy shrug. "He is three years older than I."

I clear my throat, resume: "'After his fall last month, he never quite recovered. But he passed at home, in his own bed, surrounded by his three loving sons and several of his grandchildren. We are comforted in the knowledge that he will finally be joining our mother and Our Maker.'" I pause, shift slightly on the chair. Madame remains still and silent.

"'How are you? We haven't heard any news in over a year, so I do hope you're keeping well. I still remember fondly those days I spent with you and Uncle François, just after the War. What a time that was.'" I pause again. Madame's head is tilted as if she has a stiff neck.

"'We're all fine. Nancy remains very involved with the school, even though she retired from teaching last year. Allen and Roberta visit often with their families—we now have six grandchildren! My law practice continues to flourish. Last summer we had a reunion on the ranch. Though it had been a dry summer, the place was as beautiful and peaceful as ever. Don and Rita do a great job keeping the homestead up to Dad's standards! We all have much to be thankful for. God bless you and yours, Rick.'"

I close and fold the letter, say again into the silence: "I'm sorry."

"I haven't seen him in a lifetime," Madame says softly. "It's hard to imagine." Her deep blue eyes look in my direction. "It's funny. You leave people, their lives, behind you. They begin to seem very far away, unreachable, irretrievable. But they can come back, in a flash. You haven't left them behind at all." She pauses. "Even a brother I haven't seen in over sixty years, a man in some ways I hardly know. He's still right there." She points to her chest, shakes her head. "He's still my brother. Was. Anyway, thank you for reading the letter to me."

On the way back to the kitchen, I feel like I might fall over. At the end Madame was speaking to me in English. She sounded like a different person.

"Ah," nods Germaine. "How did she react?"

"She seemed quite upset."

"Hmm," Germaine nodded. "She never went back again, you know."

"I thought she was from New York."

"Oh, no. She grew up on a ranch. In the wild west somewhere."

Up in my room, getting ready to go back down and have a bath, I am still thinking about *le rann-she*, as Germaine pronounced it. The angle from which I was viewing Madame Amenia Quinon was entirely wrong. Forget New York high society. It's Cowboys and Indians and crude manners that should have been in my mind, not some American version of Sloane Square. But Madame's fine features—that delicate nose and thin skin stretched over her high cheekbones, her seemingly effortless elegance—how could a ranch in the wild west be the birthplace of a woman who gracefully, naturally inhabits a mansion on the place des Vosges?

I slowly take my towel from the hook next to the sink. Nothing is ever as it seems.

Tuesday, 8 March 1983

I wouldn't have thought the news of Ted's death could sting so. After all these years. We were never close, even if we played together when children because there was no one else around. I was bookish; he was not. I had ideas about seeing the world; he was content right where he was. Even going to university held little appeal for him. All he wanted to do was work on the ranch, but Mother needled him, said it was a changing world and Ted should learn about new agricultural practices. As usual, she prevailed.

When I arrived at the U of W and saw Ted striding across campus, long head sticking forward, books under his arm, I hardly recognized him. Though he joined a fraternity, he wasn't much for the parties. He met Bess his first year, and right from the start, they looked like an old married couple. Maybe that's the secret to success, skipping all the youthful romance. Anyway, Bess was an angel—a person who was sweet not just in the wrapping but right to the core.

Beyond a polite, irregular correspondence, I have had no contact with my brother since I left the ranch. Yet since that letter arrived the other day, there he is, riding in front of me on the way to school. Or sitting at the table, head lowered, slowly chewing his food. Everything was slow and deliberate with Ted.

For years I told myself that one day I'd go back for a visit. And I kept saying it even when the odds of it happening decreased to almost zero. As long as Ted was still alive it seemed possible. Now it is not. And the finality of that is like another nail in my own coffin. Or, at the risk of mixing too many metaphors, a last straw. A final reason for me to be gone, to let the Seresta carry me away.

Of Ted's three children, Rick is the only one I met. He had been stationed in Italy during the War and on his way home knocked on our door. It was a shock. He looked so much like Ted, who looked so much like Mother. Ted with Bess' smile. When he walked into the *salon*, cap in hand, you'd have thought he'd just entered the palais de Versailles. I remember he lowered himself slowly onto the chair, hat still between his hands, as his eyes roamed the room in wonder.

François put Rick at ease. He always made people relax, feel comfortable. He'd ask questions, listen intently to the answers, ask more questions. But I think it was more than that. I think it was the graceful way he moved around the room, as he was preparing the drinks or opening the window, almost as if he were on the dance floor. You wanted to be in step with him.

Rick was a polite and sensitive young man. He took in Paris with his fine nose and wide eyes. What a waste, I thought. He'll just end up back at the ranch, shrivelling on a drought-stricken vine, as my melodramatic mother used to say about us. But I was wrong. Rick left the farming to his younger brother and took advantage of the GI bill to become a lawyer. He settled in Colorado. And Ted, to his credit, was immensely proud of his son, a whole state away.

It is a sharp regret, another one to add to the quiver, that I only ever learned of these things via the diaphanous sheets of airmail paper. That I never went to see with my own eyes, while I still had them.

But it's also a sign. That time's up for me too.

***

Though I still feel like a novice, I've been flying solo for a while now. Since Flora started her treatments last month and Germaine has been making supper over there. Sometimes she stays on to eat with them, sometimes she's comes back, but she's never fully here. Her face is closed, rigid. Her mind and spirit remain with Flora. It can make me a little jealous, the physical signs of the pain she feels for her daughter.

I now do all the shopping on my own, using money from the little purse, in which I then stick the receipts. The merchants are getting to know me. They ask how Germaine is while they pinch the heads of garlic to give me one that isn't rotting. And I've learned about fending for myself at the stands, making queue-cutters wait their turn.

As for the cooking itself, I've mostly stuck to dishes Germaine taught me. Scallops, chicken, lamb chops, quiche or salmon. Basic vegetables. Potatoes or rice. That kind of thing. I work on getting the timing right, not under or overcooking anything. It's trickier than it seems, getting it all to come together at once. Madame has not complained, and I have not been unhappy with the results.

When I was turning off the kitchen light last night after supper, I heard a bang, just a small one, but it had clearly come from across the courtyard. This morning, cleaning up the breakfast dishes, I resign myself to confronting him, to finding out how long his friends plan on staying. This time I must be firm. Since I do not want to run into Them, I decide the most likely place to find Thibaud on a Saturday is at the

Beaubourg. Because of his Fulbright interview, he told me, he spends a lot of time at the language lab.

And there he is. The incipient curls. The angular shoulders hunched in concentration. The high forehead and perfectly triangular nose, his heart-shaped lips. Why aren't the girls flocking around him? I've wondered this before. Meredith, who does not know about us, thinks he's gay. But as Carol says, that's what she thinks about every man who isn't falling all over her. There is something more beautiful than handsome about his face. There is also something impenetrably private. As if he were a fortress surrounded by a moat that runs deep and wide. Not unlike myself, I guess you could say, and constructed for similar reasons: both our lives are built on childhoods that cause us embarrassment. Perhaps that similar architecture explains why we were attracted to one another in the first place.

Instead of making a scene and interrupting him, I decide to let him finish. But this entails quite a wait—he is a diligent student of the English language—and by the time he puts down the headphones and returns the cassettes, impatience has smothered any apprehension at the encounter.

Thibaud is obviously still conjugating verbs in his head because he doesn't notice me until I step in his path.

"They have to leave," I say. "You're going to get caught and I'll lose my job."

"What do you mean?" I'm not sure if he's playing dumb or just lost in the conditional.

"You know what I mean. Your friends. Last night I heard a noise. A bang."

"How do you know it was us?"

"Who else could it have been?" Someone tells me to hush.

Us hit me like a dart. Like he and I are no longer on the same side. I can feel the tears rising.

"Come on," he whispers. "Let's get a coffee."

I walk to the door as if carrying two glasses of water filled to the brim. All my concentration is focused on not allowing the liquid to spill over my lids.

We take the escalator to the top floor. There are the roofs of Paris, almost engulfing me. It's dusk, what Germaine told me the French call *entre chien et loup*, between the dog and the wolf, and the sky is howling at me that the lives behind the lit windows are happier, better, more normal than mine. A few tears fall, but he's walking in front and doesn't see.

By the time we are seated and coffee has been ordered, I have regained control of my tear ducts.

"I'm sorry it's turning out like this," he says. I look hard at him, try to gauge his sincerity, but he is looking at the table, not me.

"You said they never stay long, but they're still here."

"They pick fruit from late spring to autumn. Until last year they spent winters at a commune in the Canary Islands. But it broke up and here they are."

"Which means they'll be here at least until the cherries ripen and that's a long way off. And now there's Laurent. I don't see him picking fruit. How long is he going to trespass?"

"You should get to know them. They're really nice."

"They're a direct threat to my living situation. They're scroungers."

"It's a huge, empty wing of a house. We come and go discreetly. We don't make noise."

"Yes, you do. I told you. I heard something last night."

"But no one else can. No one who doesn't know we're there."

I fiddle with my coffee spoon. Maybe he's right. Maybe I'm being a prig, but I wish he'd stop saying We like I have nothing to do with Him.

"Hey," he smiles, places his long hand on mine and it feels warm. Better than no hand at all.

***

Tuesday, 15 March 1983

Beware of the Ides of March. I have never been able to think of this date without remembering my Shakespeare professor at the U of W.

My third year was his first teaching. He was ten years my senior and had a crush on me. Not surprising, given the slim pickings in Cheyenne. Ernest Baker had come from the east to experience an America that was not beholden to Europe, that was its own person, was the way he put it. He taught Old World literature begrudgingly. We are living the American century, he would say.

America has taken over the world, hasn't it? The movies and the literature—there's certainly nothing to compare in contemporary French letters. The fiction here is as fluffy as an *île flottante*. The films are often ponderous and plot-less.

Octave visited yesterday, out of the blue. He has just been to New

York and was almost as fervent about that city as he was about life in general as a young man.

Such energy, he said. None of this morose French pessimism.

Are you ready to move? I asked.

I would if I could, Tante, he said. I really would. It was so fresh. Our soap has a big future over there. It's already selling like 'ot ca-ickes, he said in English (*comme des petits pains*, he added, in case I hadn't understood).

How odd, I said. That's what your uncle thought, and he did the same thing, expand business to the US. Until the Depression got in the way.

Really. I didn't know that. What a strange coincidence, Octave said, pleased as punch. He has always viewed François, whom he never met, through a display case window. Dead men stay heroes, unless a biographer dredges up dirt. François, as far I know, had no dirt and wasn't a big enough hero for someone to want to dig in the first place. But if one did start to excavate, would he or she get beyond the handsome, strong and brave François? Would the writer discover, for example, that temper of his? Or be able to see what it was like for me, always coming second, initially to his work, then to the War and finally to grief? At the beginning, I thought I could change him. Or that being with me, he would change—the great fallacy on which so many relationships are founded. Naturally that didn't happen, but for as long as our life was relatively trouble-free—no wars imposing prickly moral choices, no dead children—I could manage his obsessions. I had my own interests, my own corners of existence.

I have always blamed the War for the wall between us. But I must at least consider the possibility that I have been wrong. That maybe we would have grown apart anyway. One can't divine the effects of age and time on people and their interaction, with or without intervening catastrophes.

Surely Octave came to talk to me because the Horse shows no interest. Has he no friends? Men tend not to make many after a certain age. They get caught up with their professional lives and even those made in childhood and at university can be neglected. They get comfort from their wives, and when that doesn't happen, they seek the company of another woman. If Octave has lit out in that direction—and if he asked my advice, I'd strongly advise him to do just that—why would he be coming to talk to me? I guess he's stuck in the Horse's stable. There are so many ways to sell one's soul.

Meredith tosses her blond head and laughs. Next to her, PR man, otherwise known as Loïc, smiles stupidly. We are having dinner at a restaurant beyond even my new-found means, Loïc's treat. His hair is a little shorter and his suit does not shine, but he's otherwise surprisingly close to my imagined version. He's got cut-out, boyish good looks, which make him appear extremely boring. Could Meredith really have fallen for such a man?

On my plate sit two crayfish with two slices of grapefruit, a splash of salad at the side and something—parmesan, I think—that's latticed and crusty. Nouvelle cuisine, mixing sweet and savory in minuscule quantities. Visually creative, I guess, certainly ostentatious, but no way to sate an appetite. Since I've started cooking, opinions take shape in my head of their own accord. Carol, I notice, has already scarfed hers down. Meredith and Monsieur PR continue to be exclusively interested in whatever is occurring under the table.

"Low-eek says this place is where everyone wants to eat these days," Meredith had burbled when launching the invitation. With this Frenchman, she has lost her cool almost entirely.

"Lily, can you pass the bread?" Carol asks.

"Sure." I stretch, pluck the basket from behind PR man's wine glass.

"So tell me," Loïc says in heavily accented English, "what you ladies think of Par-ee."

"It's good."

"Yes. It's good."

"Méré-dite tells me your course is boring." Méré-dite, who is now applying herself to the crayfish and grapefruit, smiles vaguely.

"Sometimes," says Carol. "Sometimes it's very interesting. What did you study?"

"I studied journalism in Rennes." The silly smile has gone from his face; he is speaking in French. "But journalism, especially in the provinces, does not pay well. Writing about the mayor inaugurating a new fountain gets you nowhere."

"But Low-eek, you did say we should visit Brittany." Meredith sits back in her chair, chest pushed forward.

"Every region of France has its *charme*," he says, serving us all wine.

"Every region of Europe, we hope," says Carol. "We'll be travelling during the spring break."

The waiter arrives to take the plates and silence returns to the table.

But not for long. As always, Meredith fills in the gap, this evening with a story about a taxi driver taking a circuitous route to Saint Michel. "I kept waving my Plan de Paris at him to show he couldn't take advantage of me just because I'm American."

The next course arrives. Tiny *médaillons de veau*, rounds of veal. Tender, for as long as they last. I begin to wish that I'd eaten something before I came. Still, hungry or not, I am relieved when dessert and coffee are declined. Even Meredith cannot sustain conversation through three courses with Low-eek.

"So the guy is not only cheating on his wife," Carol whispers to me as we walk down the street, in front of the lovebirds. "He's beyond boring. He won't even speak French to her. And his English is terrible."

"She says he's good in bed." I have decided this must be the basis for the attraction.

"At least she doesn't have to talk to him once the lights are off," says Carol. "And did you see that stupid look on his face at dinner? Like Meredith was jerking him off under the table?"

I laugh. Since Meredith has taken up with Monsieur PR, we are often alone, Carol and I, and I like her a lot. The other day, at the supermarket, I came close to telling her my predicament. Carol had been banned from the flat because Meredith and Loïc were "having a long lunch." When I was preparing to pay, I pulled out Madame's little leather purse.

"That's nice," Carol said. "Where'd you get it?"

"It's not mine."

Carol's eyes darted from the purse to my face.

"I mean, it's Madame's. I buy food for her sometimes."

"Oh." Carol looked more closely at my purchases. The Maison du Café coffee, the Bonne Maman fig jam, eggs and unsalted butter for the hollandaise sauce Germaine had promised to teach me how to make, plus salted butter for the morning *tartines*. "We buy that kind of jam too, with the red-checked top."

I almost said: Usually we do not. Usually we buy a more esoteric, expensive kind but the merchant ran out and Madame loves fig jam. Fig jam on one side of the *tartine*, honey on the other. I could have then continued, told Carol everything—the big, empty house, not so empty anymore.

But our turn to pay came and the moment passed. Today, as we walk ahead of Meredith and PR, I'm tempted again. Tempted to say: What Meredith's doing doesn't hold a candle to the acts of folly I've committed.

Because I know that besides Laurent, at least one other person is over there now. Yesterday I saw a burly young man open the *portail* and act very much *chez lui*. My heart is pounding all over again, just at the memory of this problem I cannot see my way out of.

"I have a feeling," says Carol, "that I won't be welcome *chez moi* right now."

I turn and see the lovebirds intertwined, practically tripping one another up. "No, you won't." This would be the moment to invite Carol to my room. We're not far from the place des Vosges.

"Wanta sit at a café with me for a while?" Carol asks. "At night, I feel stupid alone." She buries her chin in her coat.

"Good idea," I say.

Carol says to Meredith: "Lily and I are going to walk up to Les Halles for a coffee."

"Okay," says Meredith vaguely, still too busy fawning on Low-eek.

"Thank you for dinner." I speak loudly, to pierce the love cloud. "The food was delicious."

"Yes. Thank you," says Carol. Then pointedly to Meredith: "I'll be home in an hour."

"*Ciao*," says Monsieur PR.

"*Ciao*," Meredith waves as if from the deck of a departing ocean liner.

"*Ciao*," mocks Carol as we walk away. "Jesus."

Once we're settled at Au Père Tranquil, a small carafe of red wine between us, she says: "That was quite something."

"Yes, it was."

"What a sleaze." Carol shakes her head.

"He studied journalism," I say hopefully, still certain there must be something I'm missing. Carol rolls her eyes. "But I admit it did surprise me, Meredith being with a man like that."

She looks at me with a crooked smile. "Even though he marks a new low, you haven't met some of her other boyfriends."

"Like the professor?"

"Like the professor. Pompous, loud and hairy."

"But Meredith is so cool. How could she fall for men like that?"

"Who knows. She has prime specimens streaming in her wake, good guys who would do anything to go out with her." She shrugs, takes a sip of wine. "But she's only interested in creeps."

"That's crazy," I say.

"The way I see it, either she was just born with bad judgment in men or she has some kind of father complex. You've heard her. She talks about her Dad all the time. She only goes for older men," Carol pauses. "Whatever the reason, sometimes it's impossible to see things through someone else's eyes. You know what I mean?"

"*Chacun ses goûts*, I guess."

"I don't know that expression," says Carol, rummaging in her bag for the notebook and that fountain pen I helped her choose. "I'm getting quite a list. But if I don't write it down tout de suite, I won't remember. 'Each his tastes,'" she says while writing. "So, like the equivalent of 'to each his own?'" I nod. She finishes scribbling and puts pen and paper away.

"Enough on Meredith and Ciao-man. What's it like living with an old lady? You don't talk about it much."

"It's okay," I shrug. "She keeps her distance."

"She's American, you said?"

"Yes. But she speaks to me in French."

"Sounds weird."

"She's lived here for more than sixty years. Her husband was French. So is her housekeeper."

"Still sounds weird."

"I'm used to it by now, and it seems normal." I look at Carol's warm hazel eyes, just a bit darker than Jane's. "Besides the shopping, I've started doing some cooking for her. Germaine the housekeeper's daughter is ill."

"You know how to cook?"

"I'm learning. Germaine gives me lessons. It's fun."

"Since you already speak French, you might as well learn to cook while you're in Paris. It's a pretty important part of the *civilisation française*."

"I guess that's right."

"Remind me why you wanted to do this course anyway?"

"I had a child's French. And I wanted to get away."

Carol nods. After a minute, "Away from what?"

I shift uncomfortably. The cheeks must be puce by now. "England. My family." Carol nods again but is waiting for more. "I wanted to do something different. Why did you come?" A question already asked and answered, but anything to steer the conversation away from me.

Carol fiddles with the strap of her bag. "I wanted to get away too. I haven't been very happy at college. In fact, I wanted to go to England, but I didn't get into the course there. So here I am. No regrets though." She looks at her watch, readjusts the bag on her lap. We sit in silence for a few moments, sipping our wine, looking around the café. I am sorry

I asked, sorry I took a pin, however unintentionally, to Carol's chatty mood.

She looks at her watch again. "We can go now. By the time I get back, Low-eek will have scurried back to the wife and kids."

Once we've paid and are on the street, Carol says: "Thanks, Lily, for coming along with me."

"That's okay. I wouldn't have wanted to sit in a café by myself either."

Carol cocks her head. "Hey, where's Thibaud these days? I haven't seen him in weeks."

"Who knows," I shrug. "See you on Monday?"

"Yeah, see you on Monday."

***

"Let me help you, Germaine," I say, stopping at the small laundry room just off the kitchen. I lower the rack and begin folding the dry clothes to make room for the new load.

"I can manage," she says, head still at the mouth of the machine as she extracts the last items.

I keep folding. Madame's nightdress, the shirts she wears untucked over her trousers, even her saggy, old lady underpants. My fingers feel as if they are somewhere they should not be—like rifling through her pockets or desk drawers. "I could do more work around the house, if it would help," I say.

Germaine straightens, brushes back the wisps of hair that have fallen in her face. "I find it relaxing. The routine. Imposing order where I can. You know."

"How are things?"

"Oh, the same," she says, limp and heavy as the towel she is lopping over the rack.

"How do you think Madame is, after hearing about her brother?"

"She hasn't said much. She wrote a letter to the nephew that I posted. After all those years, it's hard to know."

"I still can't believe she's not from one of those wealthy New York society families," I say. "She looks like an heiress."

"She was very beautiful." Germaine snaps a tea towel, remains silent for a long moment. "Even at sixty, when I met them, she and Monsieur—what a pair."

I wait a moment, hang up the last towel.

"How did a ranch girl end up in Paris?"

"Monsieur went and found her," Germaine smiles her smile. "Well, not exactly. He went to America after the War, the first one, to recover. His brother was killed at the Somme, and his father had just died of the influenza."

"That's a lot." But not as much as you, I would like to add.

"He worked on the family ranch for a summer and that was that." She bends down, picks up the empty laundry basket and puts it on top of the machine. "We'd best get started on supper."

I follow Germaine with her uneven gait back to the kitchen. Monsieur lost half his family, Germaine everyone. Mine may be strange, but its members are still alive, despite our mother's best efforts to the contrary.

"How would you like to make a cheese soufflé?" Germaine asks, opening the fridge. "It's nowhere near as difficult as its reputation. As long as the eggs are fresh and the timing right." Germaine pulls some *gruyère* out, hands it to me. "We'll have to keep an eye on the clock this evening."

I am grating the cheese but thinking about the death and suffering of people who have lived before me in this century. How my childhood may have been peculiar, challenging even, but not tragic.

"We have to make a *roux*," Germaine says. "I'll let you try that."

"Flour and butter, right?"

"Yes, then milk. You don't want to make the sauce too thick, or it'll weigh down the eggs."

"Here's the milk," Germaine says. "Drop by drop, at first."

While I stir, I imagine the young Frenchman and the young American galloping away on horseback. Or later, during the War, meeting secretly in dark rooms to plot against the German invaders.

"Not too fast with the milk," says Germaine. "While I get Madame her drink, I want you to whisk the egg whites, *monter les oeufs en neige*. That's an important cooking skill to acquire."

She gets two bowls, cracks an egg on the edge of one, then lets the white fall in, while holding the yolk in the half shell. She shifts the yolk from one broken half to the other, until all the white has fallen out, then she lets the yolk slip into the second bowl. "Now you try," she says, handing me an egg. "Don't hit it too hard on the edge of the bowl, or the yolk will break and fall in the white and you'll have to start all over again."

It takes a minute, to tap hard enough for the shell to crack lightly and the yolk not to break, but I get faster with each egg, and there are the four whites in one bowl, the four yolks in another.

"Now," says Germaine, fixing the bowl of whites in the crook of her left arm and holding the whisk in her right. "It's simple. You just keep going round and round at a good pace. Don't stop until they form snowy peaks." She hands the equipment over. "Add a pinch of salt. That helps firm them up."

I look down at the snotty gunk in the bowl, sure that I will never be able to make it look like snow, thus ruining dinner, but as instructed I throw in some salt and begin going round and round. Germaine fixes Madame's aperitif, then leaves. The gunk gets a little foamy. On I whisk. When I pause to readjust my hold on the bowl, I'm sure I hear a noise across the courtyard. Fear creeps up the back of my neck. Though I know it's a question of time until the intruders are discovered by Germaine and Madame, I can usually force that knowledge to the back of my head. This evening I resume beating the egg whites and let the rhythmic sound of the metal whisk against the glass bowl block out any further reminders of their presence. As the foam thickens and lightens, I beat harder. By the time Germaine returns, it's white as snow.

"Perfect," she says, not looking at all surprised that I have succeeded. She takes the whisk from my hand, curls a bit of the white with it. "Firm as a snowy peak. That's how you know you're done." I feel like I've performed a miracle.

"Now," says Germaine. "Gently fold it into the yolks, the *roux* and the cheese."

"Very good," says Madame, after her first bite of the golden, fluffy soufflé that has emerged from the oven.

"She's got the knack." Germaine looks at me proudly.

"Hmm." She slowly takes another bite of the soufflé. "Maybe you should have done a cooking course instead. One of the cordon bleu things. Many Americans, I think, pay very good money for them. You get a certificate or something."

"Germaine's a good teacher," I answer. Germaine appears not to have heard. "Right, Germaine?"

She takes a breath, comes out of her slump like an inner-tube being re-inflated. "I don't know." She rises to collect the plates with a gravitas worthy of the last supper. "I really don't."

****

Spring

"Who's Bruno?"

"The friend of Jean-Marc's cousin Laurent," says Thibaud. "The guy who is leading the crusade to 'put unoccupied space to good use.' He's the one bringing them in."

"How many?" My voice is high with panic. Though I have not wanted to admit it to myself, it's been obvious that more people have come. When I dare look out my window, I can see lights at night across the courtyard. I've seen people who look like the trespassing type when I buy coffee or eggs at the Félix Potin. Meaning that if I weren't so busy with the course work, shopping and cooking, I would have eaten myself alive with worry by now. Meaning if Madame weren't blind and Germaine so pre-occupied by Flora, I would already have lost my job.

"About ten," he mumbles. Alarm bells scream in my head. I shouldn't have asked. Putting a number to a problem always makes it more real. In this case more intractable.

"Come with me. Help me reason with Bruno."

"I don't see how I can have any effect." I look around at the square. There are no children yet in the playground. The air has a milky haze, sun burning through fog. It's got a March feel, a hint of spring floating on a chill. Birds are chirping.

"Two is always better than one," he says.

"Is it? I'm not sure."

"Please."

It feels like we're on the way to the gallows. When we reach the *portail*, Thibaud pushes open the door. "Not locked?" He shakes his head. The unlocked door seems like the final link to law and order completely broken, but I know that's ridiculous. The link was lost long before the lock was.

On the landing, we pass a tousled person scratching his head and yawning. A few steps farther and some other groggy souls are shuffling here and there, in and out of doors. Thibaud and I, with overcoats and alert minds, look completely out of place. Jean-Marc and Cécile's door is closed.

"Have you seen Bruno?" Thibaud asks someone.

The slouched figure with mouse brown hair sticking out in all directions, a sagging, torn jersey and mismatching socks, looks at Thibaud as if over a great distance of time and space.

"I'm looking for Bruno," Thibaud repeats.

"I don't know." The words seem to be a general statement, one that might apply to any number of subjects.

Thibaud looks at me and shakes his head. I realize that I am standing in a compact hunch, hands shoved in my pockets, head tucked into my shoulders. I try to relax my posture. "Now what do we do?" I ask just as a young woman and man appear. They are groomed, dressed for the outdoors and sober.

"We're looking for Bruno," Thibaud repeats.

"I don't think he's here," replies the woman. "He comes and goes."

"I believe we have you to thank," the young man says to me.

"You have no idea how hard we've looked for a place to live," adds the young woman.

Thibaud smiles self-righteously at me.

"Anyway, we're off to the library," the young woman says. "But really. Thanks a lot."

We climb the stairs to Thibaud's attic room.

"See?" Thibaud says. "They're not all drugged parasites."

"That doesn't change the fact that none of them—of you—should be here."

"I know, I know," he says. "And everything might have been okay, if Bruno hadn't appeared on the scene."

"What's he like, this Bruno person?"

Thibaud's mouth and eyes narrow. "Bruno Landereaux is the Parisian I'm always telling you about. His father is a former *haut fonctionnaire*, an over-educated civil servant, now the head of an insurance company. His aunts and uncles and cousins are lawyers, book editors and journalists. Long-standing members of the *haute-bourgeoisie* and intelligentsia. You see their names all over the media." Thibaud's eyes narrow even further, his voice drips with scorn: "*Très gauche caviar.*"

Here I am again, now months into the course, understanding the words but lost when it comes to what *very left caviar* might mean. "What on earth is that?"

"Someone like Bruno who is a member of the Socialist Party but lives in a large Left Bank apartment with hired help—often undeclared immigrants—to make his bed, do his laundry and iron his shirts. In their cavernous *salons*, these 'leftists' discuss the plight of the downtrodden working classes over champagne and caviar." He pauses, looks down at his long hands that I still can't imagine doing a day of farm work, that look more like what you'd find at one of the evenings he's just described. "What really gets me is that I'm sure this whole exercise, this 'unoccupied real estate' business," he mimics, "is just a way for Bruno to draw attention to Bruno, to further plans for his own future. If you'd like to know why I want a Fulbright, look no further than Bruno Landereaux." His face drops its sour twist, lights up. "I had my interview, by the way."

"And?" What a relief to have his eyebrows calm down.

"I think it went okay. The director is from Toulouse. He understands the Paris problem, shall we say. I wasn't great on the English part. I shouldn't have stopped spending time with Meredith and Carol. That was an error."

"Instead of wasting your time with me?"

"No," he smiles. "Without you I'd be lost."

***

Monday, 21 March 1983

Something's going on in the empty part of the house. Like a plumbing problem, you hear a noise in the walls, and despite hoping it's just air in the pipes, the sound comes back, gets louder, until you know for certain there's a leak.

Could they be people off the street? It happens, I heard a reportage about it on the radio. I suppose it could be the girl who discovered the wing and invited friends, but it's hard to believe she'd have the nerve to do that. Other questions remain. Are they just having parties, or have they moved in? Could it be the American friends? She's mentioned their ample parental funding, so why would they need those dusty, dilapidated rooms? Just for the fun and recklessness of it? In any case, I'm sure the voices were French.

But the real question is what do I do about it?

Choices:

1. talk to the girl
2. call the police
3. tell Octave and let him handle it
4. ask Germaine for advice
5. laissez-faire

Of course I should talk to the girl, find out what she knows. But that would require direct communication, and our interaction is more that of two wary animals. My fault, undoubtedly, but there we have it. As for option number two, I do not trust the French police. Not since the War. Going to them would whiff acridly of denunciation. Telling Octave—well, that's paramount to going straight to the police myself.

As for consulting Germaine, she has too much else to worry about already—the fact that she hasn't appeared to notice proving the point. Unless she's trying to protect me as I am trying to protect her.

Anyway, that leaves option number five, laissez-faire, the alluring route of inertia. The do-nothings win.

For the moment. Something will happen. It always does.

***

Tonight, I am going back to the beginning, to Germaine's first lesson: veal with creamy mushroom sauce and sautéed leeks. What decided me were the slender green and white *poireaux* lined up pertly at the market. Irresistible. Instead of the white wine Germaine puts in the sauce, though, I'm trying a splash of Madame's Noilly Prat vermouth. I find that its fuller, bittersweet taste gives the sauce more gravitas.

The cooking has distracted my thoughts away from what has otherwise been hammering my head all day. How could I have been so weak, falling into Thibaud's unreliable arms again? I am unable to resist attention from another human being. It's sick, the need to feel wanted so badly. I'm a passive shambles, that's what I am, letting life pull me along like a dog on a lead. Rather than a decisive step forward, this year of *civilisation française* is no more than a delaying tactic on the road to adulthood.

Tapping the mustard spoon on the side of the saucepan, I remind myself that there's another theory about me and Paris. That it's here I've finally started living. I have a social and a sort of sex life, a job. I am having the fun now that most people seem to have at university. Just today, after a lecture on the subtle differences in enunciation between *–an* and *–on*, I went to lunch with Meredith and Carol at the Gaulois. Trying to get Meredith to hear and repeat the differences in the vowel-consonant combinations had the three of us bent over with laughter. No matter how many ways she rounded or puckered those sensuous lips, she couldn't get it. "To me they sound *exactly* the same," she said, wiping her eyes.

I light the gas for the veal cutlets. The problem next door could ruin it all. The butter spits when I lay the two slabs of meat in the frying pan and I give the handle a shake, turn down the gas to brown the outside, leave the inside pink. Letting Thibaud in was an act of *flagrant délit*. How could I not have at least considered where it might lead? I tip the sauce over the meat.

"That smells good," says Madame, putting her glass down on the table. I put the food on serving plates, pour some wine. "Can I serve you?"

"No need." Madame approaches her failing eyes to the food. She takes a small spoon of leeks, saws off the end of an escalope. Her knobby hand takes a piece of bread. When she chews, the wrinkles around her mouth contract as they do when she's displeased. "Delicious."

"Thank you." After a long pause, Madame asks:

"I suppose you go to the *Marché aux Enfants Rouges*?"

"Same as Germaine, yes."

"Strange name, isn't it. It comes from the orphans at the nearby hospital, *l'hôpital des enfants-rouges*. They had to wear red capes because red was associated with charity. Long ago, of course."

The image reminds me of the film *Don't Look Now*, where a couple's child drowns and the parents, bereaved to the edge of madness, chase a small, red-caped figure that may just be a figment of their grief-stricken minds through the dark, labyrinthine streets of Venice. They think it might be their daughter. In the end it's a dwarf with a hag's face. The film gave me nightmares for weeks.

"Most places in Paris seem to have some kind of story like that behind their names," I say.

"Most European cities, I think." Madame wipes her mouth with the napkin. "London too, no?"

"Yes, I guess. I don't know it that well."

Madame brings her knife and fork together over a puddle of sauce. She drains her wine glass and stands up.

"Can I get you anything else?"

Madame shakes her head. "No. Nothing." She turns to the door, pauses. "Good night. And thank you. The supper was excellent."

I serve myself the rest of the escalope and sauce, cut myself another piece of bread. Positive parting words but otherwise our dialogue was worthy of an Owens family non-exchange. Why did she tell me about *les enfants rouges*? Now that scary film will not leave my mind alone. I help myself to a bit more wine too. The parents were in a way like our parents, crazed and in search of something lost. In our case it wasn't us, the children they were looking for but my mother's pre-oven self. Even if along the way, Maude, Jane and I were as good as lost at Madame Flaviche's.

I stand up. Paris is a city for fun, for letting go, and I must un-button. After cleaning up the dinner, I head straight downstairs, before my safe-haven room can change my mind. I march out and around, enter through the unlocked *portail*. Usually walking thorough this door makes me feel criminal. Not tonight. Tonight I will be bold and uncaring about authority, even if the place does stink of smoke and unwashed clothes. I will ignore the electrical wires dangling around my head. As I climb the stairs, I focus on the library-goers. Not everyone is borderline delinquent. Laurent is as bourgeois as I am. Jean-Marc and Cécile's door is open. It's just two of them and Thibaud.

"Hey, Lily," says Thibaud.

I step boldly over the threshold. He hands me a bottle of wine. I take a swig, pass on the bottle to Cécile. When I hold the hit from the joint going around, it is an effort to feel this is fun. But I stomp on my ill-ease, and soon the cannabis takes over and frees me. Jean-Marc I still find a bit creepy, but Cécile's okay. Thibaud takes my hand and leads me back to his bed. He is okay too. Just go with the flow, I tell myself.

I wake to Thibaud shaking my shoulder.

"Hey. It's ten o'clock."

"It's what?" My head is foggy.

"You've overslept. The old lady's breakfast."

"Oh my God."

What's my excuse, I wonder, raising an arm into a shirt-sleeve. What if Madame has wandered out in search of help, like that day I found her stock still under the arcades? What if she's set another toaster on fire? I button my jeans, slip on my shoes and tear down the stairs, run into the street and around the corner and back in the building through the legal entrance. When I open the front door of the flat, it smells of burnt toast and I murmur another Oh my God while rushing through the living and dining rooms, down the corridor. But I stop short outside Madame's sitting room. The radio is on. I slide quietly towards the kitchen, where the counter and table are littered with the detritus of breakfast, but there are no signs of fire.

Face up or run away, that is the question. The latter is an option I have begun to consider. Just pack my bag and leave, return to England. Madame won't die. Someone else can deal with the squatters.

What would Jane do? I feel a pang, sharp as a stitch, for her calm advice. For the days when I could lean until I toppled, and my sister would catch me. What would Jane say? She would sigh, cock her sensible head, look at me with her big hazel eyes and say: we got ourselves into this mess. I guess we have to get ourselves out of it.

"*Entrez*," Madame replies to my knock.

"I'm sorry. I overslept."

"As you can see," She points to the coffee cup on her desk, "I managed." The notebook and pen lie in front of her; the radio to the left emits vaguely dissonant music.

It's while I'm screwing the tops back on the honey and jam jars and looking at the crumbs on the table that the tears well up. What a stupid idea, to think that I could be a wild child, even for one night, even in Paris.

***

Thursday, 24 March 1983

The girl, flustered and upset, has just made an appearance. I was not nice to her—or more accurately, was even more hostile than usual, which I regret. Everyone can make a mistake. Young people oversleep. My reaction was a cover-up anyway, a tactic to hide how frightened I felt when she didn't appear as usual. When all I could hear above my head was empty silence. I waited and waited and eventually went into the kitchen, set about making my own breakfast. But oh, how frightening even your own house can be. How quickly your ability to cope alone can vanish. I felt as I did that day when I walked out of the building, teetering, off balance, disoriented.

As for whatever is happening across the way, I continue to hear the odd noise, to wonder what I should do about it. In my head, it pulls on my guilt strings, that I did not rent out all that space in this crowded city. In mes tripes, my gut, however, their presence sets me on edge. But from there to doing something about it—I can't summon the energy, the resolve.

My stash of Seresta, my escape route from this intolerable business of living, grows.

***

Saturday night I'm on my way back to the place des Vosges with Thibaud, who joined me for an evening at Meredith and Carol's, along with some others. Ronnie and Luisa. Gary, too, and the French girlfriend he's somehow managed to find. The gathering, besides being legal, was fun in a wholesome way that the squat scene is not. It reminded me of last autumn, when everything felt fresh and new and hopeful. Thibaud is happy too—on the way back we have been talking about the good old days when it was just us—and I have granted his umpteenth request to see my room. We step inside the *portail* and hear music. I can't move, can't speak. Thibaud sighs. "So much for the chief's orders."

"What do you mean?"

"Bruno ordered them to be quiet, saying that the longer the space is occupied before legal action is initiated, the harder it will be for the authorities to get them out. But I've noticed that the longer they are here, the more they feel *chez eux*. And the more noise they make."

"We have to do something."

And out we go, around to the side entrance. I keep my mind on Jane and Meredith, neither of whom would have any trouble facing down a pack of freeloaders. As soon as we push open the *porte-piétonne* the music goes down. I am tempted to leave, return to my bed, pull the duvet around my shoulders, tuck my neck into the pillow, but someone shouts *Merde!* and I keep going up the stairs.

The gathering has begun to break up by the time we walk into Jean-Marc and Cécile's room. With them are cat-shoed cousin Laurent and the elusive Bruno, the person I saw going in the door not long after Laurent moved in. He looks at me as if he's been waiting for this moment all his life. The cheeks go hot and deep pink. This man could make you feel naked no matter how many layers of clothing you were wearing.

"Sorry about the music," he says with a disarming smile, both apologetic and engaging. "I just got here myself. It won't happen again."

I want to reply: now that the whole *quartier* knows you're here? But I say: "I hope not." Instead of sounding like Jane or Meredith, I come across as purse-lipped Madame Flaviche.

"I'm really happy to finally meet you," Bruno says, continuing to hold me in his gaze, as if no one else were in the room. "After hearing so much about you." Although I do not see how this could be true, he looks entirely genuine, unflinchingly honest. "Let's sit down a minute," he says, and everyone obeys, me included. A joint is passed, but Bruno doesn't partake. He has a broad face with big eyes and strong eyebrows, a full, movable mouth and a honker of a nose. Not handsome but magnetic. A contagious laugh. A presence commanding attendance. He in fact runs the whole show, hogging the scene one minute, then handing it over to someone else and making the gesture seem an act of grace. He does not ask me any questions—like he senses how uncomfortable I am in the spotlight—but at the same time it's as if he's putting on this whole show for my benefit. I try not to be flattered but with minimal success. He feels like a force beyond my control.

When the joint that I too have resisted is finished, Bruno stretches and says: "Time for me to get some sleep." The group immediately decomposes into isolated particles. Even Jean-Marc and Cécile, usually so fused, seem cut off from one another. And I say to Thibaud: "I can't risk oversleeping again."

***

Sunday, 27 March 1983

E ven Germaine must have heard the music last night. The volume went up until someone—the girl?—forced it down, but up it crept again, then down it went again. It left me feeling an odd mix of indignant, frightened and entertained, the last not difficult to achieve, I admit, these empty days.

But I must also ask how people living in my house, people I don't know and presumably would not particularly care to know, could give me any enjoyment whatsoever? Maybe because a house needs people the way people need a house, that's what Michel used to say. When François moved here, the wing had several families living in it. The building was fully occupied and despite their being dirt poor, there was a sense then that things were as they should be.

About the time François had his *accident* the last of the families moved out. For the last decade—since everyone else has been gone—it's often seemed that the ghosts moved back into this old house and Germaine and I are the intruders.

The girl brought my breakfast this morning, as usual. I believe she lingered slightly, either waiting for me to say something, or trying to pluck up the courage to speak herself.

Later: Germaine arrived right then, as I was writing. Did you hear, she whispered, as if we were under siege.

How could I not? I answered. What do you think?

I don't know. I really don't. Roger says rents are rising, and students can no longer afford them. Maybe they're students.

I suppose it's the girl who let them in.

Lily? Germaine said. How could that be?

People might have sniffed out the space on their own, broken the lock and moved in. But the girl's acting strangely.

She must have heard them too. Every day they are louder.

Believe me, I answered, suddenly certain, she's behind it.

Maybe it's better that way. At least the people are not total strangers.

Dear Germaine seeing good in people while possessing such crippling proof to the contrary.

I'll speak to her, Germaine said, paused. Wouldn't it be better to keep the police out of it, if we can?

Yes, it would, I say. Germaine's parents were taken away by the French police, and I can still hear boots coming up the stairs that summer morning. François was at work; Henri in those days was almost never home and my mother-in-law was out for her daily shuffle with Annie the housekeeper. Solange was gone too. The building shook as they stomped, and my heart and stomach crashed together; my vision tingled. I thought they were coming for my husband or my son or me the American. But no, they stomped right past our door, up one more flight of stairs to the Epsteins, who lived right above us. The cultivated, clever Epsteins who hadn't heeded the signals. Their grown children had already left, one to England, one to America, and François had even warned them: These Germans have a grudge to bear. Get out. Sergeï had listened, nodded gravely, then said: But one can't pass one's days in fear.

Oh yes one can and sometimes yes one should. In the summer of 1942, for example, when you are a Russian Jew.

Soon they were traipsing down the stairs. I had my ear to the door and wondered why Sergeï wasn't protesting in German, one of his multiple languages, until a French policeman told him to shut up. A van was waiting in the street. When I looked down, there was his bald head and impeccably dressed person, a suitcase in either hand. Elena was a heavy woman and had trouble getting into the van and the policeman shoved her brusquely. Sergeï began haranguing them again and they pushed him roughly too. The van started up. Black exhaust belched out the muffler, as if they were disappearing in a puff of smoke, and indeed they were never seen again.

We all said we didn't know anything beyond the fact that Jews were forced to wear yellow stars, were humiliated and deprived of their rights as citizens. That they were being arrested and taken somewhere for no reason. On the British radio we heard of concentration camps, even death. But there were so many rumors flying around during the War. Exaggerations and false information worked like sparks to dry leaves. You had to resist believing everything you heard. It was impossible, living in that time of deep distrust and constant threat, to know what was true and what was invented—and who, really, can imagine the unimaginable.

I don't think I was the only one to have constructed a metal door between my mind and the world, between consciousness and conscience. It was a door that shut out any inconvenient information beyond the hard facts of our daily lives.

I say this as explanation rather than excuse. We knew enough to do more than we did. *Point final.*

***

I sit at the kitchen table, staring at the clock on the wall. The second hand judders forward like toiling feet moving under a heavy weight. Tick. Ugh. Tock. Ugh. Will this wait ever be over?

"I'm sorry." Germaine rushes through the door, still in her coat. "I couldn't get away."

She is apologizing to me? I don't answer, am not sure words will ever come out of my mouth again.

"Well." She removes her coat, hangs it on top of her apron. "I don't need to tell you why we're here."

After an awkward moment of silence, I blurt out: "I had no idea it would lead to this. I let in one friend who didn't have a place to live. It was just supposed to tide him over until he could find new accommodation. He let two of his friends in. Then it spun out of control."

"But Lily." The sound of my name makes me want to cover my ears in shame. "How did you get over there in the first place?"

"The door across from the kitchen in the service stairs. There's that cup with all those keys in it. I was curious."

Germaine nods and sighs, laces together her short fingers. "How many?"

"About ten."

"Ooh. That's a lot," she frowns. "What kind of people are they?" she asks more hopefully, as if she has every expectation that I will reel off a list of titled guests at a large house party.

"Mostly students." I think of dread-locked Jean-Marc and Cécile, itinerant workers, formerly of a Canary Island commune. Some of their unkempt comrades. "A mix."

Germaine's right hand turns the wedding band on the left, round and round on her finger. "We don't know what to do," she finally says. "We do not like the police." She pauses, sighs. "We understand it's difficult." She shakes her head. "But they can't stay."

Having expected everything but this feathery reprimand, I am too astonished to reply. I realize that part of me in fact wished to be fired, forcibly removed from the situation. But Germaine is speaking as if it's our collective problem. "I've told them that," I finally say. "To absolutely no avail."

"You have to try again," Germaine says standing. "See if you can't at least get a date. A date in the near future, the very near future, by which they'll promise to be out." She looks at the wall clock. "Now let's turn to the more agreeable task of making supper. I noticed there are lots of vegetables. We'll make soup."

What a relief it is to be cooking. Washing, peeling, chopping. The burbling of the stew pot and the steamy smell of the vegetables twined together. Here it smells nothing like the acrid stuff Madame Flaviche used to serve us. Madame comes in for her evening drink. I am chopping some spinach to throw in and do not look up from that task until she has left the kitchen.

When the soup is ready, I am about to excuse myself, but Germaine is setting a place for me. The three of us sit down. There is much silent blowing on spoons. I wish I had held firm and left. It seems to me at this moment that I never, ever make the right decision about anything. From letting Thibaud into the house to taking this strange job to coming to France in the first place.

Germaine, remembering she'd promised to phone Flora at nine, stands up and leaves in a rush. Alone with Madame, I am melting from shame.

"We have some visitors," she says after a couple of minutes, dabbing the corners of her mouth with her napkin.

"Yes."

"Germaine has spoken to you."

"Yes."

"Well."

Eventually: "I did not mean for this to happen. I'm sorry." Madame's silence is unbearable. I soldier on. "I was trying to help a friend."

Altruism seems a reasonable excuse, but this too is greeted with silence.

I get up and clear the plates, begin washing them in the sink, but she keeps sitting there. When I turn off the water, the chair scrapes the floor, and I hear: "We all make mistakes." By the time I turn around, Madame Quinon has gone.

***

Monday, 28 March 1983

Just yesterday I was regretting my imperfect humanity during the War. Ditto in earlier entries, vis-à-vis my mother. Yet here I am, at it again. I was rude to the girl. No, worse than rude. I was unkind. She's got herself—and all right us too—in a mess but there were no ill intentions. What's wrong with trying to help a friend? The boyfriend, I'd guess. My little parting comment of We all make mistakes did little to make amends. The scale and circumstances of each situation may differ, but each comes back to a flawed sense of compassion.

With luck, I don't have much time left on this earth. In the meanwhile, I must be kinder to—and a good start is using her name—Lily.

***

Thibaud is waiting for me outside the Sorbonne, and my heart sinks. He reminds me of what I want to forget, at least ignore. And I assume that if he's made the effort to remember what time I finish and come to meet me, he has something particular to say, something I probably don't want to hear.

He starts by telling me his latest woes, this time financial. He's going to have to get a job, he says. Even with no rent to pay, his scholarship money, the last installment of which arrived a couple of weeks ago, is not covering his costs.

"Maybe you shouldn't have bought the new shoes," I point to his feet. The brown suede with crepe soles look a lot like Laurent's but less finely cut.

"My old ones had holes in the soles," he mutters, looking down. "Yesterday the police came."

"The police?" I half shout.

"I was coming out of the Félix Potin and there they were. And who should appear but Bruno. 'It's illegal.' He said to them, gloating. 'You cannot force us out. We are not leaving.'"

"What do you mean, it's illegal? Aren't they the ones breaking the law?"

"Yes…and no. If the people have been occupying the property for more than forty-eight hours, the police can't throw them out. They need a court order. Do you think the old lady called them?"

"No." A phrase from my law studies floats to the surface: possession is nine-tenths of the law. Phrases like Adverse Possession, Squatters Rights and Paper Owner rise in my memory. But this seems ridiculous.

"The French legal system is very indulgent with people who can't afford a roof over their heads. It's a counterweight to other laws that are very favorable to proprietors. A lot of landlords are real *crapules*."

"Madame is no scoundrel," I say. "What happened after Bruno said you weren't leaving?"

"I went to the Beaubourg."

"And did they enter, the police?"

"No, they know the law as well as Bruno does," he says. "When I came back, everyone was congregated in the kitchen-bathroom. Bruno, of course, was holding forth: 'It's time to go public. Ordinary citizens will be sympathetic to our plight. They'll agree it's scandalous for all this space, owned by a rich old lady—an American no less—to stay empty. I have a friend, a television journalist, who would be interested in just this kind of story.'"

"Oh, great," I say. "First the police, now the press."

"Listening to Bruno made me wonder if *he* wasn't the one who called the police. Just for the attention." He shakes his head. "It's fine for people like him to provoke the authorities. He can go home to several hundred square meters, a clean bed and a full fridge." His eyebrows have gone nuclear again. "First he tells them all to be quiet, so we can 'establish residency'. Now it's make lots of noise, draw as much attention as possible. What right does he have to command homeless people? And how can they believe in him, have faith? It makes no sense." He shakes his dark head. "Yet there they were, hanging on his every word, under his spell."

"A television journalist is the kiss of death," I mutter, not wanting to address the question of Bruno's hold over people. I have rerun that evening where I felt his powers of seduction, his hold over the group, and yes, over me.

"I can see my mother and father and brother sitting down to supper, television news in the background," moans Thibaud. "My brother Jean-Marie will spot me being chucked into the street. Hey, he'll say—

c'est l'intellectuel—what's he doing there? My father will shake his head, lower it even closer to his plate, say nothing. My mother will put a hand to her mouth, possibly cry."

"I have to buy a baguette for supper," I say in front of the boulangerie.

He looks like a grave-digger as we part ways.

It just gets worse and worse, I think, climbing the main stairs with the baguette. I see no way out, if even the law won't help.

There is a letter for me on the kitchen table. It's from Maude. I don't remember ever receiving a missive from my sister, and I barely recognize the loopy handwriting. My heart picks up the pace—how could this be good news? I am out of breath by the time I've taken the back stairs two by two to my room.

Calm down, I tell myself. Make a cup of tea. I put the water to boil. Besides the whooshing kettle all is silent, as if nothing has changed since late September, when I first looked over the broken vases and mossy paving stones. Except that it feels like another life.

The kettle goes quiet. I pour the water over the teabag. "*C'est pas vrai !*" I hear, followed by laughter. Maybe Maude's letter is calling me home to help with an urgent problem. Maybe I will be compelled by a family emergency to leave this mess. I tear open the envelope.

Dear Sister,

The parents will surely tell you in their bi-weekly blah-blah—hey, finally some real news besides 'the weather was mild today'—but I wanted you to hear it from me first.

I'm leaving.

Yeah, this yoga thing has changed my life, and I've decided it's time to cut the cord. My teacher knows a place in Norfolk where I can live and paint for almost nothing since it's a working farm as well, and I'm moving there on the 1st of April.

Nothing changes here, surprise, surprise. The mother is overcome with bouts of who knows what; the father comes and goes from his practice. Joanna the Australian won't shut up about the Down Under. I can't even sketch much less paint, the vibes being as they are here, but I believe new inspiration will come with my new life. It will be a real spring this year.

Whenever you're back in this country, you'll come visit me, right?

Love, Your Sister

On the one hand, I am happy for Maude. On the other, I am thrown off balance at the thought of the house without her. No Hoopers, no sisters—so much for a family emergency calling me back. It's more a family mutation designed to keep me right here.

***

"*Venez tout de suite.*" The edge on Madame's voice is as sharp as the knife in my hand and a slice of fear runs up my spine. I hurry almost on tiptoe, to the sitting room. As if light steps could help.

Madame is sitting like a stone in front of the television news. I freeze too, when on the screen I see Bruno, one foot in, one foot out of the side entrance to this house, speaking to the camera.

"It's scandalous. Students can no longer afford to live in this city, while huge spaces like this one remain empty. We're not leaving." He steps back inside; the door closes behind him.

The television camera returns to the news presenter, who says: "The *hôtel particulier* being occupied by students stands on the place des Vosges in Paris' Marais district and is owned by a wealthy American widow. Reportage by Anne Sylvestre."

Afraid I might topple over, I grab the back of the chair in front of me. A short history of the house is given, some illustrious French names that I don't recognize are cited as former owners or tenants, then:

"The property was bought by François Quinon in 1960. He restored the front section of the *hôtel* for his own private apartments, while the back was left to languish. It is this large, neglected, unused part of the house that the homeless students are occupying.

"During the War Quinon sheltered British agents and used office printing machines in the soap company he owned to disseminate information to the Résistance network. In the late fifties he bought the place des Vosges property and campaigned for the Loi Malraux that sought to protect derelict but historically important areas such as the Marais from demolition. In 1963, a year after the law was passed, he suffered a serious accident, after which he was an invalid until his death in 1967. The house was left to his wife, American-born Amelia Quinon, who continues to reside, alone, in the spacious front apartments."

During this *récit* the camera has been showing photos of the man I recognize from the pictures in the spare room as Madame's husband. He is always in a suit, with other suited men—typical period photos— but when the journalist mentions Madame, a photo of the two of them,

Monsieur and Madame, appears. They are dressed in evening clothes, he in a dinner jacket and she in a sleeveless gown. And she's smiling, leaning into her husband's side. They are the most gorgeous, glamorous couple I have ever seen. Just like Germaine said.

"Tell me. Tell me what they're showing."

I describe the photos, the shots of the house, while Madame futilely strains her eyes at the screen.

"How did they get all this information?"

"I don't know." I am obviously suspect number one. "I really don't. I promise."

"Tomorrow I want you to buy all the French papers and go through them, see what they are saying. Please."

I return to the kitchen with the tingling numbness of fear at the base of my scalp at being caught out, of angering authority, a sensation that goes all the way back to Madame Flaviche, who would punish children by making them stand on a chair in the passage to the bathroom, and everyone had to walk around on their way to brushing their teeth. Think of Meredith and Carol, I tell myself, people who have nothing to do with this madhouse. I am going to see them this evening; they will save me. I finish chopping the parsley for the potatoes, turn on the gas for the *escalope de poulet*. The butter sizzles, the chicken browns. I stir the mushroom sauce for the chicken, then make a cheese sandwich for myself. Anything but stay here.

"Please know," I repeat while putting the food on the table, "that I have nothing to do with this."

"I believe you," she says, sitting straight as a rod before her still empty plate. "But it's gone too far. I can't have my life splashed all over the television." She looks like she might cry, and this really panics me. When my mother has crying fits, she blubbers: "It's too much for me. I just don't know what to do. What am I going to do? It's too much for me." And my father comforts her, shows a soft side rarely displayed to us his daughters. It hollows me out.

"It's way beyond my control," I almost whisper.

"So it would seem," Madame sighs and begins helping herself to the parsley potatoes. She pauses, serving spoon in the air. "I do understand, I really do, that this wasn't your intention."

When I leave her sitting alone at the table, looking stunned, almost frightened from the reportage, my heart pinches painfully. That photo. The handsome couple in *tenue de soirée*, people who have it all, smiling for the camera. A dream life, and this is how it ends. It makes me want to turn back, say a kind word, but I can't. I'm too shy, too insecure to risk a cold bony shoulder.

Cheese sandwich in hand, I fly down the stairs, out the door and onto the street and come within centimeters of crashing into Bruno.

"*Salut*," he says.

His broad shoulders pin me to the spot.

"Going out for the evening?" he says.

"Yes." I stuff the cheese sandwich in my pocket.

"I was just on my way back," he looks in the direction of the side street. "Have you got a minute? Can I take you for a drink?" In the same way his body prevented escape, so his words preclude choice.

"I'm on my way to see friends," I say feebly. Then the thought crosses my mind that maybe, just maybe, this is a chance to move him. "But I can spare a few minutes."

"Good," he smiles, like my Yes makes him the luckiest guy on earth.

We walk under the dark arcade and do not meet a soul. The café on the corner is almost empty. Bruno points to a table at the back.

"What would you like? Coffee? Glass of wine?"

"I don't know. A glass of red wine, I guess."

"*Un verre de rouge et un café*," he says and turns his attention fully on me, does that undressing thing with his eyes. "What about you? I hear that you are in Paris taking a course in *la civilisation française*. That you're American but grew up in England with a French nanny."

"Something like that."

"It sounds exotic, your life." He looks at me with what appears to be real envy, then shakes his head. "I can't imagine being anything but a member of a boring French family, locked within these hexagonal French walls." He puts his hands up, miming a box.

"Why did you do that?"

"Do what?"

"You know what I mean. Advertise on television." His eyes dart about my face, reassessing. I hold his gaze to mask my own surprise at the bold words that would have struggled to come out of my mouth in English.

"Not advertise. Inform. About unfair housing practices." He pulls out a pouch of tobacco and some papers and begins rolling a cigarette.

"What's wrong with letting private property stay private?"

"Come on," he says, tearing off a piece of métro ticket and rolling it into a filter for the rolled cigarette. "One old lady sits on more than a thousand empty square meters while thousands of people can't afford housing of any kind. It's not right."

He lights his cigarette. The wine and coffee arrive, and I regret my order. Alcohol is for weak-willed losers; caffeine for the strong and disciplined.

"But squatting Madame Quinon's house is against the law." I take a sip of wine, try to look defiant.

"The law is not always fair." He exhales a thick stream of smoke. "Inequality, the way the wealthy take advantage of the rest of the world, is unfair. Everyone should be able to afford a roof over their heads."

"But you're taking advantage of a helpless old lady."

"This has nothing to do with individuals. It's a matter of principle."

"Behind the principle is a human being. The legal owner. She has done nothing illicit, however much you want to criticise the deeper morality of it." In French, I can almost believe I studied the law.

"It is important, sometimes, to stand up for what is right." He flicks ash into the ashtray on the table, inhales again. His outrage looks completely genuine. "Regardless of *legality*."

I can, on some level, see what he means. That it's not fair for one person to be sitting on all that empty space in an expensive city, but: "What you're doing won't fundamentally change anything. The property is not going to be handed over to you. Someday they'll manage to get you out."

"Someday, yes, but it will take a long time. It's very hard in this country to remove tenants."

"Tenants?"

"People occupying property." Thibaud's words and the nine-tenths principle run depressingly through my mind again. "In the meantime, citizens without resources have a roof over their head."

"Not a problem for you, from what I understand."

"I am fortunate, but that doesn't mean I can't try and help others who are less so." He is rolling another cigarette, tearing off another strip of métro ticket.

I sip my wine. I hate contention, and I'm hardly winning him over.

"I did not invite you here," he smiles, leans toward me, puts a hand on my arm, "to argue. I wanted to thank you. Find out a bit more about you. It's not every day an American crosses my path."

I nod, vaguely, feel tired just at the thought of having to explain any of part of my uncomfortable life, so I ask: "I'm really not very interesting. What about you? Where's your family from?"

"Paris."

"I thought no one was really from Paris."

"You are learning the nuances of *la civilisation française*," he smiles, as if I've just said the most astute thing he's ever heard. "We *Parisiens* do cling to our provincial roots while scorning anyone who actually grew up beyond the city limits. My father's family comes from Normandy and my mother's from the Périgord. Which is an inauspicious pairing, according to my Norman grandmother, who says the north and the south are not compatible in any way, even physically—my father's side is all fair skin and light eyes and my mother's, well, like me. The Normans, of course, are also the reliable, hard-working types, while the southerners are lazy and hot-headed." He takes one last drag of the cigarette that he's smoked right down to his fingers, adds this butt to the other. "Though I like to think it's a coincidence, the members of our family tend to illustrate her point."

"It's hard for me to imagine you're lazy."

"I could lie around all day." His grin goes right through me. "You are very good at directing the conversation away from yourself."

I smile back—his is contagious—and he makes it seem a strength, rather than a weakness, my proficiency at dodging. A proficiency that most people don't even notice. My wine is finished. I look at my watch. I'm late for Meredith and Carol. "I really have to go. I'm late now. For my friends."

"Okay," he says, reaching for his wallet in his back pocket. "But next time I won't let you off the hook. It'll be all about you."

I begin fishing in my bag. Bruno stops me, lays a hand on my shoulder. "Absolutely not. This was my invitation."

The paw remains, squeezing me with a surprisingly delicate touch.

Outside the café, Bruno continues to look hard at me, like he's trying to see what's inside or behind my eyes. Then he leans forward, kisses me on both cheeks. His are rough, as if he has to shave every hour and still the stubble will not be tamed.

"*A bientôt*," he waves. I watch as he walks along the arcade. The straight back, the digging heels—every step radiates purpose, self-confidence, control—it's odd, adds to my confusion—his walk reminds me of my father's, on his way to the train station in the morning.

I turn quickly, in the direction of Saint Michel and my friends, wondering what, if anything, has just happened.

***

Friday, 1 April 1983

Humiliation. Complete, irredeemable humiliation: my life splashed across the television screen. Typical French, they didn't even get my name right. Amelia Quinon. But they got the basic story. A whole life in one paragraph. And what if they start digging deeper?

Well, what if? My husband was a hero; I was the obliging wife in the background, no Lucie Aubrac but no Florence Gould either. I kept a low profile. Meanwhile my husband used his soap business as a front for a vigorous back-room Résistance. It is impossible for anyone to know, now that he's dead, that he didn't approve of me and my War or for anyone to know what was festering under the glittering surface between us, the beautiful couple. So why does this distress me so?

Because it reminds me of all the things I can barely write about here, or even evoke in the privacy of my own head. It's only a question of time until they dig up Henri and that will be the last straw. Just the thought of it made me put down my pen, put my hands over my face, struggle to breathe.

I recognized the photo they used, just from the girl's description. It was a gala dinner not long before the War. An evening at the opera. I remember the photo because it got into the society pages of *Le Figaro*. François scoffed; I felt quite tickled. A ranch girl in a Paris newspaper. But that doesn't mean I want it dredged out of the archives now. Now I want my life, every damn shred of it, locked away in a dark file.

***

I wrap my blue scarf around my torso like an evening gown and look at my smooth, bare shoulders in the mirror, the protruding collar bones. That photo of Madame Quinon was so lovely. It is odd, very odd, to see a person one way one minute—good-looking for a crinkled and grumpy old bag—and in a flash, have your vision deepen, to see that once she was young, smiling, of enviable beauty. I climb into bed, pull the reassuring duvet around me, tuck the pillow into the crook of my neck.

My parents have photos in their bedroom of their first years together, and they were gorgeous and glamorous too. Not so much different, now that I think of it, from Monsieur et Madame. My mother with her slim waist and fair hair, sunglasses. My tall, darker father, also smiling, though perhaps already with the slightly awkward turn to his lips, a kink I have always linked to his having found his wife lying unconscious on the kitchen floor but that may have been there since his Oklahoma boyhood, a part of his life I know little about. They too had it all, the Fulbrighters. Until they had children. I can never chase away entirely the lurking fear that we the daughters and me in particular as the last to arrive were responsible for our mother having reached a tipping point. I mean, childless, would she have been driven to put a towel under the door and turn on the gas? Or would her life have been manageable if she'd stopped at two? Jane always told me this theory was pure rubbish and to stop, stop right away, but I never could.

I force my eyes shut. Whether my theory is true or false, there's nothing I can do about it. Here I am.

With my eyes closed, I see Bruno's brown globes. Our encounter in the café clung to me like a piece of clothing all evening. Thibaud says he's a total fake, but he didn't seem that way to me. He seemed to genuinely believe in social justice. Then that hand on my shoulder, his rough cheeks against mine. I readjust myself in bed, remind myself of all the trouble he's causing, however authentic he is or isn't. But his physical presence will not leave me alone.

The next morning the choice of newspapers is formidable: *Le Matin*, *Le Figaro*, *Le Monde*, *Le Parisien*, *L'Humanité*, *Libération*. I buy them all, depleting the resources of the little leather pouch, and return to the house. Since I am under orders from Madame, it seems right that I should do my research in the kitchen, like Germaine with the post. This project also seems a good excuse to forgo the morning's lecture on the subtleties of the subjunctive. I make more coffee, spread out the papers on the table and go right to the *faits divers* pages.

Only *Le Parisien*, *Le Matin* and *Libération* have short articles on *les squatteurs de la place des Vosges*. *Le Parisien* even reprints the photo in the evening clothes. I cut it out, put it to the side—Madame will never know that I've kept it. In reading the articles, I am surprised by the obvious sympathy the journalists feel for the squatters, the "students," they keep saying, though only a minority of the occupiers are enrolled in higher education. The articles praise the dead hero husband but don't have an ounce of sympathy for the widow, the legal owner of the property. I find myself wanting to protest, as I did with Bruno. To point out it's not Madame on the wrong side of the law.

Libération gives the most space to the back story, to François Quinon, who made soap for the Germans while concealing British spies and French *résistants* and printing illegal tracts in the basement of the factory. About his American wife Amenia who had been a translator of contemporary French literature both before and after the war and now takes up all that space for herself. It's also in *Libération* that I read: "The couple had one son, Henri, shot down by the Germans during the liberation of Paris in August 1944."

Why hadn't it occurred to me that the boy in the spare bedroom was their son? One photo on a pony, short legs splayed atop the big belly, and one—obviously the same boy but several years older—in tennis clothes. Why did I never consider it could be a child who died? But Amenia Quinon has never mentioned a son, so I won't either.

"I've read the papers."

"And?"

"Some have articles."

"Do they say anything of interest?"

"The longer ones, in *Libération*, for example, talk a little about you. And your family. I've cut them out for you."

"Thank you." I put them on the desk. She looks stunned. "It's very unpleasant, to have your life splashed all over the press. For the whole world to see." She shakes her head.

I look out the window at the lovely weather, a day stamped with early spring. Meredith's knee will be bouncing up and down, waiting impatiently for the end of the lecture. Carol will still be attentive, taking notes with her fountain pen in her messy handwriting. I'll go now, meet them at le Gaulois, where we'll linger idly because it's Friday and Paris, and I can maybe forget about everything here for a couple of hours.

***

Saturday, 2 April 1983

My greatest nightmare: to have the facts of my life recounted out loud—and in this case for the entire French nation, first on the eight o'clock news, then in print, in the daily papers. The only thing they didn't say was: Amenia Tucker Quinon is a coward. Her husband did all the right things, all the time, but not sorry-sack Amenia. Though she didn't mention Henri, when "your family" came out of Lily's mouth, she may as well have taken a board to the side of my head.

After she left, I stood next to the window with the articles, hoping against hope that on what looks like a bright early spring day, the light would allow me to make out some of what was said. The exercise just gave me a headache.

Laughter from across the courtyard, the smell of cigarette smoke. Sometimes embarrassment can act as a slap in the face, a bucket of cold water over the head. These people must go.

***

Saturday mornings, I've started helping Germaine clean house.

"Today," she says when I knock on her door, "it's time for a spring clean upstairs."

"Okay," I say, catching myself just in time before mentioning the sheets on the furniture and thus letting her know that I've snooped in this part of the house already too.

"Oh, it's musty in here," she says, as we open the wooden shutters and the windows in the *salon*. "Since you're taller, I'm going to give you the job of dusting that chandelier." She hands me a stick with a round, soft-bristled head. "This is *une tête de loup*. It's for getting cobwebs and dust from high, unreachable places. See how the handle telescopes? I'll start by giving the sheets a good shake out the window."

For a few minutes we go about our tasks in silence, the tinkling of glass beads the only sound.

"She saw the reportage on television the other night," says Germaine.

"I know."

"Shameful, the way those journalists sniff around people's lives."

"She asked me to buy all the papers, see what was said the next day."

"And?"

"A few of them outlined her life story. But when I started to tell her, she didn't seem very interested."

"It must still be painful."

"You mean her son?"

She pauses, a large white sheet pulled against her chest. "Yes. Shot down by those wicked Germans." She shudders before returning the sheet to its place over the chair. "Him. Then later Monsieur. It never seemed to stop."

I keep up the delicate brushwork on the chandelier, wait for Germaine to continue, wonder if her mind has gone back to her own multitude of sorrows.

"I must take her to the plaque again soon," she says finally. "She doesn't like going to the cemetery."

"The plaque?"

"At the spot where he was shot down. Haven't you seen them? They're all over the city, marking where men died during *la libération*. If you can call a nineteen-year-old a man. His plaque is on the rue de l'Odéon. Just meters away from where they lived on the rue de Tournon. I've always thought it's why Monsieur bought this building. To get away from all that sadness. I told you he'd already lost a brother in the First War, his father to the influenza."

I lengthen the telescope of the *tête de loup* to dust the top of the cloudy mirror over the fireplace. We studied World War I last month and finished World War II yesterday. Ronnie has noted how differently the two wars are being taught to us. While the professor stressed the pointlessness of so many deaths and so little land gained during the First, his overall tone was *la gloire de la France*. In depicting the Second, he's practically muttering, like he can't wait to get to the armistice and change the subject. Even Jean-Paul has been more muted than usual: France's role under the German Occupation, let's say, is not as clear as it is portrayed, i.e. Résistance being the rule and Collaboration the exception, the very rare exception. Ronnie pushed him to clarify. He said, which shocked us all: Read *Vichy France* by the American professor Robert Paxton. Which Ronnie told us the other night he had: Just reverse Jean-Paul's ratio of *Résistants à Collabos*, he said, and you've understood France's War better. Lara said: It's crazy that almost forty years later there's still this *omerta*, this code of silence, hanging over the War years in France, even at the university.

"It's a shame," says Germaine. "I don't think it worked."

"What didn't work?" I have completely lost track.

"Monsieur and Madame buying a new house, creating a new project, to escape grief." She hands me a feather duster. "Here, you can take this to the paintings." She pauses, starts running a cloth over the end tables. "I told you about his accident. Well, most likely he stepped in front of that delivery truck on purpose."

"Oh," I say, feather duster freezing over a portrait of a man, perhaps some ancestor, with liquid, expressive eyes and a set jaw.

"Yes," she says as if she still can't believe it. "It was the one thing he failed at, finishing himself off. And afterwards there he sat in a wheelchair, no more responsive than an overcooked cauliflower. It was very painful to see, that vigorous man reduced to a lump."

"It must have been very hard for her."

"The clock just stopped." Germaine gives her dust cloth a snap.

She fills in more blanks about François Quinon—all he did to help people during the War, how he fought to save the Marais from destruction—and he comes alive with greater force through Germaine's words than he did in the press reports. The feather duster is working on its own—I've forgotten where I am—this romantic story has wrapped around me like silk.

"And then a bout of pneumonia carried him off." She pulls the cord from the innards of the vacuum cleaner, plugs it into the wall.

There is a thud from across the courtyard. Germaine and I look at one another. She shakes her head and turns on the machine, which thankfully drowns out all other sound, and I go back to feather dusting the artwork.

We move through the lonely room with the elaborate writing table and the real stopped clock, then the antechamber with the bed. The Quinons may have looked like a perfect couple, but how could that be if they didn't even share the same floor in this spacious old place?

Is that the effect of so much War in the lives of these older people? Silence (Germaine) and separation (Monsieur et Madame)? In any case, it's hard to imagine how they keep walking and talking, acting to the outside world as if nothing troubling had ever occurred. How can Germaine spray and dust the furniture with all that tragedy in her history?

I'm relieved when we've finished and I walk outside, away from sad, confusing thoughts, over to the Félix Potin for some cheese and tomatoes. As usual Madame Dodé is on her stool like a sack of grain. Monsieur Dodé, cap on his head, stands small and straight at her side.

"We saw them on the television the other night, *les sqwa-terres*," she says.

"Yes."

"What is Madame Quinon going to do?"

"I don't know."

"How did they get in?"

"I don't know."

"It was bound to happen," interjects Monsieur Dodé. "All that empty space."

"They come in here to buy their food." Madame Dodé leans forward, whispers conspiratorially. I instinctively recoil, certain that the breath behind her picketty teeth smells as bad as the body. "At first I didn't know. Didn't know they were living right across the street." She jabs a fleshy finger towards the door, eyes bulging. "Not until the police and the journalists showed up."

"Most of them look—well—quite normal," says Monsieur.

"They say rents are so high many young people can't afford Paris anymore." I root quickly for my money. "*On verra*," I add, grabbing the loops of the plastic bag. *We'll see* is a good way out in any language. Except that there is no way out now. Everyone knows, everyone's talking. It's *un huis clos*, a dead end, worthy of the Jean-Paul Sartre play we will soon be reading for class.

At the bakery, who should tap me on the shoulder but Bruno.

"*Ca va ?*" he asks, full smile.

"*Oui, oui.*" I blush, turn to order my baguette, then to leave, but Bruno grabs my arm.

"Hey, wait for me." I cannot suppress a little bounce in my heart. I shove it back down, remind myself he is the source of the problem next door.

Outside, he breaks off the heel of his baguette, pops it in his mouth. "What are you doing this afternoon?"

"Going to visit some friends."

"Friends again? That's too bad. I am in a debate. The topic is US Hegemony: True or False. I'd like to hear what an American thinks."

"I don't have an opinion on the subject."

"Really?"

"No."

"A Disney park is opening in Japan. There's talk of the same thing happening here. The Disneyfication of the world. Did your parents take you to one in America?"

I try to imagine my parents at an amusement park. It cannot be done. "No."

"Well, it's too bad you can't come see me."

We are standing in front of the *portail*. I am worried Germaine might appear. "I have to go. I'm meeting my friends soon. But thanks for the invitation."

"Another time," he says, leaning over to kiss my cheeks, arm to the small of my back. When he pulls away, the broad hand moves from my back to my head, where he strokes my hair, just for a second. His eyes fasten me to the spot. "You meet your friends a lot," he says with a large smile that is both gently mocking and amused. "*A bientôt*," and he is off with that same firm step.

I manage to get the key out of my pocket and into the lock, but it's as if the shoulder pushing open the door belongs to someone else. I shake myself and cross the courtyard, climb the stairs with indignation and excitement switching places at every step. What does he want from me? Surely a Bruno is the type to go after a Meredith, not a Lily. Is he just playing with me? But those looks into my eyes. He saw right through my excuse. And that hand on my back. I can still feel it.

My room, as always, calms me down. Sitting at my little table, I slice into the tomato, which is pale and watery at this time of year. Germaine has taught me to salt the flesh to bring out more flavor. While I wait for the salt to sink in, I plunge the knife into the plump Camembert, which is neither too chalky nor too ripe. A bit of olive oil dribbled over the tomato slices and my mouth waters in anticipation. I pull off a piece of my *baguette bien blanche*, a slightly undercooked crust outside, soft and fluffy within. The sun is coming in the window and the convergence of light, warmth and sustenance feels like a blessing. It is hard to be frightened, angry, resentful or even to care what is going on beyond the limits of my incubated room.

But the meal regretfully comes to an end, and minutes later thick, menacing April clouds kidnap the sky. I move to the bed. What will I do this afternoon? Not see Meredith and Carol. They left this morning for what they call their spring break, their second express tour of Europe by train, where they will cover the cities and countries they missed at Christmas. I feel a small crater of emptiness at their absence. They have become my lifeline to normality, provided the kind of fun people are supposed to have at my age when they spend a year in Paris.

Still, I sometimes wonder how strong this tie is. Though Meredith and Carol like me and I like them, I'm not sure we would have become friends if we hadn't been doing the same course in a foreign city. Unusual circumstances draw people together in unusual ways. Can such a relationship last once the academic year draws to a close and they fly back to the US? Letters may migrate across the ocean for a while but for how long? In five years won't I have completely lost track of them?

And can I, really, even call them friends? They know nothing of my place des Vosges life. After the television reportage that got Madame so upset, we were sitting in the classroom, waiting for Jean-Paul and our TD. Lara, who's the only one to pay attention to the French news, was flipping through *Le Matin* and said: "This is quite a story. A big house, *un hôtel particulier*, being squatted on the place des Vosges in the Marais. It's owned by an old American woman." I could feel my cheeks heating up, my heart thumping.

"That's near where you live, Lily," said Carol.

"Yes," I said.

"Have you seen the place?" asked Lara. "I'm tempted to go have a look."

Jean-Paul walked in, and she didn't mention it again.

There have been times when I've wanted to come clean, to relate the details of this strange half of my Paris existence, but it's the kind of thing you share straight away or not at all.

And when I think about it, I have to say that my "real" Paris life, the one that is more likely to stick to my ribs, is in this house. With its floating souls—Thibaud included—it feels the natural continuation of my life thus far. Won't I always feel more comfortable with oddballs and outcasts than with the mainstream? The French normal, the kind that Lara or Ronnie, for example, have encountered in their rented rooms in bourgeois family flats, is not my fate. This pull to the anomalous is true for me and it's true for my sisters. Maude, who is now communally yoga-ing, painting and farming in East Anglia, but even Jane. She may have been my only friend throughout our childhood, but I was hers too. We leaned on one another. And since then, the friends she has made in New York, she's told me, are loners like herself. Our past, it seems, will cast its shadow in our paths forward forever.

Beyond its karmic relevance, this strange house is where the important developments are taking place. The life-changing elements of the year abroad. My real discoveries have revolved less around the course work or fleeting friendships and more around Thibaud's mattress, even if he too will move on, get himself to the US, and I'm likely to lose sight of him as well. But he is, has been or was—it's impossible to get the tense right with Thibaud—a first boyfriend of sorts. At least he is the first man to know my body and intimate details of my life.

Even that experience pales next to what I'm learning with Germaine. When I shop and put it all together in the kitchen, I feel an excitement I have never been able to muster for academics, or anything else for that matter. For once, I concentrate completely and—also a first—I have confidence in the results. It's the strangest sensation, but after I've prepared a meal, I feel a bigger, better person. A more complete version of Me.

**

Tuesday, 5 April 1983

When Germaine stopped by yesterday, I said: Enough is enough. We have been patient and they're still here. Lily is obviously getting nowhere, though she didn't mean any harm (I added in my new, last-minute benevolence). Here's my address book. Can you dial Maître Berger's number?

They make more and more noise, Germaine whispered, as if they were right at the door, which I have to say it often feels as though they are. And the cigarette smoke, she said. I can smell it even through the closed window. The other day a few of them drifted into the courtyard.

She kept muttering, and I could hear her agitation in the way she jerkily dialled the phone.

Unfortunately, my conversation with the *notaire* was less than satisfactory. When I told him the circumstances, he sighed. Paused. Well, he said. The good news is you've passed the period of *la trêve hivernale*, the winter truce between November 1st and March 31st during which you can't evict anyone in France. The bad news is you didn't declare their presence within forty-eight hours and need a court order. That can take quite a while. Assuming you win the case, the prefecture then has to carry it out. For one reason or another, that too can take some time.

I wanted to scream: I don't have time! Or: I've had too much time and now I want my time over!

Instead I asked calmly: How long?

He sighed again. Let's say they're likely to still be there when the next *trêve hivernale* comes round.

I asked him to go ahead and launch the process. A young intern in his office will help with registering the complaint at the Préfecture. I must compile all sorts of papers to show I'm the legal owner. What an affront.

We've lived through worse, said Germaine as she left.

***

"Tante, you have to fire that girl."

I freeze, door handle in one hand, shopping bag in the other.

"Why? You're the one who insisted I hire her in the first place, and now I'm used to her. She stays out of my way. She cooks well."

"But look at who—or should I say what—she's brought in off the streets. Parasites, vermin."

"Octave, really. They're students, just as you were once upon a time."

"I have never," Octave pauses, perhaps for moral emphasis, "unlawfully occupied private property."

"Not everyone has a wealthy aunt living in an indecently large building."

"I was lucky, I'll admit that. But I'm not going to feel guilty for good fortune, past or present."

"I'm not asking you to feel guilty," says Madame. "I'm asking for some generosity of spirit, a sense of clemency."

Octave exhales, exasperated.

"I am asking you, Octave de Malbert, to remember the person you were when you knocked on my door all those years ago. When you had your own housing problems in that rat-infested student hotel. To remember how lost—»

"I repeat," Octave interrupts loudly, "I never did anything illegal. These people are trespassers. They are breaking the law."

"What good will it do to fire Lily?"

"She's clearly behind it."

"No, not clearly. As I understand it, they broke in through the entry around the corner—they probably didn't even know it was connected to this part of the house on the square."

A long pause.

"I'm taking care of the situation, Octave. At the moment I do not need your help."

"I'm speechless."

This sounds like a parting comment, and I gently close the door, tiptoe rapidly into the coat closet. More agitated words are spoken, but I can't make them out. Feet stride by, the door to the apartment opens and shuts—not quite a slam but almost. He takes the stairs in a great hurry and is gone. Like the first day, when I was interviewed, I feel the air—even here in this closet—settle once Octave has departed, as if his very presence disturbs the atoms in the space around him. I stand frozen for quite some time in the rose smell of Madame's coats.

That was an unexpected exchange. Madame Quinon sounded kind and reasonable. Noble, really, the way she defended, even lied for me. And a good cook, she said. I tell myself I should not feel pride but that deadly sin cannot be suppressed. As for Octave, I can't say his take on the situation is a surprise, but until now I had not considered what role he might play. I imagine Bruno and Octave meeting, those two dark heads butting, and it does not bode well. I wait in the closet until I hear Madame leaving the *salon* then walk on tiptoe to the kitchen, wondering what she meant by "taking care of the situation" but feeling a hint of relief.

***

Saturday, 9 April 1983

What a brute Octave has become. He is of course correct that the visitors are here illegally, that they must go, but his haughty, disdainful, sanctimonious manner is insufferable. Much as I'd like to blame it all on the Horse, I know the problem is rooted deeper. Octave is, after all, the son of Agnès, and maybe that's what disturbed me so much the other day: he sounded so much like her, even the barking timbre of his agitated voice, that I was thrown back sixty years, to the time that poisonous creature, only seven years my junior, was in my callow charge.

Her mother, my mother-in-law Hortense, was no help at all. I would like to report that she was sweet and endearing in her dotage, but she veered from demanding to pathetic, always—it seemed to me—with the same intent: to make me feel I was not doing enough, that I was not up to the task of running the house, a burden I never wanted in the first place. François was no help. He was always working. For a while, instinctively aware that bad news would infect the teller, I said nothing. But Agnès succeeded in leading me to the end of my rope. I then delicately tried to describe what I was suffering to François. The things that disappeared. Or were damaged. Her defiance of my authority at every corner. He would listen and nod sympathetically, but he never seemed to absorb or retain my words. Certainly, he never acted upon them. He took a stand against the Germans but was willfully blind to wickedness inside his own four walls. The journalists won't report on that.

It's a malevolent thread—my mother-in-law Hortense to her child

Agnès to her child Octave—that has been woven through my life in Paris, and it still has the power to almost unravel me.

Nevertheless and despite the pessimistic view of Maître Berger, I must pull myself together and try to do something about those people, whose presence is very disturbing, however much I'd like to be noble and help the less fortunate. I have no intention of prolonging my existence the time it will take the lumbering legal system to do the job.

***

Cigarette and cannabis smoke wafts across the courtyard. There are no pretences to discretion anymore. The blackout shade in the kitchen-bathroom was ripped off long ago. Someone has stuck a cut-out butterfly onto a window-pane; someone else—maybe the library-goers—has even put up curtains.

I step quickly back and away, close the window, go to the Félix Potin to buy my supper. On my way back, I walk right into Bruno.

"Perfect timing," he says, looking excited, putting an arm around my shoulder, and I can smell fresh, clean clothes under his coat. "Come with me. I want to show you something." Before I can protest or walk away, he leads me through the *portail*, up the stairs.

"Sorry. Not much space in here," Bruno says. The room is very small, even smaller than Monsieur's antechamber next door. It is empty, except for a mattress with a duvet, enveloped in soft white cotton, and a small duffle bag against the wall. "It's only right that the people who need them have the bigger rooms." I try to read some of the cynicism Thibaud attributes to him into his face but see only earnest concern.

If I thought the two times Bruno kissed my cheeks made me tingle, being here in these close walls makes my skin quiver.

"What did you want to show me?" I can hear my voice wavering.

"This." He leans down, causing a gap to form between his jersey and belted jeans. The band of his boxer shorts peeps out. Thibaud wears the skimpy white things, which had led me to believe that all Frenchmen did. He pulls an envelope from his duffle bag, straightens, pulls out a photo of a couple, a couple I recognize from the photo on television and in the newspaper that I kept. Here they are standing in front of this very building on the place des Vosges. They are not touching. He is smiling; she is not. Both the square and the façade are in a lamentable state.

"Where did you get it?"

"I have a cousin who's a journalist at *Le Figaro*. It's from the society pages in the early sixties. The article somewhat ironically praises this Left Bank couple who have dared buy property in a virtual ghetto on the Right Bank. Hard to believe but there was a time when the government was considering razing the whole area." He points: "François Quinon says: 'I have faith in the future of Le Marais.' He lobbied hard for the Loi Malraux that spared historically important areas like this one from demolition. Rather perspicacious, wouldn't you say?"

All my attention, however, is on Madame, Amenia Quinon. What beauty. What grace. I forget Bruno entirely, until I feel his intense stare and look up with a start. He has long, thick eyelashes that curl. They shadow warm, brown globes.

My consideration of his features is cut short. Bruno has wrapped his arms around me, is kissing my face, my neck, with great tenderness. I know I should push him away and storm off indignantly, but what he is doing has already fuelled too many forbidden fantasies since that drink in the café. In real life, contact feels even better than I'd imagined. Before I know it, he has pulled me down to the mattress and is remov-ing my clothes with the same expert touch. His lips are all over me. It is like a whole different undertaking from the one I have experienced with Thibaud. I find myself returning his kisses and caresses with animal avidity. Then, rabbit from a hat, out comes a condom. He tears open the package and blows on it, slowly, as if he were trying to make a bubble. The fine plastic flutters forward and on it slips like silk. He is rhythmic and gentle; I encourage him with firm hands on his back. When I come it is an inner explosion of pleasure that is almost more than I can bear. But this is not enough for Bruno. He turns over, pulls me on top of him and I come again, twice, before he finally releases his own orgasm.

"Ça va ?" he asks.

"Oui, ça va." I thought I knew but I didn't. I had no idea.

He leans over me and lights a cigarette, this one from a packet, not hand-rolled. "Do you want one?"

"I don't smoke."

"You can't grow up in Paris and not smoke."

I think of country-boy Thibaud who does not smoke. I think of Thibaud, whom on some level I am betraying. On some level. Things between us are not clear, conveniently so at this moment. For once the smell of smoke is alluring. I am almost tempted to ask for a cigarette—do the whole French bedroom scene—but the time I tried a smoke at school, behind the gym, I was so dizzy and nauseous I couldn't stand up for a full ten minutes. And here I've had too much trouble with the tobacco-laced marijuana already.

"You must have a girlfriend," I say, still with my back to him.

"No."

The answer is firm, but I can't help imagining a squat and a woman in every arrondissement. Bruno leans over to tap ash in an ashtray already full of butts. His extremely hairy chest tickles my shoulder. I can now smell the acrid old nicotine from the ashtray, but my attention is distracted by his free hand, which begins to stroke my side. He leans over again, crushes his butt into the others and brings his smoky mouth, his solid body, on top of me again.

During the next cigarette, laughter comes through the door. It must be after seven now. I still have a salad to make, leftover quiche to heat up for Madame.

"I have to go."

"That's too bad," he kisses my shoulder.

I get up and his eyes are on me as I dress. Despite our skin having touched at every conceivable point, I feel self-conscious and turn away.

"I'll see you," I say, hand on the doorknob.

"Don't forget."

"Don't forget what?"

"Your shopping bag." He stands up, still naked, and wraps his woolly body around me, descends his extremely soft lips on me. "That was really nice. Thank you."

The voices are coming from the kitchen. Thibaud particularly resents their presence in that room so there is little chance he is among them. I saunter out, appearing cool and composed, while feeling anything but.

***

Tuesday, 12 April 1983

This morning I was still ruminating on Octave's visit, and it occurred to me that as my will now stands, once I die, everything I have that isn't devoured by the French state will be thrown to the vulturous nephew and his equine wife. By French law, I can't do anything about half of the house that belonged to François, but since Octave is thankfully no blood relation of mine, I can leave my half to whomever I like. So why couldn't I, wouldn't I, shouldn't I, leave it to Germaine? I must have another chat with the *notaire*.

And I have been brooding about what I can do next door. Only one option appears to have any merit: putting my age and handicap to good use. Going over there myself and evoking their pity. A desperate measure, perhaps, but I see no other. I could ask Germaine to accompany me—two older ladies might work on their consciences better than one—but she has too much else to worry about already. She would hate the confrontation. Lily can take me. She'll know the right person or people to talk to. She will be my eyes.

***

With no lectures and no Meredith or Carol, I spend way too much time rerunning the scene with Bruno, over and over again, each time with a frisson and a confused smile. Occasionally Thibaud pokes his way into my conscience. Who would have thought? Virgin one minute, two-timer the next. But I don't feel that guilty. Thibaud's loyalties have often seemed to lie with Jean-Marc and Cécile, rather than with me. Or to himself and his own future. Beyond the occupiers, no one knows about our relationship. Undeclared, therefore non-binding, that's the way our arrangement feels.

I also feel betrayal, on some level, to Madame and Germaine. Whose side am I on anyway? I thought more theirs but maybe not. The squatters' presence has changed the building. It no longer feels empty, and at moments that can make the place feel less sad. In fact, maybe that has something to do with Germaine and Madame not being harsher with me. Germaine told me that when the Quinons bought the house, several families were living over there, that her husband always said that a building is built for people. It needs us; we need it, he said. So as much as I wish these particular people were gone, I must admit the squatters, the occupiers, whatever you want to call them, have breathed life into the place. They are over there with the living, and I am over here with the half-dead.

Speaking of the half-dead, we finished Sartre's *Huis clos* before the holiday. The play is about three people who have just died and are arriving in hell. Except hell is a Paris apartment. The characters have nothing to do with one another, beyond the fact that they are locked in together. All three of them pretend to have no idea why they have been sent to hell, to this apartment, but soon they coax their crimes out of one another, leading one of them to say: "*le bourreau, c'est chacun de nous pour les deux autres.*" The henchman is each one of us for the other two.

Last week we had a lecture on the most famous line, "*l'enfer, c'est les autres.*" Hell is other people. The professor said the words have been misconstrued. Sartre didn't mean that being with people is hell. He meant, the professor said, that we define ourselves and are defined by the judgment of the Other. To illustrate the point, Sartre imagined a situation where you are listening to a conversation through a keyhole. As long as you are alone, you are completely absorbed in You. Now imagine other people arrive and see you peeking through the keyhole. Then you see yourself through their eyes, the eyes of the Other, and You are ashamed. That's hell, *le regard de l'autre.*

My recent adventure in the coat closet during Octave's visit comes to mind, as do all my acts of deceit these last months. Do I feel more guilty now that everyone knows about the occupiers, even if my name has not been dragged across the evening news and daily newspapers? And less guilty about Bruno because Thibaud doesn't know? Probably yes, in both cases. Certainly long ago, when Madame Flaviche was always casting her judgmental eyes down on us, practically as if we were criminals, it felt hellish.

But I see Sartre's message on another level too: that we're all in this inferno together, from the dead people in the Paris apartment to all of us still alive in this house on the place des Vosges.

Which may be why I find myself being led over there, as if by a force beyond my will. Once I'm standing inside the *portail*, I wonder what my objective is. Am I looking for Bruno? Or Thibaud? And if I do find one of them, what do I expect to happen? Despite his attentions, I should not be involved with Bruno. As for Thibaud, I'm not sure I could go to bed with him again. It would be like opting for an English meal after the experience of French cuisine.

I walk on because it's better than turning around and being alone in my room.

"*Tiens.*" It's Bruno walking out of the kitchen the moment I pass. He does have a way of running into me.

"Oh, hi," I say. "I was actually looking for Thibaud."

Bruno tosses his head upwards. "He's probably up in the attic doing his tortured poet thing." Then a playful smile. "Come with me." He wraps an arm around my shoulders. "I promise you it will be more fun."

There I am, back in his small room, with his soft lips on mine. I am pulled down to the white duvet. Clothes are removed. All internal activity warms to soft wax. A condom again appears and is gently blown upon. It flutters open like a soap bubble under his measured breath.

Pop. The spell is broken. I sit up.

"What's wrong?"

"This." I point to the condom, then fling my arms open. "All this is wrong." I get up, grab my scattered clothes and start to dress.

"You're not feeling guilty about the tortured poet, are you?"

"Absolutely not." I wriggle into my shirt. "What is it you have against Thibaud, anyway?"

"What is it I have against Thibaud?"

Repeating a question, the perfect ruse for gaining time. Thibaud has told me it's the classic French trick for a student in an oral exam, a politician in front of the camera.

He grabs a cigarette, lights it. "Nothing." He exhales. "He's a bit of a poser."

"He was the first one here and is no happier than I am about all of you moving in." I shove my foot into my shoe.

"His attitude injects negativity into the group. He doesn't fit."

"Why? Because he's not *Parisien*?"

"Maybe. I don't really know. But he's the odd man out."

I shove on my other shoe, shake my head and turn to leave. "I've had enough of both of you. Of this whole scene."

It is only once I'm back in my room that the anger, shame and humiliation come to a boil. How could I have let myself fall under Bruno's spell? Okay, the first time there was physical attraction plus an element of satisfying my curiosity. To see what sex would be like with someone other than Thibaud. Someone who makes my skin tingle. That part I don't regret. It was both instructive and thrilling and thank God my timidity can occasionally take the back seat. But a second time? Well, at least some shred of good sense or pluck or whatever it was prevailed. It surprises me now, that I stood up. Walked out. *J'en ai marre de vous, tous les deux*, said my bold French self. The second language creates a distance from my inner core. Or a bypass around my self-doubt and diffidence. And tempestuous outbursts are so much better adapted to a Latin language, one that came into being in the heat of the Mediterranean, rather than in the cold and damp climes of the north.

The music rises from across the courtyard and in perfect synch, my heart falls another several inches. However wild I would sometimes like to be, I am not.

Preparing the tray for Madame the next day, following the routine is a balm to fear and uncertainty: yogurt in the left hand corner, coffee in the right, jam and honey in the middle, toasted baguette right underneath. I walk down the corridor and at the door balance the tray on my left arm, knock with the right hand.

The leather address book is out on the writing table again.

"Today I would like you to phone my *notaire*," says Madame, tapping the book. "If possible, I'd like to see him this afternoon." She pauses. "His name is Maître Berger." Another pause. "Would you be able to accompany me? I believe you mentioned you have no classes this week or next."

"That's right. Sure."

"Thank you."

Back in the kitchen, the book remains closed on the table while I butter my own baguette. *Notaire*. Does that mean action against the squatters? After the music last night? I feel relieved. Maybe law and justice can work faster than I've been led to believe. An image forms of the police leading out Thibaud, who falls back on his lie to me and claims diplomatic immunity, and Bruno, who is resisting and crying *aux armes, citoyens !* I watch, unmoved from the sidelines as they are subjugated by authority.

I wipe my mouth on a piece of kitchen towel, consult the clock and sigh as I open the address book to B, move down the corridor to the phone table.

The time between now and the five-thirty appointment stretches long and wide. Staying here means thinking about next door. But leaving means facing a cold April day, a day not conducive to a long walk. I decide to go to the *Marché aux Enfants Rouges*. Prepare an exceptional supper this afternoon before going to the *notaire*.

As soon as the thought is there, all others are banished. The market electrifies me. The bustle, the expectation of finding the right combination of ingredients for a meal, the smells—from the earthy raw vegetables to the fermented cheeses—fill my head like a drug. Meaningless exchanges with the *commerçants* I now know, that feeling of recognition, add to the high.

I comb the alleys, trying to construct a meal around what looks fresh and good. As Germaine is always telling me, quality is everything. Since it's Tuesday the fish will have come in this morning ("Never buy fish on a Monday," she says. "It will always be what no one wanted over the weekend.") The sole is plentiful and reasonably priced, and I buy three in the hope that Germaine will appear. I move on. Spinach. Wonderfully tender-leafed spinach and not even too sandy. There are crates with the first Noirmoutier potatoes, small and round and irresistible. While I am keeping an eye on a woman who is brazenly ignoring the semblance of a line, I am thinking that my meal is still missing something. Dry. It's too dry and not quite colorful enough. I'll make Hollandaise sauce, I think, after asserting my rights with the queue jumper. Germaine will not be looking over my shoulder this time, but I think I can manage on my own. At the cheesemonger, I buy some eggs and butter. I leave the market cheerful and confident, a feeling that is almost punctured by a glimpse of Jean-Marc and Cécile rounding the corner just ahead of me. *Them.* But Madame is going to the *notaire* and maybe *They* will be taken care of.

By the time the two of us are going down the stairs to the taxi, I feel transformed. The soles are lined up in the fridge, ready to be grilled; the spinach is washed and roughly chopped, as is the clove of garlic I will add. I've gone over the potatoes and removed dark spots and other blemishes—there weren't many, they are so fresh—and put them in a pot of water waiting to be boiled. The ingredients for the Hollandaise are prepared and ready for me to spring into action.

The taxi bumps along over the paving stones. The *notaire*'s office is near the train station Saint Lazare, a *quartier* I do not know. The streets are very busy with shoppers and office workers. Once again, as when I babysat for Octave or Flora, it almost seems a different city from the Marais. It's very *haussmannien*, nineteenth-century buildings on wide boulevards. We studied this guy, Baron Haussmann. In the second half of the last century, he single-handedly changed the face of the city. First, he destroyed sixty percent of the streets and buildings, then he expanded and rebuilt. For lots of reasons, Jean-Paul told us. Partly because Paris was still medievally chaotic, like the Marais or the little streets of the Left Bank still are today but all over, which meant it was *insalubre*, dirty and unhealthy, and people were dying of cholera all the time. The Baron also had an obsession with the straight line, *le culte de l'axe*, Jean-Paul called it, and was willing to tear down any historical monument or church in the way of his unbending vision. "Like the boulevard Saint Michel or Saint Germain," he said, pointing to the window, "that now cut right through the core of the Latin Quarter." It is odd that the French can be so order-obsessed one minute and disorderly the next—thinking like Descartes yet incapable of forming a proper queue at the post office or market.

Baron Haussmann had another motivation that got Jean-Paul quite upset. He wanted to build fancy buildings with high rents that would keep away the workers and peasants who had caused insurrections in 1830 and 1848. To create the equivalent situation of today, you could say, where young people can't pay the rent so squat large, empty properties. The Baron also wanted to build roads wide enough for the army to trundle down. "The French state," Jean-Paul said with sad, angry eyes, "has long, strong arms and no heart."

We stop in front of a Haussmann specimen with a sooty façade. After I have paid the driver from Madame's purse, we enter a gloomy marble foyer that looks untouched since its construction a hundred years ago. The elevator is halting and small—not like the smooth one at the Malberts—and I stand stock still, barely breathing. Being confined with Madame in this tiny space is a bit creepy. We shudder to a halt; the doors groan open. The offices are imperturbably calm. The receptionist who greets us has a voice that hovers just above a whisper.

The magazines in the waiting room are all boringly linked to the law. In the Fortin's living-waiting room, at least there were *Paris Match* and *Point de Vue*, mindless gossip magazines with photos of stars and royalty that at night I took to my camp bed in the consulting room. I would pore over the pretty, famous faces, lose myself in their glamorous lives. I look around at the wood-panelled room, wood that seems to have entirely lost its connection to a living substance. The watercolors on the wall are bland to the point of bad taste—my mother would not approve. Bookshelves are filled with heavy red tomes. I do not like to be reminded that I made a three-year mistake and studied law. I do not like to be reminded of many things. Then stop thinking about them, I tell myself. Do not let The Mood pull you down. Instead, look to tomorrow's meal and what would be a good follow-up to tonight's fish and spinach. We've had a lot of meat recently, so maybe a lentil salad.

I start when the door opens and a bespectacled man with a bow tie leads Madame out.

"We've finished our business," he says. "A taxi will be here in five minutes."

"I'm glad that's over," she says in the lift on the way down. I look at the white, thinning hair. At the finely lined face and the blue eyes. It's like seeing her through a magnifying glass.

On the way back the traffic is terrible in the narrow one-way streets, and I entertain the perverse wish that the Baron had been yet more draconian in his remaking of the city. The taxi ride seems eternal in this maze. I prop my chin on my hand, look out the window, would like to get out and walk. It would be faster.

"You mustn't mention this to Germaine." Madame is sitting compactly, bony hands on her meager lap. It is the same confidential tone she used when she wanted me to phone the doctor or buy the newspapers. Or keep quiet about her outing into the street.

"I won't." I look back out the window.

"What I've done, you see, is leave my half of the house to her." I notice the driver's ear cock towards the back.

In English, I say: "You are being listened to."

"Ah, well," she replies in her ancient and rusty American accent. "I do have three nephews in the United States." She pauses, then continues as if she's looking for reassurance. "But I don't see any reason to bequeath them more than a token. It's the house. I want Germaine to have my half of the house."

"That makes sense to me." I remember something Miss Bonner once said to me: "Friends are the family you choose. Or they can be."

"Yes, exactly."

"And Germaine after all she's…well, she deserves it in a way."

"That's just the way I feel."

"*Voilà*," says the driver, pulling up in front of the building.

"Sorry it takes me so long these days," she says on the way up the stairs, back to French. I am relieved. However odd, it seems more normal.

"I'm not in any hurry. Supper is under control." I follow her into the entry, hang up her coat in the closet that recently provided me concealment from Octave. When we reach the *salon*, Madame stops. "Sit down a minute, Lily."

She settles on the same hard-backed chair where she perched that first day, at my interview. As if it were my assigned seat, I return to the same chair too.

"Leaving my half of this house to Germaine," she says, "means that the visitors absolutely must go. Sooner rather than later. Besides the fact that their presence rattles me, I cannot leave her with such a mess."

My face gets the pink thing. "I understand."

"I've spoken to Maître Berger about that too," and her head moves in the direction of the courtyard. "He said removing tenants, legal or illegal, in France can take years."

I nod, realize she can't see me and murmur: "Yes. In English, they say that possession is nine-tenths of the law."

"Here in France, it appears to be nine point nine-tenths. Maître Berger could only advise the endless legal channel, but I must do something. I can't let this drag on." She pauses, looks hard in my direction. "I'd like to talk to them. It's one thing imagining me the owner—a wealthy American—and quite another seeing me—old and blind—face to face."

"You want them to come over here?" I ask, alarmed.

"No. I'd go over there."

"To the—" I stop myself from saying squat. The place next door has never seemed more squalid than at this moment, imagining Madame within it. "To the other side?" My rigid, upright posture on the edge of the chair stiffens further; I'm pretty sure what's coming next.

She nods. "And I cannot ask Germaine to help with this. She has too many worries as it is. So you will? Help? Act as my eyes?" She tips her face at me with a hopeful smile.

"Sure. Of course." I say, but my heart pounds in protest.

"Good." She bounces her hands on the armrests, rises spryly from the seat. "Just tell me when." She turns to go, then looks back to me. "Do make sure the leaders are there. No point talking to the foot soldiers."

Back in the kitchen I take off my jacket, hang up my bag. What a turn of events. On the one hand, I feel relieved that Madame has seized control. On the other, terrified at the prospect of taking her over there. It seems dangerous, like bringing a pedigreed cat into the feral den at the Roman baths I walk by every day on the way to the Sorbonne. Could she prevail upon Bruno? Much as I can practically picture Madame being his Norman grandmother, it's hard to imagine him budging even for someone who looks like she could be family.

Fortunately, dinner calls and I can push the mess to the back of my mind for now. Maybe the spinach would be better with not just garlic but some zest from the lemon for the Hollandaise sauce.

While I am grating, Germaine arrives.

"Flora had her last treatment today. The doctors expressed optimism." She pulls the apron off the hook.

"That's great news." She looks exhausted. "Are you sure you don't want to rest?"

"You know I like busy hands."

I wish Germaine would let me go it alone. I've got this far and would like it to be my meal, start to finish.

"Germaine?" Madame asks from the doorway. "I thought I heard you. How's Flora? What exactly did the doctor say? How long until the next tests?" While she's talking, Germaine is preparing her drink. Suddenly Madame Quinon stops, looks around:

"Lily, would you like a glass of wine?"

"Thank you."

"Help yourself. Germaine, you don't need asking." I pour each of us a glass.

Madame sits down. Germaine continues to talk about Flora's last treatment, the doctor's optimistic prognosis and I am left to prepare. In the end it is as I wished, my meal. The fish is cooked just as the hollandaise is ready. Germaine pours more wine, and I serve the three of us. Strangely, I do not feel nervous. I know it will be delicious as well as I know my own name.

***

Sunday, 17 April 1983

Voices. Music. Laughter. I lay in my bed, and silly as it sounds, I couldn't help thinking they were laughing at me. At my poor excuse for a life. All the things I have done and have left undone. The noise came to a halt abruptly, but still I lay awake for a long time, the silence suddenly more of a torment than the commotion.

Germaine is knocking at my door.

***

Now all is quiet and it's hard to imagine the ruckus last night when the party spilled into the courtyard. Panic is what I'd felt, as if every organ in my body had abandoned its station, dropped to my pelvis. When I open the door to the kitchen, both Madame and Germaine are there in their dressing gowns. Germaine's hair is loose and there is something close to terror on her face, as if the Germans were back and where is she to hide. I want to vanish.

"I know you didn't mean for this," Germaine says. "But parties in the courtyard, right under our windows. They've gone too far. They really have. They must go."

"They must indeed," says Madame quietly. "Lily," she looks in my direction. "Find out if the chief is there and then you can take me over there this morning. I will try to reason with them."

"Madame!" says Germaine.

"They're not going to eat me. They might even take pity." She raises her chin. "Once they get a good gawk at me." At this moment she looks so imposing, I wonder how the old-blind-pathetic strategy could possibly work.

"But—," Germaine says.

"Let's sit down and have breakfast," Madame interrupts. "Is there enough baguette?"

"Sure," I say.

"I'll make the coffee," says Germaine.

I cut the bread, put out the butter, fig jam and honey on the table.

Eating toasted bread makes a lot of noise when three people are chewing. Especially when no one is talking. Madame, usually the motor for conversation, is particularly quiet, pensive.

"All right, Lily," she says, wiping her hands on kitchen towel. "Let's see if we can make them go quietly. I'll get dressed and you go check if the chief is there."

"You cannot go over there," says Germaine. "It could be dangerous."

"What's the worst they can do to me?" Madame has a strange look on her face, as if she wouldn't be averse to a good dust-up. "Lily will accompany me. She knows them."

I drain my cup, stand up and start collecting the dishes. "Never mind that," says Germaine, not looking at all relieved. "You go, I guess. I'll wash up."

Now it feels like I have a mission, am under orders, and it strengthens resolve. I march right over there, through the smell of unwashed clothes, cigarettes and alcohol. The library-goers are the only ones up and about, leaning against the edge of the bathtub in the kitchen, each with a bowl of coffee between their hands. I walk straight to Bruno's antechamber, open the door without knocking. He's propped up on his mattress, *Le Monde* open and blocking my view of his face. The paper comes down slowly.

"*Tiens*," he smiles.

"Madame is coming over to speak to you. You'd better get dressed." I close the door before he has time to respond. On the way by the kitchen, I repeat the words to the library-goers, suggest they round up the others.

Upstairs, Thibaud is asleep. There's an open letter with the Fulbright insignia on the little writing table he made for himself. As I get to the being accepted part, he opens his eyes.

"Madame is coming over."

He rubs his eyes, yawns. "What?"

"You heard me. She wants to talk to you all."

He sits up, runs his hands through his hair, and sighs. "Even if I leave, no one else will. They're all under Bruno's spell." A childish smile. "I got the Fulbright."

"So I see. Congratulations."

"All thanks to you."

For once I am untouched by crumbs of gratitude. "You'd better get ready. We'll be back shortly."

***

Monday, 18 April 1983

It surprised me, how galvanizing even the prospect of action is. As I got dressed and ready to face the intruders, I felt twenty—well, maybe ten— years younger, ready to take on an army. I needed no help getting down the stairs but did hold Lily's arm along the pavement. I didn't want to break my neck, wind up in the hospital before I could have my word.

They'd congregated in a room. I could feel their presence. And smell it. I suppose if they can't afford rent, staying clean is a problem too. Someone provided a chair.

This is Madame Quinon, I heard Lily say. She is the owner of the building.

Enchanté, said a commanding voice. We are pleased to have the opportunity to speak with you.

Rather a presumptuous thing to say, but what is illegal occupation if not presumptuous.

You, I said, have moved into the empty wing of this large building that is, on paper, my private property. As I understand it, that is a principle in which you do not believe, and on some level, I have to say, I agree with you. There was a murmur of surprise. I went on: I've never really thought of this place as *mine*. At the beginning, it was my husband's project (how odd the word husband sounded, like a concept I couldn't quite grasp) and I moved to the places des Vosages against my will. Over the thirty-five years I have lived here, however, it has become what I would call *chez moi*. Home. Yet I find it hard in this old building with such a long list of occupants to feel its owner. Instead I see myself as its caretaker, a person who will be no more than a chapter—perhaps just a short paragraph or even a sentence—in the long history of this Paris house.

It was all quiet as I spoke, even when I paused. It was both harder and easier, not being able to see their faces, gauge their reactions.

Furthermore, I said, I have sympathy for your plight, for people without a place to live. It's a terrible thing, not having a *chez soi*.

There was some rustling at this, some *oui, oui* (more *ouaih, ouaih* from this slangy crowd) of accord.

But it's not that simple, I continued. As much as my mind can entertain lofty thoughts about the limits of private property, the rest of me finds your occupancy of these four walls very disturbing, distressing even. Beyond the noise and the smell of your cigarettes, your being here feels like an intrusion into my most private self. I put a hand to my heart. What is a home, after all, but a protective extension of our inner selves?

Silence.

I am an old, blind woman, *sans défense*, I continued, which makes the violation feel more acute. Therefore I would beg you, please, to pack your things and go, to let me live my last days in peace.

Perhaps somewhat overdramatic that last bit, but pity-mongering requires a certain level of theatrics. It was met with more silence—but not for long. The chief said:

We understand your point of view, and our aim is not to disturb you. But we believe that sometimes the will and perhaps even the well-being of the individual must be subsumed to the greater good. All this empty living space in the middle of the city is a scandal.

More mumblings of agreement among the occupiers. So much for their compassion. It was time to move into a higher gear: I understand that most of you are here because you can't afford Paris rents. That being the case, I am willing to offer you an incentive to leave. A monetary one.

This sent the noise level up to a satisfying din. Bingo.

This is about more than money, said the chief above the commotion, but he was beginning to sputter. I forged ahead:

If all of you agree to go, and I mean all, I am willing to pay each of you fifteen thousand francs. *Wah!* said someone and there was such chatter that the chief didn't even try to interrupt. Before he could collect himself, I rose, concluding: Think about it. All of you agree to go and each of you will be remunerated. The offer is available until the eighth of May.

I took a step and Lily was there at my arm. The return trip seemed to last forever. I may have sounded feisty and immutable, but the intervention reduced me to jelly.

What do you think, I asked once we were in the street.

You were brilliant, she said. But are you sure about the money? Some of them are real scroungers.

Take any group of people and there will be the good, the bad and the oscillating middle. I can't start passing moral judgments on who is or is not worthy. Having them gone quickly is my overriding concern, I said. Dispensing with that sum will not ruin me—it's just less money that will go to the government when I'm gone. Will it work, that's the question.

It might. You created quite a stir.

At my desk a day later, adrenaline drained, I have my doubts. I know all too well that inertia, the path of no resistance, often wins by default.

***

Madame seems so shaky I walk her all the way back to her sitting room, leave her in a soft chair. Germaine is in the kitchen, pretending to be busy.

"And?" she says.

I hesitate for longer than Germaine's patience can endure. "How did it go?"

"She was incredible," I say. "She gave a really convincing speech."

"They'll go?" She sounds so hopeful I hate to break the bubble.

"Not out of good will or any pity for her. She offered them money."

"Money?"

"Yes. A lot of money."

After a minute: "Well, how much?"

"Fifteen thousand francs. Each. If they all go."

"*Mon Dieu.*" She puts a hand to her cheek.

"At least a third of them don't deserve a centime," I say. "But I'm not sure she has many options. Waiting for the legal system to get them out could take years, whatever the inherent justice or injustice of the circumstances. And she says it won't bankrupt her. That it will just be less money for the French government when she dies."

"Imagine, having to offer money to delinquents," Germaine mutters, but she is already late for lunch at Flora's and rushes off. I climb the back stairs to my room, sit down at the small table. A meeting is most likely being held across the way. Bruno is trying to convince them not to be led into capitalist temptation, but *la fronde*, the opposition, is growing. The trouble is the decision to go for the cash must be unanimous. If I consider the characters I know in this drama, Thibaud could easily take the money and run. With his Fulbright assured, he only needs a home for the next few months anyway. Jean-Marc and Cécile too would likely cash in; good weather and ripe fruit are on the way, and they like their itinerant lifestyle. As for Laurent, he doesn't have another place to live, but he has the assumption of money behind him. I'm sure his parents would have bailed him out if this squat hadn't temporarily solved his housing needs. Hard to know the effect of a cash buyout on him. The library-goers are even more complicated. They're not the squat types, would rather have a legal roof over their heads. But how far would thirty-thousand francs take them? Not very, if they have several years of study left.

As for Bruno, he doesn't need cash or a roof. Just the cause. He'll never relent. But since he's only a fair-weather squatter, they could overrule his objections, force his hand. Without them, Bruno's project crumbles.

I had very mixed emotions, taking Madame over there. On the one hand, it felt like I was leading her to the gallows. On the other, I felt bolstered, stronger and more confident with her clinging to my arm. When she spoke, my doubts dissolved. She was so dignified and equitable. It felt like a lesson in humanity, with a wily tactical twist at the end. She was amazing.

***

Tuesday, 26 April 1983

There's still an American in me somewhere: when there's a problem, throw money at it.

Though I got the idea from a French news story on the radio that morning. Just two years after the Socialist government sent shock waves through much of my France (Octave and the Horse were apoplectic) by nationalizing French banks and companies, it is now re-privatizing them. The economy was in free fall because investors weren't interested in government property. They prefer the private kind. It will make them richer.

So it came to me: offer them money and see how long their anti-private property principles stay standing. There is a capitalist lurking inside everyone, François used to say.

Germaine came in late morning to put my clean clothes away and lingered.

What is it?

Lily told me about the money. Are you sure?

I want them gone, and since I can't physically remove them, dangling a reward is my only choice. It's just money.

I guess you're right. It would be better. If they were gone. She sighed, then: I was wondering if we shouldn't go to the plaque. It's been a while.

Yes. It has. We should.

In the taxi, it felt as if we were travelling under water, in slow motion or in a dream. I knew, almost as if someone had whispered it in my ear, that this would be the last time. I asked the driver to drop us at the top of the rue de Tournon, our old street. Though I could make out no details, there was a smell from the Luxembourg Gardens in early spring, one I used to inhale with undiluted joy.

At the plaque, rue de l'Odéon, I ran my fingers along the chiselled letters on the marble, letters I know by heart. *Ici est tombé le 19 août 1944 Henri Quinon, à la libération de Paris, 1925-1944*. I felt the brass ring where the Mairie will soon, on the 8th of May, insert a bouquet of flowers to commemorate the Allied victory in Europe. When the plaque was put up, it was suggested we include *mort pour la France*, but François wouldn't have it, saying his son died, *justement*, for the path that France did not follow. His indignation had angered me. Our son was dead—what else mattered?

It came back to me with such force, standing there blindly in front of that plaque. I could practically hear the German tanks rumbling by all day, shaking the walls of our solid building. Guns popped off. Bombs boomed. I pleaded with Henri to stay home; François backed me up but as soon as he left, Henri slipped out too.

When he didn't return in the evening, it was as if a lead bullet had settled in my stomach. I knew, didn't need Henri's best friend Edouard to tell me the next day. I'd just rounded the corner, he said. But Henri was behind me. There was a shot.

His death caused the wall between us to go higher still. I resented François for if not actively encouraging Henri's Résistance activities, then virtually condoning them with mild admonitions that poorly masked paternal pride. And François, after losing his brother and his father in one war, could not absorb another such loss in the second. It was one death too many. Like Germaine when Flora became ill, he said to me, with crazed, desperate eyes: Why is it always me who survives? Why does everyone I love die?

I don't think he even realized how hurtful such a remark was to me, surviving right along with him.

How I would like to undo my life and retie it differently. It is the hardest thing about being old. The parcel is wrapped and knotted for good.

***

I am walking back from Meredith and Carol's eating crunchy, sickly sweet, chocolate-covered Délice-Choc biscuits and hoping they will improve my mood because everything seems wrong. I ran into Thibaud this morning, and whether the mess next door can be bought away is still under discussion. "Long and very repetitive deliberations, for which I have little patience," Thibaud said. Meanwhile, time is running out and I must figure out what I am going to do after the course ends in June.

As of an hour ago, on top of everything else, I feel hopelessly out of synch with Meredith and Carol. Back from their travels, they told me all about Geneva and Zurich, Florence and Milan, the Côte d'Azur, Barcelona and Madrid. The list was dizzying, the report extremely dull, though after so much time alone the company felt good.

Until Margot arrived. "We met Margot in Milan," said Carol proudly. "She's an artist."

Margot's credentials are impeccable. She grew up there, in Milan, daughter of an American and a Frenchman. She went to art school in London and for all I know, besides English, French and Italian, she somehow managed to learn German along the way too. She has long, straight hair, is exquisitely poised and beautifully dressed. Worst of all, she is very friendly. She asked me all about myself and convincingly appeared interested in the responses. Watching Meredith and Carol watch Margot, I realized that with her they have found the real thing in terms of cosmopolitan chic. What's the point of me now?

I stuff the half-empty biscuit package into my bag, put the key into the *porte piétonne*, and get a flash of Madame Flaviche gravely distributing one Rich Tea biscuit to each of us, as if she were handing out our day's wages. Though I didn't much like those insipid cookies, I would take tiny bites and make it last as long as possible. I could not understand how the others—even Jane—dunked theirs in their tea and gobbled them down all soggy.

And here I am up in my room, ten years later, stuffing a whole packet of sweeter, tastier, richer biscuits in my mouth, one after the other, with no one to stop me. Should I consider that progress or a wanton lack of self-control? I look out the window and the courtyard I no longer walk through. Debris has collected. A rush of fiery resentment rises. I am spitting mad at the whole lot of them and catch myself just before I hurl the now empty biscuit package into the courtyard with the rest of the junk.

I lower my arm, turn my back on the window, throw the packet in the waste-paper basket next to the sink. The room, as always, relaxes me. The bed, with its dark wooden frame all around, looks like a boat, the head the prow and the foot the stern, but will it save me from the shipwreck? I've eaten too many biscuits, feel sleepy. A short nap, a respite from the mess, that's what I need. What a luxury closing your eyes can be.

***

Friday, 29 April 1983

Now that I'm not trying to dislike her, I have to admit that I do like her, Lily. Her presence has made this last year better than the one before it, even if she created the problem next door. It makes me wonder why I resisted for so long. A stubborn, ornery wrinkle—the ranch girl in me that even sixty plus years of *la civilisation française* has not been able to iron out? I haven't asked her to stay on after her course only because I'm not planning to be around myself. I'll give her a good bonus for when I go.

I wonder what she will do. She certainly seems in no hurry to return home. Or to go to the US, where her favorite sister is. So she might well stay here, meaning she'll have a Paris life, as I have had, and it makes me want to scream Be careful! Or: Don't be too careful! At her age it's impossible to fathom that it's over before you know it, that it's all too easy to be left with nothing but scribbled words and sorrow.

***

"What are you going to do, after your course is finished?"

I have a bite of the first white asparagus of the season halfway between the plate and my mouth. I have prepared them with hard-boiled eggs and a lemon sauce.

"I don't know."

"You should think about cooking. If Germaine were here, she would undoubtedly agree."

"You mean at a restaurant?" Since Flora is better, Germaine will be back. I've been thinking about that.

"I don't imagine you want to be a housekeeper and besides, you can only find those jobs with old cranks like me," Madame says. She points to her plate. "You have a gift. Or at least a talent. Don't waste it." She stabs a tip of asparagus, puts the fork in her mouth and after swallowing: "It'll be over before you know it. Regret is a terrible thing."

While I am washing up, I wonder why I didn't say anything about being able to stay on here. Her silence on the subject feels like rejection, which, along with growing worry about what the hell I am going to do with my life next year, causes The Mood to hover. I counter the anxiety by clutching to her encouraging words, that I have a talent in the kitchen. Anybody can cook, comes the answer, and everybody who comes to Paris either wants to write a novel or become a chef. So what, answers the other half my head. I have to do something, and people don't need to read books, but they do have to eat three times a day. But this is Paris, comes the reply. The competition is fierce.

Yes, but when you go to the market, when you're standing over that cooker, I tell myself on the way upstairs, nothing else exists. You're in your element. That's what my father used to say about Mr Hooper in the garden. Taciturn Mr Hooper, trimming the roses or trussing up the tomatoes, would come alive, could talk about oidium and black spot all afternoon. "He's in his element," my father would say wistfully, as if he didn't quite feel the same fundamental love for the human nervous system, his life's work. And Madame said: don't waste it, avoid regret.

I open the door to my room. There is a direct correlation between thinking too much, especially about my family, and The Mood. The best tactic to combat its menacing presence is not to ponder. This year other people have been instrumental in the fight. Spending time with Meredith and Carol has worked on me like an elixir, but now there's Margot. Or there was Thibaud, but all he can think about is Thibaud. Jane's gone. Even Maude has found her way out.

Voices and laughter from the other side. In the end it's up to me and me alone.

***

Saturday, 30 April 1983

Yesterday I got Lily to renew my Seresta prescription. The stash of pills is now more than adequate. Question: should I—can I—swallow them all? Or just fifty. Maybe sixty. All at once or staggered? I have to be careful not to throw them up and survive. If only I knew how Adrienne Monnier managed it.

Germaine has just stopped by.

They've left such a mess in the courtyard, she said. I don't dare go out there and clean it up.

It's not your job to clean it up, I said. Then with a sigh: Let's hope they take the money. We should know in another week.

***

I've just pushed open the *portail*, am still sorting through the evening with Meredith and Carol. And Margot. And Giovanni, Margot's friend and another study in polyglot perfection. It was instructive to watch him and Meredith flirt. During the spring break, while she and Carol were visiting Madrid, Madame PR had found *un billet doux* in Monsieur PR's trouser pocket and that was that.

"She spared me the effort," Meredith shrugged. "He was beginning to be a bore. He wouldn't even speak French with me, and his English was terrible. As far as I'm concerned, Low-eek is history."

BOOM. I freeze, then run up the stairs, arrive at Germaine's door just as she opens it.

"Madame," she says, long hair loose again and dressing gown open.

By the time we get to the bedroom Madame is up and in her robe too. "What on earth," she says, eyes straining as if the answer were right there in the room with us, if only she could see it.

"It sounded as if it came from, you know, over there," I say.

The three of us peer out the window. Some of the rooms are strangely alight.

"Fire," says Germaine.

Suddenly a flame leaps through the roof and even Madame recoils. Panicked voices travel across the courtyard.

"Call the fire department," says Madame softly, firmly, which calms me. I run to the phone in the corridor, dial eighteen, the number that has been stuck to the wall ever since the toaster blew up, Germaine told me. "You're the fifth person to phone," says a weary voice.

"The firemen are already on their way," I say, sirens now wailing.

"We shouldn't stay here inside," says Madame. "We need to get out." Her eyes travel vainly around the room. "I have nothing worth taking," she shrugs faintly, almost apologetically.

Getting down the stairs takes forever. Germaine stops to pick up her bag, and I am left to continue the slow, silent descent on my own with Madame. We can hear the fire crackling and the firemen's sharp instructions to one another. Germaine arrives, coat on and handbag over her arm, as if she were going shopping. Once outside under the arcade, I volunteer to go see what's happening.

It is a relief to be moving at my own pace, a pace consistent with my distress. A police car and two fire trucks with swirling lights and hoses are in the middle of the narrow street. Stunned squatters stand in a group, faces tilted up towards the fire that can still be seen burning behind a couple of windows. I don't see Bruno, or Laurent. Thibaud is standing apart from the others.

"What happened?"

"You have to speak up," he says. "My ears are ringing."

"What happened?" I repeat loudly, slowly.

He points, shouts back: "The library-goers, over there talking to the police, they're pharmacy students and had ether in their room and it blew up."

"What?"

"Something about air and ether and unstable electricity. You know, all those dangling wires."

"Is anyone hurt?"

He cocks his ear towards me; I repeat the question. He shakes his head. "I don't think so. Everyone was congregated in the kitchen, arguing about Madame's proposal, when the ether exploded."

I can feel the heat of the fire on my face. The leaping flames seem to have a life of their own. The heat is soothing, the flames are riveting. Fire is complicated, like everything else on this damn planet.

After a few minutes the firemen prevail, though smoke still billows in black clouds from the windows, the hole in the roof. The police stop several squatters who are clamoring to get back in, proclaiming their right to do so.

I lean towards Thibaud's ear: "What about your stuff?"

"Everything that's important is right here." He pats his rucksack.

And I wonder what is important to Thibaud. Nothing, as far as I can tell, besides his Fulbright, his future outside of France. Maybe *Les Aventures de Huckleberry Finn*. I remember how his passion for that book had made no sense, given his diplomatic background. God, I was guileless.

"I'd better get back," I say loudly into his ear. "Where will you go?"

"I'll figure it out." He looks over at the group of squatters still arguing with the police, then at Jean-Marc and Cécile who are standing in the shadows. "If only I'd ignored Jean-Marc that day at the Beaubourg." He looks at me. "It was good at the beginning, wasn't it?"

I half nod, half shrug.

"That one decision has led to this," he opens his arms toward the black smoke.

"Or you could say if only I hadn't let you into the building. Or come to Paris in the first place."

"I guess that's right. Before you know it, you're back to the snake and the apple." Then he turns his gaze again to what was, briefly, his home.

"It's over," I tell Madame and Germaine. "We can go back inside."

***

Wednesday, May 4, 1983

I awoke to the BOOM and thought I was on the rue de Tournon during the War. Only for a second. My blind eyes brought me back to my senses. It was strange: despite my desire to have life over, a will to survive engulfed me.

It was ether, of all things, that set off the explosion, the fire. What was used to knock me out when I had Henri by Caesarean and Henri when he had his tonsils removed.

Back up in the kitchen, Lily made coffee for Germaine and me. She was about to go and let the police in, but I told her to return to her room. I was afraid her presence might encourage questions I did not want answered about how the squatters got in. Oh, how uncomfortable Germaine and I were sitting with those men in the *salon*. Technically they have nothing to do with the sins of their fathers, but some associations are like brands on cattle. They are seared into your skin for life.

Over the last two days there have been more police and people from the local town hall. Octave came with the insurers. He whispered fiercely not to mention how the occupiers got in in the first place (honestly, how stupid does he think I am?). If they discover the squatters were as good as invited, he hissed, they'll give us nothing.

What a shame I won't be around to savor the moment he discovers his inheritance has been cut in half.

Smoke worked its way into every fiber of the place. Its smell is cloying and inescapable. Soon I will make my own fire. I will burn these books and my life, except for the fading memories of a few surviving souls, will go up in a puff of smoke.

***

Sunday, May 8, 1983

Today should have been the day. The one I designated for the occupiers to give me their decision on the money, but there's no longer any need. Deus ex machina and poof, they were gone.

There's a small corner of me that wishes the fire didn't happen, that I could have witnessed one more time in my life, how humans react when presented with a prickly choice, a moral dilemma.

It's also V-Day in Europe, though that "victory" has never reminded me of anything but Henri. By then, almost eight months after he was shot down, shock was no longer numbing the pain, and the amputation was raw and throbbing. While people danced in the street, waved flags, screamed their joy and relief, I sat inside alone. Where François was, I do not remember. I do remember thinking that I wanted to kill myself but didn't have the courage. I'm not any braver now. Just unable.

***

Monday morning and the roofers have started banging even before my alarm goes off. They're covering the open parts so rain can't get in. Madame says it'll take months, at least, until the insurance approves real repair. I tuck my arm under my head, look out the open window. There's a chill but the sky is a primary blue, the sunlight a hospitable yellow. From here I cannot see the black marks licking up the walls across the courtyard, even if the smoke that got into everything is a constant reminder of that night.

Scary as it was, the fire brought Madame, Germaine and me closer together, bound us through a potent common experience, I guess you'd say. Most evenings I've been eating dinner here with them. Madame Quinon has continued to encourage my cooking, my staying on in Paris. Without offering to let me stay here. Which is strange. Germaine shakes her head when I ask her, says she doesn't understand either why Madame won't talk about the future.

When asked by others what I plan to do post-*civilisation française*, I have been feinting and hoping the subject would change. Until yesterday. Margot put the question to me at the Gaulois, and the words popped out: "Try to find a job in a restaurant."

She said: "A friend of my brother just opened a place near the Bastille. Give him a call." She wrote the telephone number on a piece of paper. "I know he's looking for people."

The alarm rings and my body jerks with fright. I'm still on edge. The smallest noise sets my heart racing.

I swing my legs out of bed, open the creaking armoire. There's a summery dress I bought with my mother last September, one of the items that I'd really thought was not *me*. All winter I'd look at it hanging there and wonder why I'd agreed to buy it. It felt like a symbol of all that was wrong in our relationship. Two weeks ago I put it on, just to see, and I've been wearing it almost every day since. Maybe she knows me better than I think.

Downstairs I prepare Madame's breakfast, a task I could now do with my eyes shut, and I wish again that she would give some sign about my future here. The course will be over mid-June, in just over a month. Carol keeps talking about seeing her dog, returning to her old summer job at the botanical gardens. Meredith was talking about getting back to her parents and the beach, but now that Giovanni's in the picture, she's stopped. There's no question he's a vast improvement on Low-eek. Maybe that will be what Meredith takes away from her year in Paris, better taste in men. Or maybe their couple will last transatlantically and Meredith will end up returning to Europe and marrying Giovanni. Maybe the crush on her French teacher in high school that propelled her here in the first place will prove prophetic. And maybe that would mean, if I stay here, that I won't lose touch with Meredith, that I will know her forever. That we really would be friends.

It's not impossible that others will end up here, however improbable it may have seemed in the beginning. There's formerly brassy Gary with his French girlfriend. Or there's Lara from California, who's thrown herself body and soul into Paris life, the language. She calls her landlords her French family, seems to have made a broad circle of normal French friends. Unlike me with my cranky expat and outcast squatters.

At least I have had a taste of men, even if not of love. Thanks to Thibaud and Bruno, I now possess experience, something I was woefully short on nine months ago. The toast pops up; I pour more coffee into the filter.

The other day, on my way back from class, I sat under the trees on the place des Vosges. It was the same spot I'd sat while waiting for my interview, last September. I remembered the two boys who had run past, one hopelessly chasing the other. The boy in second place I had called the loser, what Madame Flaviche always considered Maude, Jane and me. It occurred to me that the child who was winning there, that day on the square, might not be winning later in life, as an adult. I mean, it's perfectly possible that Thibaud makes a huge success of himself in the US—or even back here—who's to know where this Fulbright year will lead him. While Bruno might never go anywhere, might stay in Paris and always be fighting some losing cause. And my unhappy childhood, like Jane said, does not pre-ordain me to a miserable adulthood. If there's one thing I've learned this year, it's that success is not a static state. It is shifting and can be hard to define. Just ask plain-faced Mona Lisa.

I pick up the tray and head down the corridor, knock softly. No answer, no radio. Not a single sound. I knock a little harder. Nothing. I shift the tray to my left arm, look at the brass handle, turn the knob slowly. It always squeaks but without the radio it sounds like a shriek.

The sitting room is empty, dead quiet. The connecting door to her bedroom is closed. I put the tray down on the writing table, notice a thick envelope with my name on it, right next to the fountain pen. A tingle at the back of my neck spreads upward to my eyes that move around the room. In the grate are the notebooks, singed but largely intact. I creep towards the bedroom door; the old floorboards moan anyway. I knock. Nothing. Heart now pounding in my ears, I turn the handle, push the door. There is Madame Quinon on her bed. Like the night that now seems a lifetime ago, when I came down and found her asleep. This time there's no need to wonder whether she's dead. The mouth hangs open and the face is ashen. The prostrate body is as stiff as the floorboards under my feet. I turn and run for Germaine.

****

Summer

T hibaud ambles out of the law faculty, once again surprising me with his height.

"Long time..." he starts to say.

"Can I invite you to lunch?"

"Of course," he says.

"There's a little restaurant I noticed around the corner that looks good."

L'Auberge du Mont Sainte Geneviève is tucked snugly at an angle on a square of postcard charm. Inside are checked tablecloths and bistro chairs. It smells of wine sauce and garlic.

"A step up from the Gaulois, no?" says Thibaud.

"Not a difficult climb."

Once we're seated at the last available table, Thibaud says: "Sorry I've been out of touch."

I smile; he doesn't look particularly sorry. "It's the first day of summer. Our classes were over last Friday. Yours must be over soon too. I wanted to see you one more time before you disappear across the Atlantic." Whatever we had is over and done, but that doesn't mean I want to lose track of him completely. And Madame left me so much cash in that envelope. I want to share some of it with someone.

The waiter appears, takes our orders. As he walks away, Thibaud says:"I've been busy doing my own waiting on tables. Back at the café where I worked the summer I met Jean-Marc and Cécile. In exchange for serving in the evening, I get a small salary and a room at the back."

"That's lucky."

"*Auvergnat* to *Auvergnat*." He shrugs, as he pours each of us a glass of red wine from the carafe the waiter has put on the table. "I was desperate."

"Any news of the others?"

"I assume Jean-Marc and Cécile have gone south. It's cherry season. Bruno's probably back full-time at his parents' waiting for the next cause that will allow him to grab the limelight. Maybe he's putting up Laurent."

The waiter sets down my *poireaux*, leeks in a vinaigrette sauce, and Thibaud's *pâté de campagne*.

"Do you have plans for this summer?" I ask.

"Yeah," he says, spreading some pâté on a piece of bread, topping it with a pickle. "I'm going back to the farm."

"Really?"

"I'm actually, almost, looking forward to it." He finishes chewing, sips his wine. "It'll be room and board in exchange for helping out. And I'll be able to sell cheese at the Saturday market, keep some of the profits, make a bit of money before I leave." He pauses, looks half embarrassed, half pleased. "It's funny. I want to make peace with the place. Like now that I've found a way out, I'm no longer ashamed. What luck, really, not to have been born with a silver spoon jammed into my mouth like Laurent or Bruno." His eyes wander the tables. "Or the people in this restaurant."

"Or me."

"You had mitigating circumstances."

I line up my knife and fork on the empty plate. "One thing I've learned this year is that we all do."

"Maybe." He shrugs, picks up the last bite of pâté, suspends it midway to his mouth. "Anyway, my mother's really happy that I'm coming back."

Little tears prick my eyes. Maybe it's just the wine that's already gone to my head. But his willingness to return to the farm this summer and his mother who loves him get to my tear ducts. Now that he has found a path forward, Thibaud can open mind and spirit and go back. It seems like a happy ending. Or interlude anyway.

"What about you?" he asks. "What are you going to do now that you know everything there is to know about *la civilisation française*?"

"You mean now that I've barely skimmed the surface. *La civilisation française* is a lifelong undertaking. Or more. Like you said to me the first night we met, at that party."

"Did I? How discerning of me. Can you keep living with Madame Quinon?"

A half sigh, half whistle emerges from my mouth.

"You're looking really weird. What's wrong?"

"Madame's dead."

His eyes widen, his chin drops.

"A few weeks ago. She took too many of the sleeping pills her doctor had prescribed and that I kept buying for her." Germaine and Flora have told me and told me not to feel guilty, that it's what she wanted and how was I to know, but shouldn't I at least have considered what she was planning, the way she'd stuff them in her desk drawer like contraband goods? "I found her the next morning."

"*Ça alors*. And you've waited until half-way through the meal to tell me?"

"It's hard to talk about." The tears spill over this time. "In the end, she was nice to me." I wipe my eyes with the stiff white napkin. "I've been reading her notebooks. She may have been wealthy, but she didn't start off that way. In fact, she too grew up on a farm, *un ranch*." Thibaud's eyebrows arch.

"And talk about mitigating circumstances. Many bad things happened to her, to others in her life, including Germaine."

"Like what?"

Since I am reading the journals that she tried to burn, it feels an even further invasion of her privacy—and Germaine's—to provide details. "Let's just say that you and I may have some reasons to complain, but the suffering in the years before we were born—so many deaths and difficult moral choices—it never seemed to end." Even the funeral was sad. Germaine, Flora and Roger, their children. An old widowed friend. Octave and Marie-France, without their children, arrived late and wouldn't speak to us. "'This murderous century,' she called it."

Our main courses arrive. The creamy wine sauce on my monkfish releases a concentrated version of the restaurant's aroma. Thibaud cuts into his steak. "So what are you going to do? Go home?"

The word "home" clangs in my ears, causes an involuntary shudder. "No way. Next week I start as a *sous-chef* in a wine bar-restaurant that a young guy is opening near the Bastille. He's a connection I got through Meredith and Carol, strange as that may sound."

"It's been a year of strange connections, no?" He mops up his potato purée with some bread. "Who'd have guessed last September that I'd meet you, who'd help me get to Boston."

Or that I'd meet and fall in bed with you, a farmer's son, then cause a squat to occur and discover *my element* and that it would be in the kitchen. "Here." I pull *Les Aventures de Huckleberry Finn* from my bag.

Thibaud's eyes sparkle—or are they glistening with a tear or two. "That's incredible." He fans the pages of the swollen, crumpled book. Though the area was strictly off-bounds after the fire, I couldn't resist going over one more time and poking around. "It was strange. Everyone's stuff had been cleared, but somehow your book was still lying on the floor of the attic. Even water-damaged, I thought you might like it."

"My talisman," he pulls the book to his chest before sticking it in his satchel. "Where it all began."

"Do you want dessert?" I ask, even though I know the answer.

We share *une tarte fine aux pommes* with a scoop of vanilla ice cream. The apples are thinly sliced and not too sweet. The crust is delicate and crispy. I let Thibaud eat most of it.

"You're not still living there, are you?" he asks.

"Until the end of the month. Madame left her part of the house to Germaine. You should have seen her husband's nephew Octave, the man who hired me in the first place. He was furious."

"Sometimes justice triumphs, I guess."

"Roger, Germaine's son-in-law, says the only reason Octave isn't contesting the will is because he doesn't want to pay the lawyers' fees. Or wait too long for the money."

"It's the outcome that counts." He puts his fork down on the empty plate, leans back and rubs his flat stomach. "That was good. I won't need to eat for three days."

"The leeks were a bit stringy and tough," I say. "The fish was tasty. I'll have to try using capers in cream sauce. They gave an acidic edge that perked things up."

"Says the *sous-chef*."

"Says the *sous-chef*," I nod.

We order two espressos.

"No more *cafés-crème*." Thibaud smiles.

"After the fire, it was so hectic and disorganized, there was no milk in the flat, and I started drinking my coffee black. Maybe next year I'll even give up sugar."

"*La civilisation française* has worn off on you."

"Of course it has. That's what happens when you live in a place. The local ways creep up on you, seep into your system. Cultural osmosis, you could call it." I've been thinking about that, how I dress, eat and even relate to the world differently than I did nine months ago. "Who knows—after a year in the US, pumpkin pie may be your favorite food."

"Anything's possible, I guess." He half grimaces, half smiles, taps the spoon on the side of his coffee cup. "What will happen to the house? Germaine isn't planning to live there, is she?"

"No. Once Madame's estate and the insurance stuff settle, it will be sold," I say. "She hopes to buy a place near Flora and Roger."

"And you?"

"Flora found me a studio in her building."

"Your new family."

"I like them, and they seem to like me." I shrug as if it's of little importance, but their kindness this last month has felt like kinship. "It's time to get out of that house. With Madame gone and half of the building a charred mess, it's spooky. Everything I own stinks of smoke."

"For two weeks, my ears rang from the explosion. I have nightmares of trying to fight my way through flames." The waiter puts the bill on the table. I reach for the chit, but Thibaud has already grabbed it, pulled out his battered old wallet. "Now that I'm going to be a cheese magnate." He lays bills on the table.

"Thank you. Thank you very much."

"I owe you a lot. Returning the wallet to his back pocket, he shakes his head. "That night changed me." His eyes dart about, as if he can't grasp how, then settle on me. "I feel lucky to be alive."

"You know what." It's like a warm little light has switched on inside me. "So do I."

Author Bio

Mary Fleming, originally from Chicago, moved to Paris in 1981, where she worked as a freelance journalist and consultant before turning full-time to writing fiction. Her novel *Someone Else* was published in 2014 and *The Art of Regret* in 2019. She chronicles life between Paris and the Perche (Normandy) in the bi-weekly photo-essay, A Paris-Perche Diary.

Photo © William Fleming

www.ingramcontent.com/pod-product-compliance
Lightning Source LLC
LaVergne TN
LVHW010155150425
808621LV00001B/88